Books by Jo Goodman

THE CAPTAIN'S LADY
(previously published as PASSION'S BRIDE)

CRYSTAL PASSION

SEASWEPT ABANDON

VELVET NIGHT

VIOLET FIRE

SCARLET LIES

TEMPTING TORMENT

MIDNIGHT PRINCESS

PASSION'S SWEET REVENGE

SWEET FIRE

WILD SWEET ECSTASY

ROGUE'S MISTRESS

FOREVER IN MY HEART

ALWAYS IN MY DREAMS

ONLY IN MY ARMS

MY STEADFAST HEART

MY RECKLESS HEART

Published by Zebra Books

THE CAPTAIN'S LADY

Jo Goodman

Zebra Books
Kensington Publishing Corp.

http://www.zebrabooks.com

Dear Reader,

For a number of years now I have been asked by readers how they might get copies of my early romances. The answers— try a used book store, the library, or the yard sale graveyards— have never been satisfactory, least of all to me.

The Captain's Lady allows me to give readers a different response. This is a reprint of my first book, *Passion's Bride*. The only significant alteration is the title. That change wasn't made to confuse you, but to give Alexis Danty and Tanner Cloud a bit more dignity and save me from blushing every time I had to say *Passion's Bride* out loud.

I have always regretted that I didn't know enough back then to send in my dedication page with the manuscript. It's an oversight I can rectify now.

This one's for the people who believed I could do it when I wasn't sure what I was doing: my parents Klem and Joan Dobrzanski, my sister Yvonne, my brother John (who still thinks he should get a percentage), my less greedy brother Richard, co-workers at then Brooke-Hancock Group Home, Inc., and Linda Johnson who put the manuscript in the mail more than once when I thought it was working well as a doorstop.

They have all been thanked in other books but I had always meant to thank them from the first.

And I am mindful that it is you, reader, whose expressed interest has provided me with the opportunity to do so. Thank you for that.

Jo Goodman.

Prologue

The small room was already smoke-filled. As if it were their voices which gave meaning to the issues, the men in the chamber talked on. Only in one area was there silence. The seat was occupied by a purposeful young man—his movements revealed this aspect of his nature—but in this cancerous haze, where men's voices droned, ignoring signs of strain, he was uncertain what was expected of him.

Tanner Frederick Cloud had ceased to be interested in what was being said. He was familiar with all the issues under discussion: the failure of Jefferson's Embargo Act to hinder British or French forces by halting the flow of supplies from America; the subsequent setback to New England shipping firms; the British blockade extending down the entire coastline of France and making it dangerous to trade with the continent; the threat of secession by New England states if President Madison asked for a declaration of war; and the unreasonable search and seizure practices the Royal Fleet inflicted on American vessels and men.

From his own experiences he was aware of the gravity of the issues, but as a captain in the fledgling United States

Navy, he had little to do with the four other men in the room.

". . . Alex Danty."

His wandering attention was captured by the sound of that name. He glanced casually around the room, shifting his lean body slightly to see if anyone had noticed his involuntary tightening. Senator Howe's sudden decision to open the windows and clear the air let Cloud know that his reaction had been noted and now was being analyzed under the cover of innocuous activity.

It was too late to pretend Alex Danty meant nothing to him, but he chose to remain silent, concentrating on the argument that had erupted shortly after Danty's name had been introduced.

Bennet Farthington was speaking hurriedly. His fingers brushed through wheat-colored hair in a nervous gesture and his blue eyes were focused on Robert Davidson, the representative from Rhode Island.

"You're mad, Robert! Absolutely mad! How could Alex Danty help us? What possible use could we make of a pirate?"

Davidson laughed derisively at the young man. "For an aide to the Secretary of War you are singularly uninformed, Bennet. Considering Danty's been carrying on a private war with the British for eighteen months, I'm surprised Dr. Eustis hasn't kept you up to date."

"I read the papers. I know Danty's sunk eleven fleet ships."

"Twelve."

"An even dozen, then. It has nothing to do with us."

The senator from Massachusetts listened to the exchange with more interest than his casual posture at the window indicated. His gray eyes rested thoughtfully on the young naval officer they had selected for a difficult assignment. Howe was pleased with the captain's earlier contribution, an outline of tactics that would make it possible to win against Great Britain in the event of war. This young man had a succinct manner of speaking which Howe suspected annoyed the others with its decisiveness. However, it had been the captain's resolute sense of his own correctness that had convinced Howe they had made the right choice. That trait might frighten the others, but to the senator it was the flaw which made Tanner Frederick Cloud eminently suited to their purpose.

Howe tapped his cigar lightly, allowing the ashes to fall to the carpet, and returned to his chair. It only remained to be discovered what the captain knew of Alex Danty, the renegade who was the focus of their plans.

"What's Danty's purpose?" he asked smoothly. "He's not an American, is he?" Howe looked pointedly at the captain but was disappointed.

Granger, the head of a failing export business in Boston and a competitor with the line owned by Cloud's family, spoke up. "No one knows. He appeared out of nowhere a year and a half ago and has been keeping the British in a constant state of turmoil. He never takes anything from the ships except supplies and arms. He offers freedom to impressed sailors—British and American alike—then he drops the remainder of the crew on an island or within swimming distance of one and sinks the vessel.

"I've read accounts that say he makes a personal search of the crew—as if he were looking for someone. No one even knows what Danty looks like. They say he wears a mask because he was disfigured in battle. The men who were freed by him and chose not to join him have nothing to say—except that they'll never be able to properly thank him."

"I don't give a damn what he looks like or what his purpose is," said Davidson. "And neither does Madison. Can you imagine what help Danty would be if he were working with our navy? It's a thought, isn't it? One privateer putting an end to the Royal Fleet while we can barely muster the funds and forces to back a declaration of war. He must have compiled a lot of information on British movements. We could use him."

"Could Danty be French?" asked Howe. "They have just as much reason to want his help."

"French? It's possible," Davidson said thoughtfully. "Perhaps he has connections with Lafitte."

"Good Lord, Robert! How many cutthroats do you want on our side? Danty is one thing. Jean Lafitte is quite another! He has been disrupting merchant ships in the Caribbean for years—and I'm talking about American as well as British vessels." Bennet lit a cigar and drew on it deeply.

"I disagree. True, Lafitte is no respecter of flags, but New Orleans is a very valuable port. All of our products from the west have to pass through there. Our navy could use someone like Lafitte, who has a selfish interest in keeping that port open, to prevent a British blockade."

Howe stopped Farthington's reply by lifting his hand. "It's immaterial to discuss this further, Bennet. Especially when you have Madison's orders in your pocket. We have been asked to arrange a meeting with Danty and secure his help. The matter is settled."

"No, it isn't." His voice cracked slightly with the effort it took to speak after remaining quiet for so long. The eyes of every man turned to the officer, giving him the benefit of their surprised, if not respectful, silence.

Tanner Frederick Cloud surveyed their anxious faces and he tightened his smile as he returned their gazes. Did they really have orders that concerned him? His superior had sent him to the meeting telling him only that he was to do whatever they asked of him. Cloud was no longer certain of the merit of that order. Their talk made him uneasy but he could not name the reason for his discontent.

Cloud felt as if the senator, *his* state's senator, he reminded himself, was orchestrating this meeting. The captain had little doubt he had been maneuvered into making a statement. He had felt Howe's calculating stare on him more than once silently demanding he speak out on the subject of Alex Danty. Cloud wondered if his reluctance to do so would cost him his position.

He had been given command only three years ago, in 1809 at the age of twenty five. He had been offered the commission after having escaped his own impressment into British service, but not before the British had been able to leave the mark of his belligerence on his flesh. The scars from the whip could still be seen on his lean, muscular back; the lines slashed in thin white strips on otherwise bronzed skin.

For three years he had sailed his own ship with a good crew and the fear of being impressed again never left him. Frequent trips to Europe increased the possibility, but he had already decided he would take his own life before he allowed himself to be forced to serve the Union Jack again.

He lowered his heavily lashed lids, momentarily denying the men a view of his disturbing green eyes; eyes that could look at them as well as through them. When he raised his head, running his fingers through dark copper hair, he knew he could not put them off any longer. He pushed his chair away from the table and stretched his long legs in front of him until he could see the tips of his knee-high boots. He placed his hands on either side of the arms of his chair, gripping the wood. He knew without looking that his knuckles were white and that the muscles in his forearms would actually hurt later because of his tension. It was always this way when he thought of Alex Danty. And now these men wanted to know. They wanted to know what he had known since the name of Captain Danty had been mentioned to him eighteen months ago when the first of a dozen British vessels went down.

His voice cut through the silence with its sureness. He spoke firmly, softly; the steely edge in the timbre of his voice came from knowing he was right.

"Alex will not help us, gentlemen. No matter what the President has asked you to do. Bennet, you may as well keep your orders where they are. Danty is involved in the pursuit of one man. The captain will not stop until it has been accomplished."

"Why are you so sure?" Davidson thoughtfully tapped a finger on the side of his long, angular nose. "I can hardly credit he's been sinking ships to get at one man. All that destruction with revenge as the sole motive? I find that very difficult to accept."

"Then you are going to have greater difficulty accepting what I'm about to say. Danty is after one man and it is *her* quest, *her* pursuit, and *her* aid you wish to seek."

Total silence greeted his words. Howe coughed as the smoke from his cigar filtered from the ashtray toward his nose. Abruptly he snuffed it out and cleared his throat. "Are you telling us that Alex Danty is a . . . a . . ." He could not go on. His shock gave way to laughter and the others joined in.

Cloud had expected such a response. He tried to excuse them, thinking that they had only met him this evening and they could not know he never made a statement without being able to back it up.

"I am telling you Alex Danty is a woman," he said quietly. It was as if he had slammed his fist on the polished table. The laughter stopped.

Howe recovered first. "How do you know, Captain? Have you seen Danty?"

Cloud said nothing. The moment stretched into an eternity in his mind. He wanted to tell everyone to go to hell. His word should be enough. He had no doubt about Alex now but he could remember a time when it had been difficult to accept. Could he expect so much from them? They didn't know her. The truth was he did not want to remember the incident and even less did he want to share it. Alex's problems were her own, to deal with in any way she saw fit. He knew her reaction would be one of disgust if she ever learned she had been casually talked about in a meeting of this sort.

He sighed. She would never find out. At least he could be thankful for that. He would never see her again unless she wanted it, and once they heard her story they would understand why she would never join them. It was to save her from even being asked that he reluctantly decided to talk. . . .

Part One

Chapter One

"Damn 'im! Damn 'im ta 'ell!"

For all that it was whispered, the curse had a strangely virulent quality. It was born of hatred and fear, loneliness and anger, yet these emotions could not be heard, trapped as they were in an icy delivery. "Oi ain't lettin' 'im sell me! Oi ain't!" This time the cry was accompanied by the panicked movement of small hands along the length of two braids the color of beaten gold. Amber eyes, seemingly overlarge in such a thin, somber face, stared at the betraying flutter as if willing the fingers to be still. Even as Alexis quieted her hands, her mind was working feverishly. The events of the past few hours made it clear that she would have to leave if she were to avoid humiliation at the hands of the man she had called her father for all of her thirteen years.

For as long as she could remember, Alexis had been asked to be grateful to the distant relatives who had taken her in, pretending to disregard her illegitimacy and the fact that Alexis's birth had meant her mother's death. But their pretense had long been obvious to Alexis due to the ill-timed remarks and blatant accusations tossed at her regarding the details of her birth. Although Charlie and Meg Johnson provided shelter, Alexis was well aware of her own value in this family of shiftless dreamers. Among the four children she had no friend, and for Charlie and Meg she felt only contempt.

Until recently Charlie's schemes for easy money had not involved Alexis, but lately Meg complained she was not doing her share. "Givin' 'erself airs. That's wot she's doin'," Meg whined to her husband, referring to the time Alexis spent in the park, inconspicuous behind flowering shrubbery, listening to the conversations of the ladies who frequented the place. "She wants ta talk loike 'em laidies, she does." And to further condemn her Meg went on to say that when Alexis wasn't in the park she was escaping her work by walking along the river, watching the ships or simply daydreaming.

Charlie, in a typically impulsive gesture, decided to put an end to his wife's needling and Alexis's defiant, ungrateful attitude by selling her. Alexis knew only too well what that meant. Now that she was banished to her room she cursed Charlie as well as any swell who would purchase a virgin to rid himself of the pox.

Alexis shut her eyes and pressed on her lids with the heels of her hands, making everything black until fleeting sparks of color appeared. She watched the floating spectrum, a rainbow for her gray world, knowing it was hers alone to see. No one else could witness the display of fireworks she controlled. She released her hands and opened her eyes, blinking a few times to restore her vision. Reality was the cracked ceiling, the blistering paint on the walls, the streaks on the windows. Alexis laughed suddenly. This would be her reality for only a few hours more. Even before she'd reached the age of thirteen she'd known surviving meant escaping.

Her decision to leave London had been made over two years ago. A destination had been established at the same time. But the plan unfolded slowly. It depended only on one person: Alexis. She reviewed the risks and the possibility of being caught, and decided what waited for her was worth taking the chance.

There was a place for her in America. She knew it. The sailors who had become her friends during the time she spent at the river told her often about the sort of life she could have there. She had listened eagerly, anticipating what she would make of the opportunities. It was a young country. And wild. And there was a place for her there. She hugged herself tightly, pleased that she knew what she wanted and knew how to get it.

She was finished with being teased for the things she held dear. Meg laughed at her for spending time in the park. Charlie accused her of whoring when she visited the harbor. None of that mattered now. It was all part of the plan. She had learned things in both places and now she would put her knowledge to the test.

Alexis feigned sleep when she heard her sisters coming up the stairs and didn't utter a sound as they crawled into bed beside her, pushing her out in the process. Ignoring their titters and giggles, she covered herself with the blanket she'd managed to drag with her and waited until she heard their even breathing before she dared to move again. Quietly she made her way down the stairs, secure in the knowledge that everyone in the house had followed her sisters' example.

She searched through the laundry hamper on the kitchen table until she found what she wanted. Her worn and faded shift was discarded in favor of her brother's short pants and shirt. She took the best pair of stockings she could find and slipped into a pair of her brother's shoes to complete her masquerade.

Her knitted cap, a present from one of her friends at the wharf, she tucked under her belt. With the sharpest knife she could find grasped firmly in her hands, she deliberately chopped at her braids until they lay at her feet. She ran her fingers through her hair and tugged at the curls until she was satisfied she had achieved her purpose. She drew back, surprised, when she glanced at herself in the cracked glass.

Tossing her head she laughed softly at her reflection, liking her new look. Alexis pulled out her cap and placed it firmly over her head, hiding most of the stubborn curls. Taking only some bread and cheese, she left the house and walked hurriedly toward the river, never looking back.

Even late at night the area was teeming with activity. She hid away in the stoop of a shop and watched the men with interest. Men well into their cups passed by without a glance in her direction. Cargo was being loaded on several ships and somewhere in the distance she could hear the sound of a ship's bell. She leaned her head against the door of the shop and fell asleep, certain she would find a ship leaving for America in the morning and equally sure she would find a way to be on it.

Alexis woke to the sound of her stomach rumbling and the odor of fresh bread nearby. A hand held out a chunk of hot white bread to her but before she took it she examined the owner of this wonderful prize. A woman smiled down at her. Her face, smooth and round, had tiny laugh lines at the corners of the eyes and mouth. Alexis smiled back, producing the brightest smile she could muster.

"You look like you could use this, lad," the woman said. Seeing the hesitation on the young boy's face, she pressed on. "I have plenty. I made it fresh this morning. Why don't you come inside the shop and have some?"

Alexis shook her head, remembering she had her own food. "Oi can't, mum." She stopped. "I mean I can't. Oi 'aven't a shillin' . . . Oi haven't a shilling. I ain't a charity case."

The woman laughed. "Who said anything about charity? You come in and have some breakfast and you can clean my stoop when you've taken your fill."

Alexis took the bread that was offered and followed the woman into the shop. Inside, her mouth watered, and she felt an uncomfortable twinge of envy at meeting someone who didn't know what it was like to go hungry.

"Are you looking for a job on one of the merchants?" the woman asked while Alexis ate.

"That's right, mum. Oi expect ta get on a ship fer the States."

"You're very young to be traveling so far."

"Sixteen. And now I 'ave a good meal in me Oi'll be strong as any wots eighteen." Damn. It was have, not 'ave. I, not Oi.

The woman searched the intent features of the young ragamuffin. He was not the first of the children who thought they could flee London by signing up to go to sea. She doubted very many of them ever reached their destinations alive. Scurvy and foul drinking water were the demise of most of them. She wondered if she should tell him these things, then thought better of it. It would be a waste of breath if she was any judge of character. The firm set of that mouth and the determination of those amber eyes told her he would not be put off by what she had to say. His kind had horror stories of their own.

Sighing at the injustice of it, she packed him a small lunch. When he was finished eating she handed it to him. "You sweep the walk and be on your way. I know one of the Thorton merchants is leaving this afternoon for Charleston. That's in the United States."

"I know that," Alexis answered.

"Yes, of course you would," she said dryly. "Well, you may be able to get on it but don't tell them you're sixteen. Try for fifteen and if they don't want to have eyes in their head they may just believe you."

Alexis smiled and thanked her. As she swept the stoop she realized that while she hadn't passed the age test very successfully, she had had no difficulty with the gender part. Her plan was going smoothly.

The *Constellation* was not hard to find among the other vessels. Alexis was familiar with the flag of the Thorton Line as well as the type of rig they had. The *Constellation* was one of the newer merchants. She knew it had made only a few trips to America; its sides and underbelly were not encrusted with barnacles and the red-and-white paint used by the line had not peeled or splintered from the corrosive salt water. Alexis watched men loading cargo aboard for some time before she approached.

Summoning her courage, she asked one of the workers if she could speak to the captain. He brusquely pointed out the direction she should follow.

She had gone only a few steps when he called her back. "Ye lookin' fer a job?" Alexis nodded. "Then don't go lookin' fer th' captain. See tha' man over there?" He pointed to a great bear of a man presently directing the movement of cargo. " 'E's th' one wot does th' 'iring. Name's Pauley Andrews. Maybe 'e can 'elp ye."

Alexis murmured her thanks and started to climb up the gangway, trying to ignore the growing knot in her stomach. She waited for a pause in the man's activity before she sidled near.

"Sir," she said softly. He didn't turn. More loudly, "Sir, I'm lookin' fer a job."

Alexis managed to keep her feet firmly planted on the deck of the ship as the man swung around to face her. "Are you now? And what makes you think I'd have any work you could be doing?" He glanced at the pitiful specimen of a human being in front of him. They were getting younger all the time. If he had half a kindness in his heart he would send this one away. Pauley shrugged. He needed a helper for the captain and he didn't have time to search for one. "How old are you, lad?"

"Fifteen," Alexis said firmly.

"Fourteen's more like it. Your voice hasn't even changed."

"It will soon." She cracked it expertly, the way she had heard her brothers do it.

Pauley put his hands on his hips and laughed a deep, throaty laugh. "If that's a sign of your determination to get aboard, then you're welcome to cast your lot with the rest of us. Just don't ever curse me for taking you. You'll find it's not the opportunity you think it is."

Alexis looked up at him, puzzled. Finally she said, "Why would I curse you? This is my decision."

Pauley laughed louder. "Making decisions at fourteen. I hope you're prepared to bear the consequences of those decisions." He stopped laughing when he saw how the boy was looking at him. By God, the lad was serious. He shuddered to think of his own sons trying to get aboard a ship like this. And his boys were older and stronger than this mite. Still, the child seemed to know what he wanted and Pauley Andrews was not one to stand in the way of the grim determination he saw expressed in the face below him. He felt almost uncomfortable under the steady gaze of this child. He spoke to break the silence.

"What's your name, son?"

"Alex."

"Is that all? Just Alex?"

Alexis remained silent while she considered an option. She did not want to use the name of the people who had masqueraded as her family, but she had no other. Her eyes scanned the wharf, stopping when she saw the sign above the bakery. Why not? She had spent the first night of her new life on that stoop and the woman had shown her more kindness in one morning than she had known most of her life. She struggled to pronounce the name on the sign to herself. It would not do to get it wrong and her knowledge of reading was limited.

"Danty," she said. "My name is Alex Danty."

Pauley had watched Alexis as her eyes wandered along the waterfront shops and he'd also seen the object of her interest. He tried not to smile when she said her name. The sign read Pantry. If Danty was the name, then so be it.

"All right, Alex Danty. Come with me and I'll show you where you'll be quartered. You'll have to sign some papers saying that you took this job of your own free will."

Alexis was shown to a small cabin not far from the captain's. "This is yours. You get a place to yourself because the captain will be needing you at all hours. He likes to have his cabin boy within bellering range. I'll see about getting you some more clothes. I think the old cabin boy's still around." He paused. "He's dead, you know. Wasn't strong enough. That doesn't bother you, does it?"

"Why should it? Oi'm strong enough. I'm goin' ta mike it."

"We'll see." Pauley shrugged. He led Alexis to the captain's cabin and had her sign the papers. She managed to write Alex well enough but Danty was a struggle. Pauley studied the signature and remained silent. He sensed the fierce pride in the young man and did not want to do anything to spoil it. He thought if there were time on the voyage he would even teach him to read and write a little. And do something about that accent. He was beginning to like the boy; he hoped he fared better under the captain's orders than the last one.

"One more thing," Pauley added as he gathered the papers, "don't get any ideas about leaving this ship when we reach Charleston. You're in this for the duration, and that means the return trip to London."

Alexis almost lost her composure when he guessed her plan but she recovered quickly. "I know wot's expected."

"We'll see," was all he would say.

Alexis heard a lot of "We'll see" in the weeks that followed. Pauley continued to tease her with those words whenever she firmly stated she knew something. But Alexis also knew he was pleased with her answers. She was not often wrong.

Captain Whitehead had been angry with Pauley in the beginning for hiring Alexis. When the last cabin boy had been buried at sea he'd specifically stated he wanted someone older. But Alexis proved Pauley's wisdom countless times by her unwavering service.

Alexis often wondered how Pauley would react if he discovered she was a girl. She was pleased she had been able to hide the fact for so long. It helped having her own quarters while the rest of the crew slept in hammocks on deck. She was careful to bolt the door at night as Pauley suggested and she stayed away from the men who named her Pretty Boy, understanding the danger these men were to her.

She thought if there was anyone she would want on her side in a bad moment it had to be Pauley. His brusque manner softened shortly after she came to know him better and his bulk was no longer a threat. She estimated he was at least six feet tall; yet he carried every ounce of muscle on his body as if it were no burden at all. He had thick black hair and his beard was equally dark with the exception of a few thin strands of gray. The outdoors had tanned his face, but he seemed ageless when he smiled and talked wistfully to Alexis of his home and family in the north of England. She was glad he had chosen to become her friend. The other men respected Pauley, so those who still thought of her as Pretty Boy stayed away in deference to her giant protector. Pauley had adopted her as a substitute son for the voyage, and nothing could have made Alexis more proud.

Under Pauley's direction she learned to use a pistol and handle a sword as well as her young hands could. Alexis did not mind that she was slowly developing the muscles in her arms and legs. It felt good to be strong and healthy. The food aboard the ship, usually salt pork or beef and biscuits, while far from good, was more plentiful than any she had had before, so her stomach had long since ceased reminding her of its emptiness at odd times. She proved adept at climbing the rigging and soon she could reach the flattened cap before any of the others. She called it her crow's nest—so it had been named on ships long ago—and there was nothing to intrude on the contentment she experienced there. Far above the captain, the sailors who called her Pretty Boy, and the rolling deck, she found a place where no one could touch her.

It was while she was up in the nest that the *Constellation* confronted a squall and she was struck by the curse. She did not know which was worse, the storm or the curse. At first she thought she had hit something when she noticed blood on her trousers between her thighs. In her panic to get out of the nest and safely to her cabin she slipped on the slick ropes and was barely able to break her fall by clutching at the mast.

Pauley saw Alexis's trouble and he hastened to a position below her. He watched as Alexis grasped one of the loose ropes and slid down perilously to the pitching deck. Pauley broke her fall and looked at her in disgust when he saw the burn marks from the ropes.

"You're supposed to climb down, not slide!" he yelled over the rising wind. "Get down to your cabin! You can't help us here with those hands."

Alexis smiled weakly, trying to ignore the painful tightening in her abdomen. Pauley's anxiety was the source of his rudeness. Aware of that, Alexis felt strangely comforted. She turned and headed for her cabin, careful of each step because the wind and salt spray were threatening to lift her away. She gasped when she felt Pauley's strong grip on her arm. It was anything but friendly.

She looked up in puzzlement but could not fathom the reason for his very real, very sudden anger. She tried to break his hold, but he gripped her more tightly and half pulled, half pushed her toward her cabin. He practically threw her inside and Alexis had to grab at the bunk to keep from sliding to the floor.

"Wot's wrong wi' you, Pauley?" she yelled.

He shut the door violently. "I should ask what's wrong with you, missy? I don't have time to find out what's going on now. I'm needed topside. You get yourself cleaned up, and don't you dare move from this room! I'll tell everyone you were injured. In the meantime you'd better have some good answers for me when I get back." His blue eyes flashed dangerously as Alexis dropped her gaze to the blood on her trousers. He had found her out. Now she knew why they called it the curse.

When Alex was alone she proceeded to tear strips of sheet and take care of her predicament as best she could. Becoming a woman was not part of her plan and she could not decide whether she was more angry with her body, for turning traitor, or her mind, for not having taken the possibility into consideration.

Pauley did not return until the storm was over. He shut the door quickly and drew the bolt. Alexis saw that he was soaked to the skin, but her concern faded as he turned to face her. She met the fury in his blue eyes directly. She did not back away or cower as he approached and snatched the cap from her head. She allowed him to grasp her chin tightly in his hand and raise her head to study her face more closely.

Finally he dropped his hand and shook his head slowly. "I'll be damned. I'll just be goddamned." He was silent for a while as if he were thinking of what to say next. "How long did you think you could get away with it?" he asked slowly.

"Until I reached Charleston."

"Didn't you count on your monthly?"

"No."

"Aren't you afraid of what is going to happen to you now?"

"No."

Pauley sighed. "I'll be damned," he said again. He had been prepared to beat her when he'd come walking through that door. It was bad enough he had taken on a child, but to discover the child was a girl was too much even for him. She wouldn't be able to hide the fact much longer and the thought of what would happen to her when the others found out frightened him even if it didn't her. "What am I supposed to do with you?"

"Why should Oi be yer concern? Oi'm the one in trouble."

"You can say that again, Alex. Damn! What *is* your name?"

"Alexis. The last name's still Danty though."

Pauley smiled, remembering the bakery. "And how old are you really?"

She was going to lie, then thought better of it. "Thirteen."

"I'll be damned."

It took him over an hour to extract the entire story from Alexis. When she was finished he was certain there were things

she'd omitted but he did not press her any further. He ha
to admit to a grudging admiration for the girl. It was clea
she did not expect his pity, or even desire it.

"I can't take you to Charleston," he said after a reflectiv
silence. For the first time since he knew her he fancied h
detected fear in her amber eyes. Reading her thoughts h
added, "You won't go back to London either. This storm ma
be the luckiest thing that ever happened to you, Alex. Becaus
we were blown off course, the captain has decided to stop a
a few ports in the Caribbean and unload some of the carg
there. That's where we'll unload you."

"Why can't Oi go the whole way ta Charleston?" she aske
stubbornly.

"Because it will be at least three weeks before we get ther
now. You can't hope to hide the fact you're a girl for tha
long. The men who called you Pretty Boy will seem like angel
compared to the others when they find out. I can't protec
you all day and night too. You'll be safer getting off at on
of the islands."

Alexis drew her eyebrows together and frowned. "Oi don
like this, Pauley. It ain't . . . isn't wot I planned for mesel
Wot would Oi . . . I do on an island?"

"Oh, Alex," he laughed. "I'm not just going to push yo
ashore and forget about you. I have friends on Tortola, i
Roadtown. I've told you about George and Francine ofte
enough. You remember? Quinton shipping."

"I remember."

"Why do you look so unhappy? They're good people.
know they'll take you in."

"Like Charlie and Meg did," she replied bitterly.

"No, dammit! Not like Charlie and Meg! Don't you kno
me any better than that? I wouldn't put you with people lik
that. George and Francine don't have any children—at leas
they didn't when I last saw them—and they have money
Alex."

"That's na' important. Oi wasn't unhappy because I wa
poor."

"I know that. You were unhappy because you could do nothing about it there. Well, the Quintons won't present you with that problem. You'll be able to get an education and if you still want to go to the United States later, they'll see that you get there."

"Why would they want me? They seem to have everything they want."

Pauley lifted his dark eyebrows in surprise. "You can ask that? I thought you knew yourself better."

Alexis tried to puzzle that out. No one had ever expressed a desire to be her friend before and it had never bothered her. Pauley was an exception. Could it be the Quintons were like him? "Oi don' 'ave a choice, do I?" she asked softly.

"Not this time, Alex. Trust me. This is one decision that has been made for you. I'll accept the consequences." He laughed and held her hand when she eyed him warily.

By the time the *Constellation* reached the port of Charlotte Amalie on St. Thomas, Alexis had accepted Pauley's decision. During the three days between the time he'd confronted her and the time they anchored near the thriving harbor, Alexis had learned all she could about George and Francine Quinton. Pauley explained how George had left England over twenty years ago with his French bride, determined to make his fortune planting sugar cane and raising livestock on Tortola. It hadn't taken him long to realize there was a better life to be had by setting up his own shipping firm to transport the goods of the other settlers. Quinton Shipping had started slowly and suffered many setbacks before George managed to make a success of it. Alexis had seen his ships before, delivering sugar in the harbor at Bristol, their sides painted dark blue and decorated with red bands broken by the spaces of the gun ports. Alexis was intrigued by what she learned about the Quintons. That knowledge and Pauley's daily assurances enabled her to put aside some of her misgivings.

By the time the *Constellation* anchored off Tortola Pauley

suspected there was little left he could do to allay Alexis's remaining fears. But when it was time for them to leave he found her alone in her cabin, precariously close to tears, and he knew that he had not begun to touch her deepest, most secret thoughts.

"I thought you trusted me," he told her as he sat beside her on the bunk. He watched a pathetic tremor shake her body as she tried to suppress her tears. "What are you upsetting yourself about?"

"Oi ain't upset." Her attempt at defiance was lost as the words passed through the lump in her throat.

Pauley smiled. "Liar."

Alexis felt herself blush, embarrassed that his accusation was true. To hide it she threw her arms around Pauley's neck and buried her face against his chest. "Oi'm grateful to you, Pauley. Truly, Oi am. Oi know yer doin' wot ya think is best fer me."

"But?" He removed her arms from around his neck and placed his hand on her chin, lifting her face to meet his eyes. "I know there's a but. What are you so afraid of? What has you shaking?"

She drew in a sharp breath; then the words seemed to explode from her. "Wot if Oi learn ta luv 'em and they don't want me by and by? Oi'll 'urt again, Pauley. Loike Oi 'urt now, leavin' you. Oi don't want ta be beholdin' ta nobody. Nor nobody's burden either." She sniffed loudly. "Oi jest want ta go me own way. Ta America."

Pauley pulled Alexis back into his arms and held her tightly. "You could never be a burden, Alex. You will always have it in you to go your own way. It's what I love best about you."

"Truly?"

"Truly. No one who loves you would ever stop you. As for loving, it's a risk sometimes. I've never known that to scare you off." Pauley knew Alexis would recognize the challenge he gave her and be unable to ignore it. She made no reply other than to release her tears softly into the fabric of his shirt.

Less than an hour later, the incident behind them and never to be mentioned again, Pauley and Alexis left the ship during the transfer of cargo. With Alexis firmly in tow, Pauley hurried through the busy streets of Roadtown. Behind them, in Road Bay, a small fleet of fishing sloops lazily made its way to open water. In front of them, the small settlement town was the source of one discovery after another. Pauley laughed at Alexis's childish amazement at her first sight of one of the dark-skinned islanders. Her enthusiasm for the bright foliage was endless; she wanted to stop every ten paces to smell some delicious new flower. He pointed out fields of sugar cane on the terraced hillsides, and she made him halt in mid-stride to watch the cane being loaded on donkeys before it was taken to the mill. Pauley was happy to comply with her wishes. He could never have denied her simple delight in her new surroundings. On board the ship she had been so defensive, so old. Now, with someone guiding her adventure, she was almost like any other child he saw on the waterfront.

He smiled as she picked an unusual pink flower and placed it behind her ear. It refused to stay in place because her hair was too short to grasp it.

"When I see you again," he said, "I expect you to have that hair of yours grown to the middle of your back. If I find out that you've chopped it off again, for whatever reason, I'll flay you alive."

Alexis laughed at the threat. Then she sobered suddenly. She took his hand firmly. "It will take years to grow my hair that long. So you mean Oi won't see ya 'til then?" There was a slight catch in her voice but she checked it. She did not want to make a habit of crying in front of him.

"Who knows the next time I'll be here," he said lightly to hide his feelings. He took the delicate frangipani from her hand and twirled it in his own. "But when I do come I expect you to be waiting."

"Will you tell yer family about me, Pauley? Maybe one of yer boys will marry me. Then you could be me dad."

Pauley would have liked nothing better than to take her

home where she would be accepted by his wife and sons and daughters, but he pushed the thought aside, knowing George and Francine were the best people for her. "You'd frighten off my boys with those penetrating eyes of yours, Alex. The only reason I stand up to your stare is that I'm three full heads taller. I don't know what will happen when you start meeting people eye to eye. You can make a body feel tiny when you stare him down."

"Not you, Pauley. Never you. That's one o' the things Oi like about you. You never back away. Me brothers an' sisters turned from me when Oi didn't take to their teasin'. Sometimes when Charlie would beat me Oi'd stare 'im down. Ooooh, 'e 'ated that. Jest about as much as Oi 'ated 'im fer lookin' the other way. What do you suppose made 'em do it?"

Pauley did not answer her. He knew the reason others turned away from her. She didn't know that in her eyes people saw her expectations mirrored and most of them avoided her because they could not meet her demands.

Alexis tightened her grip on Pauley's hand when she felt his pace slacken. She looked up and followed the path of his gaze until her eyes rested on a house situated on a cliff overlooking the water. "Is that were Oi'm goin' ta live?" she asked, feeling her heart beat wildly in anticipation of his answer.

"That's it. Your new home." He said it without hesitation, knowing that George and Francine would never turn down the gift he was about to offer them.

The breath caught in Alexis's throat. She could not take her eyes away from the house. She had never expected so much. She blinked once, then several times in quick succession. Each time the same view greeted her. The large house, the wide portico, the thick white columns, and the red tile roof were all still there. Surrounding the house were trees so green she wondered by what right the trees in London made claim to that color. The sun touched the leaves so that they sparkled like emeralds, and the flowers here were even more beautiful than she remembered on her walk through the settlement. A coral bush, glowing like a firework display with yellows, oranges, and crimsons, demanded her attention; even as the belladonna, like a delicate yellow pinwheel, begged to be noticed. These were the colors, the sparks of light, she had seen when she'd pressed the heels of her hands to her eyes. There would be no grays in this existence. She thought she had never seen anything so clean and fresh as this place. The only thing marring it was her own grubby appearance. She held back suddenly, not certain she wanted to go on. Pauley waited patiently, sensing the reason for her hesitation. When he heard her sigh and caught sight of that determined set of her mouth, he pulled her up the hill quickly before she changed her mind.

Alexis followed him, willing her feet to take each step firmly as if she were climbing the rigging of the *Constellation* again. She knew when she reached the crest of the hill it would be like being in the crow's nest.

No one could ever harm her there.

Chapter Two

The next six years held the promise Alexis had envisioned when she first reached the crest of the hill. In the loving protection of George and Francine Quinton she found a contentment she had never known or even hoped existed. Yearning to be worthy of the love she had learned to accept and return, she challenged herself to contribute to her new family.

Under George's strict eye and encouraging countenance she learned to read and write, and was able to laugh at the mistake she had made selecting her own name. It wasn't important any longer. Alex Danty was gone. She was Alexis Quinton, secure in the knowledge that no one could take that away from her.

She retained all the perseverance of the child who had at one time dropped her aitches. George was never quite certain how he had been persuaded to allow Alexis to work in his offices, but after a time it ceased to matter.

He ignored the comments others made when he gave her tasks ranging from the most difficult to the most menial. She did them all with equal enthusiasm. George was quick to realize he had found a person capable of running Quinton Shipping. He never tried to conceal his pride when she handled difficult situations smoothly. Her self-confidence was labeled as arrogance by some but that mattered little to him. That quality was a sign of knowing what she was doing as far as he was concerned and he loved her for it.

During the years that Alexis was learning her trade she gradually became aware of her maturation into womanhood. She bore no resemblance to the gangly, tow-headed youth Pauley had introduced to the Quintons. At nineteen her limbs were in perfect proportion to the rest of her tall form and the awkwardness that had plagued her was replaced with a grace some women take years of conscious effort to learn. Francine had told her her long limbs would be her best asset, but Alexis could not help wondering if asset was quite the right word to apply to the smooth line of her arms and legs. It was getting harder to be taken seriously by some of George's associates. It had been bad enough when they had treated her as a child, but now they only seemed to see her slender waist and gently swelling hips. She never blushed when they stared at her. She merely waited until their gazes returned to her face; then she discreetly murdered them with a piercing amber glance. It was they who blushed and looked away, embarrassed for having forgotten the business at hand.

At home, with Francine, Alexis practiced needlepoint and dancing. She learned how to entertain guests and her graciousness was as natural as her arrogance.

Only on one subject did she and Francine disagree.

"But Alexis," Francine would protest, "you cannot continue to turn away every young man with a look. You frighten them."

"I don't intimidate George or Pauley," Alexis would return quickly.

"They are different."

"You mean they're special."

"Perhaps," Francine would concede.

"Don't you see, Francine? The man I want would never turn away."

And the subject would be closed until Francine caught Alexis doing it again. She was at a loss to explain Alexis's peculiar behavior. Her daughter was beautiful, intelligent, and certainly wealthy. It was known throughout the islands that she was George's choice to run Quinton Shipping in the future. And it was not as if the islands were not without suitable matches. There were planters and ranchers as well as politically ambitious men vying for Alexis's attention. She, however, seemed interested only in making friends with George's employees, the men who worked in the offices or the men who sailed his ships.

Francine finally contented herself with tutoring Alexis in social graces. Her daughter hung on every lesson with the same degree of earnestness she exhibited when George was teaching her some aspect of the business. The intensity with which she approached every stage of her education sometimes frightened Francine. Alexis was a formidable young woman, even as she had been a formidable child. The man who would have her love would have to be very special indeed and Francine had to agree with her daughter that Alexis had not met him yet.

Alexis had too much interest in the present to allow herself to dwell on the past. But she thought of Pauley's return and of her promise to him as her hair grew past her chin, then her shoulders, and finally reached the length he had commanded.

Not far beyond her home Alexis found a natural ledge on the cliff side of the hill. Overlooking the ocean, it reminded her of the crow's nest and offered her sanctuary when she watched for Pauley's ship. Here, in this rocky nest, while searching the horizon for her friend, she thought of all the pleasures that had been hers since coming to the island.

On the eve of her sixth anniversary with George and Francine, Alexis again took up her vigil in her well-worn spot. Absentmindedly she pulled at her long yellow braids. Surely he would come soon. She had so much she wanted to thank him for. Pauley had been right about so many things and now she wanted to tell him she understood.

Alexis watched the shadow of a ship nearing the harbor. The full moon gave it a ghostly appearance, and she shivered even though she told herself she was being silly. She did not believe in Francine's woman's intuition. Still, as she followed the ship into port, she could not put aside a feeling of dread. She had never experienced anything like it before, and she hoped she would never feel anything akin to it again.

Alexis slept peacefully that night, never knowing that her life in the crow's nest was about to be shattered. There was no sanctuary in 1810 from a British naval vessel in search of a crew to man her guns.

When she awoke Francine's petite frame was bending over her, wishing her happiness of this special day, and the uneasiness she had experienced before going to bed was forgotten.

"Happy anniversary," Francine whispered, laughter alive in her azure eyes. "Can you believe it is six years? George says you may have the day off in honor of the occasion. He promised to be home early. All of the servants have a holiday. I believe they'll want to thank you later for it."

Alexis smiled, trying to stifle a yawn. "It's been a wonderful six years, hasn't it? As if I've always lived here." She brushed the hair away from her eyes, wishing she hadn't unbraided it before she'd gone to bed. It had practically strangled her in her sleep and now it covered her shoulders and back like a blanket. The silky waves everyone else admired were more often a nuisance to Alexis.

She sat up while Francine reached for her brush and began to work through the tangled ends. "Where would you like me to go today so you will be able to make my favorite sweet and surprise me later?"

Francine hit her lightly on the back of the head with the brush. *"Vous êtes impossible, Alexis.* Would it not be a good surprise if this year I did nothing?"

Alexis turned suddenly, horrified that Francine might make good her threat; but when she saw those blue eyes light up she laughed at her foolishness. This day meant too much to all of them for Francine to change her ways now.

"You haven't answered my question, Francine. Where should I go?"

Francine sighed. "Why don't you go to the beach? The spot you can see from your crow's nest. I'll be able to call you when the surprise is ready." She paused. "Stay away from the rocks, Alexis. Please? I worry when you swim so close to them."

"You worry too much," Alexis scolded. "I've never been hurt before and I'll be careful now. Go along and don't fret. Give me a chance to dress." She kissed Francine on the cheek and hugged her fiercely. "Have I told you lately how wonderful you and George are?"

"Not in the last day or so." She laughed, extricating herself from Alexis's arms.

When Francine had gone Alexis dressed quickly, pulling on a light cotton shift she saved for making the steep descent to the beach. Carrying a towel, she whisked past her mother on her way out the door. The cool grass felt good beneath her bare feet as she carefully picked her way down the hill. When she had reached the white sandy bottom she undressed hurriedly and ran to the water's edge. Without pausing she dove headfirst into the clear, blue water. She swam for a short while and then floated on the water, letting the gentle current carry her along to the area Francine had asked her to stay away from.

Around the rocks the current became swifter and Alexis had to use all of her strength to avoid being tossed against them. As always, with strong deliberate strokes, she avoided the rocks and reef and returned to her starting position.

Laughing and breathless from the exertion of her swim, Alexis paused a moment before she ran from the water. She reached for her towel, and after she dried herself she put on her shift and began to unbraid her hair.

From his hiding place among the rocks Tanner Frederick Cloud's breath caught in his throat. He had seen the young woman swimming and was amazed at her daring when she ventured dangerously close to the breakers. It was as if she were taunting the strength of the water with her own. She seemed to make each stroke so effortlessly Cloud was surprised to see long, finely curving legs carry her from the sea instead of a glistening, emerald tail. He studied her graceful movements as she dried, dressed, and unbraided her golden hair. She ran her fingers through the silky tresses until they were free of tangles, then she held her hair at her head while she lay back in the sand, freeing it at the last moment so it formed a silky backdrop for her face. Cloud wished he could see her more closely, but he was almost sixty yards away and he could only guess that her face would compliment her lithe form.

"Have you seen them yet, Tanner?" came a voice behind him.

Cloud shook his head, the voice of his second in command shaking him back to the reality of his purpose on the hillside. He did not add he had been too intrigued with the girl to pay attention to the house. He was guilty of violating his own orders.

"No, not yet. But it's just a matter of time before they come for Quinton. Go back and wait. And make sure Allen and Briggs stay put until I give the signal." When Cloud was satisfied Landis had hidden himself completely out of view of the girl, he turned his attention to the house.

He wondered if it had been unwise to bring so few men. They had all volunteered, but he could not risk leaving the ship unprotected while he pursued what could turn out to be a fool's errand. There were only four of them stationed at various points along the hillside. It would have to be enough.

Cloud had been assigned to take his ship, the USS *Hamilton*, to Tortola to discuss commissioning ships from George Quinton. He smiled ruefully, looking back on his reaction to the order. What had seemed so easy, even boring, to his adventurous spirit, was quickly becoming more of a danger than he was willing to subject himself or his men to. A simple business transaction between Quinton Shipping and the

Amerian Navy had a distinctly unpleasant edge to it once the *Hamilton* noticed the British Naval frigate patrolling the waters near the harbor. The presence of the British vessel made his crew feel ill at ease. They knew it was likely the British were looking for men to replenish a skeleton crew. Being on a naval ship did not necessarily protect one from the possibility of being boarded. Cloud had learned that lesson well enough.

The British made a pretense of legality. However, once they boarded a ship they looked for the heartiest crew members and then announced these men were actually deserters from the Royal Fleet. It didn't matter that the men had never set foot in England. The British officers had false records, and there were always those who would identify the victim as a deserter. That was how it had happened to Cloud. He winced at the memory and shifted his position behind the rocks. Just recalling the incident was enough for him to feel the scars lacing his back as if they were being put there for the first time. He shrugged the memory off and watched the house more closely.

Last night, after the British had sailed into the harbor, Cloud had hidden the *Hamilton* in one of the small coves at the end of the island. This morning he took a few men into Roadtown, leaving a disgruntled crew to guard the ship. Cloud went straight to the offices of Quinton Shipping while his men acted as lookouts. There was already something of a panic in the port town as the press gang moved among the residents, selecting men from every walk of life. Cloud narrowly missed being apprehended as he waited in the outer office to see Quinton. The secretary had already informed him that George was gone for the day, something about an anniversary party for his daughter, but Cloud had remained a few moments longer to write a message for Quinton, hoping he would agree to meet later. He had never finished the letter because his men broke into the office and dragged him, bodily, out the rear exit. It was not until they were safely hidden that Landis told him the reason for the action, though Cloud suspected immediately. It seemed George Quinton and his business were the main attraction of the island for the frigate's crew. They were searching everywhere for him.

Cloud determined to get to him first. He needed those ships as much as the British, and his government was willing to pay.

He and his men found Quinton's home, but Quinton himself had not returned. They positioned themselves along the cliffs where they could watch the activities of the hill. Landis was stationed so he could see Quinton approach on the main path leading to the house, since he was the only one who knew George by sight. Cloud glanced in Landis's direction. The officer was gesturing toward the beach, but motioning that the newcomer was not George Quinton. The captain turned quickly on his heels to see what Landis was pointing out.

He watched with interest as a big, rugged man approached the girl on the beach. Cloud had a hand placed lightly over his pistol should the stranger not be welcomed by the girl. In the moments that followed he saw his fears were ungrounded.

Alexis sat upright when she heard soft footsteps coming toward her. She glanced over her shoulder and, seeing the man approaching her, scrambled to her feet, and began running toward him.

"Pauley! It is you! It really is you!" she cried. She stopped a few feet in front of him when he held out his hand, motioning her to halt.

Alexis enjoyed Pauley's scrutiny. It was evident he was just as pleased as she at how she had matured. She turned slowly so he could see the waist length hair she had grown for him, and when she faced him again she knew he remembered because she was looking into the broadest smile she had ever seen him wear.

"You're a beauty, Alexis," he said finally, stressing her name slightly.

"Oi know, Pauley," she said simply, and they both laughed.

He crossed the distance between them in two easy strides. He put his hands on her waist and lifted her into the air while she rested her palms gently on his shoulders. After a few turns they fell to the sand, breathless and dizzy.

"How has it been for you, Alexis?" he asked once he had caught his breath.

"Do you even have to ask? I have never been happier. George and Francine are wonderful—but you knew they would be."

"I knew. I've already seen Francine. She told me where to find you."

"Did she tell you what today is?"

"Of course. But I already knew that too. Your anniversary, isn't it?"

Alexis nodded, smiling at her friend. Her delight was as readily seen in her amber eyes as it was on her lips. "Did Francine tell you I never doubted you would come back?"

"She told me that and a lot more. It seems you've been accomplishing all sorts of things. Francine couldn't stop talking."

"Oh! I wanted to surprise you!"

"You should know Francine can't keep a secret long. Besides, she's very proud of you and what you've been able to do."

"She would be more pleased if I were married, Pauley." Alexis sighed.

"Only if it were what you wanted. She trusts you to know when the time will be right."

"Let's not talk about this anymore. I want to hear about you and your family. Are they all right? Do you have any more children? What about—"

"Whoa! One at a time." Pauley got to his feet and held out a hand for Alexis which she took eagerly. He led her along the beach toward the base of the cliff. "I don't want to repeat myself a hundred times so I'll answer all your questions when I see George and Francine."

Alexis laughed. "I know Francine told you to get me up to the house so she could surprise me."

Pauley gripped her hand tightly. "She said you would say

that. But you're in for the surprise; she was so busy entertaining me there will be no trifle when we get back."

"That is a surprise. I think my first real one."

"Francine said you are not the easiest person to fool."

"I've been a disappointment to her there. She wanted a little girl and by the time I met her I was already too old."

"And she wouldn't trade you for all the babies in the world."

"I know. I love her so much. And George too." Alexis stopped suddenly and looked up at Pauley's weather-worn face, a face that had changed little since she had seen him last. She met his warm blue eyes and whispered softly, "Thank you."

Pauley was saved from blushing at her simple words because he saw Francine waving frantically to them from above. "Look. It's Francine. George is probably back and she's in a fine French snit because I've kept you so long."

Alexis waved back to Francine then she began pulling Pauley along the cliff. "I'll show you the fastest way up. No need to keep her waiting any longer."

Neither Alexis nor Pauley realized until it was too late that Francine was trying to keep them away from the house.

When she reached the top Alexis stood still, shocked. Pauley, a few paces behind her, did the same. George was on the portico, pistols in hand, ready to fire on any of the six men approaching the house from Alexis's right. Francine, directly behind her husband now and also with a weapon, called to Alexis to stay back.

Heedless of the warning, she broke Pauley's grip on her wrist and ran across the yard to join her parents. "What's happening?" she cried. "Who are those men?"

"Take her into the house, Francine," George ordered sharply. "And you stay there too. Pauley and I will handle this."

Francine nodded obediently and did as she was told. She gave her pistol to Pauley then she hustled a protesting Alexis into the house, shutting the door firmly behind her.

Alexis had never seen fear on Francine's face before and the sight of it made her own stomach churn disquietingly. "Francine! For God's sake! Tell me what is going on!"

Francine answered in rapid French until she realized Alexis could not make out what she was saying. Slowly, as if she were talking to a child, she started over in English. "Those men are from the Royal Navy. They've come from English Harbour on Antigua to see George about some of his ships."

"They want to commission George to build some?" she asked hopefully.

Francine shook her head sadly. "They don't want to commission. They want only to take what is available in the harbor now."

"They can't do that! Why even if they took them they wouldn't have enough men to sail them. It's preposterous!"

"It's a press gang, Alexis. Do you understand what that means? They've already been through the settlement, taking men who were unfortunate enough to be on the streets this morning."

Alexis remembered back to the time she had boarded the *Constellation*. The Thorton Shipping Line required its men to sign a paper saying they had not been forced to take the job. Now she understood exactly what that document meant, and at the same time, the stories she'd heard from her seafaring friends about press gangs came back to her. "But they won't take George surely? How would they get ships later?"

"They don't seem to have much thought for the future. They need the ships now and they'll take George and any other able-bodied man they can to replenish their own sickly crews."

Alexis gasped. "Pauley too?"

"Pauley," Francine confirmed. "He knew about it before he came here. He warned me to be prepared."

"But he didn't say anything to me. He let me believe everything was fine." Alexis didn't know with whom she was more angry, Pauley or the limeys.

"I asked him not to. We both thought we were worrying

needlessly. In any event, we didn't expect them to come so soon. I tried to warn you to stay away, but you didn't listen." Francine collapsed into tears.

Alexis led her over to a chair and pushed her into it gently. "Francine. Quiet. We've got to do something and I can't think while you're crying."

Francine buried her face in her hands, and although she did not stop crying, the sound was at least muffled so that Alexis could hear what was being said through the closed door.

"Listen Quinton. We didn't come here for trouble. The pistols aren't necessary. If you had been in your office we could have talked this over reasonably."

George laughed. "Captain Travers, I have never heard you discuss anything reasonably. Tell your gang to put their guns away and leave quietly. We have nothing to say to one another."

"You're a British subject, Quinton. You have a duty to your king. I'm claiming those ships by right of the British Crown."

"How typical," George answered smoothly. "The King pays us no attention until he finds himself in need of a few ships and some men to sail them. Then he suddenly remembers we are British subjects."

"We can take them with or without your consent," Travers replied testily. "I prefer your approval. We already have most of the crew we'll need. We want you to join us. Your friend there, with the gun, as well. He looks as if he knows his way around a ship."

"Indeed I do, Captain," Pauley answered, raising his pistol a hair. "But I'm already employed aboard the *Constellation*. That's a Thorton merchant and my captain won't take kindly to me jumping ship."

"I know Whitehead well enough. He won't be protesting too loudly, seeing that we found some deserters on board his ship." Travers looked at the five men surrounding him, daring them to contradict his statement. None did.

Alexis left her position at the door. "Francine! Is there another pistol anywhere?"

"In George's desk," she replied before she realized what Alexis intended. In horror she watched as Alexis ran to the study and returned to the foyer in a few moments with the weapon. "You can't go out there! George and Pauley will be furious. You'll be killed!"

Alexis stared at Francine uncomprehendingly. There was the faintest glimmer of a smile on her lips as she spoke. "If I can't die for the only people who have cared for me, then what am I supposed to die for?"

Francine saw the smile fade, to be replaced by an expression of intense determination. "Alexis, the gun isn't even loaded." It was too late. Alexis had turned and was heading toward the kitchen entrance at the rear of the house.

"Those limeys won't know that!" she called back.

Moving stealthily along the side of the house she was unaware her progress was being watched by four Americans. Even while admiring her bravery they were cursing her interference because fear of exposing her prevented them from making a move to assist her family.

"What is it going to be, Quinton?" Travers's voice was impatient. He kept his narrowed eyes trained on George. The stare was as hard and cruel as the face it belonged to. The narrow, pointed chin and the high, prominent cheekbones were set so tightly that neither George nor Pauley doubted this was a duty to which Travers was accustomed. "I'll not ask again. What are you going to do? Will you have to be persuaded to do your duty by your country?"

"I'd like to persuade all of you to drop your weapons." Travers turned quickly in the direction of the voice and saw Alexis approaching his men slowly, her weapon held steadily.

"You'd better do as she asks, Captain. I assure you she can handle that pistol," Pauley said. He did not notice George wince at the sight of Alexis holding what he knew to be an unloaded weapon.

The men looked to Travers for guidance.

"Keep your pistols," he ordered them. "She can only fire once with that thing and I doubt she's as handy with it as he says."

"Would you like to discover that for yourself, Captain?" Alexis responded evenly. "After all, I have it trained at your head. Now, tell your men to drop their weapons and leave. We have no use for your kind on this island."

Alexis was so intent on Travers that she failed to notice one of his men sliding closer to her. George did and he fired, the shot catching the seaman in his leg, causing him to fall toward Alexis. She tried to move out of his way but he grabbed the hem of her shift and she lost her balance, falling to the ground and dropping her pistol. The others were on her in a moment and Pauley and George had to stand by, afraid to fire for fear of hitting her.

Alexis struggled in vain to be free of them. When she was standing before Travers he grabbed her by the hair at the nape of her neck and twisted it hard. His eyes revealed surprise when she did not show any signs of pain. She stared at him coldly, contemptuously, and when he turned away from her gaze he did not know he was not the first to do so.

"Well, Quinton? I seem to have caught a very lovely prize here. Your daughter?" He hid his confusion as both Pauley and George acknowledged the girl as his own. He did not care to whom the hoyden belonged, as long as she could get him what he wanted. "Drop your pistols and we won't hurt her. All I want is your agreement to serve."

"Don't you dare do it!" Alexis called to them. "He has no right! I'll hate you if you do it."

Both men understood what Alexis meant and they gripped their weapons more tightly.

Travers could not comprehend the situation. The girl should be begging for mercy, yet instead she seemed more than willing to be punished for her insolence. And even more confounding, the two men seemed willing to let that happen.

"Tie her up," the captain ordered. He barked the command again when his men were slow to respond. As Alexis's hands were pulled roughly behind her and bound, he asked George once more, "Have you reached a decision? Are you coming with us or do I have to punish the girl for your reluctance?"

George and Pauley exchanged glances. Neither believed Travers could go through with such madness. They looked at Alexis but she was glaring at the captain and did not turn in their direction. They only had two shots left against six men and they each made the same decision: to see what the next few minutes had in store for them.

At the same time, Cloud decided he and his men could not wait any longer. They'd heard Travers's threat and fully believed he would carry it out. At Cloud's signal they began their separate approaches. Allen chose to use surprise to cover the others' positions and charged out of the trees screaming like a banshee in the direction of the house. He didn't go far. One of Travers's men picked him off, but the confusion that followed was enough to give Pauley and George the chance they needed.

Pauley fired first, catching Travers in the arm and knocking the gun out of his hand. The force of the slug sent the captain to the ground, but in his wisdom, or his cowardice, he had the presence of mind to grab Alexis and use her to shield his body. George fired off a shot that narrowly missed Alexis as she struggled to be free of Travers's icy grip.

Two of the British seamen were pursuing Landis and Briggs, who had been sighted in spite of Allen's effort as they were nearing the house from the back. As another shot was fired, George leaped toward Travers in a desperate bid to free Alexis. He was stopped in midair by a shot that sent him to the ground with a sickening thud.

Alexis cried out as George dropped to the grass only a few feet in front of her. She knew he was dead even before his body hit the hard earth. Pauley started to move forward, but he stopped when one of the men pointed his pistol at Alexis's head. He held his position, rooted to the spot he stood in.

Peering over the edge of the cliff from Alexis's crow's nest,

Cloud was met by the grim sight of Landis being dragged, unconscious, toward the front of the house. He knew then that Allen and Briggs were probably dead. He had decided to make his approach on the cliff side, using the same path he had seen Alexis use earlier. But she had made it appear far simpler than it was, and the delay had cost dearly.

Icy rage gripped him as he raised his pistol toward the man who had a weapon directed at Alexis. He fired. He knew a bitter satisfaction when the man clutched his head and fell to the ground.

Astonishment held Pauley rigid for a moment longer, then he forgot everything but his immediate purpose. He cared little for the fact that the sailors had pulled out their cutlasses or that they had anticipated his move. He wanted Travers.

He ran toward the group and pulled Alexis off the captain, then he fell on him, twisting his collar. Pauley lifted the man's head and repeatedly banged it to the ground.

Cloud watched as the other men surrounded Pauley, weapons ready. He scrambled over the edge of the cliff and fired but Alexis was on her feet by this time and she lunged at him. The shot that was meant for Cloud's heart found its target along his hairline and the captain slipped into darkness.

Alexis was at a loss to explain the presence of any of the men who seemed to have made it their business to help. As she saw the tall, lean man whose life she had tried to save, fall to the ground, she was filled with an anger so intense it momentarily frightened her. She tried to get to her feet again but because of her bound hands her movements were awkward and she was sent reeling back to the ground by a well-placed boot in her stomach.

Powerless to stop what was happening, she watched in horror as Pauley was lifted from Travers and thrown to the ground. One of the men was ready to shove his blade into Pauley's chest when Travers's moans halted him. Alexis could hardly believe the man was still alive. His arm was bleeding heavily and his head was cut in a number of places. He staggered to his feet, dazed and disoriented.

"Don't kill him yet. We need some answers first." His voice became louder and harsher as he composed himself. Alexis thought the anger in his cold eyes could only be matched by the fury in her own. He seemed oblivious to the pain he had to be feeling.

Travers walked over to Pauley and took the sword from the seaman who was standing over him. "Who are those men who tried to get to you? How many more are there?"

Pauley narrowed his eyes and stared at the captain. He did not know any more than Travers but he wasn't about to explain that. He remained silent.

Travers moved the point of the cutlass up Pauley's chest and let it rest at his throat. He pressed lightly until the skin broke and he could see tiny rivulets of blood coming from the opening. "Who are those men? How many more are there?" Pauley chose not to answer again and Travers motioned his men to begin a search. "One of you take the girl in the house and tie up the other woman in there. I've had all I can stand from meddling females today." He grinned at Alexis as she was forced past him. His smile faded when she spit on his boots.

Alexis was pushed into the house and forced into a chair in the dining room.

"Where's the other woman?" the seaman asked her.

Alexis shrugged her shoulders. She glanced around the room. Francine seemed to have disappeared. Alexis hoped she had gotten away and into town for help. Her eyes stopped at the sight of Francine's shoes peeking out from beneath the heavy gold drapes. She looked quickly away but her captor had already seen her hesitation and he approached the window cautiously.

He was ready to pull back the drapes when a sound behind him caught his attention. He spun on his heels in time to see the object of his search coming at him with a large kitchen knife. As barefooted Francine lifted her weapon, the man gripped her wrist and twisted it hard. Francine hung on to the knife in spite of the pain and with the kind of strength only a person in terror can find, she pushed the blade closer to the man's chest.

Alexis forced herself to watch the action without making a sound. She knew if she screamed it would only attract the others, denying Francine all chance of winning, and because there was nothing she could do the struggle seemed to go on forever.

The seaman's foot caught Francine's ankle and she lost her balance. They both fell to the floor, the knife wedged between them. The man stood up and staggered back against the wall, his eyes wide and horror-filled. His chest was crimson. He looked down at Francine, then over to Alexis.

"Oi never killed a woman before," he said, the words strangling in his throat. "Oi didn't wan' ta kill 'er."

Alexis looked from his blood-soaked shirt to the cause of it. Francine was lying motionless on the carpet, the knife firmly embedded in her chest. Alexis thought she detected the slightest smile on Francine's face and she looked back at the horrified seaman.

"I think you had better kill me also," she said without emotion. "Or I will kill you."

The sailor stared at those amber eyes, and they held him motionless for a moment. He was suddenly afraid of the beautiful girl who sat without moving in the chair into which he had thrown her.

Brusquely he walked toward her and yanked her out of the chair. He led her outside, wanting only to get out of the house and into a position where he felt in charge.

Alexis gasped when she saw what was happening out there. The two men who had tried to help were both bound now, so Alexis assumed they were alive, but unconscious. Pauley was tied to one of the portico columns. His shirt had been torn up the back and Travers was issuing the order to begin the flogging.

The captain stopped when he saw the girl and his man come out of the house. "I thought I told you to leave her in there! Where's the other woman?"

"She's dead. She came after me. Oi 'ad ta defend meself." He looked at Alexis when he said his next words. "It was an accident. Oi didn' wan' ta kill 'er."

Travers said something to him that he did not hear. He only had ears for Alexis as she said softly, but with an edge of hardness that gave meaning to her words, "It doesn't matter, Sailor."

The British captain turned his attention back to Pauley. "You asked for this! You refused to answer my—"

Alexis broke in. "He doesn't know the answers!" she screamed. "He doesn't know who those men are! Wait until they wake up and ask them yourself!"

"I believe you," Travers said. "But that's only part of the reason this man is being punished. He attacked an officer of His Majesty's Navy and for that I could have him killed."

"Then do it," Pauley answered. He stared at Alexis, telling her that he was not afraid to die and that she should not interfere.

But death was not what Travers had in mind. He still needed men for his ships. Getting the ships would present no problem now, with Quinton dead, but he could use a strong man like Pauley on board. Not on his ship, of course. That was to invite death, but he could be valuable on board another. The lashes that were about to be delivered would make him more cooperative. Travers had not encountered many men who, once they had experienced a hundred and fifty strokes, ever came back for more. Most of then were terrified at the threat.

Alexis did not take her eyes from Pauley as Travers gave the order.

Cloud opened his eyes. His brain was foggy and his vision blurred. He tried to move and realized he had been tied. He looked over at Landis who was just beginning to stir. The seamen standing over them were not interested in their movements. Their eyes were trained on a sight in front of them and when Cloud looked in that direction he had to fight the waves of nausea that assailed him.

The man tied to the support had easily received one hundred lashes and still Travers was ordering his man to inflict more. Cloud could not tell if the girl's husband had already passed out. He was not moving or crying out, but sometimes that was no proof. Cloud remembered he had taken almost that many before oblivion set in. He turned away from the man's bloody back to the girl, standing motionless on the porch. Her gaze suddenly shifted from Pauley to Travers, and Cloud thought then, that if eyes could inflict death, she had just murdered Travers mercilessly.

He watched, helpless, as Alexis broke from her captor's grip and ran to Travers. She threw herself at his feet and begged him to stop the flogging. Bile rose in Cloud's throat. He knew this girl wanted to do nothing but kill the man in front of her; yet she was forced to beg instead. It was harder to look on her face as she stilled her pride, than it was to see her husband's raw and bleeding flesh. This was an anniversary she would always remember.

"Captain Travers! Please! Stop it! You'll kill him! Don't make him suffer anymore!" Her voice was soft as the whip was sharp. "You've had your revenge! Leave him alone!"

Travers ignored her and kicked her out of the way. "Shut up or you'll be feeling the lash next."

Alexis stood up. Her muscles tensed and she clenched her fists behind her back. She glared at Travers once more, allowing him to see the full extent of her hatred. He laughed at her and ordered his man to continue. Alexis was not shocked by his laughter, only his stupidity. At least the man who had murdered Francine knew that she spoke the truth about killing him. Travers was a fool to believe anything else was possible.

But not now, Alexis thought. Now she had to save Pauley. Travers would be hers later.

If she lived.

Alexis ran to Pauley and threw herself across his bloody back. The front of her dress and the top of her breasts were immediately soaked with his blood. The man holding the whip did not have time to check his movement and the stroke intended for Pauley caught Alexis across her back, tearing her shift and drawing a small, thin line of red. The seaman dropped his whip, intending to pull Alexis from Pauley and continue the punishment, but his captain stopped him.

"If that's what the lady wants," he said as he picked up the whip, "then she may have it. He has twenty-five lashes left, girl. They're yours!"

Cloud's features hardened as Alexis's hands were untied and retied around the man she was trying to protect. He heard Landis wince as her shift was ripped open from her neck to her waist.

"It seems a shame to mark such beautiful skin," Travers said as he ran his rough hand down her naked back. He raised his hand to strike the first blow but hesitated when he saw his men turning away. He yelled at them. "She wants this! If it hadn't been for her, none of this would have happened." It was a lie. He knew it and his men knew it, but they also knew that if they turned away they would be at the wrong end of his whip soon. They steeled themselves and watched.

The man who had killed Francine could not take his eyes from Alexis as she turned her head, leaning her cheek against Pauley's back, and stared at him.

Alexis's eyes closed briefly as she felt the strip of leather crease her back. She whispered to Pauley not to be afraid, that she could stand it, that she wanted to stand it. She pleaded with him to hang onto life until vengeance would be theirs. She felt the sticky wetness on her back as Travers brought down the whip again and again. She bit her lip, tasting blood, so she would not cry out. Her hair was plastered to her back as sweat mingled with the ruby creases every stroke made. She forced herself to remain conscious, wanting to remember every nuance of pain the captain was inflicting upon her. She would need that memory to keep her going in the days, possibly months, ahead. Tears sprang to her eyes and rolled down her cheeks. They were at first tears of pain, but they were fed by sadness, horror, and outrage. She could not stop the involuntary moan that came to her lips. She lost count of the strokes. She was ready to lose reality when suddenly it stopped.

Travers threw down the whip. The pain from his wounded arm was burning him, distracting him. The movement as he wielded the whip had caused blood to flow rapidly and he began to feel weak from the effort. He had stopped at twenty, when he heard her moan. That was enough for him. It was all he'd wanted from the beginning—to hear the girl cry out once. She could have saved herself a lot of pain if she had given in earlier. He had never intended to give her the full count. But she had lasted and damn near killed him in the process, he thought bitterly.

He held his wound, trying to stop the flow with pressure, and barked at his men. "Leave them all! We'll get the ships we want and get off this island." The men did not move immediately. They were still staring at the girl's back. She was not crying out or moving, but they knew she was alive by her erratic breathing and by the rasping sounds coming from her throat. They hated Travers for what he had done and they hated themselves for not stopping it.

One of them moved forward to untie Alexis but Travers stood in his way. "No. Leave her. Let't get out of here before the entire settlement discovers what has happened."

They started to move, all except Francine's murderer. He was still, held prisoner by the amber eyes that were open now, but glazed over by tears. When the lids closed over them he felt as if he had been freed and in that instant he knew what he wanted to do. He leaped forward, toward his captain's unprotected back, and threw himself on him.

Travers was not caught completely off guard; he had been suspecting the man would do something since he had first walked out of the house. Something had happened in there, and he did not think it was only the death of the woman.

Instinctively Travers knew when the moment was about to take place and he was ready. In spite of his weakened condition he managed to draw his pistol, and as the sailor caught him by the shoulders Travers spun and fired into the mutineer's belly. The man dropped to the ground and Travers faced his three remaining men.

"Don't any of you entertain the same idea," he said tightly.

The men looked away and started down the hill, each having the same desire to kill his captain; yet none was willing to risk the consequences if he did not succeed.

Cloud could hardly believe he and Landis were still alive. Alexis had saved them by her actions. Travers would never want Landis and him aboard after they had witnessed what happened, and they had not been killed because Travers had had all the carnage he could tolerate in one day.

Cloud slid closer to Landis. They began working on their ropes. The first officer managed to free himself first; then he untied his captain and together they raced to Alexis. She was alive, but barely. When Cloud freed her hands, she slid down Pauley's slippery back before he could catch her and fell in a crumpled heap at his feet. He was about to pick her up and take her into the house when Landis stopped him.

"He's dead, Captain. He was probably dead before she tried to save him."

Alexis looked up at the man who was speaking. She forced herself to answer him. "He died while I was asking him to go on living. He died in my arms." Sobs racked her body and Cloud reached down for her but she pushed him away. Every sob, every pained breath her body took, gave her additional strength.

Cloud and Landis could not hide their surprise when she got to her feet. She wavered only slightly as another spasm of pain gripped her body. She looked down at Pauley's lifeless form, then over at George. She remembered Francine in the house. Then she remembered all of them as they had been only an hour ago. Happy. Excited. Her anniversary. Pauley coming to see her. Life in the crow's nest where no one could touch her. She noticed that the two men were watching her curiously. It was obvious they thought she was half mad. And perhaps she was, she thought.

Hadn't she been half mad to believe there was a place

where she could not be hurt? Hadn't she let George and Francine soften her with their well-meaning love and protection? Hadn't she let Pauley make a decision to bring her to them in the first place? It was a decision she hadn't liked but one she'd allowed herself to accept. It was a decision on his part that was made out of concern and love for a small girl. And she had learned to love them all.

And now, the only people who had ever shown her any affection were dead. The pain that gripped her back was insignificant compared to the pain of losing Pauley, George, and Francine.

Alexis staggered toward the crow's nest, falling to her knees before she made it half the distance and crawling the remainder of the way.

She looked out over the cove, aware of the two men at her side, and she wondered if they thought she was going to throw herself over the cliff. Didn't they know she had a reason to live? Didn't they suspect?

The sky and water blended into a singular blue line on the horizon. Alexis raised her fist and made the promise that would guide her future.

Chapter Three

The meeting had been over for less than an hour. As Cloud built a fire in the hearth of his kitchen he cursed himself for ever telling them so much. He should have known from the beginning there was no way to make them alter their plans to meet Alex.

"She made two promises that day," he had told them quietly. "Only one of them affects what you are proposing." The other affected him, its nature intensely personal. "She promised she would find Travers and kill him. She vowed she would live on the sea until she had him at her mercy."

He had paused then, to allow them to consider what he had said. When he continued his voice became progressively harder. "Alex Danty is on a personal mission. She will never join us. She is after only one man and if she finds him she will stop. She doesn't kill or plunder. She offers men liberty from impressment because she happens to find them before Travers. It was never her purpose to do it, and freeing them is not what sustains her. If she joined us she would be losing time from her pursuit. Our goal is not hers."

Although they had listened, they had not accepted it. They

continued to talk as if they would be able to persuade her to join them. When Cloud questioned their ability to do so, Howe played his ace.

"She may not be an American citizen," he said. "But she is a pirate. We can hang her for that. We'll offer her a pardon in exchange for her assistance."

"That's stupid!" Cloud had spit back. "She's not a pirate. She has never even so much as threatened an American ship."

"But she's been attacking British vessels without the sanction of our government. The British could interpret that as instigating war."

"But she is British."

"They don't know that, Captain. We didn't know it ourselves until today. And reports have it that three of those ships she sank went down within the territorial limits of the United States. It puts our government in a rather awkward position."

"Awkward, hell! If you try getting her to cooperate with those charges as leverage she'll laugh in your face."

"Actually, Captain, the matter has already been decided. The President wants to meet Alex Danty and he chose us to arrange a meeting. We've chosen you. We had no idea you knew the captain, but you've convinced me that you do. Your knowledge will help you bring her to us even sooner than we anticipated—perhaps before war is declared. The President needs support and if the public discovers Alex Danty is on our side the issue won't be so unpopular."

That was when Bennet pulled out the order. "Here it is, Captain. You're to leave within the week. Mr. Madison considers it vital that you return as soon as possible. No one else, other than your superiors, knows about the decision to find Alex Danty."

Cloud reflected on their fevered approach to the imminent war. It did not seem consistent with any of Madison's policies to order him to go after Alex; yet, that was what he was expected to do. He pulled out the orders and examined them. Signed by the President and his superior, Commodore Graig. Sighing, he put them away.

Perhaps, if he had never mentioned Alexis's connection with Jean Lafitte, they would not have persisted with the idea of meeting her. He had never intended to tell them he was aware Alexis had met the notorious pirate shortly before she'd begun her hunt for Travers. At some point it had slipped out—probably when Bennet, in a rare moment of insight had guessed he was in love with Alex Danty, and had accused him of forgetting his loyalty to his country. He had wanted to slap Farthington's insipid grin right off his face. He loved Alex Danty, but he would never let her stand in the way of what was required of him. Just as she had not let him stand in the way of her goal. And he had tried. Oh God, he thought how he had tried.

As soon as Lafitte's name was out, Alexis's fate was sealed Cloud thought bitterly. He had tried to avoid being given the assignment, but they would have none of it. His men would think he had betrayed her, just as Alexis would.

He never wanted to see Alex Danty again until she had had her vengeance, until she had put to rest the thing that drove her. But now their goals clashed. He was going to be at war and her personal war could not block his way. He only hoped she did not kill him before he had a chance to reason with her.

Cloud stared at the fire. He sat down in a high-backed chair, tilted it, and propped his legs on the table. So much he had told them, he thought, and so much still remained The things he omitted were never far from his consciousness just as Alex was never out of reach as long as he was willing to retrieve the memory.

He ran his fingers through his copper hair as he recalled the sight of Alexis on the very edge of the cliff. On the very edge of her sanity, he had thought at the time. Her face was smeared with blood; her golden hair, more crimson than gold. He never knew how she found the strength to speak let alone raise her angry fists and head skyward. But she had and Landis and he had never heard anything more chilling There was a moment on the cliff when he thought she had

ceased to be human, a moment when she took on an appearance that was almost ethereal. He had heard Landis tell someone later that she was like an angel, an avenging angel; and
Cloud, having been there, was forced to agree with that assess-
ment. Alexis Quinton had died on the crow's nest that day,
and Alex Danty had been brought back to life.

At first he fought against her continuous presence in his
mind. There had been other women since Alex but they only
made him want her back. There was no other woman for
him, and he could never have her completely until she had
finished with Travers.

And then there was the matter of her second vow, the vow
that only Landis and he heard that day—a vow they had never
shared with anyone. It was the one Cloud knew he would
have to fight against. He loved Alex Danty, and with the last
of her strength she had sworn she would never love anyone
again.

A crimson spark leaped free of the crackling fire. The red
glow of the burning embers was all his tired mind needed to
vividly recall the events of that day and the weeks there-
after. . . .

Alexis finished her oath and let her arms drop to her sides.
Trembling, she raised herself to her feet and took a step away
from the edge of the cliff. Her head was swimming and the
rhythm of the tide was the same as the throbbing in her brain.
She knew she was about to faint; she thought how absurd her
promises would seem to the two men behind her if she slipped
over the hillside.

Cloud stepped forward, gathering her in his arms before
she fell to the ground. He carried her into the house and
laid her on the sofa in the drawing room. It was when he
went in search of cloths and water for her back that he saw
Francine's body lying beneath the window in the dining room.
He fought another wave of nausea and tried to remember

when her death could have occurred. He was suddenly very grateful to the limey who had rendered him unconscious.

Cloud returned to Alexis with a basin of water and bandages and began to clean the blood from her back so he could examine the extent of her wounds.

Landis watched, shaking his head so his graying hair fell across his forehead in places. "Travers wasn't easy on her. The man has to be insane to go after a girl that way. What are we going to do with her?"

"Do with her?" Cloud asked, surprise surfacing in his voice. "We're taking her with us, of course. There's nothing for her here. The British will have made a shambles of her father's business. Her husband's dead—"

"Her husband? You mean the man she almost got herself killed for was her husband?"

"I believe so. When I talked to Quinton's secretary, he informed me that George's daughter had an anniversary today. This is obviously the daughter and that was her husband. Her mother is in the other room. Did you see what happened to her?"

"I didn't see it when it happened, if that's what you mean. Here, let me do that," Landis said, as he watched his captain try to clean Alexis's wounds. "You may be my commander, but you're making a mess. Take some of the cloths and dip them in water and clean yourself up. You've got a nasty gash on the side of your head. How did it happen?"

Cloud moved aside and made room for his first officer. He had forgotten about his head until Landis mentioned it. He wetted a few cloths and did as Landis suggested.

"Slug creased me," he explained, walking to the far side of the room, where he sat down again, facing a window. He could not watch Landis working on her, remembering too well what it had felt like when Landis had worked on his back. He was glad she was still unconscious and he hoped she remained that way until most of it was over.

"You were lucky," Landis observed. He worked gently on Alexis's raw flesh. If she survived these wounds, he thought, he would not want to be in Travers's place for anything in the world. He did not doubt the sincerity of her promises for one minute.

"Luck, nothing. She saved me. That limey had me dead and buried. She pushed him just as he fired. If she had been a second earlier I wouldn't have been hit at all."

"Or a second later and I'd be burying you now."

"What about Allen and Briggs?"

"Dead."

"Damn," he said softly.

Landis winced as he cleaned the last of the blood from Alexis's back. The wounds were deep. "I don't know if she's going to live, Tanner. Come and look. He did a hell of a job and she's lost a lot of blood."

Cloud forced himself to get to his feet and walk over to the sofa. The marks were indeed deep and she would always carry the scars—if she lived.

"At least you've stopped most of the bleeding. Do the best you can for now. I'm going to get some of her things so we can take them to the ship along with her. I'll bring the bodies in here and leave it to someone in town to bury them. We just can't take the time now."

Cloud quickly searched the bedrooms until he found Alexis's; then he took the things he wanted. He placed dresses, undergarments, shoes, and jewelry into a satchel, then took it to the front entrance. Afterward he dragged the bodies into the house, placing George's and Francine's together, with Pauley's nearby. Next he brought in the man he had killed and the one Travers had murdered. He found Allen and Briggs out back and he pulled them through the servants' entrance. He did not have time to consider what had happened to the Quintons' servants. He only knew their absence had saved their lives. When he finished he went back to Landis and told him it was time to leave.

"Just a few more minutes, Tanner. I've got to get these bandages around her and it is damned hard since I can't turn her over."

"I'll help." Cloud sat down on the edge of the sofa and together they lifted Alexis's unconscious form to a sitting position. Cloud stripped away the remainder of the shift that covered her shoulders and breasts. He forced himself not to recall how lovely she was beneath her matted hair and blood-stained face. As Landis wound the strips of cloth around her, her breasts brushed against his chest and Cloud caught himself thinking that if none of this had ever happened today he would still have found a way to take her from her husband and would never have let her return to the island. He would have made love to her until neither of them could go on or would want to. When he looked up Landis was staring at him.

"She is beautiful, isn't she?" he asked as he completed the wrapping.

"Yes. Very."

"Can an old man give his captain some advice?"

"When the old man is you, he can."

"You're not going to like it, and I don't expect you to take it, but here it is anyway." He stood up and washed his hands in the basin. Drying them off on his trousers, he said, "Don't bring her with us. You heard what she said on the cliff before she fainted. If she lives she will want to be here, not aboard the *Hamilton.*"

"You really think she'll go through with it?"

"I do. Do you remember that Travers threatened to punish her earlier if her father and her husband didn't lay down their weapons?" Cloud nodded. "Then remember what she told them. She screamed she would hate them if they did as Travers ordered. And they held their pistols."

"They were fools."

"I don't think so," Landis answered. "The girl was willing to make a sacrifice for the people she loved most in the world. In her mind her act had ceased to be a sacrifice and she would have despised them for not accepting what was here alone to offer."

"What are you getting at?"

"Only this. If you take her on board and stop her from leaving when she decides she has to go, she'll hate you also."

"Christ, John, you talk as if I am going to keep her on the ship forever. We're going to take her to Washington, where she can make some kind of new life for herself. Maybe Boston. My sister would care for her. She can't stay here."

"And I'm saying that is not a decision you can make for her."

Alexis moaned softly and her head fell limply against Cloud's shoulder.

"This girl's not in any condition to make decisions for herself. You're right; I am not going to take your advice."

Landis shrugged and ran his fingers through his short silver beard.

"Come on. Let's get her out of here before she wakes up," Cloud urged.

Landis helped him get Alexis to her feet then he let his captain sling her over his shoulder. "Easy, Tanner. She's not baggage."

Cloud nodded. "I know, but she's not as light as she appears either. I'll start toward the ship while you get her things. Meet me on the beach."

Landis watched Cloud leave with the girl securely in his arms. She intrigued him too. He could understand his captain's fascination with her. If he were thirty years younger he would do what Tanner was doing now. Thirty years ago he would have had the strength to put up with the demands a woman such as she would place on him. She had not made her vows lightly. She had a powerful rage burning inside her slender body. He did not think that kind of rage could be dismissed by taking her away from Tortola. As he followed with the girl's belongings, he wondered if his friend had given any thought to her second oath. He should have. If she lived Tanner was going to find himself a victim of it.

On board the *Hamilton* Cloud gave the order to sail, ignoring his crew's curious stares as he took his unconscious burden to his cabin.

He unwrapped the bandages around Alexis, pulling at them gently to prevent any more bleeding. When that was finished he washed the rest of her, discarding her ruined clothing. He made new bandages, and after he applied an ointment to her cuts, he put them on her. He pulled a sheet over her nakedness; then washed the dried blood from her hair. Afterwards he used his fingers to untangle the knotted mass of gold and brushed it all to one side to keep it from wrapping around her throat while she slept. When he was satisfied he could do no more for her, he left her alone and went on deck to make sure everything was proceeding smoothly.

It wasn't. Landis was trying his best to explain the events that had just taken place, and he was not doing it very well. The crew was outraged at the loss of two of their mates and even more so by the inhuman treatment of the girl. Some of his men had had the distinct misfortune to have sailed with Travers and they counted themselves lucky to have escaped impressment.

"Captain Cloud?" asked Harry Young, who was familiar with Travers's discipline. "The girl? Is she going to live?" His usual lopsided grin had vanished in response to the concern and anger he was feeling. He pulled nervously at the dark brown hair curling at his ear, thinking about his years on Travers's ship. His face aged drastically, just remembering Travers's cold, black eyes.

"I don't know, Harry," Cloud said quietly. He understood what the man was going through. Hadn't he felt the same way when he saw the ship? "She's strong. She might pull through."

"Yeah," Tom Daniels added. "Mr. Landis has been telling us how she stood up to Travers. She's got to be strong." His Georgia drawl was as soothing to hear as his words.

"Or crazy," a voice broke in.

Cloud searched out the speaker and glared at him. Mike Garrison shrunk back under the penetrating stare. Mike, as rugged and bawdy as any man on the *Hamilton,* was not immune to his young captain's commanding presence. In his forty years he had never met a man who could set him in his place like Cloud. He liked it. It was better than serving a man who was afraid of his brawn and went out of his way to avoid provoking his teeth-grinding anger.

"She's not crazy, Mike," Cloud said sharply. "You'll find that out soon enough if she recovers." Mike murmured an apology for being out of line, and Cloud laughed shortly. "Don't apologize to me, Mike. You can apologize to her. She's the one who is going to prove you wrong."

"Then I'll look forward to her recovery," he answered firmly.

Cloud explained the situation more fully to his men and when he was done he ordered them back to work. When he was not needed any longer, he returned to his cabin to check on Alexis. She did not seem to need him either. She was still unconscious, oblivious to the pain that would overtake her once she awoke.

"Come in," he answered impatiently to the knock at his door.

Landis strode into the room and walked over to the bed. "You did a fair job here, Tanner," he said as he inspected the wrapping.

"You didn't come here to tell me I should have gone to medical school. What do you want?"

"It's the men. They have something to ask you. It's not my place to give them an answer. I'll stay with her until you get back."

Cloud left his cabin. It had not taken them long to gather the courage to confront him. He knew what they wanted to know. He had been asking himself the same question since he'd returned to the ship. But he also knew the only answer it was possible to give them. And the answer was no.

He approached the small group of men standing on the quarterdeck. "Mr. Landis said you have a question for me. What is it?"

"You probably already know, Captain," said Harry. "We

want to go after Travers. He couldn't have got much of a head start on us. We could take him."

Mike cut in, his square jaw tightened with purpose. "There's not a man here who won't stand behind you if that's what you decide to do."

"I appreciate that, Mike. I only hope you will understand why we can't do it. We've lost two good men to Travers's insanity and we have a young woman below who may die because of his cruelty. We're not at war with the British and we may not be for some time. To initiate an attack against Travers's ship would be to invite catastrophe. We can't start a war on the basis of one man's actions." He examined the men's faces. They were unhappy with his decision but they knew he was right. They had known his answer just as he had known the question, but he admired them for asking it anyway. It never hurt to take an extra chance, even if the outcome was changed little by the effort. "Washington may open its eyes when we return and inform them there will be no ships from Quinton. It's going to put a heavier load on our ship-builders. Until then we can do nothing but get there as quickly as possible."

The men nodded their agreement. When Cloud left they went back to their stations, each silently hoping Mr. Madison would finally realize what they had known for several years: No American ship was safe in the open water until American vessels were allowed to prove they were a match for England's sea power.

Chapter Four

Cloud slept very little during the next three nights. He stayed by Alexis's side, changing her bandages and wiping her head as a fever set in. Landis relieved him occasionally so he could catch a quick nap, but when he heard Alexis moan or cry out he invariably woke up.

The second evening was the hardest. Her fever grew worse and Landis warned Cloud she might not survive the night. The crew also grew restless, waiting for word of her condition. If she died, Cloud was going to have his hands full trying to keep the men from doing anything foolish.

She talked in her sleep, crying out for George and Francine. He thought it was strange that she called her parents by their first names. Landis, who had known George years ago, was at a loss to explain it. Her most despairing cries were for Pauley. She would try to sit up, would reach out for him, and when she could not find him, would collapse into anguished sobs.

It was on the fourth night of their vigil, when Landis had stepped out of the cabin for some fresh air and Cloud had finally succumbed to his need for sleep, that Alexis woke.

She sat up peering through the darkness at the man sprawled in a chair near her bunk. Still feverish, it took her several minutes to remember who he was. When she did, she could not stop all the other images that flashed, unbidden, in front of her eyes.

She recalled every detail of the day vividly until the moment she fainted. After that she could not remember anything. She despised the weakness that had caused her to faint, but as pain gnawed at her back she understood why it had happened. She fought the urge to moan, biting her lip instead and causing tears to spring to her eyes.

She wondered how long she had been out. Not more than a few hours surely. It was night now. It couldn't be too late. She tried to identify her surroundings. Her own room didn't roll—Oh dear God! She was on a ship and the sound of water breaking against the hull outside told her she was not in port. What had these men done? How could they have taken her away from the island?

The man in the chair was still sleeping soundly. She tried to think back. Hadn't the other man called him captain? Then this was his ship and he would have made the decision to bring her here. She started to move, only one overwhelming thought in her mind: to get away. She stopped abruptly when she heard him stir. She remained motionless until he was quiet, then she got out of bed, looking down at her body in dismay when she felt a chill. Where were her clothes? Silently she cursed the captain in a rapid burst of French, almost sorry the object of her anger couldn't hear her.

She wrapped the sheet around her body and quietly searched the large wardrobe for something to wear. She was more than a little astonished to find her own things folded neatly away among the clothing that could only belong to the captain. She dropped the sheet to the deck and pulled on a chemise. She winced at the pain as the material pulled against the bandages and she could feel the bleeding start again. She was lifting a dress out of the wardrobe when the door to the cabin swung open. She recognized the man who entered as the same one who had been with the captain. When he did not notice her immediately, she slid into the shadows.

Landis walked over to Cloud and woke him roughly. "Your turn for some air. I'll watch the—Christ, Tanner! Where did she go?"

Cloud jumped to his feet. It wasn't possible! He had just dozed off for a few minutes. She couldn't have gone anywhere. He turned when he heard a small movement coming from the corner of the cabin. Alexis was standing against the wall, holding a dress in front of her. Her eyes shone like a cat's in the dim light, and Cloud wondered if she could see them more easily than they could see her. He lighted a lamp and walked toward her.

As Alexis watched the captain's approach she pushed herself against the wall. It was not fear that made her seem to back away, but pain. She thought she was going to faint again and the wall was the only thing offering her support in the wildly spinning cabin. It would never do to faint before she had a chance to tell them to take her back to Tortola.

Cloud stopped a few feet in front of her and placed the lamp on a commode. "Ma'am, you're not well enough to be moving yet. Let me help you get back to bed. You're ready to pass out again."

What a nice voice he had, she thought as she shook her head. It was clear and deep, blanketed with anxiousness. He did not appear to want to harm her. His liquid green eyes told her that. His outstretched arms were an extension of the things she saw in his eyes and heard in his voice. They looked inviting for their strength as well as the comfort they could provide. His body was lean and firm, and she remembered being held against that body. He must have been the one who caught her when she fainted. Now the pain was almost unbearable. She wanted to be held in those arms again, but she remembered her purpose and fought the urge to submit. She recalled this was the man who had taken her away from Roadtown. She had to tell him that he must return her. She had to make him understand.

Her eyes returned to his face, and she could not help thinking what a truly beautiful face it was. Even with his dark eyebrows pulled down in worry and his face etched with lines of weariness he was the most handsome man she had ever seen. His eyes, framed by long heavy lashes, never wavered from hers, and they were as green as the dark moss that clung to the breakwaters. His nose was long and straight. Aristocratic, she thought. Quietly arrogant. His lips were full, their line sensuous and his skin was as bronzed as her own from the sun. His beard was unkempt and darker than the thick copper hair curling at his collar.

Her eyes opened wide in horror. His beard! He hadn't had one before. No man's beard grew so thickly in a few hours. She cried out as the full realization struck her. She was out to sea! It couldn't be happening!

Alexis dropped her dress and let the pain overtake her. She slid down the wall to the deck.

Cloud reached her quickly and lifted her gently, carrying her back to his bunk. He laid her down and pulled the blankets close about her; then he faced Landis. "What do you suppose happened?" he asked. "I thought she was going to say something, but she just stared at me and fainted."

Landis laughed. "You obviously haven't looked at yourself lately. You're a sight, Tanner. You probably scared her into fainting. God knows, you're scaring me now."

Cloud set his jaw firmly and glowered at his officer. "Get out of here, John, and tell the men she is going to recover; then send me some fresh water so I can clean up and get rid of this damnable growth on my chin."

Landis left the cabin, chuckling to himself. He told the men the news and then brought back the water to Cloud's quarters, trying to hide his amusement as the captain went through his drawers to find a fresh shirt and trousers but only succeeded in pulling out lacy slips and shifts.

After he finished bathing and felt reasonably presentable for his guest, Cloud decided to go on deck and get some fresh air. He was still exhausted from lack of sleep and worry;

he knew he was not doing himself or his crew any good in his present condition. He walked to the starboard side of the ship and gripped the railing tightly. There was a full moon out and his ship cast shadows onto the water. He watched the shadows, not minding the salt spray hitting his face, and thought about the girl.

Had he done the right thing by bringing her along? he wondered for the hundredth time. And what was his motive really? He could have taken her to town. She had to have friends there who would have seen to her. Perhaps she would have been better left in her servants' care. She was beautiful, but that was only a small part of his attraction to her. She was not merely lovely because of the way she looked, but also for the way she moved, the way she fought, and the way her very presence demanded that others embrace life in the same manner she did. Those eyes. Those catlike amber eyes had held him captive below deck for a few moments while they bored holes into his flesh. He had never seen so much revealed in someone's eyes before. He knew she had examined him as any trapped animal examines the hunter; looking for weaknesses, considering the danger and the risks. But he also knew she had discovered she was in no danger. She'd revealed a momentary sense of relief not only in her eyes but in her limbs as well. Then her expression had changed so quickly. He could not fathom the reason. She had been ready to tell him something; he was certain of it. Then he'd seen her tense again, looking more like a trapped animal than earlier. The horrified expression on her face signaled anger, frustration, and, a moment later, defeat. She had given up. For a brief space of time she had thought she was helpless, and he had done something to cause it.

Cloud turned as he heard soft steps nearing him from behind. "What is it, Mr. Landis?"

"I thought I'd go look in on the girl. Her bandages probably need changing. She really needs fresh air for those wounds, but I don't think she can very well walk around on deck without a dress."

Cloud smiled, white even teeth outlined in the darkness. "No, I don't think she'll want to do that. Go ahead. You go to her. In fact, stay with her until she's ready to talk. I don't think she wants to see me for a while."

"It will be morning before she's going to make much sense. She tried to move too early and caused herself more discomfort than she had to."

"I know," Cloud replied, shaking his head. "What do you suppose made her do it?"

"I think she wanted to get off this ship, Captain."

"We'll find out soon enough, won't we?"

Landis said nothing as he turned and headed for the captain's cabin.

Alexis felt warm fingers tugging at her bandages and she tried to move away. She just wanted to be left alone. To think. To plan. She turned her head and opened her eyes. After the hazy mist cleared she saw it wasn't the captain, but his friend, who was gently removing the bandages.

"You'd better lie still, ma'am," he said. "I don't want to hurt you more than you've already been hurt."

"Where is the captain?" She tried to be still but it was hard. He was as gentle as possible, and the only reason she didn't wince was because she knew it would be harder for him. "I must see him," she added, her voice muffled in the pillow.

"Later. He wants to talk to you, too, but not until you feel better."

Alexis sighed as Landis rubbed a lotion on her back. It seemed to take away most of the burning and she felt drowsy again. When he was finished she turned her face to him. "What's your name?"

"John Landis."

"And your captain?"

"Cloud. Tanner Frederick Cloud."

"A formidable name. Is he a good man, your captain?"

Landis laughed. "You'll be able to form your own opinion,

if you haven't already, in the morning. But I'll tell you now, there isn't another man I'd rather serve." He saw a small smile form on her lips. "And your name? We don't know what to call you except Miss Quinton and that can't be right since you're married." He sat back, tensing, when he saw the surprised look on her face. He wanted to kick himself for mentioning her dead husband. He hadn't meant to upset her.

"What gave you that idea?"

Landis relaxed when he realized she was only confused, not distressed, by his information. "Captain Cloud said he heard something about an anniversary. We just assumed—" He stopped. Now he knew he had said the wrong thing. Her eyes narrowed sharply and her jaw was tightly clenched.

"You assumed wrong," she said, equal emphasis on each word she spit out. "Will you please leave me now?"

"I have to wrap you again," he protested although he wanted nothing more than to go.

"No," she said forcefully. "I don't need bandages. I need fresh air. Tomorrow I will have to get out of this bed. Just leave me for now, Mr. Landis."

Landis thought better of arguing with her. He took away the strips of cloth and removed the basin of water by her side, then he left her alone.

Alexis watched the door shut behind him. When she heard him walk down the companionway she sat up and was pleased to discover the move was not as painful as her earlier attempt had been. In another day or so, she thought, she would be ready to leave. She had to get away. She realized she had been hasty in dismissing Landis. She still did not know where she was, or how long she had been away from Tortola.

The anniversary. Why had he mentioned it? How had he known? Alexis brought her legs over the side of the bunk and rested her elbows on her knees, cradling her head in her hands. She vowed no one would ever see the invisible wounds she had acquired from the loss of the people she loved. She could only share that pain with someone she loved, and that was something she would never allow herself to do again.

It had been easy to dismiss London and her childhood. Humorlessly, she laughed, wondering if she had ever really been a child. She had left nothing behind when she'd boarded the *Constellation*. Then Pauley had changed that. He had understood her, respected her; and that had made her love him. When he'd left she had known a bitter ache that had only been relieved by the promise of his return. George and Francine were different and she'd loved them differently. They had always wanted what was best for her. She'd known she loved them the moment they had realized that she knew what was best for herself.

She would never see them again. Oh God, how it hurt! She had meant what she said when she had made her oaths on the cliff. Travers would pay for what he had done. She would live to avenge their deaths.

Alexis sat up, straightening her spine. There was nothing more to be gained by reflection now. The future. She had to look ahead the way she always had. Quinton Shipping would have to wait. Whatever Travers had destroyed could be rebuilt later. George had taught her well. Now she had to get off this ship and back to Roadtown. She would raise a crew and take whatever had been left behind and start her search. The future. Every moment Captain Cloud kept her from the island was wasted time. In the morning she would talk to him and explain what she wanted to do, and then he would take her back. Landis said he was a good man; she believed he was. Cloud had apparently tried to stop Travers and he had certainly saved her. She would thank him, then tell him he simply had to take her back. He would listen to reason.

She lay back on the bunk, covering herself, and buried her head in the pillow. Sleep followed quickly.

Cloud opened the door quietly. When he saw she was sleeping he moved as softly as he could so as not to wake her. Landis had told him she was distraught over something he had said and Cloud was too tired now to deal with her anger.

He took blankets and an extra pillow from the chest. He had decided to sleep in the adjacent cabin now that she was out of danger. He stopped moving when she stirred in her sleep.

She kicked at the sheet covering her body until it slid to the deck. Her chemise had ridden up to her thighs and the moonlight provided him with a view of her long, firm calves. She moved again, turning her head slightly. Her slim fingers brushed at the golden strands of hair covering her face. Her lips parted as she took a breath and expelled the air in a sigh. Cloud wanted to capture that sigh. It was the most comforting, soothing sound he had ever heard. He wanted to protect her and never let her feel anything but what she felt at that moment. He would have to make her understand that she could not go back to the island. Roadtown would be torture for her after what had happened and he couldn't allow her to punish herself like that. He would not let her go. She must listen to reason.

He replaced the sheet and hurried out of the room. His own breath was ragged, but not from exertion. His body cried out to be touched by her. Not yet, he thought. Not so soon. He wanted this woman, but he knew he would wait. He would wait until she wanted him as well.

Alexis awoke to the sound of light tapping on the door of her cabin. She rubbed her eyes and got out of bed. "Just one minute," she called to the man behind the barrier. She found a fresh chemise to replace the one she had stained with her blood and slipped it on. She located other undergarments and put them on also. A dress was another matter, she realized. She needed something more loose fitting for her back. She found one of the captain's shirts. Not caring if he minded, she put her arms into the long sleeves and buttoned it. The cuffs came to her fingertips and the hem of the shirt covered her hips. She looked down at herself and laughed at her appearance. Her feet were bare and her petticoat did not reach her calves. It was an old one but then she could not have expected whoever brought it along to know that. She sat back down on the bunk, her feet curled under her, and told the person who'd knocked to come in.

She smiled when she saw Landis. "I thought it was you," she said. She noticed the tray he was carrying. "What do you have there?"

"Your breakfast," he answered, placing the tray on the table. "The captain thought you might be getting your appetite back. You wouldn't eat much while you were sick."

"Captain Cloud is very thoughtful, Mr. Landis. Will I be able to talk to him soon?"

"Just John, please. We're not that formal here. At least not privately. You'll be able to see the captain as soon as you want, Miss."

Alexis got off the bunk and sat at the table. She stared at the fresh fruit and realized for the first time how hungry she really was. "This looks very good, John. Will you please ask the captain to join me if he can be spared? I am anxious to talk to him and although I am ravenous, there is much more here than I can possibly eat."

"Of course. But who shall I say you are? You never told me your name."

Alexis sliced the orange in front of her and brought a section to her lips. Before she put it in her mouth she looked up at the officer, the merest smile forming on her lips. "Please tell Captain Cloud that Alex Danty would like to see him." She chewed on the juicy section of orange while she watched Landis chew on that information. Quinton was a name that belonged to her life in the crow's nest. It was the Danty name that had gotten her to Tortola and the Danty name would return her to it. It was the misnomer that had carried her from London, and now it would take her to Travers. "I'll explain everything to Captain Cloud," she said when Landis only stood there, pulling at his beard.

He nodded thoughtfully and left the room. Alexis ate slowly, savoring the taste of everything on her plate, setting some aside for the captain. She was wiping her mouth when she heard the door open.

Cloud shut the door behind him and leaned against it. "John said you wanted to see me now."

"I didn't command it," she said. "You make it sound as if I had."

Cloud did not comment. Should he tell her that even her requests had an edge of authority according to Landis? He had been warned what to expect from her. "You probably have questions just as I do," he said after a brief pause.

Alexis tried to dismiss his physical appearance from her mind. She remembered she had thought him attractive last night, but now, in the light of day, he was striking. He belonged on this ship. His features were distinctive and well formed. She could imagine him cutting through the waves with the same ease as the vessel he commanded. There was pride and a subtle hauteur in his stride as he walked over to the chair at her side. She shut her eyes a moment, not wanting to stare at him and perhaps frighten him away as Francine insisted she always had. She opened them suddenly when she realized this was the man who would not be put off by her looks. She was glad. She had found someone she could respect. He would take her back.

"I do have some questions, Captain Cloud," she said when he was seated comfortably across the table from her. "Who shall go first? It is your ship."

"Then I will," he replied, slicing an orange Alexis left for him. "Your name, first of all. We were under the impression, because you were on the hill, that you must be George Quinton's daughter. Now it appears you are not."

"I was George and Francine's daughter in every way but one, Captain. I am not their blood. I lived with the Quinton's for six years, from the time I was thirteen. They were very dear to me."

Cloud could not help staring at her as she spoke. Her voice had no inflection in it and her eyes were expressionless. She might as well have been talking about a grocery list instead of the people she thought of as her parents. He did not want a hysterical female on his hands, but neither was he prepared for her total lack of emotion after all she had been through. He raised his eyebrows slightly as he asked his next question.

"The other man, the one you tried to—"

"That was Pauley Andrews," she replied. "He was the man who brought me to George and Francine. The day I came to them we celebrated in later years as an anniversary." Her voice broke and she glanced away from the captain, cursing her lack of control. "That morning was the first time I had seen Pauley since he took me to Tortola. By afternoon—" She stopped, blinking back tears.

Cloud's face was grave as she talked. He thought back to the girl on the beach and the man who approached her. He remembered thinking then that she was in love with him. It was strange to find out the man was not her husband, but that love would have been expressed in an entirely different manner. "You don't have to tell me any more," he said as he watched her struggling for composure. He felt a great deal of respect for her as she battled all the emotions welling up inside her. When she faced him again, her eyes were clear and almost vacant, as if the light inside them had been snuffed. Her features were as placid as a calm sea. Her mouth, nose, cheeks, and brows simply existed on her face, without reflecting any of her turmoil. They were like ornaments now, pleasant to look upon but without expression. He thought he understood her desire for control. He was not moved by crying, irrational females. And yet, if she were to break down completely, he would hold her and not care that she cried. He understood what would be behind the emotions and so did she. That made the difference.

"I would like to finish, if you don't mind," she said quietly and continued before he had a chance to object. "The day Captain Travers came to my home was my anniversary. George left work early so he could be with Francine and me. The servants were given a holiday so we could celebrate alone. That is the way we preferred it. Pauley arrived quite by accident. He promised to visit me whenever his ship came near the island. This was the first opportunity he had. I don't know how much you saw of what happened, but you know they were all murdered. That is all you have to know. Do you have any more questions?"

"None that can't wait. But you must have some."

"I would like to know where I am."

He smiled. "You are on board the USS *Hamilton*. A naval vessel. We are presently headed for Washington and we should be there within a few weeks. I trust that is satisfactory."

Alexis glared at him while her fingers clenched the knife she had used to skin her orange. "It is not satisfactory, Captain." She raised the hand holding the knife slowly. Cloud did not blink an eye. She twisted suddenly and with a quick snap of her wrist she hurled the knife at the cabin door. It struck a knothole she had targeted dead center.

"Do all island girls learn that skill?" he asked, unmoved.

"No. Pauley taught me." She waited to see if he was going to say anything else but he remained silent, totally composed, his green eyes meeting her gaze solidly. "You had no right to take me off the island, Cloud." She dropped the captain to see if he would care. He didn't. In fact she thought she detected a slight curving of his lips. It infuriated her. "I have things to do there. I do not want to go to the United States." If Pauley could only have heard her say that. "You must turn this ship around and take me back."

"Must I, Miss Danty?" His tone was one of amusement but it was forced. Landis had been right. She'd meant what she said on the hill and she was still determined to go through with it. Somehow it pleased him, though he didn't dare say so aloud.

"Alex. As in Alexis. And yes, you must. You had no right to make a decision for me that wasn't yours to make. I am asking you to rectify your mistake and take me home."

"I wasn't aware you were asking me to do anything." Alex. He liked that. It suited her. "I have heard nothing but demands. Actually you sound quite ungrateful."

"I cannot be grateful to you for saving my life if you will not allow me to live it!"

"But I am giving you a chance to live it," he said patiently. "There is nothing left for you on Tortola. If you go back there and try to carry out your revenge you will die. I will not be responsible for that."

"I was not aware my life, and therefore my death, was your responsibility. It is my decision. I am the one who will bear the consequences, not you. It is not your plan, but mine, that must be followed through. What is there for me in Washington? What is there for me anywhere in the United States now for that matter? The answer is nothing. My reason for living is somewhere on this ocean—probably in Antigua by now— and I will find him."

"And if you fail?"

"I won't."

"All right. And if you succeed? What then, if vengeance is your only reason to live?"

"Quinton Shipping," she replied, taking satisfaction in the way his eyebrows lifted slightly. It was a questioning look, not one of disbelief. "George taught me everything there was to know. After I kill Travers I will go back to Roadtown and rebuild the shipping line. It would have been mine one day. Now it's mine sooner than I expected and certainly not the way I wanted it."

"You seem to have answers for everything, Alex," he said, dropping another section of fruit into his mouth.

"Almost everything," she responded quickly. "I don't know why you brought me with you."

"You needed medical attention. John has had some experience dealing with lashings worse than yours. I trusted him to help you." Cloud struggled to keep his gaze focused on hers. What he said was true, but it was not the entire truth. She would know that if he turned away. He thought she probably knew already. She was not a person one could hide things from.

"You could have left me at the settlement. There are people there who would have helped me. My friends, my father's associates, or someone who worked for him would have cared for me."

"You should have a real doctor, not some old woman with herbs and incantations," he said patiently. "You can get proper care in the States."

"I am doing just fine without a doctor. Tortola is not uncivilized. I would have had good care there." She stopped. It was obvious he was not going to tell her the real reason he had taken her away; suddenly she decided she did not want to know. And she could not ask him why he did not want to take her back since that was tied to the reason she was here now. There must be another way to make him understand she could not go any further with him.

"Cloud. I am a wealthy woman. The British may have taken some of my ships but they did not take everything. There are still Quinton vessels on cargo routes, and there is probably enough money in the office for me to start rebuilding soon. Our house was not as large as some of the planters' homes. We lived simply in comparison to most of them, but that was by personal choice, not by necessity. I can pay you and your crew a great deal of money if you will return me to my home."

Cloud stood up, picking up his own knife. With a dexterity matching Alexis's he threw the knife at the door. It stuck in the wood only a few inches from hers. "No," he answered firmly. "I do not want your money and neither do my men."

Alexis pushed her chair back and got to her feet. A sudden pain shot up her back and she tried not to let him see it. She gripped the edge of the table tightly. "Then what do you want, damn you?" The words were not said angrily, rather frustratedly, despairingly. She could not understand why he was refusing her.

"I want what is best for you!" he spit back.

She wavered slightly. The pain and his words were too much. She steadied herself when she saw him take a step toward her, waving him aside with her hand. "No. I will be fine in a moment." She waited and it passed. She walked over to the bunk and sat on the edge, hiding her bare feet under it. "You cannot possibly know what is best for me. You tried to decide that once and you failed miserably. I can tell you what is best. I have several times already, but you don't seem to think I am capable of reasoning for myself."

"After all you've been through I doubt you are really capable, that's true."

Alexis laughed bitterly. "I thought you would understand," she said through her laughter. "I thought if I explained what I wanted without tears and apologies you would see that I do know exactly what I want." She stopped laughing. It was time to make him say why she was here. It could be her link to freedom. She hated using herself to bargain. It was a horrible price to pay, especially to a man she was not sure she liked anymore. She thought she could actually hate him, and that was strange because she was not even certain she hated Travers. Travers was not worthy of her hate. At the moment she simply did not care about him. That was why it was going to be so easy to take his life. Indifference was a potent weapon.

Cloud could not fathom her change in moods. She had stopped laughing as suddenly as she'd started. He did not like his loss of control when she tried to bribe him with her money. Didn't she realize what she wanted to do was madness? He could not go along with it. If she thought he would not be held responsible for her death she was wrong. He wished he had not said she wasn't capable of knowing her own mind because he truly thought she was. But that was because he had met her. He had seen what she was like. Who else, not knowing her, would believe a nineteen-year-old girl—woman, he corrected himself—would want to take on such responsibility? He eyed her carefully as she stood and leaned against one of the posts of his bunk. She looked like a waif in her strange outfit. Her petticoat was too short, his shirt too big, and yet none of it detracted from her beauty. Her hands went behind her back and she held on to the post. She rubbed one of her slim legs lazily against the other. He thought if she were anyone else he would not tolerate the unhurried seduction another moment. He held his breath for a second:

he knew what was coming. He did not know if he would be able to hold his temper as easily.

Alexis smiled slowly at Cloud. She hoped it was not a little-girl smile. That would not do at all. She tried to picture Francine in her mind and the way she had looked at George when she wanted something. Sometimes it worked and sometimes it didn't. Alexis could never abide the deception, but Francine assured her George was well aware of the game and he only gave in when it suited his purpose. Alexis did not think the captain was one to play games, but she could not name his purpose and she had run out of alternatives.

"You think I am beautiful, don't you, Cloud?" Dammit! That was not something Francine would have said. She wished she had paid closer attention. Francine said she was too blunt, too direct. Alexis was relieved when the captain did not.

"Yes. Very beautiful." He fought the smile that was trying to force its way to his lips. Even in her seduction she was cool and determined. It was refreshing because it was so unusual.

"And you would like to take me to bed, wouldn't you?" She tried to keep her voice even, but she lowered it to give the effect of a self-assurance she did not have. Emerald eyes stared back at her.

"Yes. Very much." Cloud wondered if she could fully appreciate what his honesty was costing him. He wanted her more than she could possibly realize, but he would not allow her to use her body as a bribe. And he knew that was her next move. He tensed, trying to gain some control before she went on.

"Then I will allow you to take me to bed if you will return me to Tortola."

He could not hide his surprise. He had not expected to be propositioned in quite that manner. He thought she would lie and say she wanted it as much as he. He thought she would say something about how she had hoped to get him into bed from the moment she had first seen him. He could have hated her for that. But for this he could not even be angry.

"You will allow me to take you to bed, Alex?" he asked incredulously.

"That is what I said."

He stepped closer to her. He could reach out and touch her now, he thought. He could caress her and hold her if he wanted, and she would not be able to stop him. He could force her into his bed; she would be powerless to prevent it. "I could take you if I wanted, Alex, whether you permitted it or not." He saw her eyebrows raise in astonishment. "You hadn't considered that, had you?"

"No," she whispered.

"Take off your clothes."

"Turn your ship around."

He laughed, turning his back on her and headed for the door. He opened it, but before he walked out, he said, "I'm going on deck to give the order. When I get back I expect to find you in that bed and prepared to back up your statement. Do you understand?" He smiled at her when she nodded her head and then walked out.

Once on deck he gave the command for the ship to make a slow circle. His men scratched their heads but no one said anything to him. Even Landis remained quiet. Cloud hoped he was right about her. What she had proposed as a test for him was also a test for her.

He waited until the *Hamilton* had started its slow revolution then he returned to his cabin. Alexis was standing exactly where he had left her. She did not seem to have moved a muscle.

She waited until he stood directly in front of her before she spoke. He did not appear to be angry with her. Instead she thought he looked pleased. "I couldn't do it."

"I know. I was counting on it."

"But the ship," she stammered. "I can feel it changing direction."

"A circle. I never intended to do what you suggested. I didn't think you could either. I had to make sure you knew it too. I'm glad I was right."

Alexis was confused, and it showed before she put it into words. "You're glad? But I thought—I mean, you answered my questions. You don't want me?" She finally got it out.

Cloud put his hands on her shoulders and drew her toward him, halting his protective gesture before their bodies touched. He placed one hand under her chin and lifted her face so he could stare down into the bewildered amber eyes. "I did not lie to you, Alex. You are very beautiful and I do want to take you to bed. But not in trade. Not as a bribe. Not when the thing you ask for in return is something I can't give you and still be able to live with myself. I want you. But not on the terms you set."

"There are no other terms, Cloud."

"Not now, perhaps. But later. When we reach Washington."

"When we get to Washington it will be too late for either of us. I will hate you for blocking my way." She paused, watching his lips close tightly. She could feel his anger in the increased pressure his one hand placed upon her shoulder while the other pressed harder against her jaw. She refused to be intimidated by his fury or his show of strength. "Then I am to be your prisoner until we reach Washington. Is that what you intended?"

He pulled his hands away so quickly Alexis wondered if she had suddenly caught fire. He took a few steps backward. "You are not my prisoner," he replied sharply.

"Take me back."

"No."

"Then I am your prisoner."

"If you wish to term your stay aboard this ship as being in prison then you may do so," he answered in a barely audible whisper. He tried to maintain his composure. He wanted to slap her for comparing his ship to a prison.

"You will accept it also? That I am your prisoner?" She walked over to the heavy oak table and sat in the chair he had occupied. She picked at what remained of the orange on his plate, peeling back the skin slowly.

He also sat down. Sighing he said, "I will accept it. Anything to see this conversation at an end. You are my prisoner."

Alexis heard the humoring tone in his voice and she refused to be humored. She put down the orange and held out her arms, crossing her wrists so they appeared to be bound by an invisible rope. "Lock me up."

Cloud jumped to his feet. "What!"

Alexis regarded him with the patience only a mother has for a child. "I assume you have a place on this ship where you keep men who have done something wrong. I want you to take me there."

"I won't do it."

"But I am your prisoner."

"You know that isn't true."

"Then take me back," she repeated.

"No."

"Then I am your prisoner."

"Damn! Are we back to that again? You are free to go anywhere you want," he said.

"Anywhere but where I have to go. This entire ship is a prison for me, Cloud. You don't even have the decency to call it what it is. You balk when I ask you to lock me up. That would make it very real, wouldn't it? You want me to pretend just as you do that I have my liberty. Well, I don't, and since I do not I will do what any prisoner would do. I will escape." She put her hands at her sides and waited to see if he would laugh at her decision. He said nothing, taking his seat once more and propping his boots on top of the table. He appeared to be thinking this over and for a moment she knew he was actually considering her proposal.

"I'm curious about something, Cloud. If I am not your prisoner, what exactly am I while on board?"

"You are my guest," he answered.

"Hardly. I would prefer a different arrangement."

Cloud laughed. "I suspected as much. What arrangement would you like?"

"I want to pay for my passage."

"I cannot accept money. This is not a passenger ship. We do not take on civilians."

"Then you do have a problem." She smiled. "I am certainly a civilian. It is worse than that actually. I am not even American. Really I'm a British spy." She said it seriously, then laughed at the thought.

"Stop it! What do you want?"

"I want to work off my passage. I know something about ships. I can be of help to you."

"And why should you want to do that?"

"Because it would be helping me. Last night I thought every minute I stayed away from Tortola was a waste, but I see I can use this time. Since I am going to go after Captain Travers I will need to sharpen my skills. My crew will have to be able to trust and respect me. I think there are things I can learn from you and your men."

She just did not give up. Everything she said or did had Travers as the motive. And what did she know about a ship anyway? "I suppose your father taught you all about navigation from the inside of an office," he said sarcastically. "Do you think your knowledge of running a line will help you command a ship?"

"Not at all. George taught me a lot, but something else prepared me for what I want to do now." She decided not to tell him about her voyage as a cabin boy until he was ready to hear it. "Do you have something I can do here?"

Cloud was amused now. It was a small request and infinitely preferable to her suggestion of being locked up. He would give her some work and wear her down quickly. It would not be long before she gave up the idea that life on a ship was a romantic adventure. She would realize soon enough that going after Travers was only a temporary goal. Even as he thought it he wanted her to prove him wrong.

"I think I can find something for you to do. Mr. Landis has been seeing to my personal needs for entirely too long. It is hardly befitting for my second in command. You may have the vacated position. My cabin boy. Do you know what your duties will be?"

"I believe so," she answered, barely suppressing her smile. "Where will I stay? I have used your quarters too long already."

"I won't give in on that, Alex. This is to be your room until we reach port. I have some of my things in the cabin forward of here. No, don't argue. You will have earned the right to stay here. I'll see to it."

"Good, Captain. Now if you will find me some proper clothes."

"But I brought your dresses and things from your home."

"Dresses are hardly appropriate attire for a cabin boy. No, I'll need some trousers and a smaller shirt. You'll get those things for me, won't you?"

"Certainly not. Don't press the issue either or I may change my mind and take the job away."

Alexis smiled. "I won't mention it again, but I think you'll see the necessity of my request soon enough. I hope you will not be too stubborn to admit you were wrong."

"If you have nothing else to ask me, I suggest you get dressed and meet me on the forecastle. I will show you around the ship so you'll know where everything is." He stood and started toward the door. "I forgot to ask you," he said, facing her. "Are you well enough to start immediately? I don't want to be accused of putting an invalid to work."

"I can manage, Captain," she replied. "And thank you."

That made Cloud laugh. "Save your thanks, Alex Danty. You may change your mind tomorrow." He left her then.

Alexis stared at the closed door. "We'll see," she murmured in her best imitation of Pauley. "We'll see."

Chapter Five

As the captain walked down the companionway Alexis swung her legs over the arm of her chair and leaned back, thinking. He was so damned stubborn. Why couldn't he admit he had been wrong for taking her away? Didn't he realize that yet? She was no better than a prisoner, whether he thought so or not. And worse, she did not know her crime. He had said he wanted her. Was that why he insisted she go with him to Washington? Was she his prisoner because he found her desirable?

She could imagine it would be very pleasant to have him touch and caress her. She could almost feel his fingers, lean and strong, in her hair, at the nape of her neck, at her throat, her breasts, sliding down her arms . . . she stopped. She wanted him as much as he wanted her, but they would deny themselves until one admitted error. If only he would say he knew she would go through with her vow to find Travers in spite of every obstacle he set in her path, it would be enough for her. When she realized the only way to have her was to acknowledge her right to decide her own course, even if he was not ready to let her go, then she knew she would seek him out. She would join him in his bed when he understood he could not hold her prisoner there either.

Alexis rose and washed her face in the basin on the commode then she braided her hair in one plait behind her head. After removing Cloud's shirt and laying it aside, she found her lightest, most comfortable dress among those he had brought for her. It rubbed against her back but it was bearable. She found a pair of shoes with low heels suitable for wearing on a slippery deck, and when she had put them on she went to find the captain.

Cloud had already told his men of the arrangement with Alexis and had insisted they treat her as one of them. He thought if they made no concessions for her she would stop insisting that she work off her passage. Beside him, as if reading his thoughts, Landis was muttering under his breath. Obviously, Cloud realized, John was not convinced she would give up.

When he saw Alexis walk across the deck toward him, he wondered if anyone, including himself, would be able to treat her as they would any cabin boy. She was lovely in her pale green dress and she moved forward in a manner that declared her a woman even while the single yellow braid and eager anticipation on her face named her a child. He watched her respond to the men who leered at her with an icy glance that sent them back to work in short notice. Those who smiled and wished her good day received a ravishing smile in return. He wondered what kind of reception he was going to get from her.

"Well, Captain Cloud," she said when she stood in front of him. "I am ready for duty. What do you want me to do?"

Cloud smiled at her seriousness, secretly applauding her determination. It seemed to surprise her. "I think I will take you on the tour I promised first. Then you can help Jack Forrest, our cook, with the meal. I'll want to eat shortly after noon. You can bring it to my new cabin. Afterward you can move my things from your room to mine."

"Anything else? That will hardly keep me occupied for more than a few hours."

"Oh, there will be lots for you to do. The crew will see to it." He held out his elbow. "Shall we?"

"I wasn't aware that captains offered their arms to cabin boys, sir."

Cloud dropped his arm to his side. "As you wish, Alex." It was not going to be difficult to think of her as one of the crew. She was going to remind them of it every chance she had. He considered the fact that he may have been wrong about different clothes. The tour lasted more than an hour. He was surprised and pleased by the questions she asked. They told him she did know something about ships. When she appeared satisfied with everything he took her back to the galley and introduced her to Forrest. He left her alone to get acquainted with the surly cook by herself.

Alexis and Forrest got along well from the beginning. He did not disguise his reluctance to have her around and she informed him by way of greeting that he maintained the worst galley she had ever seen. But they became friends quickly, and by afternoon the tall, lanky cook admitted he did not know how he'd gotten along without her.

"Don't you dare say it's a woman's touch, Forrest, or I will take a meat cleaver to that skinny neck of yours and show you exactly what a woman's touch really is!"

He laughed so heartily his meager frame trembled and his mouth formed the first smile she had seen him make. He had nothing but short grunts and tight grins even for the captain.

"I wouldn't dream of it, Alex!" he said, wiping grease from his hands on his trousers. "Where did you learn so much anyway? You've been on board a ship before, haven't you? And I'm thinking it was not as a passenger either."

"Oi 'ave an' it weren't," she said in a brash tone reminiscent of young Alex Danty.

"Does the captain know?" he asked, handing her Cloud's tray.

"No, and don't you tell him. He still doesn't believe I'm serious about working for my passage, but that's how I got from London to Tortola six years ago."

Forrest's bushy black eyebrows raised in surprise and his low whistle was admiring. "But how? You couldn't have been more than fourteen."

"I was thirteen and it was a lot easier then, hiding the fact that I was a girl."

The cook motioned her to be quiet. He heard someone coming. Landis walked into the galley.

"It's all right," he said. "I heard what she said." He looked at Alexis. "Your secret's safe if that's the way you want it, but I don't understand why you won't tell the captain."

"I will later. But he doesn't think I can do it now. He will not believe I did it when I was thirteen."

"I take it you are not satisfied with my opinion of the captain as a good man."

"Oh, he is a good man, Mr. Landis, and from what I have seen he is an excellent commander. But he presumes to know what I want better than I do. We do not see eye to eye."

Landis laughed. "Well, things are not going to get any better for you if you don't hurry with his lunch. He thinks you've given up already."

Alexis gripped the tray tightly and cast the two men a purposeful glance. "We'll see about that."

When she left the galley Forrest shook his head slowly. "I don't know about you, John, but I almost feel sorry for the captain. She is going to make his life miserable until he takes her back to Tortola."

"She told you about going after Travers?"

"Yeah. Can't say that I blame her. I can understand the captain not wanting to return her though. She'd end up killing herself going after him."

"Maybe," said Landis, tugging at his beard thoughtfully. "And maybe not."

Forrest regarded his friend curiously for a moment, then

he remembered his reputation. "John, get the hell out of my galley, will you? I got work to do."

Alexis knocked on Cloud's door. When he answered she walked in briskly and placed his tray in front of him on a small table. "Do you want anything else, sir?"

"Yes," he said, annoyed. "Stop the sir. Captain or Tanner or Cloud is all that is necessary."

"Will there be anything else, Captain?" she asked blandly.

"Some wine, Danty. You'll find it in a cupboard in your cabin. Bring me the bottle and a glass."

Alexis nodded and obediently went to get the wine. Returning, she poured him a glass. "If there is nothing else, I would like to move your things. I will get your tray later."

"There is something else," he said, peering at her with sharp green eyes over the rim of his glass. "Sit down."

Alexis pulled out a chair and did as she was told. She held her body rigid, hands folded in her lap. She returned his stare, willing herself not to be controlled by it.

Cloud put down his glass. "Another, Danty. Pour yourself one if you want."

She refilled his glass but refused to take any for herself. "You said there was something else, Captain."

He nodded. "You never asked me what my men and I were doing on Tortola. Weren't you curious?"

"I was. I would have asked you this morning but our conversation took a decided turn for the worse. I didn't want to know then, but I'll ask you now. What were you doing on the island?"

"I was sent there to arrange for your father to build us some ships."

"Oh." She stared at him blankly.

"Dammit!" Anger gripped him and he released it by throwing his glass across the room. "Doesn't that help you understand why I cannot take you back? I have to get to Washington and tell my commander what happened. They will want to know as soon as possible there will be no ships coming from Quinton."

"It only explains why you won't turn around now," Alexis said calmly. "It does not explain why you ever took it upon yourself to take me in the first place."

"I already told you why. You needed medical attention."

"That is what you told me." She leaned forward in her chair, putting her hands on the table, intertwining her slim fingers. She looked at him expectantly. "Cloud," she said softly, liking the stressed intimacy of his name on her lips. "I asked you earlier what there was for me in Washington but I answered my own question. I said there was nothing. I have been thinking I would like you to answer that question. When I get to the United States I will still want to return to Roadtown. Will you help me?"

"No."

"So what is there for me in Washington?"

He drew in his breath. "I don't know any longer. I only know I can't let you go yet."

Alexis smiled tentatively, almost shyly at him. Her eyes searched his face and she was pleased to know he spoke the truth. "Thank you for being honest." She wondered if he knew it was the thing she valued most.

She stood, her posture resuming its former stiffness. She was the cabin boy in the presence of her captain. "Am I dismissed now?" she asked.

"Yes. When you come back to move my things be sure to clean up the glass." He watched her leave. When the door shut he cursed softly under his breath. He knew then she was everything he wanted. He couldn't let her go! He couldn't! Would she understand that he respected her for trying to fulfill her vow but that he could not allow it? He admired her strength, her determination, her honesty, and her beauty. How could he let her slip from his grasp?

He remembered his own desire to escape from the prison of the British Navy. He had been punished for it twice and only Landis's skills had saved him after the second flogging. But still he had tried a third time and he had made it. And why had escape been so important? The answers pressed against him with almost physical force. Because he had been taken against his will; forced to serve without regard to his own purpose. What he had wanted to do with his life was not what the British wanted. Was that how she saw him? Was he the enemy to her? If that was true, then she had no choice but to escape from him. Still, he would do everything in his power to see that she failed.

It did not take Alexis long to complete her assigned tasks. She began immediately after she heard Cloud leave his cabin and in a little more than an hour she was finished. She had cleaned his quarters, made up his bunk, and put his clothes away. She had taken special care in transferring his navigational charts and equipment. Even his liquor had been carefully removed from her cabin to his. When she was satisfied her work was completed she went back to the deck to ask what other chores he had for her.

She saw Landis first and went to him. "Captain Cloud—where is he? He might have something for me to do."

"He is in the hold, checking some crossbeam supports," he replied. "Some of them are rotting. He won't be needing you for a time now."

"Then do you have something I can do?"

Landis shook his head. "We're having some trouble with the main topgallant right now." He pointed high over head. "Harry's trying to fix it. It's caught in the—"

"Yes," Alexis interrupted. "I see what the problem is. I can take care of it."

Before Landis could utter a word in protest Alexis had kicked off her shoes, thrown the skirt of her dress over her arm, and was climbing the rigging. In a moment all work on board had ceased as the men watched her nimbly make her way to the top.

"Alex! Your dress!" Landis called after her. "Come down and we'll find you something else to wear!"

Alexis shook her head and laughed. "I told the captain I

would need a pair of trousers and he refused me! If the sight of my legs is so distasteful, then don't look!''

Landis joined the laughter of the others in response to her suggestion. There was certainly nothing wrong with her legs. They all tilted their heads back as they watched her climb higher.

"I wouldn't have believed it if I hadn't seen it with my own eyes," Mike Garrison said admiringly when she joined Harry at the top. "She didn't falter once. And wearing that dress too. Don't think I could have done it in a dress."

"Maybe she'll let you borrow one so you can find out," Tom Daniels drawled. He cut off the laughter around him. "You'd better have your apology ready when she gets down. She's got spirit, not craziness."

Mike nodded his agreement and continued to stare upward.

Harry was as surprised as anyone when Alexis clambered beside him.

"What possessed you to come up here?" he asked, astonished. The captain had said treat her like one of them but Cloud wasn't going to like this at all.

"I thought you might want some help. Don't be so shocked. I know what I'm doing."

"God help us all if you don't!" he answered, crossing himself.

"If you could pull that rope over there and hand it to me, I will take the knot out."

"What do you think I have been trying to do?"

"My fingers are smaller. I can work at it more easily than you. Now hand it to me."

Harry heard the order in her tone and he responded. He smiled when he saw her struggle with it, but the smile faded when she undid the knot.

"I don't know who is responsible for this mess," she said, "but he needs a few lessons. Change me places—what is your name?"

"Harry Young, ma'am." He smiled lopsidedly at her.

"And I'm Alex. Now change me places, Harry, and I'll fix

this." Carefully they maneuvered their positions until she was closest to the mainmast. Alexis retied the rope and placed it where it belonged. Then she proceeded to work on the others. "Harry," she said, tugging at the caught sail, "you do not have to stay here. I can finish this myself."

He hesitated. "Are you certain? I don't want to leave you stuck up here. You won't be afraid to come down?"

"Nonsense. I am in more danger with you hanging over my shoulder than I would be if I were alone. Go on. I'll be down shortly."

Harry scratched an imaginary itch at the back of his neck. Shrugging, he began his descent. When he got to the deck he sighed, looking at his mates. "The lady knows what she's doing." He said it as if he couldn't quite believe it himself.

The general murmur of approval ended suddenly when they became aware that Cloud had joined them on deck. They shifted their gaze from overhead to stare at one another. They felt like accomplices in some foolish scheme, yet none of them knew why he should feel that way. They were only following orders. Alex Danty was one of them now.

Cloud approached the group. "What is going on? Do I have to be on deck every minute to see that you men are working?"

The men shook their heads sheepishly, but with a hint of a pleased smile on their faces, and went back to their stations. Harry and Landis remained with Cloud. He turned to Harry. "I thought you were going to fix the topgallant. I don't see it down yet." Before Harry could form a response Cloud addressed his first officer. "Have you seen Alex? She is finished in my cabin and I have other things for her to do."

Harry swallowed hard but Landis answered calmly. "I think she's found more appropriate work." He pointed upward.

Cloud followed the path of his arm. He would not speak for a moment and when he did, he bellowed. "Dammit, Mr. Landis! Why did you allow her to go up there?"

"She said she could do it."

"In a dress?"

Landis laughed softly. "Offered her something different to wear but she said you refused her trousers. She told us if we did not like what we saw we weren't supposed to look. Not a man turned away."

Cloud shot him a venomous green glance. "Harry, why did you leave her alone?"

"She said she could do it; then she proved it. You told us to treat her like one of us, Captain."

"Dammit! You know what I meant! If anything happens to her I will hold you both responsible!" He took a few steps backward so he could see her clearly. She was working diligently, oblivious to his presence below. He cupped his hands and yelled to her. "Alex Danty! On deck at once!"

Because she was almost finished, Alexis pretended she had not heard. He called again and she ignored him, working faster.

Cloud lost patience. He knew she heard him and had chosen to deliberately disregard his command. His cabin boy was about to learn something about following orders. He grabbed the rigging and began his ascent. Each foot he climbed made him more determined to see she did not try any more tricks like this one.

Alexis finished untangling the last rope at the same time that she noticed the captain coming after her, his face livid with anger. She looked around her for some means of escape. There was not any place to go but down. She thought if she could do it quickly she might be able to get by him. She wanted to thrash out this difference in private, not in front of the entire crew.

Alexis started down, catching a rope, and slid past the captain. She regained her footing on the rigging below him and continued downward. The crew below stopped their work again to see what their captain's next move would be. The game of tag had interesting implications for many of them. They thought their commander may have just met his match.

Cloud was furious with her action until he found a way to stop her. He wrapped his foot around a free rope and let his hands loose from their hold overhead. He fell backward. His crew had seen his action so they only grinned at his ploy. Alexis, however, had seen nothing and she screamed when she saw his body suspended in midair. His back rested against the rigging and the rope around his foot was the only thing keeping him from falling to the deck.

"Cloud!" she cried out as she scrambled up to help him. "Oh, my God! Are you all right?"

He stilled his smug laughter and enjoyed the view of Alexis's long, slim legs above him. "Take my arm," he said when he thought he had terrified her long enough.

Alexis reached down and pulled him up. When he was able to grasp the rigging once more she set about freeing his boot. As soon as she untangled it, she felt a strong arm go about her waist. "What the—" She could not say more as he lifted her in one arm and threw her over his shoulders. "Put me down!" she screamed as he started down. "You are going to kill us both! Cloud! Put me down!"

She heard his laughter and it served to make her angrier. She pummeled his back and tried to kick at his legs, not caring anymore if they both plunged to the deck. She could see the smiling faces of the crew below her; they were enjoying the spectacle. He paused long enough when he reached firm footing to tell the men to go back to their stations; then, without missing a beat, he carried her to her cabin. He kicked the door open, crossed the room in a few strides, and tossed her on the bunk.

"What do you think you are doing?" she spit at him when her body hit the mattress. She did not let him see that he had hurt her back with his carelessness. She knew it had not been his intention. She sat up on her knees and tried to move off the bunk but he caught her by the shoulders and pushed her back.

"I could ask you the same thing!" He released his grip when she stopped struggling. After he shut the door he returned to the bunk, sitting on the edge, and stared into her furious amber eyes. Her features were as hard and as tight-set as his own and he thought in some ways she was an accurate reflection of his own determination.

"You cannot do that!" she stammered in indignation when she caught her breath. "You can't carry me and throw me around as if I were a piece of baggage!"

"I can and will do whatever I want! You forget that this ship is under my command and you are to follow my instructions!" His voice was like thunder and her eyes were like lightning. He was pleased she did not back away from him. She deserved this lesson in discipline. "That's what you agreed to when you took the responsibility of being one of the crew! Isn't that right? Isn't that the way you wanted it?"

"Yes," she whispered. "But you did not order me not to go up there. You only ordered me to come down."

"An order you disobeyed!"

"Yes," she admitted. "I was wrong. What are you going to do?"

He ignored her question. His voice softened when he spoke, carrying only a hint of his displeasure. "What did you think you were doing anyway?"

"I was fixing the sail."

"And did you?"

"Yes."

"Didn't it occur to you that you could have been killed climbing up there?"

"The only danger I was in was from this damn dress!" Her voice and her eyes dared him to say otherwise.

He took the dare and placed the blame squarely on her. "Then you should have known better than to attempt the rigging dressed as you were."

"Perhaps. The risk seemed warranted so I took it." She gathered the folds of her dress in her arm and moved off the bed, taking a small amount of pleasure in the way his eyes dropped to her bare legs as she brushed past him. She dropped the material and crossed the cabin. She sat on top of the table, bringing her feet to rest on the seat of a chair. "There was another alternative I considered briefly. Since you refused to give me the trousers I requested I thought perhaps you would rather that I make the climb with no clothes at all."

When Alexis moved from the bed Cloud lay back, his hands folded behind his head, one leg stretched over the length of the bunk while the other hung lazily over the edge, his foot resting on the deck.

"Well, Cloud?" she asked impatiently when he did not rise to the bait.

He sighed. "I would have rather you hadn't attempted the climb at all, Alex. But you know I find the thought of you naked very appealing. That is what you really wanted to hear, isn't it?"

"Yes," she admitted miserably, feeling defeated that he would understand and express it so simply, easily, as if his desire was the most natural aspect of his personality. Why could he respond so easily to her needs as a woman, needs that only he made her aware of, but refused to respond to the other facets that made her what she was? Why didn't he see the things that made her want to be free, to go on with her life in the best way she could? She tried to read his face, wondering if he understood more than he was letting on, but she could see nothing in the immobile features. Nothing made sense to her. How could he want only part of her? How could he accept her body so easily and not the rest of her? Then she remembered he really had not accepted her body, even when she offered it. Did he want something more from her? Alexis did not know the answer and she avoided his gaze for the first time since he'd brought her into the cabin.

Cloud did not notice Alexis's lapse into silence. His mind was taking another turn entirely. "I was wondering, Alex. Wouldn't you have been afraid of what the crew might have done if they had seen such a sight?"

"Your men would not have dared to touch me!" She practically spit out the words.

Interested, Cloud raised his head slightly to see her better. "You are pretty certain of yourself. Why wouldn't they?"

"Because they think I am your woman! And you confirmed that in a grand manner when you carried me from the rigging. It was a barbaric display of your strength and my weakness! You couldn't have been more effective if you had carried a club and dragged me away by my hair!"

He had to laugh at her description. There was truth in what she said. "But what would make them think you were mine in the first place?"

"The same thing that makes you think I will come to you! Gratitude!" The last word came out as a snarl. "They think since you brought me aboard you saved my life. From there they think I will demonstrate my thanks in your bed."

Cloud considered what she said briefly. "That may be what my men think, but I doubt it. Once you know them better you will understand that. And Alex," he continued gravely, more serious than she had ever known him, "I do not think it at all. I don't want you in my bed out of gratitude. I don't want you as part of a bribe, a trade, or as thanks. I don't expect you to be thankful for what I've done to you. Not while you are my prisoner."

Alexis raised her eyebrows in surprise. She leaped from the table, knocking the chair over and ran to the bunk. She knelt on the deck by his side and placed her hands on his chest. "Then you do understand! You know what it's been like for me since I found I was being taken away! Oh, Cloud! Take me back! You must! If you really understand that I'm a prisoner here, release me!"

Cloud held her hands a moment, letting the energy in her trembling fingers pass from her into him. When her fingers were still he removed them from his chest and sat up, brushing a golden curl from her expectant face as he did so. His finger traced a line from the corner of her eye across her cheek and finally touched her lips lightly. Her eyes dropped away from his but he caught her chin and gently forced her to look up at him. When he held her eyes with his own he gave her his answer.

"No," he whispered softly, firmly. It was his final answer. He could not let her go.

She nodded her head slowly as if accepting that he had no other choice. Cloud released her face and stood up. She was still kneeling at his feet when he became the captain once more. "Danty, you will have to see about my dinner soon and later you can polish my boots. See Mr. Landis about getting something more appropriate for you to wear. He should be able to find something suitable. I will inform the others you are permitted to climb the rigging as long as there is a good reason for it."

Alexis stood, tossing back the braid which had fallen over her shoulder. "I'll see to everything," she responded evenly putting the last few minutes out of her mind. They walked out of the cabin, he going first, and parted in the companionway.

Alexis helped Forrest in the galley until almost everything had been prepared. With his promise that he would find her when the captain's dinner was ready, she went off to look for Landis. She found him on the upper deck, supervising the cleaning of the guns.

He stepped away from the cannons and motioned her over to the railing. "What is it? A problem with the captain?"

Alexis frowned. What did this man know? "No. Nothing like that. Just the opposite in fact. Hasn't Captain Cloud spoken to you?"

He shook his head and leaned back on the railing.

"He said I was to have some regular clothes like the rest of the crew wears. He said I should come to you and you would be able to get me what I need."

Landis eyed her figure critically, scratching his head behind his ear. "You're kind of tiny," he said finally. "But you're taller than most women. I'll see what I can find you. You look to be about Frank Springer's size. That's the lanky young man over there." He pointed to the forecastle.

Alexis turned and saw the fair-haired man grin at her. She smiled back, assessing his lean, wiry frame. "I think something of his would fit," she said to Landis. "Will he mind?"

"I doubt it. I'll put what he can give you in your cabin later."

"Thank you, Mr. Landis."

"I thought it was John."

"But I'm a worker now."

He smiled. "That you are. Well, save John for private. Was the captain very rough on you this afternoon?"

"He let me know I was wrong."

"And do you think you were wrong?" he asked, pulling at his silver beard.

"For going up? No. But for not coming down when he told me to, yes, that was wrong."

Landis dropped his hands to his side. "Did he ask you how you came by that skill?"

"No, he didn't," she said slowly, considering that fact for the first time. "You didn't tell him, did you?"

"No, and Forrest didn't either if that's what you're thinking. That cantankerous old fool doesn't have two words to say to anybody."

She had to laugh. The cook was no fool and he was the same age as Landis. Cantankerous she could agree to. "Why did you bring this up? Are you saying the captain thought I could do the work all along?"

"Not exactly," Landis explained. "This morning after he gave you the job he thought you would fail, but he wanted you to try anyway. He told me about the tour he gave you and that you asked intelligent questions. He said perhaps your father had taught you something after all. I think that's when he began pulling for you."

"I did not get that impression from his actions this afternoon."

"That is because you couldn't see his face down here. He was angry with you for going up there, but not because he didn't think you could do it. He was angry because you could have hurt yourself by trying it in a dress. Then you compounded everything by refusing to come down."

"I don't understand, Mr. Landis. What made the captain

believe I knew what I was doing in the first place? I thought
I had to prove it to him."

He laughed briefly. "You're not giving yourself or him
much credit. One does not have to know you very long to
know that you do not say things you don't mean, that you
do not attempt things without giving consideration to the
consequences, and that you do not allow others to determine
what is best for you."

"But if he knows all that, then why—"

"No. Let me ask the question. Why do you think he brought
you along?"

"For those reasons?" she asked haltingly.

Landis nodded. "He will tell you sooner or later himself.
He knew it the afternoon he took you. He brought you for
the very reasons I asked him to leave you behind."

"You asked him not to take me?"

"I did, but he was already determined to do as he wanted.
You and he are very similar in that way."

"Why are you telling me this, Mr. Landis?"

"Because someone has to."

"And why doesn't the captain tell me for himself?"

"Because for him it would mean admitting he was going
to lose you."

"I suppose I knew that," she conceded softly. "In some
ways he has been telling me all along."

Landis merely smiled, his eyes searching her face for an
understanding of what had just been said. When he found it
he left her and went below.

Alexis remained on deck, helping some of the men clean
out the guns, while she mulled over what Landis had said.
His interest in her predicament confused her. She could not
understand his special friendship with the captain although
she had glimpsed it several times during the day. Thirty years
separated the two men but there was a bond between them
that nullified those years. "Because someone has to" he had
said when she asked why he was explaining the captain's
actions. He wasn't meddling in a private conflict, she realized.

He was pointing out the truth and she secretly thanked him for it.

In the early evening Alexis returned to the galley and ate her own dinner before she took Cloud's tray to his cabin.

She knocked firmly on the door.

"Yes?"

"Your dinner, Captain."

"Bring it in." Cloud did not like the irritation in his voice. He did not want to see Alexis alone again today. It had been so hard to control his desire to make love to her this afternoon when she had run to him, first demanding then pleading that he return her.

He wanted to whisper "no" softly against the hollow of her throat, "no" against the curve of her naked arm, "no" while his head lay gently at her breast so his breath would kiss her tawny skin with its warmth. He would have formed the word while his fingers caressed her golden hair, while his hands slid along the length of her slim legs and traveled over the smoothness of her flat stomach. He wanted to sigh his refusal against the glistening flesh revealed by her parted thighs and to say it firmly while his lips brushed against the center of her womanhood.

He glanced at the charts in front of him. The lines on the paper fused and he blinked to clear his vision. He heard the door open quietly behind him.

Alexis set the tray on the only clear space on the table she could find. She hoped he would not notice her trembling hands. They trembled every time she thought of all Landis had told her. They trembled now, as she watched Cloud push back his dark copper hair with the heel of his hand, in anticipation that he would say those things to her. They trembled in anticipation of what awaited her when he did.

She hid her hands in the folds of her dress. It was an unnecessary gesture because he did not look at her when she spoke. "I will come back for the tray later. You said you wanted me to polish your boots. Should I get them then?"

"Yes, yes," he answered impatiently. He dismissed her with

a wave of his hand but he watched her out of the corner of his eye as she walked past him to leave his quarters.

Alexis went to her cabin to put it in order. She had not had a moment to herself since joining the crew. Landis had placed a pair of trousers for her on the bunk and she eagerly snatched them, putting them on under her dress. Delighted that they fit she quickly discarded her dress and looked for a shirt. He obviously had not been able to find her one, but she remembered she still had Cloud's shirt. She slipped it on, rolling the cuffs up to her elbows. She glanced at herself in the mirror, satisfied with her appearance. The clothes no longer could hide the truth of her sex as they had when she was thirteen. In some ways they actually accentuated her femininity. Even a haircut and a knitted cap would no longer help, she thought with pleasure. She had not asked for the clothes in order to deny being a woman, only to aid her in doing her job as best she could. The captain's white linen shirt could not conceal the outline of her breasts in its folds and the trousers, while they gave her ample leg room, fit snugly across her abdomen and hips. Reluctantly she took off the clothes, deciding to ask Cloud if she could have the shirt before she wore it. She washed her face to remove the smudges of gunpowder and grease, and washed her hair, rebraiding it while it was still damp. She put on a clean dress. When she thought Cloud had had plenty of time to finish his meal she returned to his cabin to get the tray and his boots.

He had not touched his food, and she commented on the fact.

"Since when is it your concern if I choose to eat or not?" he countered, leaning back in his chair and folding his hands across his chest. He eyed her warily, not believing she would care.

"In truth, Captain, Alex Danty does not care why you haven't eaten, since the reasons could hardly concern her. Your cabin boy is concerned because not eating, and the way you are studying those charts, could have something to do with this ship."

Cloud picked up a pencil and tapped it lightly on the table. There was something in her tone he had never heard before. A false sweetness. And he was leery of it. "Would the cabin boy accept the fact that I am just not hungry?"

"Yes, of course," she answered. "Though I doubt Forrest is going to believe it when I return a full tray to him."

"You can set Forrest's mind at ease, as well as your own. There is nothing wrong with the ship or the course we are taking. I doubt he will say anything."

"No, you're right. He won't say anything," she said innocently. "But your cabin boy had to know for sure so he could tell Alex. She won't be pleased that she possibly upset your appetite." Alexis jumped back as Cloud snapped the pencil he was holding in two. The sound echoed in the room, but the silence that followed was even more frightening.

She saw his features harden, his jaw stiffen, and his lips pull tight in a thin line. Her hand flew to her mouth at the realization of just how horrible she had been. What a stupid game to play! He hated her for it, but not nearly as much as she hated herself.

Cloud pushed his chair back with a sudden jerk and stood. In a few short strides he narrowed the distance between them. He grabbed her brutally around the waist with one arm while his other hand reached for her braid. Finding it, he tugged it hard, forcing her head back, tilting her mouth toward him.

"Of all the things I thought you were," he whispered menacingly. "A coy bitch was not one of them." His mouth came down on hers, crushing her lips. She kicked at him, pounded his back, as he ravaged her mouth with his tongue. Her lips were bruised under his brutal kiss. There was no tenderness in the way he held her or in the way he forced her body to press against his. Alexis was glad. This was her punishment for being something she wasn't; to be taken in a manner that repulsed her, just as her words had repulsed him. She deserved this, she thought. And then she fought him with all her strength. She had her answers now. She had not meant to bait him into admitting that she was the reason he couldn't eat, couldn't concentrate, couldn't think without thinking of her. By his actions he was naming her crime, naming the reason he had brought her with him. He had brought her for everything she was. Now he was proving that by using her as a man would use any woman he no longer respected.

She felt his hand travel from her hair to her breasts. He slipped it into her bodice and pressed his fingers cruelly against her flesh. Suddenly he pushed away. Startled by the loss of support for her body, Alexis fell to the deck.

"Was it enough, Alex?" he asked, breath rasping, green eyes hard and biting as he stared down at her limp form. "Did you find out what you wanted to know? Did the consequence suit the action?"

"Yes," she whispered hoarsely.

"I didn't hear you, Alex. Was that yes? To which question?"

"Yes," she repeated louder. "Yes! To all of them!" She stared at his face, unable to avert her gaze. His disgust was evident and she tried to memorize exactly how he looked at that moment so she would never cause anyone to look at her like that again.

His disgust faded and he seemed to accept her answer. He held out his hand to help her to her feet. She was being harder on herself than he could ever be. His lips parted in surprise when she refused his outstretched hand. She remained motionless on the deck and he dropped his hand to his side.

Alexis spoke quietly, but with a firmness that came from conviction. "Cloud, I want to be the cabin boy now—only that. I hurt you just now—me as well—by playing one part of myself against the other. I was wrong and I can only tell you that it will never happen again. Will you do that for me? Will you be the captain?"

"For how long, Alex?" His tone was almost that of a plea. "How long can either of us keep up the pretense, wanting each other as we do?"

Alexis shook her head. "I don't know. Perhaps only long enough for me to get out of this room." She knew he still wanted her and she, him. If she could not leave quickly she might never be able to leave at all. It was hard admitting that she needed his help to do it. She was afraid for the first time since she met him that he might be able to hold her prisoner after all.

Cloud knew she was punishing herself by denying what she wanted most at this moment. She wanted him now, not in spite of what he had done, but rather because he had done it. It was the only reason he granted her request, and even while he did it he knew he would have to pay for letting her go. He walked over to his chair and sat down, sliding his foot in her direction.

"I believe you came for my boots as well as my tray, Danty. You may have them now." His voice was cool, arrogant.

Alexis stood and walked toward him. She knelt in front of him and removed his boots. Cloud struggled with himself. As he looked down at her lowered head he wanted to tell her to stop, that this was not necessary. He did not want her to do any more penance. Yet he allowed her to continue, knowing she had never done anything so menial in her life and it was more difficult for her than him.

She took the boots and the tray, and started for the door. Cloud went back to his charts. When she reached the door she hesitated, remembering the shirt.

"What is it, Danty?" he asked tightly when he noticed the brief pause in her step.

"Mr. Landis gave me the trousers I needed but no shirt," she explained in low tones. "I still have the one I took from your things this morning. May I wear it?"

Cloud stared at the papers before him, but he only saw images of Alexis attired in those clothes. He turned to her and scanned her figure slowly. He knew he was about to pay for having let her go. "You'll look very beautiful in them, won't you?"

"Yes," she answered truthfully. She opened the door before she was unable to.

"You may have the shirt." He turned away, closing his eyes,

and listened for the sound of the barrier shutting between them. How long until she would come to him? He looked at his charts and books, and put them aside, his interest gone.

Alexis went to her cabin and polished Cloud's boots with a vengeance that yielded a high gloss when she was through. It was settled between them. There would be no more tests. Her goal remained the same: to escape his hold and carry out her promise for revenge. A faint smile crossed her face when she thought of his goal, unchanged except for a brief lapse a short while ago: to stop her.

Alexis placed the boots outside his door, then went for a short walk on deck. She welcomed the cool ocean breeze that whipped at her hair and face, and when she turned in that evening she fell into a peaceful, dreamless slumber.

Chapter Six

The following morning Alexis woke early, rested and ready to perform her duties with a new interest. As long as it was unnecessary to prove anything more to Cloud she felt comfortable in assuming a student role and becoming more knowledgeable in areas where she had little experience.

She washed and dressed quickly, wearing the clothes Landis and Cloud had provided. She brushed out her hair and hastily redid the yellow plait. When she reported to the galley Forrest informed her sourly that the captain had already eaten and gone on deck. She stayed and helped the cook until he complained she was getting in the way. Alexis thanked him and went topside.

Cloud's first impulse was to look away when Alexis stepped on deck from the hold. He forced himself to keep sea green eyes trained on her lithe and graceful form as she approached him. Her shirt—his shirt, he reminded himself—was open at the neck, revealing the soft hollow of her throat. As wind swept past her it caught the extra material, pressing the linen against her chest so he could make out the rounded outline of her breasts. Her hips swayed gently as she walked. He bit his lip remembering this was the way she always walked, only now the trousers accentuated the easiness of her gait. He looked around at his crew, taking in the obvious pleasure on their faces as they also watched Alexis. It was part of the price he knew, that not only should he be compelled to watch her but that he had to share what he saw with others.

Harry Young, high atop the ship, saw Alexis walk across the deck and he called down to her. Alexis put one hand over her brows to shield her eyes against the bright sun as she tilted her head and bent her body back at the waist to look up at him. Smiling, she raised her other hand to wave.

"Come on!" He called. "I could use you up here!"

Alexis glanced hesitantly at Cloud for a sign of permission. He gave her a short, impersonal nod and she scrambled up the rigging to help Harry.

"She does it pretty well, doesn't she, Captain?" Landis asked.

Cloud took his eyes from Alexis's diminishing form and turned to his friend. "Damn well, I'd say. She doesn't do a bad job on boots either." He leaned against the taffrail, stretching out his legs, and lifted one foot a few inches off the deck.

Landis's gaze dropped to the shiny black boots, and when he looked back at Cloud his eyes registered mild horror. "You didn't," he whispered, his voice betraying his disbelief.

Smiling, Cloud put his hand on the older man's shoulder. He squeezed it with firm friendliness. "I did," he replied, no guilt in his tone. He released Landis and walked away, leaving him to sort out the reason he would order Alexis to do such a thing. Landis would be pulling at his beard for hours. And he would get no more information from Alexis or him.

The morning and afternoon passed quickly for Alexis. She found the men were more than willing to answer her questions about guns and battle strategy. At first it was a game for them, relating stories of famous sea battles they had either been in or heard about. When they saw the earnestness with which Alexis hung on every word, they hesitated to tell her any more. They were reluctant to play any part in what could ultimately be her death. Alexis wore them down gradually, one at a time, satisfied each time she convinced a man of her determination.

She knew every man she won over helped make her escape less difficult. Cloud would anticipate her attempt to get his men on her side, and he would counter her gains at every turn. Time stood on the captain's side. He had already earned his men's loyalty and she had only a short time to do the same thing. If there was no opportunity to leave the ship before she reached Washington the crew would be of no help, no matter what they thought of her.

She brought Cloud his dinner and, as at lunch, no unnecessary words passed between them. She went to her cabin to wait for him to finish his meal. Lying on her bunk, she surveyed the room. She looked at the rapiers mounted on the wall against a blood-red velvet backing. Before, they had been merely decorations on an otherwise bare wall. Now they screamed purpose at her. She took one down, testing the weight and balance. She took a few short sweeps through the air, assuming the stance and grip Pauley had taught her. The hilt was too large for her hand; she knew her arm would tire easily. She put it back and tested another. When she had tried them all she chose the one that seemed an extension of her arm.

She had handled such a weapon many times since Pauley had instructed her. George had expressed an interest in teaching her for his own exercise. Though Francine had protested loudly, and always in French, Alexis and George found opportunities at the office. She was grateful for those lessons now as the proper moves came back to her. She knew she needed practice and more instruction, but surely among the crew there had to be someone skilled with a fencing épée. She touched her finger lightly to the point and pulled back quickly when she drew blood. She replaced the blade in its place on the wall. Then she went to get the captain's tray.

"Captain," she said, pouring him the wine he requested.

"There are some fencing blades in my room. Do they belong to you?"

"Yes, Danty." He took a sip of his drink, not at all amused by what he knew was coming. He also knew he would not refuse the dogged determination in the amber eyes presently appraising him.

"Would you give me permission to use one of them if I can find someone to instruct me?"

"You have my permission. Who will you look for to teach you?"

"The best on this ship," she said certainly.

"Then you better get this back to Forrest," he pointed to the tray, "and start your search." He allowed himself a wry smile when she left, sure of where her search would lead her.

Alexis quickly finished her work in the galley and got the weapon, eager to take advantage of the few hours of light left. When she went to the upper deck she saw Landis and several others sitting in a small circle, finishing their dinner. They motioned her to come over.

"You can sit here," Frank Springer said. "If you promise not to use that thing on any of us."

Alexis laughed. "Not my intention at all, Frank. In fact I came to find someone who would be willing to teach me how to use this properly. Who's the best among the crew?"

"With all due modesty, ma'am," Tom Daniels spoke. "You are lookin' at him."

"I'm not interested in modesty, Tom. I'm interested in skill."

"He's your man," Landis told her. "He's the best." There was a murmur of agreement and Tom grinned.

Harry looked at Alexis's weapon as a ray of light caught the thin blade. It glittered for an instant as she changed its position. He spoke to her while he looked pointedly at Tom. "Daniels is the one you want unless you are including the captain. Don't protest, Tom. You know it's true. Captain Cloud is the best."

Tom shrugged. "He's right, Alex. He makes me look like a fumblin' backwoodsman."

To Tom's chagrin the others readily agreed and Alexis thanked them for their information.

"I suppose I should have known," she said, examining her sword. "I'll ask him when he comes up."

Harry laughed soundlessly, pointing behind her. "He's coming now, and from the looks of it you are about to have your first go at it."

Alexis spun around and saw Cloud coming toward her, carrying one of the swords she had found too heavy and awkward for herself. When he reached her he took the weapon out of her hand, placing his own on the deck, and tested the blade she had chosen.

"That was a good choice, Danty," he said, giving it back to her. "It was mine when I was first learning. It's not right for me now but when I was about your size it was perfect. I take it you are somewhat familiar with using one of these."

"A little, Captain. You should have told me when I asked for it that you would be my instructor."

"Would that have dissuaded you?"

"Not at all. Only saved me time."

"Then there's nothing to be learned by any more talking," he said, bending to pick up his sword. "Let's clear a place and begin."

She nodded and Landis, Tom, and the others moved from their places, forming a larger, interested circle around where she and the captain stood.

"You'll have to show me what you know," he explained. He took the beginning position and thrust his sword in her direction. She blocked it easily and began advancing. He allowed her a few forward moves, then he rapidly sent her back to her starting place and a few more steps beyond that. He stopped to adjust the sword in her hand. "If you place your hand like so," he said, repositioning her slim fingers on the hilt.

She nodded. "That's better."

"You can feel the difference?"

"Yes."

"Good. Now let's go at it again." He continued advancing, and she parried with increasing confidence. She attempted another advance, but he stopped and called a halt. "Danty, I know every move you are going to make before you make it. Your eyes are giving you away. Try not to make it so obvious that you want to drive your point through my heart." He smiled when the men around him laughed. "A well-placed cut on the arm or leg will put your opponent out just as easily. Sometimes they are even more devastating because they are so quick and clean he will not even realize he's been sliced. When the pain strikes it will take him off guard for a moment."

"I understand," she said. "An arm or a leg."

"Yes, but not the captain's," Harry called.

"Don't worry," Alexis grinned. "I'm not after him."

Cloud and she began again. This time they remained in combat longer than before. He talked as they fought, pointing out her mistakes as they happened rather than halting at her every error.

"You move too often to the same side, Danty. Keep me off guard. Don't let me anticipate your next move. Get your arm up higher—use it for balance. That's good. Relax. Don't hold yourself so stiffly. Like that. Right. Watch me, Danty. Try to anticipate me. What am I going to do?" He knocked the sword out of her hand. It clattered to the deck. She bent to pick it up, wiping the sweat from her brow with the sleeve of her shirt. "Let's rest," he said.

Alexis agreed and sat beside Tom while Cloud leaned back against the mast. "It's hard," she said breathlessly.

In a low voice Tom replied, "You'll be happy to know he isn't going easy on you, Alex. He's done a couple of things with you he wouldn't use on a beginner and you handled yourself pretty well."

Alexis smiled, thanking him for his encouragement. She drew her knees to her chest, wrapping her arms around her legs, trying to catch her breath.

Cloud watched her uneasily. She was obviously tired and probably a lot more than she was even letting on. She had worked hard yesterday and today and he was certain she still experienced pain in her back. Perspiration was clinging to her forehead; the tiny beads glistened in the sun's waning light. He saw her wipe her forehead again on the knee of her trousers. If she was exhausted she would get careless, and although he had no intention of getting close to her it still could be dangerous. He wished the others were not watching. She would probably feel obliged to go on even though she might realize she shouldn't.

Alexis looked over at Cloud and signaled her readiness to continue. The brief rest made her feel better though there were occasional shooting pains along her back. She dismissed them and concentrated on the correct grip of her sword instead. He hesitated when she stood up and returned to the center of the circle. "I think just one more lesson tonight, Captain," she said, letting him know she was aware of her limits.

Cloud joined her, checking her grip. Finding it satisfactory he commenced the lesson, holding back until he could adequately determine her strength. She sensed his reluctance and planned her attack accordingly, thrusting and lunging at his slightest hesitation.

"Good, Danty," he praised her strategy. "But a worthy opponent will recognize his own weakness and respond quickly." He sent her on the defensive in short notice.

They went on for several more minutes, Cloud alternately criticizing then praising her every move. "That was a good step, Danty, but get that other hand up. Try placing more weight on your right foot. You're still moving that way too often."

Alexis's smile at his approval and seriousness vanished completely as a grabbing, twisting pain took hold of her back. Her weapon fell to the deck and her eyes filled with agony at the sharp, burning sensations controlling her body. She was powerless to stop her body's instinctive convulsing just as

Cloud, although immediately aware something was terribly wrong with her, was impotent to stop the sweeping motion of his sword. Alexis felt nothing as the point of his sword sliced through her shirt at the shoulder; she only knew it had made contact with her skin because his face immediately went pale and he dropped the sword from his hand. The pain in her back was momentarily forgotten as a fresh network of torture spread up from her shoulder. She felt something wet and warm trickling toward her breast and she glanced to her side and watched the path of blood with detached interest. She looked up at Cloud who was standing not more than a foot from her and smiled bravely. "I have had enough for one lesson, Captain." She dropped all pretense, holding out her arms as the pain defeated her. Then she felt herself falling into a black void.

Cloud caught her in his arms and lifted her. Her head fell back and her long braid whipped against his thigh. He was surrounded by his men but they quickly cleared a path to let him take Alexis to her cabin. Landis followed while the others remained behind in silent misery over what had just taken place.

Cloud placed her gently on the bunk while Landis went to the orlop to get bandages and medicine. While he was gone Alexis woke. She tried to sit up but Cloud pushed her back against the sheets.

"Lie still," he ordered.

"It's only a scratch, Cloud," she protested weakly. "It was stupid to faint."

"Let me see it." He unbuttoned a portion of her shirt and slipped it over her shoulder. The thin red line extending for almost five inches directly beneath her clavicle had stopped bleeding heavily since she had lain down. Landis returned with the bandages and Cloud washed the cut and inspected the severity of the wound. "It's a little bit more than a scratch, Alex, but I think it is safe to say you'll recover to have another lesson soon."

"Good," she murmured. She bit her lip as he washed out her cut with alcohol.

"You can cry out or faint if you want, Alex."

"No, Landis is here," she replied in a voice so low he had to bend close to her mouth to hear it. "He thinks I'm very brave."

Cloud placed a finger on her lips, stilling their trembling. His hands were trembling as well. As he looked at the gentle curve of her naked shoulder and then the harsh, ugly scratch across it, he knew it was not one or the other causing his fingers to shake, but both, because they were part of this woman lying quietly beside him. He looked away and motioned Landis to go. "Tell the men she will be all right. She needs a rest more than anything." When Landis had gone he turned back to Alexis. "You don't have to be brave for my sake," he told her. "I already know—" He stopped, seeing that it was useless to continue. She had passed out again.

Cloud removed her shirt completely and wrapped her shoulder with clean strips of cloth. He got her another shirt from his room and put it on her. She woke briefly while he was fastening the button at her throat. Her eyes had the smile her lips could not manage.

"I think I just need to sleep, Cloud." She placed her hands over his and held them. "It was not your fault." He said nothing, but she saw the disagreement in his eyes and felt the tensing in his fingers. She wanted to ask him to stay with her so she could continue to assure him each time she woke. She wanted to thank him for teaching her, for taking her seriously, for understanding her purpose. Her eyes closed, and her last thought before she fell asleep was that she would go to him later and tell him that she wanted him, now more than ever.

Cloud waited until he was sure she was in a deep sleep before he left her. As soon as he opened the door to his cabin he knew what he was going to do. He was already quite drunk when Landis joined him. He poured a glass for his friend and took another for himself.

"Dammit, John," he said, more to himself than to the man sitting across the table. "I should have known better than to let her have the weapon."

"That's what she wanted, wasn't it?"

"Of course that is what she wanted! I wanted it for her too!"

Landis took a quick sip of his drink to hide his smile. "Why?" he asked.

Cloud shook his head slowly, thinking about it before he answered. "I can't let her go, John," he replied softly. "But I still want her to try. And if she is successful I want her to be prepared for Travers. I guess you already knew that, didn't you?"

"I knew. I had to find out if you knew it too. Why are you drunk, Tanner? Who are you feeling sorry for?"

"Alex," he replied without thinking.

"It's a good thing she can't hear you. She doesn't want your pity. She would hate you for it."

"Myself then." He finished off his drink in one long pull.

"She would hate you for that too," Landis said, placing his hand over Cloud's glass and preventing him from pouring another.

"Christ, John! What do you want me to say? I knew she was getting tired. She hasn't had enough rest since she first came on board. Her back isn't even healed for God's sake! Are you forgetting I know what kind of pain she's in?" He said the last through clenched teeth. The memory of the leather hitting his back returned. He could hear every crack of the whip and the sound of tearing flesh. He removed Landis's hand from his glass and emptied the bottle into it. His voice was low and controlled when he spoke again. "It could have waited. I wanted to teach her, but it could have waited until she was stronger."

"I suppose. But she thought she was ready or she would not have asked."

"She was wrong."

"Yes, she was. It was her mistake. Why are you taking the responsibility?"

"I almost killed her."

"But you didn't. And she doesn't blame you for anything that happened, does she?"

"No." Cloud stared into his glass, his fingers gripping it tightly, causing the tips to turn white.

"Get some sleep, Tanner. It's after midnight and she'll probably rest until morning. You'd better hope she does. She will not want to see you the way you are now." Landis got up and left quietly. He whistled softly to himself on his way to his own quarters.

Cloud took the advice of his friend. He fell into his bed, fully clothed, and shut his eyes. His head throbbed and the cabin tipped dangerously. In spite of that he fell asleep, dreaming of Alexis.

He saw her approach his bunk hesitantly, dressed only in the white linen shirt he had given her. He could just make out the bandage beneath the material and he winced at the sight of it. His eyes traveled downward to other, more pleasant sights. Her breasts rose and fell gently in time with her breathing, their soft swell noticeable because the collar of her shirt was opened wide. Her hands were all but invisible, the only evidence of their existence being the slender fingertips peeking out from under the long sleeves as she walked. Her legs and feet were bare and his eyes swept down them in a single continuous motion. She stood beside his bed and placed his hand on her thigh and held it there for a moment before she let it drop, allowing it to graze her leg as his eyes just had. She leaned her head toward his face as she sat beside him and whispered something so lightly he could feel the words more than hear them. Her breath caressed his cheek. He wanted to hold her, molding her form to the curves and hollows of his own, but his arms felt as if they had been anchored to the bottom of the ocean floor. The blood in his head was pounding and he fought for breath even as he

ought for control over what was happening. The alcohol was
still in command and he saw horror and disgust wash over
her face. He could not stop her when she pushed him away
and fled the cabin. He returned to oblivion.

Cloud woke a few hours later, before the first signs of the
morning sun had reached his cabin. Holding his head in his
hands, he rose and cursed himself for his stupidity. He washed,
shaved, and changed his clothes, not recalling the dream until
he put on his shirt. He buttoned it slowly, each movement
bringing him closer to the truth. It had not been a dream,
or even a nightmare, as he would have labeled it now if he
did not know better. His hand flew to his head, his fingers
coursed through his hair in a sullen, bitter motion. He paced
the cabin for several minutes, stopping suddenly when he
knew what he had to do. He left his quarters, slamming the
door violently behind him.

Once he entered Alexis's cabin he was calm, no hint that
inside he was burning from anger directed solely at himself.
Leaning against the door, he extended his legs in front of him,
supporting his weight with his back pressed solidly against the
wood. His thumbs hung in his pockets and his fingers rested
on his hips. He remained still, content to observe Alexis in
the last stages of sleep.

Her face rested in the crook of her elbow, the other arm
hidden somewhere beneath the blanket. As before she had
kicked away the part of the blanket covering her legs, and
the smooth flesh of her calves appeared even softer in contrast
to the rough woolen blanket lying beside it. When she stirred
Cloud walked toward the bunk, pulling a chair with him. He
placed it within an arm's length of her bunk and sat down,
waiting for her to wake.

"It wasn't a dream, was it?" he asked when her eyelids
opened and amber eyes met his own.

"No," she answered harshly as she sat up, pulling the blanket
around her as if the gray wool had the same qualities as
tempered steel. "Why are you here?"

Cloud smiled, tiny lines forming at the corners of his mouth.

"To do what I was in no condition to last night. To do what you wanted me to, and what I wanted to, and could not."

"You were drunk," she said flatly, revealing none of the anger, disgust, and loathing she had felt when she'd realized that earlier. "Why?"

"I blamed myself for what happened. I know you said it was not my fault and I realize that now. I realized it last night after too many drinks."

"I took on too much, too soon. I came to your room last night to make certain you knew that and"—her voice dropped but her eyes did not waver—". . . and to tell you I wanted you."

"And has that changed?" His voice was just above a whisper.

"Not if you understand what you've just said—and what it means about me." She dropped her protective armor, ready to welcome him into her arms as he murmured his comprehension, but she pulled back sharply in the next moment when she heard his words.

"Let me make love to you, Alex."

A frustrated cry escaped her throat and muffled itself in the blanket as she covered her mouth with it. Cloud snatched the gray wool away from her.

"What's wrong with you?" he demanded, searching her face for some answer.

"Don't call what we are going to do making love!" she spit, her eyes narrowing. "I don't want to be made love to! I don't want to be loved at all! I don't love you!"

Cloud stood over her and placed one hand firmly at her throat, his thumb extended vertically, supporting her chin and forcing her head upward. "But I do love you, Alex. You can't change that." He pulled his hand away when she laughed at him. The vibration of her scornful chuckle as it rose from her throat seemed to burn his hand even before it could be heard by his ears.

"Have you forgotten I made two vows, Cloud? I haven't. Neither of them were made lightly. I will never love you! I don't want you to love me! What you call love is suffocating, binding, restrictive. Your love is holding me prisoner more securely than any chains! And I hate you for it, Cloud! If you really knew what it was like to be kept from something you had to do, you would recognize your love for what it is. You would know why I hate you for it and why I am going to punish you. Here. In my bed. Your love is like a yoke around my neck so use me in the manner of an animal. That's what I want. Use me! Take me! But don't call it love!''

He said nothing. She continued to stare at him while her fingers moved to the buttons of her shirt, unfastening them coldly, deliberately. He sat down beside her and removed his boots, matching her purposeful approach. There was silence until a hoarse gasp escaped her lips as he shrugged off his shirt.

She had just seen the scars on his back. He remained motionless, waiting for her reaction, knowing those scars would say more than the explanation he had denied her. He felt her weight shift as she moved directly behind him. The depression she made told him she was kneeling. He felt her palm close to his skin but not touching it yet. He knew it was there by the heat emanating from it, the warmth caressing his flesh across a small space of air. She touched him lightly with her fingertips and drew back quickly, as though she was unsure if she wanted to do it at all. He felt a single finger trace the line of a single scar, causing them both to draw in breath simultaneously. He, from the sensation of pleasure; she, from the sensation of pain. She stopped abruptly. He felt both her hands press flat against his back in an attempt to absorb all the suffering he had gone through. Her hands slid down his skin. When they were gone she replaced them with the cool flesh of her cheek. She held her face against him for a long time, then added her hands, placing them on his shoulder blades, on either side of her head. He closed his eyes as he felt a single tear try to wedge its way between his back and her tightly pressed face. He knew the outline of her cheek as the tiny drop of salt water ran along its edge until it fell in a straight line down his back. Her voice, when she spoke, was broken like pointed slivers of the finest crystal, sharp and clean.

"I didn't know how well you do understand." She released him, and he turned to face her. "Tell me," she said. He shook his head and wiped away the wet line on her cheek with his thumb. "Not now," he answered, pushing her gently against the sheets. "Later. First this."

He brushed her lips lightly with his. "I love you," he whispered, knowing how much it hurt her to hear it. He clamped his mouth down on hers hard then, insistent, demanding. She responded fiercely, pressing her lips tightly against his own, searching for an outlet to the pain of his words. His hands slid down her neck, and lower, parting the material of her shirt. He heard her moan as his fingers circled her breasts, spiraling inward until they touched her nipples and her flesh stood erect under his caress. He took his mouth away from her lips and kissed her eyes, her nose, and followed the line of her jaw from her chin to her ear. He put one hand under her back and lifted her until she was sitting up, her head resting on his shoulder while his fingers quickly undid the braid lying against her back, freeing her golden hair until he locked it in his own hands, memorizing the texture as he curled it between his fingers. He slipped the shirt from her unresisting body, and when his eyes caught sight of the bandage he took it off also, so he could see all of her and know everything she was.

He laid her on the bunk once again and Alexis remained passive while he removed his trousers and slipped in beside her. Once his hands touched her skin the passivity was gone, and she trembled in response to his stroking. There was no place he could touch that did not answer to him. His kisses were alternately brutal then fragile, and his hands were as often cruel in the pressure they applied as they were tender, sometimes barely coming in contact with her flesh. It did not matter, she realized as she returned his kiss, matching his savagery of the moment. It did not matter what he did, only that he did it, and that her body responded to it. She held him tightly. Her fingers could feel the rough line of the scars on his bronzed back. Her legs could feel the power and strength in his thighs as naked flesh touched naked flesh.

Soft moans escaped her throat and she liked the sound, liked the fact that it was he who forced those sounds from her. His mouth was on her breast, evoking the same sensations he had with his hands, and now his hands were moving along her inner thighs, slowly parting her flesh. She tried to move away from the incessant motion of his strong fingers at the junction of her legs but he would not allow it and then she was pushing her body against him, demanding more of the exquisite pleasure shooting through her; pleasure so intense it was almost painful in its grip over her body. She felt him release her breast and his mouth moved down her quivering flesh to the place his fingers had caressed.

"Cloud," she murmured between ragged breaths. "No. Not yet. No one . . ." She tried to grab his hair and push him away but it was a useless motion that ended with her flinging her arm over the edge of the bed in defeat.

"Shhh," he reassured her. "I know that." His body shifted and his mouth returned to her own, his lips hovering above hers. "Everything about you is lovely. I want to know all of you." Then he kissed her and she responded greedily, hungrily, glad he liked what she had to offer.

Cloud moved between her parted legs, brushing against her gently. Slowly he moved into her, watching her carefully to assure her in that moment of pain. When it came, her eyes opened wide in shock and she looked at him as if he had betrayed her. Then as he gently continued his movements and the pain washed away, her face revealed an odd mixture of emotions. He saw her struggling with her own desire; a desire to be free of him and a desire to never let him stop what he was doing. The struggle was the conflict between her body and her mind, and her wish to give him one or the other, unaware that with him there could be no such division—that when she'd surrendered her body, she had already given him her mind. She began moving with him, catching his rhythm, working toward a single instant when she would allow him to have all of her.

Alexis gasped as he carried her toward the edge of fullfillment once more and kept her there until she cried out. Then as he thrust deeply inside her a final time, she felt herself tumble over the precipice, her body convulsing in free fall, her limbs making wild thrashing movements designed to protect herself once she hit bottom. And once she hit, once the fiery, burning sensations no longer controlled her, she lay motionless beneath him and a warm glow spread over her flesh. It was warmer than the heat from the sun, only now making its presence felt in her room, casting its rays more fully over their bodies. It was warmer than his breath, close to her ear; breath that caused wisps of yellow hair to part at the force of life within him. She heard his words again, the same words he'd spoken earlier, the same words that had hurt her before hurt her again, but she listened, wanting to be hurt by him. "I love you," he said.

"Tell me now, Cloud," she said after a long stretch during which the only sound had been their soft breathing. The sheet was pulled over them and Alexis liked the coolness of it next to her perspiring flesh. She moved under it, bringing her body close to his, touching his chest lightly with her breasts.

Sighing, he pushed her away. "I won't be able to tell you anything if you insist on moving like that."

"So soon?" she asked, surprised. She could not imagine it. The last sensations still caressed her limbs.

"So soon," he assured her. He remained lying against the pillow as she lifted her head and supported it with her elbow so she could look down on his face.

"Tell me," she said gently.

"Are you familiar with the *Chesapeake,* Alex?" Her sudden stiffening answered his question. "I'm glad you know. It makes it easier to explain." He continued flatly, without emotion, reciting the story as he had so many times before. The memory was etched permanently in his brain. "It will be three years ago in June. I had been with the navy for two years when I was assigned to the *Chesapeake*. We were leaving Norfolk, Virginia, on our way to Europe. We had not gone more than ten miles when a British frigate hailed us."

"The *Leopard*," she whispered.

"That's right. Our captain, Commodore Barron, thought they only wanted us to carry dispatches to London so he permitted one of their officers to board. The officer produced a copy of an order from the Vice Admiral—Sir George Berkley, I think. He was the Commander in Chief of the American Station at the time. The order was to allow the *Leopard* officer to search the *Chesapeake* for deserters. Barron refused and all hell broke loose after that. The British met our decision with a ten-minute cannonade which we were defenseless against. Those ten minutes seemed to drag on for hours then. When the smoke cleared and the fires were put out we had lost three men and eighteen were wounded."

"Friends."

"Some." He knew she heard his bitterness slowly surfacing, and he searched her face for the first signs of pity. He only saw understanding. He kissed the fingers that were resting lightly on his shoulder before he went on. "Barron had no choice but to submit to a search after that. He fired off one defiant shot for our flag, then he allowed a second boarding party to search the *Chesapeake*. The British produced the usual false documents and claimed four men as deserters. I was one of them." He paused, seeking the words to continue with the part of the story he did not often share. Her fingers curled around his arm, offering support and the tightening in his throat eased.

"I stayed with the *Leopard* for almost six months. During that time my family went through every channel open to them to find me and have me released. They nearly managed it, but then I was put aboard the *Grenada* and British officials informed my family they were unable to trace my whereabouts. The furor over the *Chesapeake* incident gradually died down in the States and my parents and sister found every door shut to them.

"At first I could not accept what had happened to me. I believed my family would be able to locate me and the nightmare of serving the British would end. Others had been that fortunate. When I never heard anything I realized I could not depend on either my family or my government to rectify the situation. I took the matter into my own hands as I should have done in the beginning—as I had always done before."

"You tried to escape?"

"I did escape."

"And the lashings?"

"The punishment for being unsuccessful—twice."

"Twice?" she said, barely concealing her horror. "Two times they did that to you and you still tried again?"

He nodded. "I was on the *Grenada* eighteen months before I managed to get away. That's where I met John Landis. And, Alex, I would have tried a fourth and fifth time if the third had not been successful."

Alexis dropped her head to the pillow and at the same time moved the hand that had been resting on his shoulder across his chest so her entire arm lay against his skin. "Then you know I will try to escape."

It was not a question but he confirmed it anyway. "Yes," he said softly.

"But you will still try to hold me."

"Yes."

"Because you think you love me." The words were forced out slowly with a pause caused by the word she did not want to say.

"Because I know I love you." His response was quick, sure, no hesitation.

She shivered in spite of the warmth of his flesh. "You will still take me to bed, knowing it may be the last time each time?"

"Yes." He waited as she moved closer to him; her head rested on his shoulder now and her leg intertwined with his.

When she was quiet he said, "And you will still allow me to make love to you, knowing it will be more difficult for you to let it be the last time."

"Yes."

They were silent. She listened to the sound of his ship cutting through the water outside while she felt the pulsing of his heart against his chest with her arm. They were perfectly synchronized, she thought, and wondered why it surprised her. He was at home here. He belonged with this ship. She was the one displaced, the piece that did not fit, the one who had to leave before she could belong to him, to anyone, to anything.

"Take me now, Cloud!" Her voice ripped through the silence, shattering it with its intensity, its desperation, its frustration. The only thing absent from her voice, absent from everything she would do from now on, was confusion. She knew what she wanted. She was more sure of it than ever before. The thought of her liberty burned into her brain even as Cloud was branding her, chaining her with invisible white-hot shackles as his mouth moved along her throat.

Their coupling was fierce this time and finished sooner. For each the intensity was greater, the desperation more obvious, and the frustration intolerable until they reached climax. It was as if the qualities of her voice which had snapped the silence had taken possession of their bodies and demanded physical expression.

When it was over she saw she had added new scratches to his back and he had caused the wound on her shoulder to open again. It frightened Alexis because it seemed to be proof that their relationship was fated to hurt them. She looked to Cloud and, finding her fears not mirrored, selfishly took the reassurance he offered.

"I have to be going on deck," he told her after he had bandaged her shoulder.

"So do I." She saw he was about to protest and she cut him off, placing a finger to his lips. "I have work to do. I had a good rest last night although it was cut short this morning in a rather spectacular manner." She pulled her finger away when he caught it between his teeth. She smiled at the sound of his laughter, spontaneous and unrestrained.

"Then you are back to being the cabin boy?" he asked lightly, forcing himself to hide the effort it took to ask the question.

"Yes, when we are with others," she replied. "But Cloud, never, never when we're alone."

He nodded and helped her on with her shirt, taking delight for the first time in fastening buttons. While she braided her hair and washed her face, he dressed. She was ready first and sat in a chair, smiling, as he put on the boots she had polished so furiously. He noticed her gaze and returned her smile. "I never did tell you what a fine job you did."

They went to the door together but she hesitated before she opened it.

"What's wrong?" he asked.

She laughed. "I was thinking: what if anyone sees us leaving together?"

"And?"

"We'd only be confirming what they saw as inevitable all along."

Cloud grinned and kissed her forehead. She opened the door and they went out together to face the others as cabin boy and captain.

The crew was pleased to see Alexis again. She put their worries about the incident aside by going about her work with a fresh enthusiasm that almost tired them out. As she performed her duties she talked freely with the men as she had done the day before, telling them what she planned to accomplish once she got away from the ship. She continued her incessant questioning, delighted to find more and more of the men willing to answer her with the seriousness her questions demanded. She saw Cloud watching her covertly from the quarterdeck but she knew he would make no attempt to stop this part of her education.

By noon she was exhausted. Her shoulder pained her beyond her tolerance. She sat down on the deck, leaning against the box that held the signal flags for support. She drew her legs up, sitting in a cross-legged fashion and scanning the ship for some sign of Cloud. She wanted to tell him she was too tired to go on for the rest of the day, to ask to be excused from her duties. When she did not see him she closed her eyes for a moment, determined to get up and find him just as soon as she felt stronger.

Quite unintentionally the moment stretched to a few minutes and Alexis had no choice but to give in to sleep.

Cloud and Landis stood over her, smiling at her sleeping form. "It seems as if your cabin boy is shirking her duties," Landis said with mock severity.

"Looks that way," the captain replied. "I'll have to be getting my own lunch today." He bent to pick her up.

Through the hazy existence of almost-sleep Alexis felt strong arms sliding under her body and she relaxed against them. Her arms went around the neck of the lean, hard body pressed against hers. She felt her head fall a few inches and come to rest comfortably on a firm shoulder.

Landis shot his friend a knowing glance and turned away to hide his chuckle when Cloud responded with a murderous look of his own. "Come on, Mr. Landis," Cloud said, sighing in resignation. "Go on ahead of me and open the door to her cabin." Under his breath he muttered, "Sometimes you see too damn much."

Landis heard the comment and laughed. It was obvious something had changed between Tanner and Alex and yet, he wondered, had anything changed at all? They were both strong-willed individuals with purposes that conflicted. Had each finally accepted the other's purpose? Landis opened the door to Alexis's room and as Tanner walked past, Alexis held securely in his arms, he knew it was true. He looked from one to the other and for a brief moment allowed himself to feel their pain before he shut the door and went back to work, humming lightly to himself.

Cloud placed Alexis on the bunk and drew the covers around her. He was almost to the door when she called to him.

"Cloud?" It was only a whisper but it riveted him to attention. He returned to her side. "What is it, Alex?"

"I'm tired, Cloud. I was going to tell you, but I couldn't find you."

"How is your shoulder?"

"It hurts dreadfully. I don't want to work any more today, but I wanted you to know why."

"I already know. It isn't simply because of the pain, is it?"

"No. If I strain myself much more it may cost me my—" She paused, wanting to hear it from him. "You say it. You say what it will cost me."

"Your escape," he answered slowly. He allowed her to see by the tightening of his lips that she had punished him. "Get some sleep, Alex. I'll check on you later."

Chapter Seven

When Alexis woke she saw Landis placing a tray of food on the table. She sat up in her bunk and smiled warmly at him. "What time is it? I feel as if I have slept through the night. I hope that isn't breakfast."

Landis laughed. "No, it's your dinner. Captain thought you might like some. He said you needed a good meal in you as much as you needed to rest."

Alexis agreed and sat at the table. "Where is the captain now, John?"

"I see you remembered," he said, referring to her use of his name. "He's below. He's trying to figure out a way to add support to those crossbeams. He's been working with the men for a couple of hours now."

Alexis took a sip of her soup. It was as delicious as it smelled. Obviously Forrest did not need her around. "You mean he's supervising the work," she corrected Landis.

"Meant what I said. It's one of the reasons the men like him so much. He's not above helping them out when there's a problem. He knows a lot about ships—but I suppose he has already told you about that."

"Actually he has told me very little," she replied, setting her spoon on the table. She leaned back in her chair and looked at Landis with interest. "He did say he met you on the *Grenada*. Did you escape together?"

Landis took a seat on her right and folded his hands in his lap. "We did. I couldn't have done it without him."

"I find that hard to believe. You would have found a way."

"I'm not so sure. I had already been with the *Grenada* for more than a year when they brought Tanner aboard. I had exhausted every alternative for escape I knew."

"And what did Captain Cloud do?" Her head tilted to one side to punctuate her sentence.

"He thought of three more alternatives." He laughed, his chuckle thick with admiration. "He would have thought of more but by the third time we did okay."

"And what did you do? I mean why did the captain put an extra burden on himself by helping you escape?"

"Have you seen the scars on his back, Alex?" he asked softly.

"I have." Her voice was bland but she had to force the unemotional response.

"I made sure he lived to think of the third alternative."

She was silent, thinking what it must have been like for the two men, and she understood why they were such good friends now. They had earned one another's respect and that, she decided, had to be the most sound basis for a friendship. She also began to understand why Landis had taken such an interest in her problem aboard the ship. He knew what she was going through.

"You were saying the captain knew a lot about ships," she said, making her voice airy in this attempt to change subjects easily. "Don't all officers learn about the ships they command?"

"Of course. But not like Tanner. He got his command as a result of his escape from the *Grenada* but he's been around ships most of his life. That's what I thought he had told you. His family owns Garnet Shipping of Boston."

Alexis's lips parted in surprise. "I didn't know," she said when she found her voice. "They are one of the very best. George told me often about them."

"So you're familiar with their business."

"Very." She lifted her spoon and took a few more mouthfuls of soup. "Why is the captain in the navy when he could be working for his family?"

"There was a problem about what his family wanted him to do and what he wanted for himself. He won't talk about it much but from the little he told me it seems his parents wanted him behind a desk in the office and he wanted to be behind the helm. They put up with it for a while, humored him by letting him sail on some of their ships. Tanner is not the kind of man you can humor like that. He never wanted to go back to the office again. They would not hear of it, so he joined the navy. They disowned him for a time after that but when the *Chesapeake* incident happened they really fought hard to get him back. His sister, Emma, never did give up. Things are still not too good between him and his parents but they are beginning to accept his decision."

"It would appear the captain had previous experience making escapes before the English took him."

"As I recall from what you said the other day in the galley, you have also had an escape."

"I guess that's what it was," she replied. "I never really thought about it like that before. I just thought I was running away but I always knew what I was running to."

"You haven't told Tanner about it?"

"No. There hasn't been any reason to. I don't like talking about the past any more than he does."

"Why?" he asked.

"It is not because I can't, if that's what you're thinking, John."

"I wasn't. I was just curious as to what you thought."

"Most people dwell on the past and say 'if only.' But when a similar situation arises in the future they never remember their 'if only.' They never try to recall the past in a way that can help them. They feel trapped by it. That's why their faces are full of pity when they hear someone else talk about what's already taken place. They think nothing will ever change. I hate it when people look at me that way. I can see 'poor Alexis' in their eyes before they say the words aloud. I don't regret my past because I learned something from it. I understand it. It's that understanding that guides me, not painful memories. I would be lying if I told you I am never bitter about what has happened to me. I am bitter. But I know why and because I do I can do something about it. I don't have to let things just happen.'' She paused and pushed away her bowl of soup. ''And that's why I don't like talking about my past. I never want to hear 'poor Alexis' again.''

Landis rubbed at his beard with the back of his fingers. ''And you know Tanner feels the same way?''

''I do.''

''Then why don't you tell him about London? He won't pity you.''

''I know. I'd never tell him if I thought that,'' she said. ''There has been no reason to. There is no reason he should know.''

''He'll understand, you know. Just the way you understood about him and his family and his need to get away.'' Landis stood and crossed the room to the door. Before he left turned to her. ''It's strange, isn't it, Alex? How understanding can be infinitely more binding than pity. Not many people realize that, but you do, don't you?''

''Yes,'' she whispered, staring at her plate. How well the old man knew, she thought when she was alone. She was reluctant to talk about her past to Cloud, not because he would pity her, but because he would understand. And that would be another link in her chain of bondage.

She picked at her dinner while she planned out her evening. When she remembered the charts and maps in Cloud's quarters she dismissed everything but her purpose from her mind. After she was finished eating she went to his cabin. Finding him absent she laid out his charts on the floor and began studying them, her head propped on her elbows, legs bent at the knees and raised off the floor. She was so intent on the lines and markings she did not notice Cloud's presence in the cabin until he sat on the deck beside her.

"Have you been here long?" she asked without looking up.

"Long enough to know you are much more interested in what's in front of you than what's beside you."

She laughed and rolled onto her back so she could look up at him. Her head rested on the charts she had been studying. "You're right. I want to learn more about these waters. Will you teach me?"

"The first thing I'll teach you is not to put your hair all over North America. The continent has never looked so inviting."

"I'm serious, Cloud."

"And I have never been more serious about anything," he replied, his eyes caressing her slender form in one continuous motion. It was always like that, he thought. There was no place for his eyes to stop. His glance was forced to take in all of her. Her oval face, the tangent line that formed her neck and branched out at her shoulder, curving over her breast, curving in at her waist, down her thigh, her calf, and extending past her feet into infinity. "There are a few things you have to learn about me, Alex." He stopped. Her eyes had narrowed and she held his glance in the only way it was possible, shooting amber flecks of fire into his face. He sighed. "I suppose that lesson will have to wait. What do you want to know?"

Alexis smiled. "Everything," she said, sitting up. "Currents, places where storms are especially fierce, how to maneuver a ship in tight places. I already know trade routes. George taught me that. And I know where Lafitte and his men are likely to strike. We had to know because we sometimes carried cargo from Spain and that made us his target. I am familiar with the Caribbean. I know the dangerous reefs, like Horse Shoe, but I'm ignorant of the Atlantic. I want to know about conditions around France and England, and islands that are available for fresh water and supplies. And fighting. Don't forget to tell me about strategy.''

"In short, everything.''

"That's what I said.''

Cloud persuaded her to move the maps from the deck back to the table. She sat in the chair and he sat on the arm, one foot propped on the part of the seat she would allow him while the other stretched out beside him. She grilled him with questions. He answered them concisely and clearly, aware of her reason for asking, her purpose not far from either of their minds. When she had no more questions, he asked some of her. Alexis answered instantly, and when she did not know something she would struggle with the problem at length until she could find a solution by studying the charts. He was pleased that more often than not she arrived at the correct answers. When she did not, he explained her errors in detail so she might learn from them.

Finally Alexis held up her hands in surrender. They had been working for almost three hours before she had heard all she thought she could assimilate.

"No more, Cloud. Not tonight,'' she said, leaning against her chair and rubbing her back on the hard wood.

He watched her curiously. She had made the same movement earlier while he was explaining the currents off the coast of France and later when she was stuck on a particularly hard problem. It was distracting and he told her so.

Alexis leaned forward, resting her head in her arms on the table. "I'm sorry if it bothers you but my back is itchy. Those cuts are beginning to heal and I want to scratch them.''

He rubbed her back lightly with his palm. "Is that better?''

"Infinitely,'' she sighed, closing her eyes.

"Where is the lotion John left with you? Have you been using it?''

"How could—Right there . . . up a little higher . . . How could I apply it to myself? I haven't used it since he last put it on me.''

"Then I'll get it. Where is it?''

Alexis told him and when he returned she was already lying face down on his bunk, her shirt and shoes on the deck beside it. She moved toward the middle to give him room to sit at her side. She felt his weight on the bunk and when he did not do anything for a long time she said, misunderstanding his hesitation, "If the sight of my back is repulsive to you I can have John do it."

Repulsive? he thought. Hardly. He did not know if he had ever seen anything as beautiful as the harsh, thin lines across her otherwise flawless skin. It was a symbol of her strength and a reminder to him of how much she had loved one man. He gripped her braid tightly and twisted her head so she could see his face and know the truth. He placed his mouth over hers and kissed her hungrily, almost brutally. He whispered the words she hated against her breasts as he turned her over and her arms folded around him.

Alexis knew the truth and thought that truth had never been at once so painful and so liberating. Their bodies clashed, sweat-slick, hunger demanding to be fed. Alexis pushed against him, wanting to feel all of him pressing close to her flesh. His strong hands that could easily strangle the life from her body she wanted to feel tight against her skin, squeezing into her lungs breath that she could emit in short gasps and brief moans. His powerful legs that walked the deck so surely she wanted to feel, hard on her own, strength against strength. His mouth that said cruel things to her ears she wanted to have on her mouth, at her breasts, on her stomach, and finally at the place between her legs where nothing he said mattered any longer, where only the pressure of his tongue against her inflamed flesh was of any importance.

When it was over Alexis lay beside him and listened to their ragged breathing grow calm in unison. Cloud took her braid and undid the golden strands, amusing himself by running his fingers through the wavy mass. He picked it up and arranged it over her glistening shoulders and breasts; then he brushed it away to reveal what he had hidden. He kissed her on the neck then, more an expulsion of air than actual pressure of soft skin on equally tender flesh.

"You have lovely hair," he said, brushing a wisp of it from the corner of her eye.

"Thank you. I grew—" She stopped, realizing she was about to tell him she had grown it for Pauley, a promise in a previous existence it seemed now. She looked up into his emerald eyes. They were the exact color of the leaves on the trees around her home on the first day she saw them. Your eyes should not be that color, she thought. You should not remind me there was a time when I was free to make the promises of a little girl in love with someone who loved me back. I will punish you for that, Cloud. "I grew it as a promise to Pauley. When I met him I had very short hair and he told me if I ever cut it again he would take a switch to me. The threat was idle. He knew I grew it because I wanted to please him."

Cloud's features tightened. He kept his fingers wrapped around the yellow tresses for a moment. Abruptly he released her hair and fell back against the bunk, staring at the ceiling. "I'm glad he told you to do it," he said after a long silence. "I thought there was something special about the way he looked at your hair that morning on the beach."

"You saw Pauley and me?" she asked. "You were there then?"

Cloud nodded. "We were waiting for your father to come to the house so we could warn him about the British. It was too dangerous for us to wait there so we stationed ourselves at points around your home."

"There were others, besides you and John?"

"Two. They were killed in the firing."

"I didn't know," she said softly.

"No reason you should," he said, unknowingly echoing her earlier sentiment to Landis.

"How long were you there, Cloud? Were you there before Pauley came?"

"You were swimming when I first saw you," he replied, a slight catch in his breath as he remembered the girl battling the waves. "I thought you were a mermaid at the time. I expected you to have fins when you got to the beach."

Alexis laughed. "That's exactly how I feel when I'm swimming. As if I am part of the water, as if I belong to it while I'm in it. I sometimes think that I do have fins. But, Cloud, the best part is—"

He turned to face her. Her amber eyes were glowing, her mouth was turned up in a smile, remembering. He returned her smile but there was sadness in the sensuous curve of his lips. "The best part," he said, "is when you decide to get out and find that you can. The best part is heading for shore and making it. The best part is finding your fins have disappeared and your legs will carry you on land."

"How did you know?" she asked breathlessly.

"I saw it," he said. "I saw all of it that day."

"What did you think then?"

"That I wanted you."

"Oh." She moved closer to him then, nestling her head on his shoulder. In a short time they were both asleep.

Alexis woke Cloud with the constant movement she made by rubbing her back against the sheets. Her hand went to her back as she tried to scratch it and he slapped it away, waking her.

"Stop it, Alex," he said roughly. "You're going to make it worse. I'll have to wrap your hands if you can't keep them away."

Alexis was still half asleep and did not have the vaguest idea what he was muttering about. She smiled through her haze and wrapped a leg around his. She closed her eyes, almost asleep again.

Cloud pushed her leg away, mumbling about a lesson she still needed, and got out of the bunk. He lit the lamp that had gone out hours ago and searched for the lotion he had forgotten in the wake of more important matters. He found it under the table where it had rolled in compliance with the motion of the ship.

"Cloud?" Alexis demanded wearily as she began to wake more fully from all his noise. "What are you doing?"

"Got it."

"Got what?"

"This." He held out the bottle.

Alexis groaned. "The last time you tried to put that on me we did something else entirely. I'm too tired, Cloud. Let me sleep." She buried her face into her pillow in an attempt to block out the light from the lamp.

"Why you little tart! Sleep is exactly what I had in mind, mainly mine, I'll admit. Only I can't get any with you constantly moving around trying to scratch your back." He heard Alexis's muffled laugh through the pillow and he nipped her lightly on her arm with his teeth. She squealed and he kissed her shoulder, brushing the hair away from her back at the same time. She relaxed under his tender caress and it was with great difficulty that he kept to his purpose and opened the bottle.

"You're not making this very easy," he cautioned her as he began to apply the lotion and she squirmed invitingly beneath his warm hand.

"I am not trying to do anything," she retorted. "It just feels so damn good."

He slapped her bottom through the sheets. "Lie still while I see what kind of damage you have inflicted with all your scratching." He put the bottle back on the floor and rubbed the remainder of the lotion into her cuts. She did not move an inch. "Alex," he said when he was finished. "You have some other marks on your back that weren't made with any whip." He touched her in one of the places. She moved slightly, her wince inherent in her movement. He took his hand away. "I didn't notice them before. They're very faint. Were you a terribly clumsy child?" He knew it was not the answer.

"Please, Cloud. May I have my shirt now? I would like to put it on." Her arm went over the side of the bunk and she groped to find it, her face still resting in the pillow.

Cloud snatched it away from her the instant her fingers curled around the material. Alexis sat up and reached for it but he held it out of her grasp. "Why?" he asked, his voice strangely hard. "Why do you want it, Alex?"

In answer she attempted to claw at his face and chest. Why didn't he just let go? Why did he want to know everything? Why did he have to see so much? Understand so well? As he gripped her wrists tightly together and pinned them above her head, forcing her to lie back on the bunk, she knew she could never be with him now if he were not capable of all the things she despised him for at the moment. She struggled with him a few minutes longer until she was exhausted.

"Alex." He said her name gently but loudly enough so she could hear it over her heavy breathing. When she had quieted he said her name again and went on. "I have already seen those marks on your back. Hiding them doesn't make them any less real." He paused and helped her sit up then he slid the sleeves of the shirt over her arms. "You may have it now," he said. "Now that you know nothing has changed."

Alexis nodded dumbly and began to button the shirt. He stopped her with his hand and unfastened it again. "Let's not try to hide everything," he said, pulling her against him and slipping an arm under the open material to encircle her waist. He let her have a moment to feel his strength, allowing her to take some of it before he questioned her again. "The marks. They look as if—"

"From a belt. My father's belt. Not George," she added quickly when she felt him tense. "Not even my real father for that matter. Charlie and Meg took me in when I was very small and raised me with their own children. They never let me forget I was an extra mouth to feed and that they had made hundreds of sacrifices in order to keep me with them. It was hard to find work in London so I couldn't bring in extra money but I did almost everything else for them. He beat me anyway."

"London? You lived in London? But how?"

She put a finger to his lips to silence him. "Oi was a real

street brat, Oi was. Oi spent me toime at th' 'arbor. Th' sailors tol' me stories about all th' plaices they seen an' they taugh' me a little about ships." She laughed at his widened eyes. "The rest of my free time I spent in the park listening to the fine ladies talk and trying to imitate their speech. Charlie and I had an argument one day and it ended with him deciding he was going to sell me. Do you know about things like that, Cloud, or do I have to explain what it meant?"

"I know," he said, his voice barely above a whisper. "How old were you then?"

"Thirteen." His arm tightened around her waist. "I decided to run away before anything could happen. I chose the United States as my destination and the *Constellation* as the means to get me there. I cut my hair, stole my brother's clothes, and took a new name for myself. I managed to get aboard the ship and fool Pauley almost the entire way to Charleston."

"What happened?"

Alexis laughed, remembering the storm and the curse. "My stint as cabin boy to—"

"Cabin boy?" he asked incredulously. Then he began laughing.

"Cloud, will you please let me finish?" He nodded and kissed her cheek, pressing his smile against her skin. "I was cabin boy for Captain Whitehead and I was a good one too," she said defensively, then laughed at herself. There was no reason for him to think otherwise. "Anyway, it all ended when my body decided, quite against my wishes you understand, to make me a woman. Pauley saw the blood and that was the end of everything."

"Was he angry?"

"Furious at first. Later I think he liked me better for what I had tried to do. He made a decision, though, not to allow me to travel the entire way to Charleston. He told me about George and Francine and said I could have a home there. I objected at first. I thought I could get away with the charade a few more weeks but Pauley was firm. He insisted I should go with his friends. He wouldn't let me . . ." Her voice trailed off as she remembered some of her fears and her friend's challenge.

"Wouldn't let you . . ." Cloud encouraged her.

"Nothing."

Cloud remained unconvinced. "Nothing? What is it you can't share with me after sharing so much? I thought you trusted me." He had no idea that his last words duplicated Pauley's words in a similar situation. He was totally unprepared for the frightened and hurt child he released in Alexis. There was no fight left in her to ward off the memories or to hide their impact. Her eyes glazed over with tears and she could not turn away quickly enough. She clung to Cloud fiercely. She burrowed against him, seeking solace and shelter in his embrace.

"It hurts so much sometimes," she cried. "I can't take the risk again. I never win. Oh, Cloud . . . I never can win."

Cloud could barely make out the words but he heard her pain and despair and he hurt for her too. With one hand he cradled the back of her head while the other stroked her back, easing the tightness between her shoulders. He would have held her all night in just such a fashion if she would have permitted it. He would have offered her anything within his power in the hope of easing her ache. But the little he understood from her garbled speech told him that she would not allow that privilege. It seemed too soon to him when she began pulling away, breathing deeply and slowly while she fought for control.

He refused to allow her to move from the circle of his arms and she didn't struggle. She would not meet his eyes, concentrating instead on fingering one of the buttons on her shirt. "I hate it when you remind me that the people I loved are no longer with me," she told him in a husky whisper.

Suddenly so much seemed clear to Cloud. "No, you don't." When she looked up at him belligerently, daring him to explain himself, he continued. "You like it when I inadvertently say something that reminds you of the pain you associate with loving. It supports your logic that loving can only hurt you. It gives you another reason to leave me.''

"I don't need another reason. I have Travers. He's enough."

"And afterward?''

Her inability to respond was the confirmation of all that he had said. Her fear of losing again made her cling tightly to the vows she had made in her island crow's nest.

"Sometimes I wish I could be different," she told him sadly.

"I know," he said, pushing her to the mattress. "But it wouldn't make me love you any less." She smiled at that and he held her for a long time, neither of them moving, then he made love to her, slowly and gently, so that even after the pinnacle was reached the fall from it was unhurried and languorous. His hands were merely a soft whisper next to her skin and her kisses were fragile wisps of air that burned his flesh like a thousand exquisite brands. When it was over he heard her sigh and he chuckled, the sound muffled and subdued against the silky texture of her breasts.

"What is it, Cloud?" she asked, brushing his copper hair from the side of his face so she could see the outline of his cheek pressed to her breasts.

"It was your sigh. I heard you make it once before in your sleep when you didn't know I was there. I thought then I wanted to capture that sigh so I could hear it whenever I wanted. I have it now."

"Now," she repeated so he would know he could not hope to possess it forever. His arms went around her and his head rested more closely on her chest. She continued to stroke his hair with her fingers until she heard the sound of his steady breathing. Then she went to sleep too.

For Cloud the next week passed too swiftly. His only consolation was knowing that for Alexis each minute was like an hour. He watched her make friends with his men and felt the same sense of pride she did when she earned their admiration.

He continued tutoring her in reading maps and using a sword while Harry Young and Mike Garrison taught her how to use a pistol.

Standing on the forecastle he watched as she successfully hit the targets Harry and Mike had placed on the railing. Harry picked her up by the waist and twirled her around while Mike laughed at her astonished face. Cloud found himself smiling as well when she insisted on being put down.

"Harry!" she cried. "This instant! Put me down this instant!" She laughed at herself when Harry let go and dropped her to the deck. She stood up and brushed herself off. "You could have been a bit gentler than that, Harry."

"You wanted down!" he defended himself.

"I never wanted up! Sometimes I think from the way you act you don't expect me to hit those blasted targets!"

Harry tried to look hurt but his slanted grin gave him away. "I couldn't expect you not to hit them since I'm the one who taught you."

Alexis chuckled when she saw Mike's pained expression. "That's enough, Mike. Harry may not give you any credit, but I do. Let's set them up again so we can make sure the last was not a fluke."

As Mike set up new targets Cloud went down to join them. "You are doing very well, Danty," he told her when he stood beside her.

"Have you seen, Captain? Mike and Harry are very good instructors, don't you think?"

"They are and they have an excellent student," he replied easily for Mike and Harry's benefit. Alexis was the only one who noticed the slight wince of his mouth and eyes. It was always that way when he saw her learning skills that were for a purpose in which he had no part.

He would remind her of it later, Alexis thought, when they were in bed together. He would not say anything; he rarely ever did now. But he would tell her just the same. He would tell her with his hands, his arms, his mouth. He would say it all in that brief moment when he completely possessed her.

And afterward there would be a strained silence as each of them thought again of their individual goals. Alexis looked up into his face and saw her thoughts boldly displayed in his eyes, his slightly parted lips, and the arrogant tilt of his chin; and she knew she would not be strong enough to put off an encounter in her bed tonight.

"They're ready, Alex," Mike called to her, breaking the spell of Cloud's gaze.

"Then step aside, Mike! I can't believe you trust me enough to stand so close!" She ignored Cloud's presence as she concentrated on the targets. She fired on the first bottle and sent glass flying into the water and onto the deck. Cloud no longer existed as she reloaded and successfully hit the second target. On the third she saw only her crow's nest and she smashed it to nothingness.

Cloud remained silent while she thanked Harry and Mike for their time and promised to help them with some of their work the next day.

"How do you plan to do it, Danty?" he asked as soon as they left. He walked over to the targets and began pushing the broken glass off the deck and into the water.

"Do it?" she asked.

"Escape. How do you plan to do it?"

"Captain, I hardly think you can expect me to answer that question."

"I am not asking you as the captain," he said, his voice strained. His fingers gripped the railing tightly. "I am asking you as Cloud."

Alexis shook her head sadly. "Whom do you think I'm trying to escape?"

Cloud ran his fingers through his hair, brushing back the strands that were flying in the breeze. He turned away from her and looked out over the water. "I shouldn't have asked."

"No. You were right to ask." She sat on the railing beside him, facing the ocean and letting her feet dangle out over the water. "I will tell you this much: I may not wait until we get to Washington."

"Alex! It would be insane for you to try anything while we're at sea."

"If the risks are outweighed by the possible chance of freedom then I will take them. You really don't expect me to do otherwise, do you?"

"No."

"When the chance is there you will recognize it also. You may even be able to take it away from me. But, Cloud, you cannot hide the opportunity from me."

He continued to stare out at the water, but his mind was wandering back several evenings ago. Caught up in his reverie he did not see Alex's face, did not see she was remembering too. . . .

"My shoulder is fine, Cloud," she had said. "Now are you going to teach me or not?"

"Not so soon, Alex," he had answered wearily. "I do not want to have a reoccurrence of what happened before."

"And I'm telling you that will not happen. If it will make you feel better we'll practice here. That way no one will be watching." Cloud said nothing in return and Alexis could feel her anger rising as he propped his long legs on the table and continued to stare at her arrogantly. Arrogance, she thought, brought on by the fact he was so sure he was right. Well, she was right this time. She was ready to start again. She picked up the rapier from the bed and started toward the door. "I'll not beg you, Cloud. Tom or someone else will teach me what I have to know."

Before her fingers were on the handle of the door she felt his strong grip on her elbow. "Let go of me!" she told him through clenched teeth. She twisted her face and looked up at his dark angry eyes. His fingers still bit into her skin cruelly. She forced herself not to show him that he was causing her real, physical hurt. "I don't understand you," she said finally when he offered nothing in defense of his actions.

He released her. "I didn't like what you said," he explained, returning to his seat. Alexis followed him and stood in front of him, leaning against the table. She frowned, still not understanding. "What you said about not begging me," he answered her expression. "I don't want to see you begging, especially not me. You acted as if that's what I wanted."

"Cloud, I only want you to teach me. If you don't want to I can't force you. It's just that a moment ago you were so righteous thinking you knew what was best for me. We've been through it before. I didn't see the necessity of going through it again. It's terribly hard, isn't it? Teaching me things you hope I will never have a chance to use."

"You know it is."

"And that's the reason you don't want to do it tonight, isn't it?"

"Yes." He spit it out.

Alexis put her hands on his shoulders. She could feel the tension in his muscles through the smooth linen shirt. "Then tell me that. Don't say it's because you don't think I'm ready. Tell me it's hard. I can respect that, Cloud. I don't have time for excuses any more than you do." Alexis removed her hands from his shoulders and sat on the table, placing her feet on his chair, on either side of his legs. She leaned forward until they were almost at eye level. "You told me I was wrong for trying to cover up the marks on my back with my shirt. You were right about that. I accuse you now of doing the very same thing. You try to hide your hurt with excuses. It is not any more effective than the shirt was for me. I understand, Cloud, but I have to hear it from you."

"We're wasting time then, aren't we?"

"Not if we understand each other now."

Cloud stood and reached for his sword. Alexis pushed the table, desk and chairs to one corner of the cabin and the lesson began.

He tried to keep her off guard by talking about the ship, the weather, the navy, but she would not listen. She kept her attention on what she was doing and successfully managed to back him against the wall twice.

"Very good, Alex. Your concentration is excellent and your balance is better than before," he said while he advanced on her. "Keep me guessing. No, I knew what you were going to do that time. You have beautiful eyes, Alex, but they are making it very easy for me to anticipate you. That's better. You really do have beautiful eyes. Like fire sometimes. Gold. Like your hair. I like to touch your hair."

"You are not playing fair, Cloud," she answered angrily as she parried his next few moves.

He ignored her. "Your legs are very nice too. Long and lean and strong. I like the way they feel next to mine." He pressed her to the wall and with a strength he did not know could exist in a woman she pushed him away and went after him furiously. He laughed. "A much better subject than the weather, I think. Mmm, what else can I say? Oh, yes. Your mouth. Don't move so often to the right. Where was I?"

"My right," she answered, sidestepping his next move easily.

"That was very good. Your move and your answer. But I was on your mouth. It's exquisite, you know."

"For what it says or what it does?"

"Both," he replied, feeling a slight catch in the single word. He lost his momentum and Alexis was quick to take advantage of it.

She advanced on him, catching the sleeve of his shirt. She heard the material tear as she said, "My mouth, Cloud. You were on my mouth. What is it you like best? Do you like it when I kiss you on the neck or on the lips? Do you like it better when I press my mouth against your ear or your chest? Perhaps you like it best when I use my mouth to give you pleasure elsewhere?" Her sword swept through the air to the object of her talk but he blocked it.

"Now who's not playing fair?" he demanded huskily.

"Oh, but I have a very good teacher. He taught me everything. Everything." She said the last word with suggestive finality.

"Get your arm up!" he said firmly, trying to regain his

composure. This was a lesson for him as well, he realized. There were some subjects not to be discussed while fencing, especially with a partner as skilled as Alexis was becoming.

"Yes, Cloud," she replied obediently, regaining her balance. "I think we have discussed my mouth long enough. Shall we discuss my breasts now?" She caught the frustration in his almost horrified glance and she pressed her advantage. "Yes, I think we should definitely discuss my breasts."

"Not unless I can see what we're talking about!" In a quick move that she had no time to block the tip of his sword picked off the two top buttons of her shirt in rapid succession. "That's better," he said evenly as he surveyed the swell of her breasts against the open collar.

Alexis did not miss a beat. "Now that you can see them what do you have to say? Perhaps you would like to touch them? Not with the end of your sword dammit! Let's stop this nonsense. Watch me. Try to anticipate me. What am I going to do?" She knocked the sword out of his hand.

Cloud stood motionless for a moment then he threw back his head and laughed. He held out his arms to Alexis and she eagerly ran to him. "I'm so very proud of you," he said breathlessly, partially from exertion, partially from the laughter, and partially from what was about to happen.

He lowered her to the deck, tearing away the remainder of the buttons from her shirt. "Cloud, you're ruining it," she protested. "It's mine, remember?" he answered, his lips covering her mouth. She returned his kiss and helped him remove his clothes, taking a little more care than he did with hers.

For the first time since they were together the mood was laughter. Alexis nipped at his chest and giggled at his falsely pained expression. "Giggling?" he asked, pretending to be appalled. "See how you like this?" His mouth surrounded her nipple and he bit it tenderly. Alexis moaned. "Did you say something, Alex?" he asked as he repeated the procedure on her other breast. This time she managed, "That was very . . ." Then another short gasp drowned out her words.

"Maybe we should talk about fencing," she suggested as his mouth moved lazily over her stomach. Cloud groaned and rolled off her onto his back. His head rested on their discarded clothes. "Oh dear," Alexis said in feigned distress. "I didn't realize that was the response I was going to get." She moved close to him, brushing his chest with her breasts. She felt his breathing quicken but he made no move to touch her. She kissed him on the mouth, her tongue outlined his lips. Then her mouth began its own unhurried journey down his throat. At his chest she stopped. "Fencing can be quite an exciting topic actually." She kissed him again when he rolled his eyes at the mere suggestion. Her lips continued to move while her hand touched the inside of his thigh lightly. "Swords," she said as she began to fondle him. "I imagine there are all different types of swords." She watched his eyes and grinned at the response her words and her actions were evoking. "I told you it could be exciting. Where was I? Blades. Yes, blades. All different kinds I would think. Although my experience is limited, I think I've chosen well, in spite of my lack of—" She was cut off from further discussion as Cloud pulled her away and practically threw her onto her back. He kissed her hungrily. "Fencing indeed," he said when he had to break for air. "There are times when I have to question your inexperience, Alex."

He took her then. The laughter was replaced by driving passion that consumed them both. Alexis clung to him fiercely, the desire to feel all of him against her urging her on. She called out his name as he brought her crashing against wave after wave of pleasure that she had no will to fight even if she had had the inclination. She kissed him softly after she felt him relax against her, succumbing to the same sea of fiery gratification.

She thought after it was over she could never leave him if all their times together could be like the moment just passed. But she knew that would not be, for she knew she would never allow it to happen in quite this manner again.

Cloud lifted her to the bunk and slid in beside her, covering them both with his sheet. He was also silent, knowing the laughter could not be recaptured, knowing she would fight against it.

"You might just be able to make it, Alex," he whispered, to give her strength.

"And you might just be able to stop me," she said, returning it.

Cloud savored the memory as he watched Alexis now. She was squinting in the bright sunlight, her face upturned as she looked toward the horizon. Determined in her path. Wanting him to see that determination. He knew that if her opportunity came he would allow her to see it. He did not know then just how hard it was going to be.

"Danty," he said sharply, almost laughing when his voice made her lose her grip on the railing and she nearly tumbled into the foamy waves around his ship. He grabbed her by the waist and set her firmly on deck. "Don't you have some work you should be doing? This is not a free trip anymore."

"Yes, Captain." Her serious response was broken as a wide grin crossed her face. She hurried away to find Landis, leaving Cloud muttering about insubordination.

That was the only laughter between them now, he realized. The laughter between a cabin boy and her captain, sharing a secret in the manner of small schoolchildren.

Harry looked down from his perch high above the ship on the mizzenmast cap. He did not see Cloud immediately so he rechecked his sighting with his scope before he yelled for Landis.

"Hey! Mr. Landis! We have company! Five, maybe six miles out!"

"What flag?" he called back.

Harry looked again. "Union Jack. But she's a merchant.

You are not going to believe this but she's one of the Quinton line. His markings are on it."

Landis found his captain immediately. "Harry says it is one of Quinton's, Captain. Probably coming from Boston."

Cloud swallowed hard. "You sure, Harry?" he called up.

"Yes, sir! Sure as I'll ever be about anything!" He did not add there was something strange about the ship. He could not be sure about that until it moved in closer.

"Very well," Cloud sighed. He did not move. He leaned forward against the railing and stared at the ship in the distance.

"Are you going to tell her?" asked Landis. Alexis was in her cabin cleaning Mike's pistols. The ship could pass and she would never know.

"I'll tell her," he said finally, his voice so low Landis could barely hear him. He started toward Alexis's cabin.

He was just out of sight when Landis saw Harry scrambling down from the cap. "Mr. Landis, there's another ship out there too. It's following Quinton's but at a safe distance. I think it's one of Lafitte's."

"This far north?" he asked incredulously. "You sure, Harry?"

"Can't be, not yet. Something strange about Quinton's ship though. She should be loaded with cargo on this run and yet she's moving too fast and too high to be carrying much. I think she's already been raided and boarded. Most likely he's got men on both of the ships."

Landis nodded but said nothing.

"Where's the captain? He should be told. There is a reward for Lafitte. We could bring him in."

"Oh, we could, could we?" Landis was patient. "Which ship is he on?"

"Don't know sir. Can't be certain he's on either one. Maybe his brother."

"I'll tell the captain, Harry. You did what you had to do. My responsibility now."

Harry walked away then he stopped suddenly, spinning

on his heels. "Does Alex know? Does she know one of her
merchants is coming close?"

"The captain is telling her now." Landis smiled when Harry
walked away, whistling softly.

Alexis did not put her work down when she heard the door
open behind her, but when that same door slammed violently
to its former position she dropped the pistol she was cleaning
in surprise. She stood quickly and turned to see the intruder.

"Cloud!" Her voice held relief. "You scared me. You
shouldn't—What's wrong? Why are you looking at me so
strangely?" His eyes were so dark Alexis ceased to think of
them as green. Now they were black and biting. She could
not tell if they were angry, she had never seen him like this
before. He leaned against the door, saying nothing, simply
staring at her as if this were the first time he had ever seen
her. His jaw was set so tightly a muscle twitched in his cheek.
She thought she recognized determination, but never this
degree of it. Never like this. "Cloud?" It was a soft question
and her voice was strained with apprehension.

"Don't say anything, Alex!" he cut in sharply. Then more
gently, "I want to look at you." He kept his gaze focused on
her as she placed her hands behind her and held on to the
table edge tightly. His eyes traveled down the smooth line of
her arm visible through the fabric of her shirt and rested on
the white knuckles pressed against the wood. Even the
strength of her grip was not enough to hide the trembling
of those slim fingers. Her feet were set firmly apart, rooted
to the floor, and yet he could detect the merest quivering in
her long legs. Her breath was coming in short spurts and he
watched the rise and fall of her breasts as the tempo of her
breathing quickened. Her head was tilted to one side, still
viewing him with curiosity, but her eyes were regarding him
as the hunter again. Just as they had that first night she'd
awakened. Only this time he saw she recognized danger—
and he was the danger. Her eyes wandered about her quarters,
averting from his gaze only an instant, but in that instant he

saw she was planning escape and he crossed the cabin to prevent it.

His hands rested firmly on her upper arms and he buried his face in the curve of her throat and shoulder. His lips pressed hard against her smooth, tawny skin and he whispered hoarsely, "I want you now, Alex. Now!"

Alexis struggled to be free of his grip but he was firm. "Cloud, tell me what is wrong!" Despair made itself heard at the last moment. He began to unbutton her shirt. "Stop it!" she cried as his head moved between her breasts. "Not like this, Cloud!" She pulled at his head until he raised himself and looked down at her. "What is it, Cloud? I have never said no to you before. Why are you doing this? Why are you treating me this way?" She was breathless but she persisted even while he was bending her back over the table, even while she thought he would snap her in two. "You're hurting me! Why do you want to hurt me this way when you can do it so easily by saying you love me?" Her next words remained a thought, unheard by him as his mouth crushed hers. She bit him. His head snapped back but then his lips were on her throat and his hands held her motionless against the table. "Cloud! No! I don't want you like this!" She tried to kick him. "Let me go, damn you!"

He eased his grip slightly. He lifted his head and stared into her catlike amber eyes. He had never seen her confused before. It was confusion that lent itself to terror. "A ship," he said quietly. "One of the Quinton Line. Your line now. It will be passing us soon." That was all that was necessary. She understood immediately and the terror was replaced by a gentle light in her eyes.

She shook her head sadly. "I cannot hate you for what you tried to do, Cloud. But you can't hold me this way." She started to move only to find he would not let her. "Let me go." As his mouth moved to her breasts Alexis wrapped her fingers around the barrel of one of the pistols at her side. Even while he was exciting her body with familiar practiced hands she raised the pistol as high as she could.

Cloud saw her movement and hoped it would be quick. If she hesitated one instant he would never let her have another.

While his legs were pressing tightly against hers Alexis marked her target. As his mouth bruised her tender flesh with his final white hot brand she brought the butt of her weapon crashing against his skull.

Cloud knew nothing but darkness sweeping over him. Alexis knew nothing but his mouth and hands grazing her skin as he slipped to the deck.

Landis found Cloud still unconscious an hour later and brought him around with a liberal amount of cold water.

"Did she make it safely, John?" he asked, rubbing the back of his head gently.

"She did. Quite a sight too. You want a drink, Tanner? It couldn't hurt your head none." Cloud nodded and Landis poured him some brandy. "She really knocked you out," he whistled softly.

"Do I detect a bit of admiration for her in your tone?"

"You should detect a whole lot," he laughed. "I want to know something."

"What?"

"Did you let her do that to you?"

Cloud chuckled then winced from the pain. "That, old friend, is something neither you nor she will ever know." He was silent, thinking she was really gone. After a while he said, "Tell me about it. How did she do it?"

Landis eased back into his chair, stroking his beard, preparing to tell a good story. "She came on deck just as natural as you please, like nothing had happened down here. She walked over to the starboard railing and waited until the ship was closing in. Harry and I knew what she was up to so we warned her it was possible that . . ." His voice trailed off. Tanner was not ready to hear that they knew for certain Alex had gone to Lafitte. "We warned her that it would be dangerous. She just looked at us with those blasted eyes of hers, daring us to try and stop her. Harry and I looked at each other and then at the other men who were watching and we knew no one was going to stop her. At that point we were giving serious consideration to hailing the other ship for her.''

"You didn't.''

"No, we asked her where you were and she finally told us she had persuaded you to understand she knew what was best but that you still would not help her leave. She told us not to hail the ship.''

"Damn fool,'' Cloud said, smiling. "Well, she didn't lie to you exactly. She did persuade me.''

"You should have seen the pained look on her face when she said it. She wasn't happy at all with her explanation. She got on the railing then and just before she dove in she told me to check on you, that she had hit you pretty hard. Next thing I knew she was over the side. The men all went to the railing and yelled to her to keep going. She swam and swam and there were a couple of times we thought she wasn't going to make it. Harry signaled the other ship and made sure they pulled her in. There was no return message. We have to be satisfied that she is all right.'' His voice dropped. "It's what she wanted, Tanner.''

And, Cloud thought, heading for his cabin, he had finally come to terms with that. He rested his head against the pillow and stared through the darkness, wondering if he had imagined her cool hands on his face after she had rendered him unconscious, wondering if he had really felt her soft lips brushing his, wondering if she had really said the words she hated to him. It was probably just a dream of what he would have liked. Even if she had said, "I love you,'' that was going to change very soon.

If only he understood this assignment better. He was going to have to stop her in spite of his own doubts. How was he going to keep her prisoner when he was no longer sure he wanted to, not in the way Howe and the others demanded. She was going to hate him for stopping her and he would have to accept that. He and Alex Danty were going to be together again; still the time was not right.

Part Two

Chapter Eight

Alexis took off her ring and dropped it into the velvet lining of the ivory case on her bureau. The ring and the box were both gifts from Lafitte and she treasured them as a symbol of her friendship with the pirate.

"You were wonderful, Kurt," she said to the man standing in the doorway of her cabin. "They never suspected for a moment you were not the captain of this ship."

Kurt smiled. He leaned against the frame of the doorway, almost filling the open space with his muscular bulk. He crossed one leg casually in front of the other and eyed Alexis as her fingers closed around the jewelry case. "I wasn't bad, but it was you, dear wife, who kept them from searching the hold. Vapors indeed. When did you ever have an attack of the vapors?"

Alexis's eyes narrowed as she peered at the handsome, brawny seaman. Then she broke into laughter. "Wasn't I convincing? I thought it was quite effective."

Kurt Jordan nodded and crossed the cabin in a few strides, taking a seat on the edge of Alexis's bunk. He rubbed a spot of dirt from his boots before he said anything. When he looked up at Alexis his blue eyes were bright with laughter. "You were quite effective, but I thought the crew was going to give it away. It was all anyone could do to keep a straight face when you started to sway. The men have seen you in so many dangerous situations I believe they thought you incapable of fainting."

"It seemed like the only solution. The British are getting too serious and too close in their search for Alex Danty. Imagine them boarding a private merchant looking for that brigand! When I saw they were ready to make a thorough search I had a vision of Alex Danty swinging at the end of a rope and that is something she is not ready to do."

Kurt shook his head. "Neither is anyone on Captain Danty's crew."

"And none of us will if we keep our heads as we did today. Were the others upset by the prospect of being searched?"

"They were prepared to fight if our explosives and extra guns were found, if that's what you mean. But I don't think they doubted you would find a way out of it. It worked well— me as the captain and you as my wife."

Alexis smiled at her second-in-command and sat at her desk. She smoothed the folds of her dress with her hands then she placed them on the arms of the chair, curling her fingers around the ornately carved wood. When she spoke her voice was deep, serious, almost weary. "We can't stay here long, Mr. Jordan. It's too dangerous for us to remain in England long. We'll put into port tomorrow and as soon as we can find where Travers has been reassigned we leave."

Jordan nodded. "Are we taking on new cargo?"

"I've made arrangements to carry tea and cloth to Boston. We are going to get rid of the rum presently hiding our contraband."

"No one will be able to say this was an entirely fruitless venture even if we never find Travers. You've been able to make a bit of money in the last eighteen months."

"The money is secondary," Alexis replied shortly. "Travers is the main thing."

"I did not intend to imply otherwise, Captain," he said earnestly.

"I know." She paused, remembering Jordan had just as much reason for wanting to see Travers as she did. "I want you to assign a half dozen men to discover Travers's whereabouts when we dock tomorrow. It will only take us about eight hours to exchange our cargo. Make sure they know that is all the time they have. You will remain on deck as captain. I will not go up at all unless it is necessary to have another attack if a search is threatened."

Jordan stood and beamed at his captain. "If I ever get married, remind me to make certain my wife takes better to the sea than you."

"It will be my pleasure," she returned, matching his bright smile.

"Anything else before I leave?"

"Find Peach and tell him I would like some of that fresh rain water for a bath. And, Mr. Jordan," she added softly but with the same firmness present in all her commands, "those men you pick to find Travers. Make sure they're volunteers."

He laughed. "That will be easier than finding Peach, Captain."

When he was gone Alexis examined the cargo manifest, checking off the list with sharp strokes of her quill. As she finished, there was a hesitant knock at the door.

"Your water, Captain," the voice announced timidly.

"Bring it in, Peach," she answered. "Fill up the tub, then take this manifest to Mr. Jordan and ask him to verify it. If it is satisfactory, slip it under my door. I do not want to be disturbed until we reach London."

Peach filled the tub quickly, in spite of the heaviness of the buckets he had to carry from the companionway. Peach, at twelve, all arms and legs, was a little in awe of his captain and his hurried pace was due as much to his anxiousness to please her as it was to remove himself from her presence. He took the paper Alexis held out to him and almost ran from the cabin, missing her murmured thank you.

Smiling to herself over Peach's actions, Alexis unfastened
her dress and hung it in her wardrobe. Tossing her other
garments aside, she slipped into the tub. When tepid water
greeted her, she noted it was time to have a talk with her new
cabin boy about hot baths.

She leaned her head against the edge of the large copper
tub and shut her eyes. The full weight of the responsibility
she carried for her men and her ship consumed her for a
second. She shuddered involuntarily. The end had been so
close today when they had been boarded.

The British were anxious to call a halt to her activities, but
this afternoon had been the closest they had come—and
they'd left, never knowing they had been face to face with
Captain Danty. The *Sea Jewel* matched the general description
of the vessel that sunk a British sloop six weeks ago. Of course
Flying Tempest, The Wicked Lady, and *Ariel*—the other names
of her ship—also matched the description. *Dark Lady,* the
name under which the search had begun, had flown with just
as many different flags and the safe was full of documents
proving ownership to different shipping lines—Garnet Shipping among them.

Alexis sighed, lathering her shoulders and face. She had
managed to fool them today because they were looking for
a scarred man, not a scarred woman. But how long would
she be able to keep the secret? Her men would never tell;
they had as much to lose as she did. The crew of the *Hamilton?*
No, they had wished her well. And Lafitte? She laughed lightly.
Lafitte would never speak a word.

Her mind went back to the day of her escape from the
Hamilton and from Cloud. . . .

She had held out her arms and allowed the men to pull
her out of the boat and onto the deck of the ship. Then they
had pulled their arms away suddenly, as if they had no right
to touch something they could not explain. And a woman,
half drowned from the torturous swim she had just finished,
was beyond their comprehension.

Alexis, swaying at the loss of support for her tired, aching limbs, would have fallen if other strong arms had not reached out to stop her descent. She thanked the man, who was regarding her more curiously than the others; then she gently released herself from his secure grip and edged toward the railing, leaning against it until she could catch her breath. She observed the startled faces, especially that of the man who had broken her fall. He seemed to be mildly amused. His narrow lips were set in a taunting half-grin as if he had already accepted her being aboard and was merely waiting for some sort of explanation. His blue-green eyes sparkled mischievously, holding some secret he was not ready to share. Alexis's gaze wandered past his handsome face in search of the captain of her vessel.

"I would like to talk to the captain," she said when she finally caught her breath. Most of the men continued to stare at her blankly. Alexis persisted. "Thank you for bringing me aboard, but I would like to explain my presence to your captain. It is Mr. Samuels I believe. May I see him?"

There was a murmur of confusion before the man with the taunting smile stepped forward to ease Alexis's bewilderment. "I am the captain, demoiselle. *Je m'appelle Jean Lafitte.*" He made a low bow but looked up quickly to watch Alexis's reaction.

Alexis was unperturbed. She smiled, holding out her hand. Lafitte took it and kissed it lightly. "Monsieur Lafitte, may I inquire what you are doing aboard my ship?" she asked casually.

For the first time she read surprise on his dark face, but he masked it quickly, breaking into a wide grin and laughing heartily. "Demoiselle, that was my question to you. Perhaps you read minds?"

"Not at all," she answered easily. "My name is Alexis Danty Quinton and this vessel belongs to me. If I may see the real captain, the one my father put in charge, he will be able to verify my identity."

"That is not necessary even though your request is impossible for the moment. Captain Samuels is aboard my own ship.

Quite safe, as is the crew." He thought he detected a hint of relief in her champagne eyes. She was most unusual. Beneath her wet and tangled hair, beyond her dripping men's attire, there stood a singularly beautiful young woman. In addition to her physical attributes she seemed to have an aura of strength and sense of challenge about her. He could hardly believe she was standing in front of him quite calmly, demanding to see Samuels.

"Je pense, Mademoiselle Quinton—"

"I would prefer Alex, Monsieur."

"Alex, then. I think you will have to answer some of my questions first; then we will make a determination as to whether you will see Samuels. Would you like drier clothes?"

Alexis looked down at herself and laughed. *"C'est une bonne idée.* I am afraid my rather unusual appearance has done little to confirm my identity."

Lafitte nodded amiably and led Alexis to Samuels's cabin. "You might be able to find something suitable among his things until your own clothes dry. I will return shortly and we can trade explanations, though I assure you that mine is very simple." He started to leave but stopped, remembering something. "The ship you left sent us a signal to pick you up. Is there a return message?"

Alexis was silent. She thought of Cloud lying unconscious on the floor of his cabin and of Landis and Harry and all her other friends aboard the *Hamilton.* They would want to know. She shook her head. This was a new beginning, and they had to be forgotten for the time being. "No," she said softly. "There is no message. I'm sure they know I was pulled aboard. They will know I survived." She paused. "And, Monsieur Lafitte, it would be best if you got under way immediately. I was warned before I jumped ship that you might be in possession of this one. Someone on board may change his mind and come after you."

Lafitte smiled brightly and bowed his head. "I am honored that even though you knew I might be here you still came." Then, with the slightest edge of mockery in his tone, he added,

"But somehow I have the impression that if the USS *Hamilton* were to follow it would not be me they were after." He turned and left her alone, but not before he was able to catch surprise in her eyes.

Alexis searched through Samuels's wardrobe and found nothing that would do. She finally gave up and stripped off her wet clothes, wrapping a sheet around her shivering form. She had just finished when she heard Lafitte at the door. "Come in," she answered, laying her clothes on the wide window bench.

"Ahh, Alex," he murmured appreciatively at the sight of her profile outlined by the sun's rays through her white covering. "Most suitable attire indeed." Only thirty, Lafitte had a discerning eye for objects of value.

Alexis turned quickly and saw he was only teasing her. His dark eyebrows were raised and they matched his mocking tone. His eyes gleamed brightly, but not rudely, alternating from blue to green as the light caught them. He was not much taller than she and slightly built, making Alexis think this could hardly be the man who was such a terror in the Caribbean. She thought of her own goal and realized she would make an equally unlikely terror. It amused her and she laughed.

"I did not mean to be amusing. Rather complimentary."

"You are not quite what I expected, Monsieur," Alexis explained, taking a seat.

"And you are hardly the sort of fish one usually finds in these waters." He took a seat opposite her, folding his arms across his chest. "I believe it is time you begin your story. There is much I do not understand." He watched her face carefully as she began her explanation. The amber eyes captivated him as did her tale. There was a common ground in the revenge each of them sought.

Alexis told Lafitte briefly about her home on Tortola and how she arrived there. She explained the deaths of her parents and Pauley and Travers's part in all of it. His face was grim as she mentioned being whipped by the captain. She misunderstood his look and offered to show him her back.

Lafitte was genuinely angered by her suggestion. "That will not be necessary," he said coldly. "I am quite capable of determining the truth without absolute proof."

"Then you are an exceptional man."

"And you are an exceptional woman, Alex. I do not believe you lie."

Alexis smiled at the statement. "I do not want to disappoint you, but I have been known to shade the truth." He seemed satisfied with her remark. As Alexis continued her story she began to understand how this man, different from Cloud in many ways, was capable of commanding his men with the same ease. "I was taken aboard the *Hamilton* by Captain Cloud and the first officer, John Landis. Their intention was to take me to Washington and give me medical attention for my wounds, but I managed to do well on my own. I asked to be returned to Tortola but I was refused." Alexis went on to explain how she had worked for Cloud. The incident when she had climbed the rigging in her dress was not left out and she saw it amused him. She mentioned the mishap while she was fencing and how Harry and Mike had taught her to use a pistol. "The captain of the *Hamilton* was aware I wanted to leave and he knew I would escape if given the chance. His crew was a bit more encouraging than he—that is why no one stopped me when they saw I was ready to jump."

Lafitte nodded in understanding. "And where was Captain Cloud when you made your escape? Surely he did not change his mind?"

"No, the captain did not change his mind. I had to persuade him."

"Shading the truth?" he asked slowly, bright eyes narrowing slightly.

"I knocked him out." Her voice was soft, but her eyes were hard.

"You are very determined, Alex," he noted when her expression gave nothing away except that fact. Still, he thought, there was something she was not saying. He could only guess as to what it was but the next few minutes gave him his answer.

"I have been told that before," she stated flatly.

"By your captain?"

Alexis's eyes flashed gold ice for a second, then she composed herself. "By Captain Cloud and a few others. You imply in your question there was something between the captain and myself. I do not know where you got that impression."

"He would not let you go, you told me that much." His mouth formed the slanted half-grin, delicately taunting her.

"Because he thought it was too dangerous and that I did not know my own mind when I said I wanted to kill Travers," she said quickly.

"If that is what he told you, then he is also guilty of shading the truth. For if he did not realize you know exactly what you want then he must have been a fool." He saw her eyebrows rise slightly. "Or," he continued, "he must have loved you very much."

"Captain Cloud loved me, Monsieur Lafitte. He was not a fool." She lowered her voice to hide the trembling as she spoke. "In the end he proved his love in the only way I could have accepted it. He allowed me to hit him and gave me my chance to escape."

"You know this?"

Alexis nodded. "I am sure he knew what I intended."

"And you did not hesitate?" Lafitte asked quietly.

"Only afterward. Only for a moment. Just to say goodbye." She waited to see if he would comment, but he said nothing as he continued to observe her. The mocking grin was gone and she saw he understood. She pressed on to her present problem. "There is nothing more to say except I have escaped one ship and seem to have found myself in a similar predicament on this vessel."

"In what way, Alex? I do not intend to hold you prisoner. You are my guest. I would not have picked you up otherwise."

"Then you will return me to the island?" She could not hide the hope that crept into her voice.

"*Naturellement.* It is not far out of our way."

"And my ship, this ship, you will return it also?"

Lafitte chuckled. "You ask a great deal."

"Only what is mine. You may have the cargo. It appears you have transferred some of it to the other ship anyway. You were making too great a speed to be heavily loaded. I want the original crew returned to this vessel as soon as you are safe from being spotted by American Naval ships."

The taunting grin returned. "You are most kind, Alex, to be thinking of our safety."

Alexis curled her lips in the exact image of Lafitte's smile, and she did not alter it when he broke into laughter, seeing the expression and realizing it was his. "I was thinking of my own safety, Monsieur," she said. "I have no desire to be captured with your men and thrown into a prison or perhaps hanged."

"Always practical."

"Always."

Lafitte stood and walked toward the door. "This Captain Travers, Alex. Do you think you can accomplish what you plan?"

"Yes."

"But you want this ship to aid you."

"Yes, but I will do it with or without this ship. It would only save me time if you would return what belongs to me."

"Do you have something you would like to offer in trade for the ship?" He scanned her slender figure, wrapped tightly in the sheet.

Alexis chuckled softly. "I made that offer to Captain Cloud for my return to the island. He refused. I think you would do the same."

Lafitte sighed. "But you are not sure."

"No. I am not sure. Therefore I will not even suggest it."

"*Bien,* because I am not sure either, demoiselle." His eyes sparkled brightly at a game played and lost. "I have already said I would take you to Tortola, but we shall not discuss the return of your ship again."

"That is fine. I do insist upon working for you, however," she said with finality.

Lafitte suddenly realized all that Cloud had been up against but he was already prepared to help her. "Of course. But wait until your things dry. I would be as angry as Captain Cloud if you chose to climb the rigging in that sheet and I cannot vouch for your safekeeping among my men."

"I can take care of myself."

"That," Lafitte said firmly, "I never doubted for one moment."

During the time it took to reach Tortola, Alexis proved Lafitte's judgment correct again and again. He continued the fencing instructions until he declared she was as good as many of his men and better than some. He refused, however, to allow her to fire a pistol, telling her he had seen too many misfire. Alexis wondered if that was the complete truth. She thought it was possible he feared her taking back her ship by force. She let it pass and concentrated on the other things he could teach her. Because he seemed to understand her need for the kind of justice she had chosen, he encouraged her to learn methods of deception that would enable her to board a ship before her intent was made clear.

It was in the Roadtown harbor that he revealed his wish to return her ship.

"Why are you so surprised, Alex?" he asked when her eyebrows arched in an astonished curve. "As you pointed out so quickly when we first met, the ship does indeed belong to you."

"I was not aware it made a difference in your profession," she answered.

"It usually does not. You, Mademoiselle Danty, are an exception."

"Merci." She thanked him for seeing her as an exception, not for her ship.

"I will hear from you?"

"You will hear of me, Monsieur. You can be sure of it."

They parted then, quiet *au revoirs* sealing their friendship and leaving the possibility of meeting again to chance.

After she left the man with the mocking grin and taunting eyes, the real preparations for her quest began. Samuels and his crew were returned to the ship and the townspeople welcomed them home. Alexis made herself comfortable in the Quinton Shipping Line offices instead of staying in the home that held such painful memories for her.

She visited her home on the hill, though, and oddly felt nothing. She looked at the graves of George and Francine and Pauley and felt a passing sadness. It was not until she sat in her worn spot of earth, her crow's nest, that all the events of the past weeks seemed to gel into a hard, cold cancer in her belly and she cried.

She did not resist the tortured moans that sounded foreign to her own ears. She welcomed them as the symbol of the relief and release she deserved. She thought the tears cleansed her body and her mind, and when she heaved the last gasp she was ready to begin again. It would be Captain Alex Danty from now on.

From her new home Alexis directed the outfitting of her ship. It was gone over from bowsprit to taffrail to make it seaworthy for the long months ahead. Extra guns were placed on board and carefully disguised so the vessel maintained the illusion of being no more than a merchant.

Alexis relied on Frank Grendon, George's secretary, to make arrangements for cargo to be taken on board. He was the one who saw to it that she had the necessary documents to protect her in the event of being boarded. His wife, Sally, along with other women in the settlement who were grateful to Alexis for bringing their husbands home after an encounter with Lafitte, sewed flags of different countries which would enable Alexis to disguise the purpose of her ship even further.

After more than four months of intensive labor and intricate planning Alexis decided she was ready to begin her search. She chose Grendon to run the line while she was gone and together they devised a system which allowed either one of them to have messages taken to various ports by the remaining Quinton merchants.

Alexis sat in the dining room of Frank and Sally Grendon on the evening before the *Dark Lady* was to sail. She sipped her wine slowly, thinking how much she preferred the company of this quiet couple to that of the wealthy planters and land-owners who had assailed her with invitations to celebrate the completion of her work on Tortola.

"They would have tried to talk me out of it," she said, thinking aloud, unaware she had spoken until Frank tilted his head in her direction.

"You said something, Alexis?" he asked. He crossed his long legs at the ankles and eased his thin form into the leather-backed chair. A shadow crossed the deep cleft that slashed his chin perpendicularly and disappeared when he lifted his head and smiled.

At one time Frank had given serious consideration to buying into the business of his close friend and employer to assure its continuation if anything should happen to George. That had changed when Alexis came to the island. At first Frank assumed, as did everyone else, that George would see Alexis's husband took responsibility for the line. Gradually it became apparent that Alexis herself was capable of overseeing the business. Frank bowed out, not disagreeably, certain that working for Alexis would be no less a privilege than working for George.

"I was thinking how much I wanted to be here with both of you instead of the others," Alexis said. "They would have tried to stop me, even at this late date."

"And you knew we wouldn't."

"I'd never have come if I thought you would, Mr. Grendon."

"Good. Sally has a surprise for you. When you see it you will know just how seriously we are taking this venture."

Sally leaped to her feet and left the room. She was the perfect physical foil to her husband. Where he was a series of triangles and parallel lines she was a succession of curves and graceful arcs. His eyes were scalenes filled with silver while hers were circles of violet. His mouth was almost a straight line while hers, more often than not, was given to an expression that pulled her lips in a small *O*. It was this expression that greeted Alexis and Frank when she returned to the room with a large bundle of clothes in her arms. Alexis helped her clear a place for her bundle on the table.

"They are for you," Sally announced with breathless pleasure. "The other women and I did a little more than make flags."

"Oh, Mrs. Grendon! It's wonderful!" Alexis ran her fingers down the stack of soft shirts and trousers. "How clever of you! I thought I was going to have to borrow clothes."

"Look on the bottom, Alexis. It's something special."

Alexis picked up most of the pile and put it to one side. She knew what Sally was referring to. The black material had caught her attention immediately. Her fingers lingered over the dark silk before she held up the shirt in front of her and looked to both of them for approval. The billowing sleeves were clipped at the wrists with gold cufflinks she recognized as George's.

"Thank you," she said quietly.

"Look beneath the trousers," Sally fairly squealed. "There's also something of Francine's."

Alexis lifted the trousers and found a crimson satin sash below. She placed it around her waist over her dress. "Mrs. Grendon, Lafitte will be absolutely envious of my attire. He prides himself on being the best-dressed brigand on the seas." She caressed the sash longingly.

Sally laughed, a small tinkling sound. "It was not our intention to see you well dressed—only well hidden. There is a mask also and a bandanna to keep the British from seeing your face and hair."

"You've thought of everything," Alexis sighed, removing the sash and sitting down. "How did you choose the color? Why black?"

"The captain of the *Dark Lady* in pink? Hardly," she scoffed. "There are boots for you too. Frank saw to them. You can get them when you go to the ship this evening."

"Why? Why is everyone so eager to help me?"

"Many reasons, Alexis," Frank answered. "Some because George and Francine were dear friends. Some because Quinton Shipping is the livelihood of so many here and Travers nearly ruined it for us. The men you chose think you can do it. It is not just because of Travers that they are willing to follow you. Part of it is their protest against impressment and an incident that should not have been allowed to take place."

"Just so none of them feel sorry for me."

"Feel sorry for you?" Frank rubbed the cleft of his chin with a thin finger. "What man in his right mind would risk his life because he felt sorry for someone else? I believe you weeded those fools out. Some of those men have been your friends since you came to Tortola. They might want to protect you—that could be part of the reason they agreed to help. They are—we all are—saddened by what happened to George and Francine, but none of them would use feeling sorry for you as a replacement for loyalty."

"You're right, Mr. Grendon. They are good men. That's why I am going to have them back working for Quinton Shipping in no time at all."

Most of them did return, although not because Alexis found Travers. His whereabouts eluded them time and time again and the Royal Navy suffered with each vessel Alexis destroyed. The seamen and officers were always given the opportunity to swim for land before the vessel was set afire. In nearly every instance the captain had to be bodily removed from the ship in order to save his life.

It was on the very first inspection of a captured frigate crew, when Alexis was looking for some of the men who had been with Travers, that she made the decision to allow the men pressed into service to board her ship if they wished it.

For the trapped seamen it was not a hard decision to make. They came to the *Dark Lady* willingly and without trepidation in spite of the fact its captain never uttered a word or revealed his face to them. They already admired the distress ruse which had enabled the slender man, dressed entirely in black, to trap their vessel and render it defenseless without firing a shot. The men, some English, most Americans, were eager to leave behind their forced servitude and take their chances with the man identified to them only as Captain Alex Danty.

Once on board the *Dark Lady,* after Danty's crew had sunk their prison, their eyes riveted on their dark avenger. Danty himself remained mysteriously silent while their questions were answered by the second-in-command, Scott Hansom.

"All it is necessary for you to know," Hansom said imperiously as he scanned the confused faces of the eight men who had been offered their liberty, "is that Captain Danty is interested in only one man and seeing this man brought to the end he deserves. We are not interested in waging war with the entire Royal Navy. We told you the truth before you agreed to come aboard. You may leave at the nearest port or you may stay with us and help us find the man."

There was a murmuring among the thin, shirtless men. Their unhealthy leanness was evidence of the poor food and sanitary conditions aboard their ship. Their backs, in most cases, showed some sign of their unwillingness to obey their jailers in all ways. After a few moments of silence one of them spoke out.

"Who are you searching for?"

Hansom looked to Alexis for a sign. She shook her head slowly. He fixed his sharp gray eyes and authoritative countenance on the man who asked the question. "You will have to agree one way or the other before you are told. Any of you choosing to be left in port will learn nothing."

"You're asking a lot," replied a man with a crisp British accent. "It's treason, you know."

Hansom clenched his large brown hands at his sides. He was kept from advancing on the men by another slow sideways movement of his captain's head. He held his position, saying his next words loudly to be heard over the outraged protests the other men made to their mate. "To save you any more questions I will explain a few things to you." He glanced over at Alexis, calmly sitting on the edge of a water barrel, her golden hair neatly hidden beneath a black bandanna and her face covered with black silk. She motioned to him and as he walked toward her he felt the gaze of the eight men pressed against his back. He leaned close to her mouth so he could hear her low whispers. He nodded several times and when he returned to stand over the men on the deck he was smiling.

"The captain wishes me to explain the reason for the disguise. He was disfigured badly by the man he seeks and by revealing himself completely he would be endangering himself. He also has no wish to see you try to hide the shock of seeing his face."

The eyes that had been resting on Hansom focused quickly on the captain and Alexis's second-in-command could barely suppress his amusement at the tale he had spun. Every man in front of him was assuming the scars were on Alexis's face. Those who chose to leave would spread the story while those who remained would be sure to keep the secret.

"We will be nearing Port Elizabeth on Bequia soon. You have until then to make up your mind." He turned to leave but he was addressed by the same man who thought his liberty was gained at too high a price.

"Why doesn't the captain speak for himself?" he asked loudly, his eyes throwing a challenge to the small form on the water barrel.

There was total silence from all on board. Alexis's crew watched her carefully. They wanted to come forward and shut the man up. They did not understand how he could continue to press his good fortune after being offered so much by Alexis. She did not understand either. She did not expect gratitude but neither did she expect insolence. With a wave of a gloved hand she motioned Hansom to stand aside and at the same time she glanced at her crew, letting them know she would handle the problem.

She slid off the barrel and approached the sitting men slowly. More than one of them thought she moved like a dark predator. Some looked at the golden eyes behind the mask, fascinated; such unusual eyes held their lives in limbo. Alexis walked around the group, keeping her gaze fixed on the man who spoke. He had no marks on his back. It was not a confirmation, but it warranted closer questioning. She walked to Hansom and addressed him softly.

Hansom stared at the man with contempt. "The captain wants to know if you were actually impressed or whether you just maneuvered yourself into this to avoid a swim?"

Caught, the man answered foolishly, resting his eyes glaringly on Alexis. "If the captain wants to know he'll have to speak for himself. Why don't you talk, Captain Danty? Or did the man you want take your tongue too?"

Alexis stopped Hansom's move toward the man and, stepping in front of him, approached the group of men once more. Those around the scarless man moved aside to let the captain pass. Alexis's gaze only left the man's once and that was to focus on some of the ruins of the sunken British vessel. She thought if she threw him over now he had a good chance of relying on one of the drifting pieces and paddling for land. It was better than he deserved, but he had a chance this way and she would not deny any man his chance.

She reached down with her gloved hands and pulled the astonished sailor to his feet by the band of his trousers. Hansom was not alone in his surprise at Alexis's strength. The rest of her crew was similarly amazed. They knew her to be accomplished with pistols and swords but did not expect her to have the strength she was exhibiting now. The freed sailors had not thought it of the slender captain either. But no one was more surprised than Alexis. Her anger was so great that this man felt like a sack of flour in her grasp. He backed up until he felt his back against the rail and only at the last second, when he saw the fury in those eyes did he know what

Alex Danty intended to do to him. Alexis raised her knee and placed it firmly in his groin. As he doubled forward she grabbed his legs and flipped him over the side. When he surfaced safely she called to him, her voice deep and husky from exertion, "Captain Danty does not speak to scum!"

Hansom and the rest of them laughed loudly, and Alexis smiled beneath her black silk. When the laughter died she whispered instructions in Hansom's ear and went below.

Hansom turned back to the mildly amused, slightly frightened men. "Port Elizabeth. Your decision then. None of you will be shown the same treatment as your friend." There were murmurs of "no friend of mine" but Hansom ignored them.

Out of the eight men they had taken aboard, five remained with them. All of those refusing harbor sanctuary were Americans. The two who left voluntarily spread the story of the horribly disfigured and vengeful Captain Danty, sealing Alexis's identity beneath half truths.

Alexis's men looked forward to the unveiling, as they called it, with the eagerness of small boys waiting for their caterpillar to become a butterfly.

"There are five who want to stay, Captain," Hansom told her after they were safely away from Bequia. "When are you going to show your face on deck again?"

"I do believe you and the others are enjoying this greatly," she grinned as she pulled off her mask and let her hair fall around her shoulders.

Hansom chuckled. "When you lifted that man over the side it was all we could do to keep our jaws in place. We want to see the faces of the others when they realize it was a woman who did it."

Alexis ran her fingers through her hair, untangling the ends, and deftly arranged it in one braid behind her back. "Very well. You can pass it along that I will make my appearance shortly," she sighed. "You have earned your fun. I hope you won't be disappointed."

"Hardly," Hansom said, stepping out of her cabin. While Alexis changed from the black uniform to a pair of tan breeches and a cream-colored shirt, word was passed quickly and discreetly that Captain Danty was soon to come topside.

Alexis did not disappoint her crew. She stumbled through the hatch and onto the deck, searching out Hansom immediately. She ran to him, her arms flung out and her eyes wide in terror. Neither Hansom nor the rest of the crew could believe what they saw. The Americans were surprised to see a woman aboard and outraged when they heard her scream at Hansom.

"Keep him away from me, Mr. Hansom! He's horrible! Damn Danty! I won't stay with him another moment!"

The Americans were confused and angered when Hansom only laughed at Danty's mistress. Not only did he laugh at her distress but he nearly doubled over from the pain in his sides.

Alexis was not stopped but she found it difficult to maintain her terror. She ran to another of her men and beseeched him with the same plea. His reaction was identical to Hansom's. Alexis looked around at her crew. All work had ceased and there were secret smiles giving way to unrestrained laughter. The Americans were the only ones not smiling. She decided it was time to end the charade, though she enjoyed seeing the astonished faces of her men. Now they would get to see the astonishment on the faces of the Americans.

She returned to Hansom and smacked his bent form soundly on the back. "All of you! Back to work! Mr. Hansom! Since when has anything I said ever been so funny?" She glared at him while he tried to choke back more laughter. The men had returned to work, but she knew they were all watching the five Americans surreptitiously.

As Alexis walked toward the men she did not realize the first dawning of truth was coming over them. With their eyes they followed her movements and they shared the same thought: the predator was gone but it was inherent in those long, lean legs approaching them in purposeful strides. They looked to one another as if to confirm their nagging suspicions that the whole world had suddenly gone crazy.

Alexis saw their looks and she smiled at each of them in turn. Hansom was directly behind her, still trying to maintain some composure. She poked him in the ribs with her elbow, never taking her eyes or her smile from the men in front of her.

"I usually run a pretty tight ship, gentlemen," she said. "You will have to excuse our meager attempt to have some fun at your expense. I am happy you decided to stay with us."

She held out her hand, but the men could not find one among them who would take the extended greeting. Alexis dropped her hand to her side, fully understanding their reluctance and confusion.

Hansom stepped forward brusquely. "Captain Danty has just given her welcome to you. I think you had better reciprocate."

As expected when the truth was revealed, Alexis's men had the enjoyment of five mouths simultaneously dropping open. A new roar of laughter shook the ship. Alexis heard the sound and she smiled. It had the sound of pride.

"You should do as Mr. Hansom suggests," she said firmly. "Or I will have to throw you over the side as I did the other gentleman."

Jaws snapped shut and hands were promptly extended. Alexis greeted them with the same grace she would have used in the drawing room of her home on Tortola. She assigned tasks to each new crew member but they all seemed reluctant to move. This she did not understand for she was used to having her orders obeyed.

She looked at them for an explanation and Ned Allison spoke up. "Captain Danty, I mean no disrespect but I feel as if I'm the victim of a joke. Are you really what Mr. Hansom told us?"

"I am. Everything you heard was true. The proof of the marks of the man I seek are not on my face. They are on my back. He murdered three people I loved. I intend to bring him to my justice."

"And may we know who the man is now?" asked Ned.

"Of course," she replied. "His name is Travers. Captain Gordon Travers of His Majesty's Royal Navy." There was a gasp of surprise from one of the men and Alexis turned to him. "You know of him, Mr. Jordan?"

"Yes," he whispered. "I served with him for eight months, then I was transferred." He started to turn, to show her Travers's discipline on his back but she halted him.

"That will not be necessary. I am familiar with his handiwork and the work of his men. Mr. Hansom, find these men some shirts and get them a decent meal before they start work. Mr. Jordan, when you are through, report to me. I want to discuss what you may know of his present assignment."

"Yes, Captain," he answered quickly.

And that was how Jordan, Allison, Redland, Wilkes, and Ford joined the *Dark Lady*. At the next unveiling, this time on the *Ariel,* these five were part of the laugher when Peters, Randall, and Davie Brandon stared at Alexis with slackened jaws and wide eyes.

After she had added twelve new members to her crew and was still no closer to finding Travers, Alexis made the decision to return to Roadtown and give the members of her original crew an opportunity to leave. Ten of them did, returning to their jobs on other Quinton vessels. Hansom was among those who left, satisfied Alexis had found a crew who was fiercely dedicated to her and skilled in battle strategy.

In his place Hansom recommended Kurt Jordan and Alexis agreed. Jordan, an experienced seaman with twenty-five years behind him proved himself a valuable addition. He worked tirelessly, poring over charts with Alexis, plotting new courses, and seeing that her orders were obeyed to the last detail. He amused her with stories of Charleston when she mentioned it had been a destination of hers at one time. At forty-five he was a rugged man, with hair bleached almost white by the sun and deep lines creasing his face around the mouth and eyes as if they had been etched there by repeatedly defying the biting spindrift.

* * *

Jordan's reassuring image faded from Alexis's mind when she heard Peach slip the approved manifest under her door. She stepped out of her bath, wrapping a towel around her, and picked it up. She glanced at Jordan's scribbled corrections and placed the paper on her desk, assured everything was in order for tomorrow.

Going to London was a desperate gamble she hoped would give her the information she needed. During eighteen months of searching for Travers in dangerous ports, eluding French privateers as well as the British ones, it seemed as if he had disappeared completely. She and Jordan decided he must have been reassigned and she wanted to get word of this from the Admiralty in London as well as news from Frank Grendon about Quinton Shipping.

She dried herself briskly and discarded the towel. In her bureau she found her nightshirt. Invariably her thoughts drifted to Cloud as they always did when she readied for bed and slipped on the one concrete reminder of him. She liked to think of him now as she lay her head against the cool coverlet. It was only during the day when his memory came unbidden to her—when one of the men said or did something that made Cloud's image leap to her mind—that she forced the memory back. But night was different. She touched the collar of the shirt lightly, enjoying the feel of the soft material beneath her fingers. She rested her head in the curve of her elbow, breathing in the scent of him that seemed to cling to the material. She had repaired the worn elbows and replaced the buttons several times but never considered parting with it. After Lafitte had returned her to Roadtown, she never wore the shirt except at night, deriving comfort from it as if she slept with him.

And there were nights she required his comfort, required the closeness and strength he had always been able to give to her. During the day, she missed his company, missed his conversation and guidance. At night she missed his love-making and the little intimacies of sharing a cabin and bunk with him. She fondly recalled the times Cloud had unwound her plaited hair and brushed it until it crackled and shone. She could almost feel his fingers gently tugging at the short hairs at the nape of her neck and the sensation was so real, and so powerful in its realness, that she shivered. She could clearly remember how his fingers would lazily shift their concentration from her hair to the contours of her shoulders and back; how they would be delicately massaging at first then become increasingly sensitive in their contact, exploring and sensuous.

At that point she would turn to face him and boldly offer her mouth, breasts, and hands for his pleasure and hers. There were occasions when he sought what she offered greedily, unable to resist what he thought his alone. There were also those occasions when he was able to draw out their pleasure, teasing her with his sensitive mouth. His lips would alight on a particularly receptive area below her ear, her neck, or her elbow; and she would tense in anticipation of his next soft contact. His lips would circle her nipple lazily, and her breast would swell and harden in response as if reaching for the rough moist flicks of his tongue.

Sometimes he would pull her onto his lap so that she straddled him and tease her still further with what she could feel straining against his trousers. She would squirm indelicately in this position, trying to make him break his rigid control, trying to make him understand as she narrowed the space between them that she was ready for him now. He would lower her to the floor or take her to their bed and the teasing would end as their naked bodies met. The union of their flesh was invariably exciting and heated, loving and satisfying. And later they would whisper phrases lovers universally share or sleep lightly, resting, until fresh desire woke them and urged them on to new pleasures.

The memories made Alexis restless. She shifted her position slightly, kicking aside part of the blanket until one leg stretched free of the confining wool. Cloud had always laughed at the way she kicked the blankets around, but he never seemed to mind when she pressed closer to him for warmth.

She wondered how he would be involved in the impending war. The Americans were at a loss to find any other alternative to the infringement of their rights. Did he know that after she found Travers she would come to him and fight beside him? Yes. He would know.

The moment he had freed her she knew her second vow on the cliff had been broken. She told him once, in a whisper, when he was still unconscious. After she had Travers she would tell him again.

She sighed and heard the sound he wanted to possess. After Travers. Everything is yours after Travers.

Chapter Nine

On the other side of the ocean, thousands of miles from Alexis in distance, weeks from her in time, water lapped gently at the sides of the newly completed addition to the riverscape. The USS *Concord* seemed to wait restlessly in her temporary home as if she were eager to head for the open sea and attain the thirteen knots she was reputed to be capable of.

In a tavern just north of where the *Concord* was anchored, some of her crewmen formerly of the USS *Hamilton* were less than anxious to be breaking in their new ship on a mission that meant the capture of Alex Danty. They had come to the tavern in hopes of tipping a few ales to forget what Cloud had told them earlier. They had all warily eyed the orders in their captain's pocket, but none of them dared refuse to assist. Each of them knew that no matter how hard their orders would be to carry out, their burden was enormously less than the one Captain Cloud carried.

As an evening of relaxation and forgetting, this one was not a success. Already Mike Garrison and Harry Young had shared an interesting conversation with another seaman. They knew they would have to report it to Cloud. They both wished

Matt Jones had not been quite so talkative in his cups. Then they wouldn't have learned anything from the young man who sailed on the Quinton Line. Now they were duty bound to tell their captain that Quinton Shipping was being run by a Mr. Grendon, although Matt was careful to point out that Grendon didn't own the line. It seemed the owner had made two trips to Roadtown in the past eighteen months and kept in contact by sending messages through other ships on the line. Worst of all it appeared that one of the points where messages were picked up was Washington. Harry and Mike shuddered to think that Alexis could be right under their noses and therefore close to being captured. They were only slightly relieved to hear Matt mention that the owner had taken on some cargo and headed for London. He wouldn't have thought much of it, except some of his mates thought it was dangerous. Harry and Mike didn't explain that they understood the danger, that Alexis's desperation to find Travers was driving her.

Shortly after Matt had wandered off, leaving Harry grinning sadly at his tankard and Mike gritting his teeth in frustration, they were joined by a brawny stranger who had listened interestedly to the information they'd gleaned from Matt.

He boldly invited himself to their table and told them bluntly, "My name's Scott Hansom, and if you have any questions about Quinton Shipping or the owner, then I'm the one to ask."

"Don't want to know anything else," Harry told him. "Take your information straight to Captain Cloud."

Mike kicked his drinking companion under the table and muttered, "Your tongue's a little loose there, Harry."

Scott Hansom was glad his crewman wasn't the only one who talked too much after a few drinks. "What was that name?" he asked Harry, his voice low to conceal his surprise.

"Captain Tanner Cloud," Mike answered for his friend. "Harry and I served on his ship, the *Hamilton*. We've been with him for three years." Mike added the last, realizing if

Hansom knew anything about Alexis then he would know they did too.

"That so?" he responded lightly. He was wary of the two men and their motives. He knew Alexis was skirting danger from all directions these days. Her status as a merchant vessel made her prey to French and English privateers when she tried to run blockades. And now the Americans were interested in her. He chose to take their interest as a threat to her safety. "And why are you so curious about Quinton Shipping? We haven't broken any laws."

"None that we're aware of," Mike said. "Matt was just telling us about your mysterious owner. He's never even seen the man. It was interesting, that's all."

"That's a lie and you know it," Hansom replied angrily. "You were the ones asking all the questions. What are you after?"

"Look," Mike said, leaning forward across the table. "We know Alex Danty and you know we do. She must have told you it was our ship she got away from to return to Roadtown. We were trying to find out how she is and if there is anything you know about Travers." It was true what he said, Mike thought later, but none of it went down well.

"So you know Captain Danty," Hansom answered smugly. "Then you know why no man who has ever sailed for her will tell you one damn thing!"

Much later that evening Mike Garrison told his captain, "She's got some good men. Hansom left right after that but Harry and I knew he'd be worried so we followed him, figuring he'd give something away. Sure enough he passed a message to the captain of another Quinton ship. Their destination is Roadtown. That means Hansom knows Alex is planning to return to the island."

"That is a fairly big leap of imagination. How can you be sure she will go there just because that's where the message is headed?" Cloud eyed their slow grins and knew what was coming before Harry reached into his pocket and extracted the folded paper.

"We managed to get it," Harry said, handing it over.

Cloud took the paper and unfolded it slowly. Not looking at his men but at the words on the paper he said, "And I don't want to know how, although I suppose it explains the bruise on Mike's face."

Mike's hand quickly went to his cheek and he grinned. "He didn't miss the note while I was there."

Cloud nodded as he read:

April 3, 1812

Miss Quinton,

Men who say they are from the *Hamilton* have asked about you in Washington. I know the man you want is patrolling the waters around New Orleans. You will know the source of that information. With any luck at all you will have found this out in London. Be leery of the Americans. I do not like their sudden interest in your activities after almost two years of silence.

Your servant,

Scott Hansom

"It explains a great deal," Cloud sighed when he finished reading. "The least of which is how Quinton Shipping has been thriving in the Caribbean when no one else can get by Lafitte. Captain Danty has some powerful friends and as you said, Mike, some very good men." He slipped the paper in beside his orders and tapped the pocket lightly. "Our course has been decided. If we are fortunate she may bypass Tortola completely in her anxiousness to get to Travers and never receive verbal confirmation of this message. We'll have surprise working for us. Tomorrow we leave on the *Concord* and start scouting the same waters as Travers."

"When we find her, Captain," Harry said, frowning, "you'll explain how it is, won't you? That we have a job to do, too."

"I'll explain, Harry. And she'll understand. But she is not going to cooperate."

Cloud returned to his home later that evening and reread Hansom's letter to Alexis. The message had been hastily scrawled but Cloud could see genuine concern in the haste. Her men obviously were committed to her and he dreaded the possibility of having to fight them in order to get to her. He had slowly come to the conclusion that many of her men were now Americans. According to the stories that had surfaced it seemed a number of them had been willing to join her. Where would their loyalties lie once war was declared? With their country, which had been so slow to act on their impressment, or with the woman, who by taking matters into her own hands, had given them their liberty?

Cloud dropped the message into the hearth and watched the flames lick at the paper until after a sudden burst of heat and light it crumbled into ashes. He knew the answer. They would never permit him to take her without a fight, and she was the only one who could prevent it. Alex, he thought, must there always be this battle, always something to stand in our way?

In rebellion against the turn his thoughts were taking he allowed his mind to drift to a point in the future when everything was settled between them. He permitted himself to think about a time when he would not have to concern himself with keeping her, because she would stay with him willingly, even eagerly.

He imagined he heard her laugh, more precious to him because it had been so infrequent while on board the *Hamilton*. He imagined he felt its lightness against his skin while she uninhibitedly enjoyed the tender tickling forays his fingers made across her abdomen or down her spine. He liked to think that she would curl into him, rubbing against him to ease the tingling of her flesh, and discover anew the taut smoothness of his body as well as the rigid warmth of his manhood. She would stop laughing once she felt him seeking entrance at her thighs, but she would smile, a lovely, womanly, knowing smile, and she would open to receive him, open to embrace him, and she would rock with him, loving him with her hands and mouth, holding him tightly with her slender arms and legs, holding him tightly inside her, seeking the same end he sought. And they would find it together, clinging and soaring, living and dying in the same moment. Above all, she would say that she loved him and when he told her the same he would no longer cause her pain.

Alexis stood, her feet planted firmly apart, on the deck of the *Diamond Maria.* Her hands were clasped behind her back and her head was tilted toward the upper reaches of the mainmast, where some of the men were busily repairing the main topsail yard after damages incurred by a late spring storm. She dropped her head when she saw Jordan approaching.

"Captain Danty, some of the men wanted to know if we are still going to stop in Roadtown."

"No, we're not. We've been blown far enough off course without losing time on Tortola. We are on Travers's stern now. I do not intend to lose him after coming this close."

He smiled. "That's what we were hoping you would say. Do you anticipate any trouble with Lafitte in these waters?"

Alexis laughed. "Hasn't anyone ever informed you about Lafitte, Mr. Jordan?"

He shook his head and listened with mild amusement to her story. "I suppose he is a fine man to have on your side, Captain."

"That's what I don't understand," she replied. "When I left him there was certainly no agreement between us that he would leave my ships alone and yet from the reports I've received, especially the one in London, it seems he has made Quinton Shipping exempt from his activities. Even our cargo from Spain is safe. It pleases Mr. Grendon to no end but it makes me uneasy."

"Perhaps it simply amuses him."

She recalled that mocking smile. "Perhaps." She dismissed the subject with a wave of her hand as she also recalled he had named her an exception. "What is the extent of the damage?"

"Minimal. We'll have her at ten knots in no time at all, providing the wind holds up. Within a week we'll be close enough to New Orleans to begin taking a close look for Travers."

"It's almost too good to be true. Wilkes certainly brought back good news from the Admiralty." She turned to face the water, fascinated as it turned to white foam when it hit the side of the ship. Smiling, she turned back to Jordan. "It won't be long now," she said with sudden fierceness, then more softly, "what are you and the others going to do once it's over?"

"I suspect once war has been declared most of us will join up," Jordan answered.

"I want you to tell the other Americans aboard that once the United States issues a declaration your ties to this ship are at an end. That goes for whether we have Travers by then or not." Her tone was so serious Jordan was taken back.

"We have already discussed it among ourselves, Captain Danty. Knowing how you think, we figured you would say that. None of us has any intention of going until we see this through." In her face he saw reluctant agreement, and in his own he knew she saw there was no changing their minds.

As Alexis walked away, Jordan watched her. If anyone had told him he would serve a woman captain he would have probably responded that he would rather serve the British. Now that he had tasted both he knew that the former was infinitely preferable to the latter. There was not one of them who could consider leaving her. Even if they did not achieve their end soon he knew everyone would still choose to stay.

He had been pledged himself to follow her since she'd invited him aboard the *Dark Lady*. Though it had surprised him, discovering she was a woman, that had not made him waver in his pledge. She was proof that skills, knowledge, ability were everything. He supposed at one time or another there was not a man aboard who had not fancied himself in love with her. But the way she carried herself, the way she was always in command, the way she handled her responsibilities, told them all it was futile to pursue a personal relationship. Jordan was sure there was only one man in her life at the moment and that man was Travers.

Ten days later he discovered he was wrong. Much later he decided he was not unhappy about it.

At the first sign of the British frigate, its sides painted Nelson style in black and yellow, Alexis issued orders that set the deception in motion. Afterward she hurried to her quarters and discarded her trousers and shirt, replacing them with the black silk uniform. Having secured her hair in place under the bandanna she tied the red sash about her waist and hung her sword from her side. As she walked out of her cabin she caught sight of herself in the mirror and paused for a moment, pulling on her gloves. So this is what they saw, she thought. Then she realized it was not precisely what any of her victims saw at all. Without the mask pulled over her face there was no denying she was a woman. The midnight outfit was suddenly very striking. The trousers were not tight enough to reveal her curves and yet they clung to her legs, showing a smooth, muscular power. Her shirt was loose enough to conceal her breasts, with the aid of a binder, but there was something about the open neckline that seemed to scream farce. She changed her stance and her reflection obliged. The woman was gone for a moment, replaced by a swaggering, arrogant figure. She laughed at the change, marveling that one movement could so easily fool the eye. She looked at her face and the woman returned. She pursed her lips, attempting a grimace, but it was a young woman in false pain who returned her gaze. The mask was everything. She quickly pulled it on. Now the mysterious Captain Danty stared back with fierceness in his amber eyes. His smile, however, was well concealed.

Alexis strode on deck and watched the activity with satisfaction. It was hardly necessary to say anything for the men were all drilled in what was about to happen. A distress signal had already been sent and the Union Jack was whipping high above the ship on the signal gaff.

"Is it Captain Travers?" Alexis asked Jordan.

"Randall seems to think so. She is still too far away to be sure. He can't make her name yet."

As if Randall had heard his captain's sigh of disappointment he called down from the mizzen cap. "It's the HMS *Follansbee*, Captain Danty! And she's seen us! She's coming this way!"

The low rumble of approval at the approach of Travers's vessel would have erupted into pandemonium if Alexis had not quickly issued orders that returned things to normal and quenched some of the excitement. The crew returned to their stations and attacked their work with a new vengeance. As the ship continued to approach, the *Diamond Maria* remained almost motionless in the water. Her sails were caught but ready to be unfurled at a moment's notice if Travers should see their ruse. Men were dropping empty crates over the side to give the impression their heavy load was in part responsible for their floundering. The hurried, frantic movement of the crew was only for illusion. The *Diamond Maria* was a sound vessel.

"Mr. Jordan, give the order to stand by stations and ready the guns. It won't be much longer." Alexis watched Travers's ship with the intensity a spider views a nearing fly.

"Thought you might like to take a look, Captain," Randall said, handing her the scope. He had abandoned his position in the cap to carry on his duties at the guns. It was part of the procedure. All hands were needed now.

"Thank you," Alexis said. She glanced through the instrument and felt a chill pass through her as she made out the familiar form of Travers at the helm. She handed the scope back to Randall, neither of them realizing this transaction signified the only error Captain Danty had made. If Randall had still been in the cap he would have seen another ship approaching in the distance. The name would have meant nothing to him. But the Stars and Stripes on the gaff above the *Concord* would have given him sufficient warning.

"You make her yet?" Cloud shouted to Frank Springer in the cap.

"It's a Quinton ship all right!" he called back. "I can tell by her lines. She's been painted differently and she's in some sort of trouble!"

Cloud cast a wary glance at Landis. "What do you think? Could it be her?" His voice was calm, hiding the anxiousness knotting his insides. He turned his attention back to the ship.

Landis was slower to answer, but finally he said, "If it's her then she's up to something and if it's not, the ship needs assistance. Shall I straighten course and move in?"

As Cloud was nodding another voice caught his attention. He looked up to see Frank shimmying down the mast. In a few moments he was standing in front of Cloud.

"Another ship, Captain," he said breathlessly. "Flying a Union Jack too. A frigate, heavily armed. They are going in to help the Quinton vessel."

"Travers?" Cloud's tone almost belied the fact it was a question.

"Most likely, Captain." Before he was told to do so Frank swiftly reassumed his station above the ship.

"Damn!" Cloud muttered. He heard Landis echo his sentiments and he smiled wryly. He was glad Frank had the foresight not to yell the information down to him. It was hard on all of them, knowing they had to take Alexis, but knowing they were about to deny her her moment of triumph—or death, he thought suddenly—was more than he was willing to burden them with. For now only three of them would shoulder the responsibility of knowing.

"Hard to port!" Cloud's order seemed more like a curse

to his ears. As the ship maneuvered, the command was given
to ready the guns. Soon the *Concord* was as busy as the *Diamond
Maria,* but the activity was no illusion.

"What's that you say?" Captain Travers asked Ian Smith.

"Another ship. American. Forty-four guns. Have they
declared war?"

"I haven't been given word," he answered. He looked at
the *Diamond Maria* again. She was in difficulty but he knew he
could not hope to protect her and her crew if the Americans
decided to engage him. The British merchant would be useful
as a decoy though. She could provide the necessary time the
Follansbee required to get away.

He issued his orders to Smith and the frigate began to
change its course drastically. Travers was not prepared to start
a war if one had not been declared. He wisely remembered the
Chesapeake-Leopard affair. As his direction changed he never
realized he had had a hand in it a long time ago.

Alexis clutched the taffrail. Her fingers whitened from the
grip. She thought she could break it if she could have maintained her hold. She released the rail and in the same motion
one hand whipped to her face and tore at her mask. She
looked at Jordan and saw he was at a loss to explain what was
happening.

"What is he doing?" she cried, expecting no answer but
wanting to hear a voice give their situation some reality. She
gave the order to start a pursuit, Travers's sudden actions still
a mystery. By the time the men moved to their stations and
the sails were ready she saw the problem. "Randall!" she
commanded. "Get to the cap and make that ship!" Pulling
her mask back in place, she and Jordan went to the other
side of the quarterdeck to get a closer look. The *Concord* was
bearing down fast.

"It's American!" Randall cried. "Navy! And she must be
making twelve knots!"

Alexis paled at Randall's words. "What do you think they're doing?" she asked Jordan.

"Maybe they were coming to help us," he replied. The shudder that ran through his body told him otherwise.

There was a jolt as the wind caught the sails and the *Diamond Maria* began its course toward the *Follansbee*.

"They're armed and they look like they're ready to use everything they've got!" It was Randall again.

"Are they changing course?" Surely, she thought, the Americans would see that her ship required no assistance and they would put about or move toward Travers. If war had started then he was the enemy, not her cargo ship.

"No, Captain! They're still coming for us and they couldn't have missed the *Follansbee!*"

The American's actions made no sense to Alexis but it did explain Travers's sudden aversion to coming to their aid. She put the American frigate aside and focused all her energies on pursuing the *Follansbee*.

"She wasn't in trouble at all!" Smith told his captain. "She's pursuing us!"

Travers's normally composed, chiseled features twisted in a brief moment of surprise as the *Diamond Maria* glided through the water toward them. He grasped his telescope firmly and examined the ship more closely. She had more guns than necessary for an ordinary merchant, even in these waters. And the distress. It was a ruse.

"Danty!" The name was like a curse violently pronounced.

Smith stared at Travers. "Danty." He merely mouthed the word.

"It has to be!" Travers said tersely, ignoring his officer's confusion. He thought then the *Diamond Maria* was a decoy of the Americans. It crossed his mind to stand and fight, but another look at the *Diamond Maria* and her heavy arms changed his mind. He could fight one or the other, not both. He did not know he was the target of only one of the vessels.

* * *

"She's giving us a good run, sir," Harry said. The men were now aware Alexis's ship was pursuing what had to be Travers's frigate.

"She certainly is," Landis whistled softly, ignoring Cloud's scowl. "Considering she was practically sitting there when Travers made his move."

"The *Follansbee* is pulling away, Mr. Landis, and we're gaining on her." Cloud took another look at Alexis's ship and caught sight of her arsenal. Now it was he who whistled. "Take a look, Mr. Landis. You too, Harry. You might as well see what we're up against if she decides to turn and fight."

Landis was not a praying man but he sent up a distress signal of his own. From Harry's face he got the impression he was not alone.

Cloud chuckled softly to himself. "We'll know soon enough if anyone heard you. But it's Captain Danty who is going to give us the answer."

He looked out again at the ship. They would be on her soon. The question no one would dare ask aloud was: would she fight?

"We can't outrun them, Captain," said Jordan.

Alexis had already known that but hearing it from him was like a period at the end of her thoughts. Final. Travers was slipping away and the Americans were gaining rapidly. "Why doesn't the *Follansbee* engage the *Concord?*" she asked. "Do you think Travers knows what we're doing?"

"Had to," Jordan answered. "And if I were Travers I'd be thinking we are part of a scheme that includes the Americans. He knows he can't fight both of us."

"Then why aren't the Americans giving him chase?"

"Because they probably think we are in it with him and we're a damn sight easier to get."

Alexis shook her head. "You make it sound plausible but

I want to be sure. Order the guns pulled in and see what the Americans do. Drop our flag and put up the Quinton banner. Let's give them every reason to believe we are only hauling cargo and see what they do."

The order was given while the *Diamond Maria* maintained a steady course toward the *Follansbee*.

"It won't work, Alex," Cloud whispered as he watched her maneuver. He ordered another hard to port to catch the wind and the *Concord* moved within firing range.

"Damn!" Alexis swore for the fifth time when she saw the *Concord* was not giving up. "We have lost Travers and I don't know why, Mr. Jordan." The despair was gone, only bewilderment remaining. She grimaced as if she were in physical pain as the *Follansbee* moved far beyond their firing range. Had Travers realized it was Alex Danty who was chasing him? She fought the urge to laugh. Even if he knew he would never suspect the Americans had saved him from certain death. It was almost comical. But not quite.

Alexis sighed and tugged at her mask. "I'm going below to change. You're the captain now, Mr. Jordan. Let's see what these Americans want. Since they have probably already seen our guns make sure you convince them they're a necessity because of Lafitte. Have some of the men secure our contraband. I don't want a search or they will never believe us. And for all our sakes, remember you're supposed to be British this time. No drawl!"

Jordan smiled but it was an unconvincing effort. There was a sadness in his grin as well as in his sharp blue eyes. His limp smile faded as he shouted the new orders. He was now addressed as captain and as he watched Alexis move toward the hatch he noticed there was something unfamiliar about her gait. A tremor interrupted her normally smooth stride and he wondered if his wife's seasickness was going to be an act this time.

He ordered the men to heave to. While the *Concord* moved to broadside he prepared himself for his new role.

"They're not going to fight!" It was Harry who loudly spread the news.

Cloud sighed patiently at his exuberance. "That is because she doesn't know it's us. Keep busy and try to hide your faces until it's too late for her to change her mind."

The men did as they were told when the *Concord* drew beside the *Diamond Maria* and used grappling hooks to pull the two vessels closer.

Cloud stood on the monkey rail with Landis, holding on to the main chains. "The *Concord* requests permission of your captain to board and search your vessel," he called. His eyes searched the deck for some sign of Alexis but he could not find her.

A tall man with sun-streaked hair stepped forward and called to him.

"I am the captain. Permission to board is granted but you will have to state your reasons for a search."

Cloud gripped the hilt of his sword as he jumped. He was followed by Landis, Mike, and three others. He did not allow his confusion to show as he approached the man who called himself captain. Watching the man's reaction, he spoke, "I am Captain Tanner Cloud of the USS *Concord*." Nothing. The man's face might as well have been made of stone. His name meant nothing. Had Alexis really kept his name from her men? He decided to change his tactics in the event this was all a gross mistake. "You gave a distress signal, Captain. What is the problem?"

"There is no problem. We were simply trying to warn the *Follansbee* of your presence." He smiled smugly. "It worked. You came after us and the frigate is safe from your guns."

"Your name?" Cloud asked brusquely.

"Jordan. Kurt Jordan."

"And your guns, Captain Jordan? All these guns are not

usual for a merchant, if that's what you truly are." His green eyes left Jordan's face. He was not interested in the answer to his question. He already knew what Jordan would say. He continued to scan for some sign of Alexis and he saw his men doing the same.

"Surely you must be aware Lafitte is in this area, Captain. We are bound for New Orleans with a cargo of material goods. That pirate would love to get his hands on our hold."

Cloud nodded. It was what he expected. They were not aware he knew Lafitte did not prey on Quinton ships. "You have a manifest and proof of your destination?"

"Of course," Jordan answered easily. "But you have not given me sufficient reason to allow you to see it. We are not in the territorial waters of the United States. You have no reason for stopping us, especially when it was obvious we were not of any mind to fight you." Jordan stared at Cloud, trying to guess the game. "Why did you not engage the frigate, Captain? You are wasting your time here."

Cloud was about to answer when a voice drew his attention to the hatch. He turned to face the owner.

Alexis had carelessly thrown her clothes on the bed and quickly changed into a dress. She'd purposely chosen the one with the lowest neckline, determined to keep the officers' minds on things other than the arsenal in the *Diamond Maria's* hold. She had unpinned her hair and unwound the braid, brushing it until it surrounded her shoulders and back like a golden cape. As she readied herself she'd felt the shifting of her ship, signaling the *Concord's* arrival alongside. She'd put on stockings and shoes knowing they were probably already aboard. Then she had cleared her mind of Travers and concentrated on the best way to divert the Americans. When she thought she had decided on a way, she went topside. Jordan was facing her but he gave no outward sign that he noticed her presence. He allowed her to make the first move.

There was something familiar in the stance of the turned American seamen and as she cried out her suspicions became a horrifying reality.

"Kurt!" she called out. "Is it Lafitte? I'll die if it's that pirate!"

Jordan was ready to move toward her and offer her comfort as any husband would, but as the American seamen turned to face Alexis he saw the forced terror on her face fade, only to be replaced by a twisted look of real pain and frustration. He stopped in his tracks as Captain Cloud moved forward.

Every man aboard both ships watched Cloud's slow approach to Alexis. Every man had a hand at his side, fingering his cutlass lightly, waiting for a word from either captain that would place the weapon firmly in his grip.

Cloud could not take his eyes away from the piercing golden stare he was walking into. He could read anger, frustration, confusion. The hatred was not in her eyes. It was in the tight line of her mouth, the firm set of her shoulders, and in the hands that alternately clenched and unfolded at her side. When he was a few feet in front of her he stopped. His eyes dropped away from hers and they swept her tense form. If she was aware of his scrutiny, she gave no indication that it bothered her. He glanced at the swell of her breasts and followed the golden wave of her hair down her arm to where her hand was once more curled in a tight fist. Only two years, he thought, and she was more of a woman than his memory had done justice to. But she was also Captain Alex Danty, the target of his assignment, and he erased the image of the heroine from his mind, replacing it with the cold business at hand.

Alexis's only thought as she watched Cloud's approach was how could she have wanted to tell this man she loved him. Beyond the sea green eyes, beneath the subtly arrogant features, underneath the tailored uniform that proclaimed his commitment to another, was a man she loathed. Even as he studied her, she wanted to strike out at him, scream her contempt at the top of her lungs. She held herself back. She had to be sure he knew what he had done before she would grace him with her disgust. She stepped forward.

"Captain Danty," said Cloud. His voice was icy, impersonal,

and the crew of the *Diamond Maria* shivered, not only because of the way he said her name, but because he said it.

"Captain Cloud," she answered clearly. She lifted her chin as she stepped still closer so she could maintain her gaze on him.

"I would like to explain . . ." he faltered. Her eyes would not let him continue.

As his words died, Alexis smiled. It was anything but a sign of friendship. She thought if he had been anyone but Tanner Frederick Cloud he would have shuddered at the insincere placement of her lips. Some part of her was glad to have him back. There was no other man like him. But she despised him for reminding her of it now.

"I only have one question, Captain Cloud," she said evenly. "I would like the answer to it before we discuss the reason for your presence on my ship."

Cloud nodded, bracing himself for the query he knew had to be answered.

"Were you aware of the presence of Captain Travers aboard the *Follansbee*?"

He met her quiet fury directly. "Yes, I knew." There was no apology in his voice. He saw Alexis relax briefly only to gather all the anger she held in reserve. She raised her hand. He made no move to restrain her as her palm swept through the air and made contact with his cheek.

Alexis's hand dropped to her side and she watched, fascinated, as the imprint of her hand on his face changed from white to red and then faded completely as his sun-bronzed color returned. She held her ground as his muscles tensed. Still, he made no move toward her. Instead his grin taunted her and his emerald eyes mocked her action.

Mike started to move toward Alexis. His hand held his blade tightly. No matter what she meant to him and the others he would not let her get away with striking his captain. If he had seen Cloud's smile he would have known, as Alexis did, that she would pay for it later.

Alexis dropped her gaze from Cloud when she saw Mike's

threatening stance and subsequent movement. Cloud followed her glance and ordered Mike to hold. Alexis looked at her crew. They were prepared to fight if Cloud had not stopped the advance of his man. Tension hung all around them and both captains sensed it was on the verge of erupting into violence.

Alexis held up her hand and addressed her crew. "Men! This is Captain Cloud. His name is not familiar to most of you but his old ship is. Captain Cloud and his men are formerly of the USS *Hamilton*." Her men understood the significance of her statement. They all knew of the *Hamilton*, but until now, they had never been given the name of her captain. "I do not understand the presence of the *Concord* any more than you but we will hear the captain out before we take any action." She turned to Cloud, signaling it was up to him now.

Cloud wanted to talk to Alexis in private, but there was a question of Jordan's that had to be answered first. "Mr. Jordan asked me why we did not engage the *Follansbee*. The answer is the United States has yet to declare war."

Ned Allison called out. "But you'll make war on a private cargo ship!"

Alexis started to interrupt her man but Cloud motioned her to be quiet. "I am well aware of the sort of cargo this ship carries. Your Boston accent betrays you, sailor. It would seem a lot of you have been making war on the British without the sanction of your government."

Jordan dropped his clipped accent and when he spoke it was his Charleston drawl that stilled the silence. "And where was my government when I was shackled and serving His Majesty?"

"Enough!" Alexis's voice broke through the rousing voices of agreement that followed Jordan's words. There was instant silence. "Captain Cloud and I will discuss the nature of his visit in my quarters. It would appear we were his objective all along. Mr. Jordan, see that all the captain's men are extended our courtesy. This will not take long."

She motioned to Cloud and walked toward her cabin. He

followed without hesitation, watching her purposeful, angry strides. He remembered, suddenly, the things revealed in her eyes when she had first seen him. Anger, frustration, and confusion. All the emotions that would lead to hatred. How long before he had to see that in her eyes the way he had felt it in her palm?

Alexis opened the door and waited for Cloud to step through before she shut it. Instantly he had her pressed against the door, his face hovered over hers. Just as he had made no attempt to halt the slap she had delivered, she made no attempt to halt his kiss. His lips covered hers, bruising them with the same force her palm had exerted against his cheek. Just as he had given her no response on deck, she gave him no response now. When he removed his mouth she calmly pointed out a chair and told him to sit; her cool taunt was in the way she said it.

As she placed a crystal goblet before him and poured them both wine she said, "Someday, Captain Cloud, I will have the same control you do." She sat down and sipped her drink. "I humiliated you in front of your men earlier. Thank you for waiting until we were in private before you humiliated me."

Cloud lifted his glass in tribute. "You always understand, don't you, Alex?"

"Not always. I am Captain Danty now and I understand none of this. I would like an explanation." She turned her goblet in her hands and leaned back in her chair, waiting patiently for Cloud to begin.

"I have orders from President Madison to escort—"

"Escort?" she asked snidely.

"To arrest you and take you back to Washington." There was no reaction. Not a flicker of surprise or fear in her face. Cloud went on. "You will be granted a pardon should you agree to aid us in the upcoming war. Your knowledge is considered valuable by the President and some others and they want you on our side."

"What grounds do you have to arrest me?"

"Forcing the issue of war with Great Britain."

"But I am English. They are the ones who should arrest me for treason."

"Many of your men are not, Captain. By acting as privateers you have helped to precipitate war." He recited the reason by rote.

"You know that is not true. The United States has a list of grievances a mile long now."

"I know it. But you asked why I was arresting you. Those are the charges."

"And you would arrest me to give credence to a lie?" She placed the goblet softly on the table and folded her hands in her lap. Her voice had not altered in the least as she continued questioning him. It was still soft and lilting, and it had the edge of a steel blade that was cutting through this mockery swiftly and surely.

"I would do what I was ordered, Captain. My approach would not have been the same but I do not intend to use that to justify myself."

"But how would you have approached me?"

Cloud wanted to tell her he would have waited until she had Travers. It was of no consequence now. He wanted to tell her he had done everything to avoid this confrontation. That also was of no consequence. "It does not matter," he said finally. "I happen to agree you could be valuable in helping us win the upcoming war."

Alexis's lips curled slightly at the corners. "The end justifies the means."

"Never!" he said fiercely. "But where no choice is given as to the means, the end becomes everything."

Alexis was ready to tell him he could have resigned his commission, but she held back, knowing that was something he could not do, any more than she could give up her search. Instead she asked, "Are you satisfied?"

"Who are you asking, Captain Danty? Are you asking the commander of the *Concord* or are you asking Cloud?"

"I was asking Cloud, but I had no right. As captain you do

not have to answer that question. I already know the answer is yes."

"What do you plan to do? Are you going to permit me to take you into custody or are our men going to have to fight?" He finished his wine and held his cup, tensely waiting her response.

"What is the agreement again?" Her brows drew together over closed eyes.

"If you decide to help us fight this war by giving us information that will aid our side all charges against you will be dropped." Cloud knew he had told no lie. What was it Alexis had told him once? Various shades of the truth? He frowned. It was a lie. He had not mentioned Lafitte, nor did he intend to. Not as long as there was still a chance he could get Howe and the others to see how senseless that part of the bargain was.

Alexis kept her eyes closed, her face serene. "My men? Are they also under arrest?"

"That depends on you, Captain. I have no orders for their capture. In the event you do not come I will take it upon myself to see that every American on your crew spends time in prison for his actions aboard your ship."

Alexis's eyes flew open and she stared at him to see if he meant what he said. She discerned, with no effort at all, that he was serious. "That's a large hammer you have held over my head. And what if we choose to fight? You may not win."

"Is the risk acceptable?" he answered tersely.

Alexis hesitated only a moment before answering. Her or her men. Certain death for many on both sides if she did not agree to go. And Travers? He was gone for now and preparing him for another trap would take months of careful planning. What would she gain if she fought and won? A chance to pursue Travers? No. If her attack on the *Concord* were known she would be hunted down by the Americans. They would see that Quinton Shipping was destroyed. Cloud thought he was only using the lives above him as leverage. But it was the

Grendons and Hansom and all the others that depended on
Quinton Shipping that she included in her answer.

"The risk is not acceptable. It appears I am to be your
prisoner once again. There is no other word for it this time,
is there?"

"There was none before," he replied.

"Good," she said with finality. "Then you also know the
same option exists for me as before. I will go with you now
but I give you my word I will escape."

"I understand."

"And, Captain Cloud," she added thoughtfully, "I realize
it will be more difficult this time. But at some point I will
succeed. I do not consider it likely that I will be interested
in anything your superiors have to say to me. They must know
my methods are quite different from anything the navy could
use in good conscience. The information I possess is available
to any seaman. Why are they not using you to their advantage?
You were once my instructor. You know as much about British
movements and tactics as I do."

Cloud smiled, fully relaxed for the first time since they sat
down. "I am being used to their advantage. I have Captain
Alex Danty, don't I?"

"And you really think I will help your side? Now? Before
I do what I have to do and after you threaten me with the
imprisonment of my men?" She raised her eyebrows in an
arch that feigned interest.

"I never thought it for a moment. I was ordered to bring
you to Washington to meet with the President and the four
men who explained this assignment to me. What you tell
them is your own affair." His voice achieved the blandness
it strived for.

"I see." Her eyes blazed contempt for him.

Cloud met her gaze and waited for her hatred. When her
face still did not become distorted by that emotion, he knew
the extent of the love she'd once had for him. Love he had
never been able to know fully because in order to have it he

had had to release her. He knew then, just how difficult it was going to be to keep her a prisoner.

"I will go on deck and tell them what you have decided while you collect the things you want to take," he said.

Alexis went to her desk. Without looking at him she said, "That would not be very wise. You shouldn't return without me. My men may not like it." She smiled when Cloud remained seated. "I have an entry to make in my log; then I will go with you and explain to my crew. Peach will pack my things." She sat at her desk and opened the log. Dipping her pen into the inkwell, she began writing. "It is the eighteenth of June, Captain. I will not forget that."

Cloud said nothing but thought he would not forget it either. In Washington there were many who also thought the date of significance. Not because they had Captain Danty—that they did not yet know—but because Congress had acted on Madison's written proposal. War had been declared.

Alexis finished writing and shifted in her chair to face him. "Shall we go?"

Cloud nodded and followed Alexis through the companionway to the hatch. When they reached the deck Alexis said to him, "Please take your men to one side. I wish to talk to my men alone."

"I want to hear what you have to say," Cloud answered. "I will not allow you to enlist the aid of your men for your escape attempt."

"That was not my intention, but you may listen if you wish. I want my men to stand far away. I will escape from you on my own."

Cloud motioned his men to the side and they went reluctantly. Since their captain and Alexis had gone below not a word had passed between the two crews. They had filled the silent void with sullen stares.

When Alexis's crew had gathered around, she called Peach to her side. "I want you to go below and gather my things. There is a duffle bag in my wardrobe. Put my clothes in. I am going with Captain Cloud." There were loud protests from her men that drowned out the sigh of relief from the *Concord* crew. Alexis barely noticed either. She only had eyes for the boy in front of her. He looked at her in bewilderment, completely at a loss to understand why she was leaving. "Go on, Peach. I will need those things right away." She knew she had disappointed him. He had not been with her long enough to know all that was involved in her decision. She searched his thin face and dark brown eyes. He was willing to fight and she was not. Yet it was she who made the decisions. She watched him hurry off, and faced the others.

"I have been placed under arrest for acts the United States government thinks have helped to precipitate war with Great Britain."

"Captain Danty!" Jordan cried, making no attempt to conceal his anger. "You are English! This is a mistake! They can't take you on those charges!"

"Mr. Jordan! I am fully aware of my citizenship as you no doubt are aware of yours!" Her statement halted all protests as the men realized she was offering herself in their place. She continued softly but none of them questioned that what she said was an order. "I have agreed to go with Captain Cloud. I have not agreed to go as far as Washington, however." She smiled as her men laughed softly. "This ship is now under Mr. Jordan's command, and my last order to him is that none of you interfere with the *Concord*'s progress from here. I want no man doing anything to help me escape. When you return to Tortola explain to Mr. Grendon what has occurred and inform him he is now in complete charge of Quinton Shipping. Each of you is free to decide to stay with him or to return to the United States and fight on her side. Whatever you commit yourselves to, I know it will be the right choice for you. Because I have no intention of aiding the United States after what has occurred here today I will not be granted a pardon. Therefore I expect to be spending a great deal of time in prison—if they can get me that far." She faced Cloud. "That is all I have to tell my men. We can go now."

Cloud was silent, grimly observing her crew. He spun

around when he heard quick, light footsteps behind him. It was Peach, carrying Alexis's bag of clothes. He held out the bundle to her, and she took it firmly in her arms. Cloud knew better than to offer assistance. He started for his ship and Alexis followed, her chin held a narrow margin too high. Instead of her crew seeing their captain being proudly led away, they could not help notice her quivering chin and trembling lips. They were glad Captain Cloud, in front of her, could see none of it.

Cloud jumped to the side while Alexis threw her bag to the *Concord*. She accepted his outstretched hand because of her dress but she refused assistance in making the leap. Cloud shrugged and jumped first, followed by Alexis, Landis, Mike, and the others. Aboard the *Concord,* Cloud ordered Alexis taken below. While she was being led away by Harry and Landis, Cloud gave the command for the *Concord* to sail.

Alexis was shown to a small cabin. When she was inside Landis shut the door and she heard a bolt slide into place. A prisoner, she thought, in all respects. She leaned against the locked door and slid down its length. When she reached the deck she dropped the bag she'd clutched so tightly when she'd left the *Diamond Maria* and she clasped her arms about her knees, drawing them close to her chest. She closed her eyes as she felt the *Concord* pulling away. Above the sound of water breaking against the hull she could hear the familiar voices of her crew cursing her old friends. She dropped her head to her knees, sighing as the tears came again, for the first time in two years.

The curses died and silence remained as Jordan and the others watched the *Concord* slip from view. Alexis would not have been surprised to learn it was Peach who expressed his opinion first.

"Mr. Jordan . . . I mean, Captain. How could she leave us? Why wouldn't she fight? Is she a coward after all?" His large brown eyes stared helplessly at the new captain, waiting for an explanation of Alexis's behavior. He wanted to hear something that would vault her back to the pedestal he had placed her on. He did not flinch when Ned Allison shook him roughly by the collar of his shirt and threw him to the ground.

"You simple brat! You—" Ned started and stopped, interrupted by Jordan who stepped forward and lifted the boy to his feet.

He set Peach firmly on the deck and turned to Ned. "He doesn't know what she did, Allison. She sent him away." He looked down at Peach's thick mat of brown hair and lifted the boy's chin so he could see those confused features clearly. "How long have you been with us, Peach?"

"Three months, I came on the last ship."

"And do you think it was Captain Danty's cowardice that got you away from that frigate?"

"No, sir."

"Captain Danty saved us all from being thrown in prison, Peach. No one would have cared that you're only twelve or that you're as English as she. If she had decided to fight, and she knows we all wanted to, most of us wouldn't be here right now. Do you understand?"

Peach nodded and said hopefully, "Then we're going after her, aren't we? We can't just let her be taken. We could help her get away somehow."

"Captain Danty's last order was that we not interfere in what is happening. She'll want to get away on her own. She knows how dangerous it would be for us to help her." Jordan shook his head slowly, realizing what she wanted to do was virtually impossible. The Americans would never give her an opportunity to escape.

Peach's jaw went slack and his mouth formed an O but no sound escaped his throat. He quickly placed a hand over his mouth.

Jordan and the others looked at him curiously. "What's wrong now, Peach? What's upset you?"

He did not reply for a time. He had never disobeyed one of Captain Danty's orders before and now he wondered if he had done the right thing. With all the men staring down on him he felt obliged to speak. "I didn't know . . . about what the captain said . . ." His voice faltered but he tried to go on bravely. "I didn't know she didn't want us to help her or I wouldn't have done it. Honest!" He hurriedly crossed his heart with a thin finger.

"Well, what did you do?" Peters asked impatiently, tapping his large foot against the deck.

"When I packed her things I put her dagger in the folds of her clothes," he explained in an anxious whisper.

No one said anything for a time. They stared at Peach in amazement then at each other in amusement. "Out of the mouth of babes," Wilkes whispered reverently as if he had just received an oracle. Everyone stared at Jordan for confirmation of what they intended to do, either together or individually.

Jordan ran his hand through his hair as he scanned their faces. "We've never disobeyed an order before, have we, men?" There were sly grins among the shaking heads and a sound of hope among the low murmurs of "no." "Then why does this mutiny feel so damn good?"

A cheer went up from all of them. She was not going to like it but there was nothing she could do about it now. Peach found himself atop Peter's broad shoulders as Jordan gave the order to put about. He was smiling happily as the ship started her turn and when he looked around he saw every man was going about his work with the same expression.

"We are going to Roadtown first," Jordan told them. "We'll tell Grendon what's happened. After we've followed her orders that far we'll head for Washington. If she's going to get away then she'll need something to get away on!" The others nodded. "She'll be furious, you know." He said it seriously but he could not help laughing. "She'll probably have us all keelhauled!"

No one seemed to mind. It would be worth her wrath, just to see her again.

Chapter Ten

An hour passed, but to Alexis it seemed an eternity since she had been brought aboard the *Concord*. She brushed away the last traces of tears with the back of her hand and opened her eyes to examine her quarters. Her frown was evidence of the grim sight greeting her.

The cabin Cloud had chosen for her was so tiny she thought she could probably cross its length in a few strides. The bunk occupied most of the available space and the rest was taken up by a nightstand and commode. There was a porthole and this is what Alexis decided to examine more closely. She walked over to it, discovering she was correct about the few steps it took to reach it. She tried to open it and met resistance. After a few minutes of struggling, and with the strength of renewed anger at her predicament, she forced it open. It was not large, barely adequate to fit even her slim figure through. Barely adequate was not the same as inadequate, she decided. She shut the porthole again, but not before she availed her senses of fresh air and salt spray. She sat on her bunk and stared at the bare wall facing her. There was nothing, she thought, nothing but the porthole as an alternative, and that would do her no good until the *Concord* reached Washington. There would be no escape at sea this time.

Washington. Why did the President want to meet her so badly? Arrest! The charges were absurd! They were fools! She would have helped them. A little more time and she would have stood by—

Her head lifted in the direction of the door when the release of the bolt caught her attention. "I don't want to see anyone," she called as the door began to open. When it continued to fan into the room she turned away and rubbed at her tear-stained face, wanting to refuse the intruder the sight of her despair.

"You do not have any choice in the matter, Captain Danty," answered the man she would have stood by. He shut the door and the bolt was immediately thrown into place on the other side. "There is a guard in the companionway," Cloud told her when she raised questioning eyebrows. "You do not have to fear because I am locked in here with you."

"I do not fear you," said Alexis. The fingers hidden in the folds of her dress trembled from a fear she could not identify, but not one caused by the man standing over her, crowding the small space with his presence.

Cloud did not comment on her swollen eyelids or reddened cheeks, wanting her to form the impression that either he had not noticed what he had driven her to or that he cared nothing about it. His eyes fastened on the dress she was wearing and he wished she had changed her clothes. She looked vulnerable inside the yards of material. He thought it only briefly. Her eyes locked on his and her vulnerability vanished. She was not a helpless creature to be pitied. Her golden eyes reminded him of that even as they reminded him she was the woman he wanted and could not have. His voice was hard and biting when he spoke.

"There are some things we had better straighten out, Captain Danty. Harry told me you would not speak either to him or John when they brought you here. I won't have you treating my men as if they are of no account. They respect you and you're making them feel miserable about what they've done."

Alexis was off the bunk immediately. She stood with her hands on her hips, feet firmly planted, and tossed her hair over her shoulder as she raised her chin defiantly. "Yes, Captain Cloud, we will straighten these things out. First of all I was not aware a prisoner was expected to make witty conversation with her jailers. Second of all I refuse to take the blame for their guilty feelings. It is their own reluctance to go through with this that is making them feel guilty, not I."

Cloud did not answer her. She had echoed all their sentiments.

Alexis calmly walked past him and went to her duffle bag. She motioned him to have a seat while she began to take out her clothes. She saw him hesitate and she laughed. "You will have to sit on the bunk, Captain. The accommodations you have for your prisoners leave no room for visitors."

Cloud stretched out on the bunk, placing his hands behind his head. He was unaware Alexis wanted to scream at him for the possessive manner in which he took over her bunk. "It may not be much," he said, glancing around casually, "but it's secure."

"If you say so." She smiled derisively. "Tell me, Captain. Why didn't you let me go after Travers? You knew I was close. You could have waited and taken me afterward."

"You might have been killed," he said carelessly.

"That was always my risk to take."

"Not when my orders hold me responsible for bringing you back alive," he said harshly.

She did not answer and continued to fold her clothes.

Watching her, Cloud found himself fascinated once again by the easy grace with which she moved, the fluid elegance of her limbs. She smoothed out the legs of a pair of fawn-colored trousers with her slender fingers, folding them gently, and laid them in a drawer; then she turned and retrieved another article and went through the same process again. He could not take his eyes from her hands caressing the material any more than he could resist recalling what it was like to have those fingers touch his naked flesh.

"I've missed you, Alex," he said suddenly. He was instantly sorry. Her reaction to the words he spoke was quick although she said nothing. She halted in midmotion, her profile frozen. He saw her, kneeling on the deck, one arm outstretched reaching into her bag. It was only a second. She pulled her hand out quickly and composed herself.

Alexis had heard him speak, but it was not only what he said that produced her reaction. The coldness of sharp metal beneath her fingers had also taken her by surprise, and sudden clarity almost made her laugh. Peach, of course! Silently she thanked him for his effort; then she placed her hand inside the bag again, this time deftly sliding the dagger into one of her boots before she retrieved them. As she placed them at the foot of the bed, she remembered Cloud had spoken to her. The full weight of his words clutched her. He was still watching her, curiously now, at odds with his admission.

Alexis stared at the man occupying her space so easily, so naturally. His thick, penny-brown hair was a little longer curling at his neck, feathered back at his temples. Beneath his dark blue jacket and white trousers she knew his muscles were as firm and tight as she remembered and his flesh just as warm. The open collar of his shirt revealed the pulsing of his blood through the vein in his neck, and as she stared she saw it grow stronger while his chest heaved suddenly, then was still as the breath caught in his throat. His sea green eyes were like whirlpools that drew her closer even while she fought against them. His lips were parted as if he were going to speak. Or kiss her.

Alexis turned sharply and went back to her task. As she bent over the black silk trousers and shirt of her month aboard the *Dark Lady* she whispered softly, "I missed you also Cloud."

He closed his eyes and stared into the blackness provided. She could not have wielded more pain if she had carried a whip. He wondered how much it would hurt to hear her response to what he'd held back. The silent I love you.

His eyes opened wide when he heard her small gasp. He sat up and saw her pulling a shirt from the depths of the bag. His shirt! Alexis glanced over and saw he recognized it. She wanted to take it and fling it in his face, but she could not bring herself to part with it. Where was it? Where was the hate she professed to have for the man who had stood in her way once too often? Why did she not feel it deeply? She struggled to find the emotion, but it was not there. Neither was love. The desire to tell him what she had felt for two years had been obliterated the moment she'd seen him on board her ship, but she could not stop wanting him. No! It was a silent scream; her mouth, as if by its own volition, formed the word on her lips. It hung there as Cloud stood and crossed the distance to her. He took the shirt from her trembling fingers, noticing the patched elbows and shiny, worn material.

"You have worn this often?" he asked quietly.

"Yes." She tried to retrieve it. Her hand brushed his and the contact seared their flesh. She pulled her hand away at the same time he did, and the shirt fell to the deck between them. Alexis watched it fall and settle in a careless heap. She bent to pick it up but two strong hands, insistent yet gentle, prevented her downward movement. She paused, looking up into Cloud's face.

"Why?" The simple word when it left his mouth brushed against Alexis's cheek, warming it, and Cloud imagined he could see the imprint of his breath there.

Alexis touched her cheek lightly with the palm of her hand, then removed his hands from her shoulders, taking a step backward at the same time. She felt suffocated by his closeness and his questions and her own brief response to his touch.

She stooped, gathering the shirt in her hands and folding it with more care than any other article of clothing. "It was the only thing I had of yours. The only thing to remind me you were not out of my imagination." She paused, turning her back on him as she put the shirt with her other belongings.

"I only wore it at night, Cloud. To sleep in. I liked to think I was sleeping with you." Her last words were barely audible.

"And that has changed now?" It was hardly a question; only the tiniest inflection at the end made it so.

"You know it has," she answered, turning once more to face him, letting the hammer drop with hushed grace.

There was nothing more to say. He had known there could be nothing between them until this assignment was over, only he knew now that he had never wanted to accept it. Abruptly he turned, no longer able to look at the soft light, sheathed in pain, emanating from her amber eyes. He rapped loudly on the door and the silence, already broken, was further split by the bolt sliding across the catch. He left the cabin without looking back and Alexis felt, rather than heard, the shudder of the door as it slammed closed. Heavy steps in the companionway assured her that her words had had their anticipated effect. Barely conscious of the movement she bent over her boots and took out her dagger. With a calculated flick of her wrist she sailed it across the cabin to sink into the blank wall of her prison.

When the hilt had ceased vibrating from the force of her toss Alexis threw herself across the bunk and stared at the porthole, willing her lips to stop trembling and her tears to stay unshed.

Hours later Cloud brought her dinner. He did not stay while she ate and he sent Frank to get her tray. The porthole continued to provide her one diversion until the sun went down and the light disappeared, plunging her prison into darkness and obliterating even the opening to the sea from her view.

She closed her eyes and pulled her knees close to her chest, covering herself with a blanket. When she fell asleep she did not dream of Washington, her escape, or Cloud. She dreamed of a young girl whose world was the color of gray soot.

As she slept Cloud kept watch for some sign of her ship. She might believe her men would not come after her, but he was not so sure. He had seen the way they'd all looked at her, recognized their respect and admiration and their reluctance in the very end to submit without a fight. She had been magnificent while she told them what was happening. There was no martyred look, no indication she was sacrificing anything for them. Her voice had been calm, self-composed, and margined with just the right amount of firmness to give her unquestionable authority. He stared out over the water. Her men would come, maybe not now, but they would try to help her, sooner or later. Cloud hoped it was sooner.

He thought of her in his shirt, naked beneath the soft, white linen, tugging at the sleeves the way she always did, trying in vain to uncover her hands as the material slid past her fingers. He thought of how she looked when only moonlight shared the cabin they slept in, casting its delicate blue light over the shirt, causing shadows to reveal the curves beneath. Her smile could only be seen in her eyes, her willingness apparent in the slight tilt of her head, the position visible only because it was followed by the gentle swing of her hair, soft and blue-gold in their silent companion's light.

He stopped, inwardly bracing himself. No matter what she meant to him she was still Captain Danty. If her men came it would be the captain he would have to fight for; Alex was not his any longer. Maddeningly, wonderfully, she still belonged to herself, a prisoner only by virtue of the four walls and locked door he had forced upon her.

"I'm your relief, Captain," Landis said, jerking Cloud back to reality.

"Good. I was getting tired."

"Do you think they'll come?" he asked as he took over the watch, allowing Cloud the freedom to close his eyes for a moment.

"Wouldn't you?"

"Yes. So would Harry and Mike and everyone else."

"Then why should her men be any different?"

"I'm not looking forward to it," Landis said, shaking his head.

Cloud laughed weakly. "You think I am?"

"Yes," came the reply.

Cloud's eyes opened wide in surprise. "What makes you think that?"

Landis peered straight ahead through the darkness, the palest sliver of moon aiding his search. "You know as well as the rest of us she can't hope to get away this time, no matter what she says. Her men would provide an easy way out for all of us."

Cloud's voice was sharp and cutting. "Let's stop this immediately, Mr. Landis, once and for all; and feel free to pass it on to the rest of the men. The woman below is Captain Danty and that is who we are taking back to Washington. Forget Alex ever existed. Stop feeling at odds with your assignment. It does none of us any good. As long as any man feels guilty, we'll have trouble. We'll get careless. And she'll use it against us. I'll have the first man who so much as hints at turning her loose hung on the yardarm without a moment's hesitation." He strode away, missing the smile that sprang immediately beneath Landis's silver beard.

Landis looked up at Tom Daniels at the wheel, and from the shrug of Tom's shoulders, Landis knew he had heard the entire conversation. Individually they wondered if the captain could take his own advice.

As Cloud readied for bed he thought about what he had said to his friend. Who was he trying to convince with his outburst, himself or Landis? How could he expect his men to forget the Alex they knew existed when he could not? How could they pretend the prisoner was Captain Danty when he could not bring himself to do it? She could not be split apart like that. She was both things to all of them. He fell asleep, dreading, then praying for the moment when her men would make their move.

Several days passed, monotony the thread holding them together. Alexis knew the number of planks forming the deck of her cabin. She had named all the knothole faces in her ceiling. She could tell who was coming to replace the guard at the door or to bring her meals by the step he made. There was a step indelibly etched into her memory to go with each face. Frank Springer was the light, airy bounce, just like his name. Mike Garrison was the heavy plodder. Harry Young had a hesitant shuffle that somehow seemed to match his lopsided grin. Tom Daniels was slow grace, his drawl and his fencing skills combining to make a whisper step. She never could visualize Forrest's approach. He announced himself with loud grumbling instead.

Cloud never came, but she knew his stride better than those of the others. His was a step that issued a quiet challenge, a step that announced itself with unassuming arrogance. It had the sound of unsought applause.

She heard those hands clapping now as his boots made contact with the planks in the companionway. She stared sullenly out the window.

"I'm bored," she told him when he entered the cabin.

"Do you always greet visitors so amiably?" asked Cloud.

"I knew it was you. I made an exception," she said coldly.

"But how did you know it was me?"

"Your audience announced you." She turned and saw he was staring at her blankly. "Having nothing else—Never mind. I just knew. I said I was bored," she repeated impatiently.

"Where is the toy I saw a few days ago?" He greeted her blank stare with a chilling smile. "The one that was in the wall."

"It's in my boot. It's yours, if you want it."

"No, you keep it. If it hasn't found its way to my heart yet I guess I'm safe." They both moved at the same time, like gladiators sizing up an opponent in the arena. He sat down on the bunk while she took the opposite side and sat on the deck. Where did you get it in the first place?" he asked, making himself comfortable on higher ground.

"Peach, my cabin boy, must have put it in my bag." She

rested her chin on her knee and continued to stare at him as if she were calculating the strength of the enemy.

"Oh, the little thing with the love-sick eyes and his heart on his sleeve."

"What's that supposed to mean?" she snapped. "All right, I guess I knew he was a little in love with me. He was only with us a few months before you came." Alexis closed her eyes and pressed a smile into her knee, remembering the way Peach always hurried by her and his inability to prepare a hot bath.

"Did they all fall in love with you?" Cloud asked slowly.

"No!" She jerked her head up. "What gave you that idea?"

"Well, if Peach is any indication then—" His voice dropped off suggestively.

"Stop it!" she answered tersely. "Just leave, Captain."

"I thought you were bored? You don't like my company?" The sarcasm was unbecoming.

"I'd like to be by myself. I don't want to talk right now."

Cloud ignored the gentle plea almost hidden in her acid tone. "I did come here with something in mind," he informed her brittlely. "I have decided you can have the freedom of the ship, if you will give me your word you will not try to escape."

"You'd take my word?" She felt herself softening.

"Of course. You've never lied to me before."

Alexis was torn for a moment. Being able to go on deck was almost like being free when compared to four walls. She looked around the cabin, then at Cloud who was studying her intently, burning her with emerald sparks. "I can't give my word, Captain. I'll still try. You had better keep me locked in."

"You hesitated. Why?"

"Then you expected my answer?"

"Yes, but more quickly."

"Why do you want to test me?" she asked angrily. "Just leave me alone. Your company sickens me."

"It didn't used to," he said, teasing, taunting.

Alexis stood, glaring at him. "Comments like those are what make me sick. You make inane remarks about Peach and lewd suggestions about my men and myself! And stop smirking at me! You remind me of Lafitte. On him lifted eyebrows and slanted grins were natural and charming. On you they are fraudulent and anything but enchanting!"

Cloud's dark brows automatically drew together at the mention of the pirate. "You shouldn't talk about Lafitte. It would be better if you never admitted knowing him," he said seriously.

Alexis did not catch the warning tone. "I will talk about anyone I want to. He is my friend."

"You would be better off not having friends like that."

"I never would have met him if you hadn't taken me from Tortola."

"Then you would never have known me." He paused, then added, "On intimate terms." .

Alexis had had all she could stand of his mocking. She ran to her nightstand and began throwing clothes on the deck until she found what she wanted. She grasped the shirt, her reminder of Cloud, and strode over to the porthole. Jerking it open she tried to throw it out but she was stopped by cruel fingers on her wrist. "Let me go! It's mine to do with as I please."

He pried her fingers open and took it from her; then he raised her chin and stared down at her face. She was fighting back tears of anger. "It's mine now," he said firmly. "I didn't give it to you to be thrown away!"

"Then take it!" She spit out the words. "Get out of here! And make it fast or my dagger may find your heart yet!"

Cloud turned sharply and left, taking the shirt with him. Mike was standing guard outside the door. His nervous stance and embarrassed smile were enough to let Cloud know he had heard everything.

"You're relieved, Mike," he said shortly. "Go on. I'll be here for a while." When Mike left Cloud stared at the closed door for several minutes, holding the shirt in a viselike grip, before he made his decision. He folded the shirt with the same care he had seen Alex use, and he walked back into her cabin.

She was standing exactly where he had left her, but the fury and tension had disappeared. Her mouth offered a greeting instead of scorn, and her eyes were liquid gold rather than amber ice. A small tremor shook her body in anticipation of his words.

"It won't work, will it?" he said quietly.

"No. You can't make me hate you."

"I can't stop loving you." He saw her wince almost imperceptibly. "We have to talk, Alex." He placed the folded shirt on the nightstand and sat on the edge of the bunk. She hesitated, then sat beside him. They half-turned toward each other, preparing for a tentative peace. She started to speak but he stopped her with a look, just as firm and tender as if he had actually brought his fingers to her lips. "There are some things I have to explain to you," he began gently, "that I should have explained during the first few hours you were here. I have been unfair to you and I should not have avoided you. Did you know I was the one who told the men giving me my orders all about you?"

"I supposed it had to be you."

"I thought you would, and I wanted you to believe that's all there was to it. I wanted you to believe I betrayed you. What I want to tell you now is I explained your story in order to keep them from enlisting your aid. I failed. I asked not to be given this assignment. Here I am. The more I explained about you the more determined they were to have you. In that they are not unlike me." He returned her trembling smile. "We managed to trace your whereabouts by intercepting a message to you from Scott Hansom. When we sighted your ship and saw you trying to trap Travers, I made the decision to take you before anything could happen. I don't regret it, Alex."

"It was right for you to do. From your side it was right," she interrupted softly.

"Alex," he went on as if he had not heard her. "There is only one man on the *Concord* I did not trust not to help you escape. Me. I can't stop wanting what you want for yourself even while I know I have to keep you prisoner. I thought if I could make you dislike me enough you would try harder to get away."

"Why are you telling me this now?"

"Because I realize you will try to get away no matter what you think of me." He paused and forced himself to say the next words slowly although he wanted to release them as a single gasp. "And because I know what you think of me will determine whether you'll ever return to me."

"You're right." She placed her hand over his. "I don't understand your orders, Cloud. But I do understand you have to follow them. I would expect it of my men. It is expected of you. I can understand that. I can even respect your decision not to allow me to get Travers." This last admission was torn from her but she offered it to ease the burden he was shouldering.

Cloud's intention, when he moved to kiss her, was only to halt her words. When his mouth met hers he knew that it had been a mistake. It had been too long since she had responded as sweetly as she was doing now. He wanted more than a memory beside him at night.

He might not have been able to pull back if he hadn't felt the tremors shaking Alexis's body. His lips left hers reluctantly then brushed their dewy softness once more, twice more, and still he saw she did not have the strength to turn her head to avoid him. The reproach was in her eyes and in the trembling of her slender frame. She was frightened by what he could still do to her and frightened by that part of her that wanted him to go on doing it.

"Please . . . don't ask me to love you now," she told him. "I can't. Don't even ask me to go to bed with you. I can't. I will try to escape and you will try to stop me. It is the only part of our past that will be repeated while your orders are between us."

"I understand." And he did. He watched her head bow slightly as if feeling the weight of her decision.

"Can you just hold me, Cloud? I think I just need to be held."

He didn't hesitate to pull her onto his lap. For a long time they sat in silence, her head on his shoulder, his arms around her waist. Once she moved to get more comfortable and he warned her, "Stop wiggling. You can only trust me so far."

She quieted immediately but he could feel her smile against his neck. "Don't worry. I've learned a few things since I put my hair all over the Atlantic."

Cloud groaned softly. "Then that explains it. Your geography is as bad as your memory. It was North America."

A week passed, then another. Although Alexis remained adamant in her desire to escape she was permitted on deck for brief periods each day, always under close supervision. If another vessel approached, she was taken below. The crew still guarded her door at night, but during the afternoon they sat with the door open and talked to her, sharing stories to ease the boredom.

As Washington drew closer Alexis's hostility increased toward the men who had ordered her capture. Cloud could do nothing to soothe her apprehensions, especially since he was guarding apprehensions of his own, and after one discussion the subject was closed.

Alexis saw Cloud frequently now. They sat in her cabin in the early evening when there was no pressing business on deck for him to attend.

"I thought I would take over Garnet Shipping after my parents died," he told her as she sat at his knees, her arms folded on his thigh, "but there was too much chance of war. I could not abandon the navy when they needed me most. Especially when I have a sister like Emma and a brother-in-law like Blake Crafton to keep things going. They understood.

Emma said she didn't want me brooding around the offices anyway."

"Emma understands her brother very well," Alexis said, lifting her head to meet his eyes.

Cloud sighed. "Emma is an angel. You'd like her, Alex."

"No doubt." There was a short silence; then she asked, "Cloud, are you glad you didn't stay in Boston?"

"I'm glad. I wouldn't be here with you now, would I?"

Alexis smiled. "No, you wouldn't."

"We're going to be in Washington by morning, Alex," he said, removing her arms from his lap. "I'm putting an extra man by your door tonight until I have you safely in dock. After that you'll be watched closely by several of the men."

In spite of herself Alexis laughed. "Thank you for taking me so seriously."

"And when have you been anything but serious when it comes to your word? You said you would try to get away and we all expect an attempt. You are not going to disappoint us are you?"

Alexis shook her head. "I'll not disappoint you." She gave him a sly grin. "And I'll not give you any information either, Captain!"

Cloud chuckled and casually ran his fingers through her hair. "Then it's a challenge, Captain Danty. We'll see which commander meets it." He kissed her lightly on the top of her head, and before either one of them had time to wish there could be more he left her.

Alexis drifted off to sleep still feeling the pressure of his lips on her head and the sensation of his fingers in her hair. She tried to imagine, in the last moments before she succumbed, how Cloud would look when he returned to her cabin in the morning and found she was gone.

The sun was barely up and already the wharf was teeming with activity. Cloud stood on the quarterdeck as the *Concord* sailed up the last part of the Potomac to the harbor. His smile was grim, reflecting the attitude of everyone aboard his ship. He thought of Alexis in her cabin. She would be awake now and dreading their approach into Washington. He had spent a sleepless night trying to determine her next move and had come up with nothing.

Landis stood beside the captain, a thin smile hidden beneath his beard. "All over," he pointed out to Cloud when the order was given to drop anchor. "She's here."

"Mr. Landis," Cloud responded sourly, "you are a master at stating the obvious. If you really wanted to help you would tell me what she's going to do next. She won't come without a struggle."

Silver eyebrows drew together. "I wish I knew," he said reluctantly, loath to admit his ignorance. He too had spent a night of tossing after his watch was completed. Now, with morning almost full on him, he had no answers.

Cloud realized the men had become quiet in expectation of his next order. The ship had been secured in record time so all hands were anxiously awaiting Alexis's appearance on deck.

"I'll go to her," Cloud said slowly. "Tell the men to stand by and be ready to stop her if she should try to make a run for it." As he walked away he felt the eyes of every man at his back, and he knew they were glad he had chosen to bring Alexis forward himself.

The men ignored the cries of greeting from the crews of the vessels on either side of them. They ignored the tightening of their own stomachs as they silently watched the hatch. Occasionally a pair of eyes would stray from the entrance and scan the horizon, hoping beyond hope Alexis's men would still come for her and then, perversely, hoping they would not. They tried to put themselves in the place of her crew, wondering if they could have followed her orders not to aid her and each found the same answer: he would have moved heaven and earth to get her back.

Tom and Frank jumped to attention as Cloud approached

them. He saw dark lines beneath their eyes and knew they also had spent a sleepless night.

"Wait here," he ordered. "When I have her out, follow us on deck. Tom, after I have her off the ship, I want you to gather her things and take them to my home. Do you know where it is?" Tom said that he did. "Well, if you have any trouble, it's the one that will look like a fortress. I plan to have everyone take shifts guarding the place until Senator Howe tells me what he wants done with Captain Danty."

"Do you expect her men?" Tom asked.

"I expect anything. Stand aside."

Frank moved off to one side and Cloud unbolted the door. He stepped inside and his breath caught in his throat as he surveyed the empty cabin. He saw the makeshift rope tied to the leg of the bunk and drawn through the open porthole. For a moment he did not speak. The joy, as well as regret, he felt at her absence did not allow for words. When he found his voice he yelled for his men. "Tom! Frank! She's gone!" They were in the room before he finished and were equally aghast.

Frank spoke first. "Captain! We didn't hear a sound. How did she squeeze out that porthole?"

Cloud did not bother to answer. He strode over to the porthole and pulled in the knotted strips of sheet, throwing them on the bunk. "It doesn't matter how she did it, only that she did. Damn her!" He stared at his men, daring them to show that they were not unhappy about this development; then deciding it was unfair to ask them to feel any differently he swept past them and went topside. When he was on deck he walked into the wide-eyed stares of his men. "She's gone! She got out through her porthole sometime during the night. Every man who was on watch I want to see immediately! I want the name of every ship we passed within her swimming range!"

Within minutes Cloud had the information he asked for. There had been only two ships during the night, both Garnet merchants. He winced at the news. How ironic if Alexis had chosen to flee to one of his ships. "Make ready to sail!" he commanded. "We're going after her!"

The *Concord* was a blur of activity as the crew quickly responded. They saw the looks of wonderment from the seamen on the wharf. They had only just secured the ship and without so much as a second to try out their land legs they were leaving again.

"It will make it easy for us to get her if she is on board a Garnet ship," Cloud told Landis as they went below.

"That's if she made it to one of them," Landis cautioned. "She took a hell of a risk. At night they might not have been able to see her. She could just be out there somewhere."

Cloud opened the door to her cabin. "I've already thought of that," he said bitterly, holding up the rope Alexis had fashioned. "Look at this. Can you believe she did this?"

"I believe anything of her," Landis grinned, walking to the porthole. "Why the rope? Why didn't she just jump?"

Cloud sat on the bed, absentmindedly undoing the knots. "Too dangerous," he answered. "She didn't have room to make a safe leap outward. She could have been pulled under the ship. With this rope she could have climbed most of the way down and used the side of the ship to push herself off. She knew what she was doing."

"When doesn't she?"

Cloud ignored him as he stared at the rope in his hand. The knot wasn't tight. How could that be? Her weight on it would have either pulled it tight or it would have given way. She couldn't have used it. She couldn't have—

He jumped to his feet, swearing as the ship gave a lurch. Ignoring Landis's stare he ran out of the cabin and raced for the deck. "Take the *Concord* one mile down river and drop her anchor! Right in the middle of the Potomac!" The men looked at him as if he had gone mad. "Tom! Harry! Come with me! Captain Danty is still somewhere on this ship! We'll start searching now!"

"How can that be, Captain?" Tom asked incredulously. "She never came out the door!"

"Don't ask me, Tom! All I know is she didn't use that rope of hers to go over the side. It fell apart in my hands. She could have been hiding under the bed when I went in. After we left she could easily have gone out."

"I'll be damned," murmured Tom.

"That's what we'll all be if we don't find her! Start checking all the cabins. We'll work our way down. Don't miss anything. The only point in our favor is she couldn't have made it to the deck yet. Don't let her get a chance!"

Tom and Harry nodded and separated to begin the search. The undersides of bunks were checked. Locked cabins were opened. Trunks were lifted and the orlop scoured and there was no sign of Alexis. Harry was investigating a small storage compartment when he heard a noise above him. Alexis's cabin, he thought. The captain must be searching for something there. He ignored the noise and started out of the cubicle when he bumped into Cloud.

"Oh, Captain. I thought you were in her cabin. Did you find anything yet?"

"Nothing." He stepped into the compartment and heard footsteps. "Must be Landis," he said looking up, drawn to the sound. He was beginning to think he had been wrong about Alexis. Perhaps she had gone over. If that was so they were wasting valuable time by remaining stationary. Still, if he was correct, they could not afford to have the search in the harbor. There were too many chances she might slip through their fingers. He was thinking this when his eyes caught a sliver of light in the ceiling. He moved directly below it, examining it more closely. He jumped and pushed at the wooden plank. He was not surprised when it moved.

"Harry! Look at this! She pried these planks loose with that damn dagger of hers!" Cloud sighed heavily thinking he should have known Alexis would see the dagger not only as a weapon, but a tool. He and Harry quickly removed several of the planks that were part of Alexis's deck. "Mr. Landis? Are you up there?"

"Captain? Where are you?" The reply was muffled.

"Below you!" Cloud turned to Harry. "What's directly above us?"

"Part of her nightstand. Maybe part of the bunk."

"Move out her bed, Mr. Landis! Then look for some loose boards!"

Landis did as he was told and soon he was staring in the captain's face. "Well, we know how she did it," he offered, trying to hide his mirth.

"Thank you, Mr. Landis. I was quite incapable of knowing that for myself. Harry, go on deck and tell about ten of the men to stay there and watch for her. Have the others join the search. They are to go over all the places we've been. I'll find Tom and continue below."

Alexis shifted in her uncomfortable position and tried to stretch. The powder storage compartment had not proven itself to be much of a hiding place. The first moment when the *Concord* reached harbor, she had tried to get off the ship. She had wanted to go over the side then, but before she'd reached a cabin with a porthole large enough for her to get through the *Concord* was moving again and she realized they were putting out to sea to search for her. Once she found a place to hide she faced the problem of how long she could stay there while Cloud began a fruitless search of the vessels they passed. She had expected him to go out to sea again to look for her, but not so soon. All her thoughts were broken when she heard the sound of approaching voices. She moved behind a barrel, making a last effort to be as invisible as possible when she heard Cloud tell Tom to start checking the storage areas.

Was Cloud being cautious or did he really know she hadn't left the ship? She waited quietly as Cloud's self-congratulatory stride neared her hiding place. She closed her eyes and allowed herself only to feel the motion of the *Concord*. When she interpreted what she felt her eyes opened wide in shock. Cloud knew! He knew! The *Concord* wasn't moving any longer.

He had put down anchor away from the harbor to do the search. A small moan of despair escaped her throat.

She heard the movement of the door and she stood up. There was no escape for the moment. It would have to be later. The door swung open and Cloud stood at the threshold, holding a lantern. Alexis smiled as the soft light passed over her. She could see Cloud was smiling also.

"Hello, Captain," she said quietly.

Cloud hung the lantern on a hook and shut the door behind him. Slowly he walked toward her and when he was directly in front of her he took her in his arms. Alexis did not attempt to pull away, rather she pressed herself closely to his warm, hard form and slid her arms around his neck.

"You tried," he whispered as his hand pulled tenderly at her braid, forcing her face to lift to his. Her eyes were soft, glistening with unshed tears of defeat. He kissed them gently. He felt her shudder in his hold and he tightened his arms around her. "I love you," he said, pressing her head once more to his chest. They remained silent, oblivious to the commotion outside as the crew continued the search. Finally, carefully, he put her away from him. "Are you ready to go, Captain Danty?"

"I am ready."

"You first," he said, motioning her to step in front of him.

Alexis opened the door and took a hesitant step into the passageway. It was empty. The men were still searching other cabins. As Cloud was calling that he had found her, Alexis pushed back against him, knocking him off balance and sending him into the storage compartment. Quickly she shut and bolted the door and ran down the companionway, heading for the deck. She heard Cloud's laughter above the commotion and in spite of her situation she found herself smiling. She was just reaching the first landing when she felt strong arms around her waist. Struggling hard, she wrestled out of their grip only to find her progress blocked by Frank and Forrest. She looked up at them, holding her hands up in surrender, and then flashed them a bright smile. They each took an arm and turned her so she could see Cloud coming up the companionway, followed by Tom, who had rescued him. Harry was brushing himself off at her side.

"You're strong, Alex," he muttered, a little embarrassed that she had been able to get away from him.

Alexis shrugged her shoulders in response, and her movement caused the two men holding her to grip harder. She hid her wincing reaction.

When Cloud reached them he was still laughing. "It was a good try, Captain."

"Not good enough," Alexis said coldly.

"No, you're right. It wasn't good enough." He turned his attention to his men. "Take her to the deck and bind her hands behind her. Tight. And if she makes one move before we get into the harbor again, tie her legs too."

"At least you've stopped laughing," she said to Cloud as the cook and Frank forced her toward the hatch.

"I never was laughing at you, Captain. Only at myself. I should have expected you would not come so easily and yet I didn't."

Alexis ignored him. "Frank. Forrest. I am going to have your fingerprints branded on my arms if you don't let up. How is Mr. Madison going to like it when he finds out I've been treated so horribly?"

Forrest guffawed loudly. "Won't work. I'm not in any mood to face Little Jemmy and tell him I was party to your escaping."

Alexis sighed and twisted her head around to Cloud, who was chuckling softly to himself once again. "I don't give up," she grinned.

Cloud nodded, but before he could make a reply they were on deck and Harry was reaching for a length of rope to tie her hands. Forrest pulled her hands behind her back while Harry looped the hemp around her wrists. She struggled briefly against her bonds and Cloud thought he detected fear in her eyes, but it passed quickly. He had no choice now. He knew she would do anything to get away.

As Harry led Alexis over to the mast, Cloud gave the orders

to sail. Alexis sat on the deck, leaning her back against the mast, Harry standing over her. Her fingers dug at the knots while she was momentarily forgotten in the activity of getting under way.

"Alex," Harry's voice pleaded above her. "Don't. I tied it tight. You're going to make a mess of your wrists."

Alexis's shoulders sagged and she quit her work. "You don't miss much."

"Not much. Would you feel terribly slighted if I took the dagger from your boot?"

Alexis laughed and stretched out her leg. "It's yours, Harry. A bit dull now, but you can have it."

Harry bent down and retrieved the dagger. "I'll sharpen it and just keep it for you, Captain Danty."

Alexis could only nod, her silence due to an effort to prevent the inevitable cracking of her voice. She tried desperately not to think of the only other time she had been bound, but visions of Travers appeared before her, unsummoned, unwanted. She lost all concept of time and place as she counted the strokes of the biting leather. Eyes closed, she pressed closer to the mainmast, her cheek against the pine. It became Pauley's bloody back and she was unaware of the tears streaming down her face.

Harry watched in confused silence, unsure of what was going through her mind. He heard her whisper a name, and then her tears ceased as suddenly as they had started. She lifted her head and glassy amber eyes stared at him helplessly. This was not a look he was used to seeing in her eyes. He wanted nothing more than to cut away the rope binding her wrists.

Alexis saw him finger the blade of her dagger delicately, and reading his thoughts she shook her head. "Don't do it, Harry," she said softly, hiding the trembling with low tones. "I'm all right now. Don't do anything that endangers your own mission."

Harry knelt beside her. "If you ever need an extra man for your crew, Captain, I would like you to remember me."

We have 4 FREE BOOKS for you as your introduction to KENSINGTON CHOICE! To get your FREE BOOKS, worth up to $24.96, mail the card below.

FREE BOOK CERTIFICATE

Yes! Please send me 4 Kensington Choice (the best of Zebra and Pinnacle Books) Historical Romances without cost or obligation (worth up to $24.96). As a Kensington Choice subscriber, I will then receive 4 brand-new romances to preview each month for 10 days FREE. I can return any books I decide not to keep and owe nothing. The publisher's prices for Kensington Choice romances range from $4.99-$6.99, but as a preferred subscriber I will get these books for only $4.20 per book or $16.80 for all four titles. There is no minimum number of books to buy and I may cancel my subscription at any time, plus there is no additional charge for postage and handling. No matter what I decide to do, my first 4 books are mine to keep, absolutely FREE!

Name _____

Address _____ Apt. _____

City _____ State _____ Zip _____

Telephone ( ) _____

Signature _____

(If under 18, parent or guardian must sign)

Subscription subject to acceptance. Terms and prices subject to change.

KF0898

4 FREE
Historical Romances
*are waiting
for you to
claim them!*

(worth up to
$24.96)

*See details
inside.....*

KENSINGTON CHOICE
Zebra Home Subscription Service, Inc.
120 Brighton Road
P.O.Box 5214
Clifton, NJ 07015-5214

She smiled weakly. "You wouldn't leave Captain Cloud, would you?"

"Never!" he said fiercely. "I mean when my service is up."

"Then I would be honored to have you on the *Dark Lady*." Fresh tears threatened to spill over the rims of her eyes, and she blinked in rapid succession to hold them back. When she composed herself she spoke again. This time her voice was laced with renewed determination that had no regard for the bonds relegating her to prisoner status. "And I will have the *Dark Lady* again, Harry. Captain Travers will learn I do not make idle promises when I have him at the end of my sword." The golden braid which had coiled around her neck was tossed to her back in a defiant gesture and she lifted her chin arrogantly to punctuate her statement.

Harry grinned at her. "I would like to be there when it happens, Captain Danty. I sure would like to be there!"

Alexis returned his slanted smile, remembering Harry also had his reasons for wanting to kill Travers. Her smile faded completely when she heard Cloud approaching. "Harry, wipe my face!"

He carried out her request immediately, using the scarf wrapped loosely about his neck. He tucked it into his pocket before Cloud was beside them, knowing Alexis had too much pride to let the captain see she had been crying. Alexis thanked him with a smile for helping her recover and got to her feet. She turned to Cloud, intending to look for some sign that he knew the depths of her recent despair, but he was not looking at her. Instead he was addressing Harry, ordering him to go ashore and get transportation for her. His words jolted her senses, making her realize they were already in the harbor and it would not be long before she was taken from the ship.

After Harry left them Cloud glanced at Alexis. He noticed her controlled features, the tight mouth curved in a suggestion of a smile to hide the clenched teeth behind it. She held herself stiffly, proudly, her arrogant bearing a covering for the traces of fear he had glimpsed earlier.

"If you will give me your word that you will not escape on the way to your quarters I will untie your hands," he said.

"No, Captain."

Cloud sighed, understanding her decision. "Very well then. We will be leaving shortly. You will be staying at my home until you see the President, which should be in a few days. Your decision then will determine whether your future quarters will be on board a ship or in jail."

"I understand." She glanced around her and saw the men working at a frantic pace to secure the *Concord*. They were as anxious to get off the ship as she. "It won't be long now," she added, watching Harry walk across the dock.

Cloud also followed Harry's movement until he disappeared. "I will have your things brought to you later today. Harry, Mr. Landis, and I will accompany you to my home. I must see Senator Howe afterward. You realize the men will be guarding the house."

"I expected it," she said.

Several minutes passed with no words between them. Alexis knew the futility of trying to escape at this moment and Cloud sensed she knew it. There was no way she could avoid the confrontation with the President and Alexis thought she might even be able to look forward to it. It was going to be such a pleasure to tell them all to go to hell. She smiled, glancing up at Cloud when she heard his laughter.

"I do not want to know what that smile means. It is enough for me to know it signifies trouble."

"Of course," she said airily. Alexis stiffened involuntarily when she saw Harry approaching. She did not pull away from Cloud's hand as he placed it on her elbow and led her toward the gangway. His hand did not force her movements, rather it was a grip of support and she allowed herself the benefit of his strength.

Harry pointed to the wagon on the wharf. "It was the best I could do, Captain. Are you ready to go?"

"Take Captain Danty down. I will be along in a few minutes. There are some details to attend to."

Harry nodded and Cloud released his hold on Alexis. She moved beside him and they walked toward the wagon together. She ignored the curious stares of the naval officers and seamen crowding the dock, while Harry fended them off with a murderous look. She refused his help getting into the rear of the wagon, managing to do it gracefully.

Cloud could not take his eyes from her as she walked away. Her steps were light, easy; and the braid at her back swung softly with her movement. As her long legs carried her with sure strides toward the wagon, she seemed oblivious to the men around her. He shook his head when she refused Harry's help and chose to climb in the wagon herself. She sat stiffly on the hard bed, and as if she could feel his gaze at her back, she glanced over her shoulder and smiled.

He had no smile in return. He hated what was happening to her now. He turned to his crew and saw that they were also staring after Alexis—not rudely, as the seamen on the wharf were doing, but with pride in their eyes; respect for her because she had been able to hold up so well against all they had done to her. Gradually they returned to their work, and Cloud went to his cabin and packed some of his belongings hardly aware of what he was doing. Tossing his bag over his shoulder, he went to the quarterdeck and gave his last commands. He ordered a skeleton crew to remain with the ship and stay alert for Quinton vessels.

"Mike, you and Frank pick out a few others and come to my home at dusk. It will have to be guarded. Captain Danty is not very cooperative in spite of her resignation at the moment." He smiled when his statement brought a round of low chuckles from the men. "Not a word to anyone of who she is. The less known about her the better. Her crew will no doubt be looking for her—we've been fortunate so far—but it can't last. Understood?" After he was assured that it was, Cloud headed for the wharf. Landis followed, seating himself beside Harry in front while Cloud chose to sit across from Alexis in the rear.

The wagon had just gone from sight when the crew of the

Concord was assailed by questions from the curious men on the dock.

"Hey Garrison! Mike!" one of them yelled.

Mike looked up from his work and saw an old friend standing among the group of seamen. He waved and returned to his business, ignoring the questions and catcalls flying in his direction.

"C'mon Mike! What the hell's going on? You come in, you leave, you come in again. Since when do you take women prisoners?"

Mike stood up and glanced in his friend's direction. He was in no mood to reacquaint himself via tiresome explanations he had no right to give. "None of your business," he answered gruffly.

He heard one of the men whistle and call out, "Sure wish I got orders to take on women! I wouldn't mind beddin' down with prisoners if they all looked like that!"

All work stopped on board the *Concord*. They glared at the men on shore. Oblivious to the sudden cessation of activity, the seamen continued their taunts.

"Who was she, Mike? The captain's whore? Can't he keep her in line without tying her?"

Mike could not ignore the comments any longer. Glancing in Frank's direction, he saw he was not alone. Before they moved toward the gangway they heard another voice call out.

"If I knew being at war could have these kinds of rewards I would have started one on my own!"

Mike stopped in his tracks. "At war?" he asked incredulously. "Since when?"

"Where have you been? We've been at war since June eighteenth. I'm surprised you didn't meet up with any of their ships. Isaac Hull already had a run in with the *Guerrière*. The *Constitution* won it too!"

"Yeah," called another of the men, "but don't worry about it! With the kind of cargo you've been carrying you probably didn't have time to worry about the limeys!"

Every man on the *Concord* knew the significance of June

eighteenth. Anger swelled inside them as they realized they could have pursued the *Follansbee* themselves and Alexis would have had her revenge. They turned their attention to the men on shore. The anger they felt was demanding to be released and their targets were waiting on the dock.

Mike and Frank moved down the plank carelessly, enjoying hiding their purpose a little longer, and approached the group of men.

"Tell us, Mike," one of them said. "About the woman. Where did they take her? Is Madame Carlton finally getting a few whores with class?"

"I don't think I heard what you said, sailor," Mike said calmly.

The young tar was unaware of the danger associated with Mike's forced calm, or he would have backed down instead of repeating himself foolishly. He was barely through with the statement when Mike's right fist made further speech impossible.

The man who said, "What's it to you, Mike?" found himself plummeting to the water as a result of Frank Springer's actions.

Taking their cue from Mike and Frank the other men aboard the *Concord* came running off the ship to take on anyone who so much as dared to look at them.

When it was over, almost as abruptly as it had begun, Mike sported a swollen eye and a cut lip. He surveyed his mates and found most of them nursing some wound. The unfortunate seamen who had managed to say the wrong things at absolutely the worst time were in no better shape. Mike could do nothing but laugh at their folly.

"Hey Frank!" he called between gasps. "What do you suppose the captain would say, seeing us now?"

Frank shrugged, grinning. "Which captain, Mike?"

This brought fresh laughter from the *Concord* crew and nothing but blank looks from the defeated men. Mike helped one of them up. "I'm not going to apologize," he told them. "But I will buy you a drink." The rest of the crew followed

Mike's example and in a short while they had relieved their remaining tensions in a few rounds at the nearest tavern. The other sailors thought the *Concord* men remained strangely quiet about the woman they'd brought to Washington, and no amount of liquor would loosen their tongues. They forgot about the woman eventually and contented themselves with bringing the *Concord* up-to-date. Mike and the others listened quietly to the news of the first month of war, all of them wondering how Alexis would receive it when she was informed.

Chapter Eleven

Harry slowly wound the wagon through the streets while Alexis took in the sights.

"It's not much, Captain," she said. "Muddy. Cheap boardinghouses. Dull. I expected it to be bright."

Cloud chuckled. "It's a new city. Newer than the country. Those boardinghouses you call cheap are where most of the senators and representatives stay when they are in Washington. A lot of important decisions are made in those houses."

"Is that where I am going to meet the President?"

"No, I doubt that. Mr. Madison has a pleasant home. So do Howe and Davidson. We'll probably be going to one of their places."

"Good. I have no intention of conducting business in squalor any more than I will discuss it during dinner."

"You seem so surprised by everything. I thought you had been here before."

"I've been here twice since I started searching for Travers," she told him. "But I never left my ship. Too dangerous." She smiled at Cloud and he returned it warmly when he saw her eyes were full of a pleasant memory. She winked at him. "I thought I might be captured by a certain naval officer."

"And so you have been," he answered.

"For now." It was Harry who spoke, taking his eyes off the road for a moment in order to glance back at them. "How long are you really with us this time, Captain Danty?"

Alexis and Cloud both laughed.

"Do you see what I am up against?" Cloud asked her. "Harry doesn't just speak for himself. My men don't expect you to be at my home when they arrive there this evening. Landis and I expect you to leap out of this wagon at any moment."

Alexis did not hear what he said. Her eyes were riveted to a handbill posted on a tavern wall. "Stop this wagon, Harry!" she cried. Without waiting for him to do as she commanded she scrambled to her feet, easily avoiding Cloud's outstretched hands, and leaped over the side. She fell as she hit the ground, her balance strained. Before Cloud could catch her she was running toward the tavern. Harry started to pursue her but Landis's hand on his wrist stopped him.

Landis pointed to the notice Alexis was studying intently and said, "She's not going anywhere, Harry."

Harry read the handbill. His stomach tightened. It stated that war had been declared and the date screamed injustice at him. June 18, 1812.

Alexis stood motionless, mesmerized by the black lines on yellowing paper. She sensed Cloud's presence behind her though he made no move to touch her. Her shoulders sagged briefly as she realized the implications of the date. "It didn't have to be," she said softly, more to herself than to Cloud.

Cloud moved closer to her, resting his hands on her shoulders, lean, tanned fingers giving her the support her frame denied her. His eyes betrayed his pain and he was glad there was no one around them to see it. He could see the *Follansb* as clearly in his mind as if the frigate were directly in front of him. He knew he was not alone in his vision; Alexis was seeing the same thing. He cursed the lack of communicatio that prevented him from taking the ship and wondered who or what Alexis was damning.

Alexis leaned her back against his hard chest. She felt his hands slide down the length of her arms and begin tugging on the ropes at her wrists. She pulled away, swinging around to face him.

"Don't you dare feel sorry for me, Captain!" she said bitingly. "Don't you dare make it easy for me and hard on yourself!"

Her harsh words were barely heard as Cloud saw angry tears form in her eyes. An effort to blink them back proved futile and they slid in tiny rivulets over her cheeks. She tried to brush them aside with her shoulder, but the positioning of her arms made it impossible. She lowered her eyes, mainly to avoid the terrible anguish in his.

Cloud reached for her elbow and drew her toward him gently. "I wasn't feeling sorry for you, Alex," he said, leading her to the wagon. "It was worse than that. I was feeling sorry for myself."

Cloud lifted her into the wagon, once more seating himself across from her. She avoided his gaze as she allowed tears to course down her face. The remainder of the trip passed in silence; neither Harry nor Landis looked back more than once, not wanting to see her face.

Alexis glanced up, dry-eyed now, when Harry brought the wagon to a halt. Cloud tossed a key to Landis. The old man jumped down, hurrying up the walk toward a large red brick house.

Alexis could only stare at the imposing two-story structure. The windows were all closed with clean white shutters, four on the second floor and two larger ones on either side of the porch on the first. It did not have any houses on its sides as so many of the others did. It stood alone; large, bold, arrogant. Impressive because it was alone, like the man who owned it.

"It's a wonderful house," she said, looking at Cloud and not his home. She followed him up the short walk, with Harry close behind, carrying his captain's belongings.

"Hold your compliments until we get inside. It's been closed for two months and I don't have any servants. I can't imagine you are going to find it very pleasant."

After a little fumbling with the key Landis managed to open the door. Swirls of dust greeted them as they stepped in. Alexis choked and gave Cloud a grim smile.

"Wouldn't it have been easier to keep me on the *Concord*?" she asked. "Or did you bring me here to do your cleaning?"

"It might have been easier for us to have you on the ship, but you would have had to stay below the entire time. A woman on board would have created quite a disturbance, or perhaps you didn't notice the stares you received when Harry brought you off the ship." Alexis's wide-eyed stare told Cloud that she had not and the three men laughed softly. "As to cleaning this place, that is up to you. Usually I hire someone to take care of that while I'm here. I suppose that is not a good idea this time."

"Well, if you would untie my hands now, I think I can manage to do a few things."

Cloud motioned Landis to undo Alexis's wrists, and when they were free she rubbed them to return the circulation. "John, you and Harry can show Alex the house. Tom should be coming by soon with her things. She can stay in any of the guest bedrooms, and take one yourself. If she wants to start cleaning she can, and you help her. Just don't let her out of your sight. I have to see Howe right away. If I am not back before the others arrive, make them comfortable and let them know that under no circumstances is she permitted out of this house."

"Captain," Alexis said as he turned to go. "I have changed my mind. I have no intention of going anywhere until I meet with your President. He and I have a score to settle."

Cloud grinned. "I'll make sure the senator relays your message." He left then, and Harry shut the door behind him.

Alexis clapped her hands, signaling the beginning of the task that lay ahead. "John, would you show me to the kitchen. I would like to wash my face and start working."

Landis led her to the back of the house and she worked the pump until she had cool, clear water gushing out. She briskly patted her face, removing all traces of her tears. When she turned back to Landis she was smiling brightly, invitingly. "I think I will start in here, John. You and Harry uncover the furniture in the other rooms."

Landis glanced toward the rear door and looked at Alexis uneasily. "I'm not so—"

"I said I wasn't going anywhere, John, and I meant it. Don't worry."

"All right. I'll leave you on your own. I'll do the drawing room and send Harry after some food. When the others get here they are all going to be hungry."

"That's fine. You take care of all those details while I start working." She gently pushed him aside and began wiping down tables and doing the dishes that had been left out.

She could hear Harry and Landis moving furniture and choking on the dust left in their wake. She was on her hands and knees, scrubbing the floor, when she heard Harry. She looked up to see him place some cartons of food on the floor at the entrance to the kitchen.

"I didn't even realize you had gone out yet," she said, surveying the contents of the boxes. "I believe you have enough here to feed the entire crew for a month!"

"Not quite," he answered. "It will keep food in our bellies for a few days though."

"I'll put it in the pantry after the floor dries. How is Mr. Landis coming along?"

"He's got most of the rooms on this floor done. I doubt if they will meet your standards."

"If he's working that fast, then I suspect you are right. Never mind though. You go and help him with the upstairs and I'll clean after you."

Harry started to go; then he paused, looking back at her. She was already back to scrubbing the floor and didn't notice his hesitation. "Alex, I want to say something to you."

Startled by the seriousness of his tone, Alexis looked up

immediately. She wiped her wet hands on her trousers and partially sat up. "What is it, Harry?"

"It's you, Alex. Here, in this house. I feel strange calling you Alex or Captain. It's as if I should call you—" He stopped, unable to continue. "I talk too much. I'm going to find Landis."

Alexis could only stare after him. She knew what he was going to say. She had felt it too. She tried to dismiss the feeling and what it meant while she put the food away. There was a sense of coming home that she associated with the house, something she had never experienced anywhere before. She was surprised Cloud owned such a large home when he probably had very little opportunity to use it. She wandered through the rooms on the first floor, noticing the expensive furniture, the rich rugs and fine paintings. The study was full of books, many of them ornately bound. She did not have to remember he was a wealthy man because of Garnet Shipping. Every room subtly stated that fact.

A knock at the door interrupted her from further exploration. She went to answer it. Tom Daniels stood grinning on the threshold, holding her bag of clothes under his arm.

"Tom, thank you," she said, taking the bundle from him. "Come in. Did something happen to your jaw? You're holding it kind of oddly."

"No, ma'am. I have a little toothache, that's all." Embarrassed by his lie he avoided her gaze. He did not want her to know about the fight.

"Well, if that's all it is, then I'm going to put you to work. You can help us with the cleaning."

Serves me right, he thought, as he allowed himself to be saddled with a feather duster and began working. "It seems I came too early," he muttered under his breath.

Alexis ignored him, laughing to herself, and went upstairs to see what the other two were doing. She dropped her possessions in one of the rooms they had already cleaned and found them in another bedroom, struggling to make up the bed. Looking around the room she realized it was Cloud's. A shiver passed through her as she glanced around her. Navigation manuals were neatly stacked on a bureau beside a hairbrush and razor. One of the men had thrown his duffle bag carelessly on the floor. Alexis bent to pick it up, setting it on a chair by the window.

She helped Harry and Landis make the bed. When they were done she told them to rescue Tom downstairs. Both of the men gave her gratified looks and went off to give Tom the good news.

Alone now, Alexis began unpacking Cloud's bag of clothes. She neatly folded his things, placing them in drawers, and hung his dress uniform in the wardrobe. She noticed his carelessness with it meant it would have to be pressed if he intended to wear it while he was in Washington. The contentment she felt being in this room, touching things belonging to him, caused her to feel a longing she had tried to put behind her. Knowing he was fighting the same desire did not make it any easier.

She smoothed the thick spread on his bed, her fingers lingering on his pillow for a few moments longer than she had intended. Caressing the coverlet lightly, she felt as if she were caressing the hard planes of his face, willing them by means of her feather touch to relax and forget the orders which had come between them. She wanted the pleasure she had found in his arms and she wanted to return the pleasure he had known from her.

She stepped back from the bed and ran from the room, slamming the door behind her, as if by doing so she could shut out all the room and the man who slept there meant to her. She knew she could not go to him, nor he to her, as long as she was his prisoner. It was different before, she thought, when he had held her captive because he alone wanted her. Now she was being pulled in different directions. While he had no choice in what had transpired, he was still pulling her in a direction she did not want to go. Now it was not only Travers who stood in their way, but also this war.

She thought how easy it would be to tell him that she would

agree to help his cause; how easy it would be to fall into his arms, into his bed, after such a decision. But he would know better, and she was glad he would. She asked herself why she was holding back from him, why she was determined not to allow him more than a brush against her flesh or a gentle kiss. She knew the answer almost before the questions had formed concretely in her mind. If she lay beside him again and experienced all he could do for her, she knew she would not have the strength to do battle any longer. She knew she would give up everything in order not to have to leave Cloud. He must know it also, she thought. She remembered how he had weakened in front of the tavern. He had almost freed her then. If she had not stopped him, he would have put her on a ship for Tortola himself. She knew how hard he was fighting the conflicts within him. As Cloud he wanted her to reap her revenge and be free to be with him in every manner possible, but as the commander of the *Concord* he had to see his mission through. And yet, he had a power at his disposal to see that she joined him, the power of his maleness, and he refused to use it in order to achieve his ends.

She smiled, recalling she had accused him of believing the ends justified the means, but here was her proof he would never willingly agree to such a thing. The realization carried with it something that frightened her for a moment. She had lied to him on the *Concord*. He had bared his soul to her and she'd responded with a lie. She did love him, desperately, totally, irrevocably. Even as she thought it, she knew she would not tell him. His burden was already too great without the additional weight her words would carry.

She put her own things away, lingering over the worn linen shirt he had refused to let her throw away. Though she owned the shirt, she knew there was nothing more symbolic of Cloud's ownership of her. When she slipped it on tonight she would be more of a prisoner than when he had had her tied. She pressed the material close to her cheek. When she pulled it away she saw, with a small shock that caused her body to tremble, that it was wet, and that she had been crying.

She erased the tears with the back of her hand and put the shirt away. Quickly, as if activity formed a substitute for her thoughts, she undressed, putting on the only dress Tom had had the foresight to pack. It was the same one she had worn the day Cloud had taken her from her ship, the day war was declared, the day she had seen revenge slip through her fingers. After smoothing out the wrinkles she brushed her hair and decided against redoing the braid. When she looked in the mirror and saw the hair fall around her shoulders, she thought of Pauley and the promise she had made to him. Quietly she reaffirmed one of the promises she had made to herself, knowing the other had been broken when she'd first met Tanner Frederick Cloud.

After a two-hour wait that left Cloud impatient and irritable he was ushered into Howe's office by his secretary.

The senator rose from his chair and walked around his desk to shake hands with him. He stared pointedly at Cloud for several moments, gray eyes coldly assessing the man in front of him. When he spoke it was as if the pause had not taken place. "Sorry to have kept you waiting, Captain. I was only informed of your presence a short time ago. I concluded my business as rapidly as I could."

Cloud smiled grimly and seated himself in a chair at the corner of Howe's ostentatiously carved desk. He refused the drink he was offered and remained quiet while Howe fixed one for himself. He was fully aware of the senator's guarded appraisal. Rather than making him uneasy, it made him want to laugh.

"I hope your being here indicates you have Captain Danty in your custody," Howe said, taking his seat.

"I do." Cloud noticed Howe's thick lips curl slightly.

"Good. I knew we sent the right man. This is the first piece of encouraging news I have had all morning. Where do you have her?"

"She's staying in my home for the present. I have men

guarding the house to prevent her escape." The senator's eyebrows rose slightly and Cloud chuckled softly. "You didn't think she would come of her own free will, did you? I thought I had made that rather clear from the moment the subject of Alex Danty was brought up."

"You did," he said, taking a pull of his drink. "I was hoping that once war had been declared she might prove to be more cooperative."

"Congress could not have chosen a worse day to act on Mr. Madison's proposal, Senator." The eyebrows lifted again, and Cloud explained everything that had taken place since he'd left Washington. He put special emphasis on Alexis's escape attempt so Howe would understand precisely how determined she was to refuse them. "The last thing she told me today was that she had no intention of leaving Washington until she meets with the President. She believes she has a score to settle with him."

Howe's eyes narrowed. He tapped the side of his large nose thoughtfully. "I imagine she wants to tell him to go to hell." Cloud nodded and Howe added, "Little Jemmy might like hearing it straight to his face for a change, instead of behind his back."

Cloud got to his feet, uneasy with the derogatory tone in the senator's voice. He wanted to end the meeting swiftly. "Senator, are you and the others still insistent upon using Captain Danty to provide a means to Lafitte?"

Howe gave no indication one way or the other. "Why do you want to know?"

"I think it is unwise to pursue the subject with her. She has already mentioned Lafitte in passing, but it is easy to see she will not use her friendship, even to save herself."

"Does she know that by bringing Lafitte to us she can gain herself a pardon?"

"In the first place, Senator, she has correctly surmised that we have no right to keep her. In order for her to be brought here I had to threaten her with the imprisonment of her men. She knows these charges are false. I have only told her we require her assistance, that her knowledge of British movements, of running blockades, would be of value to us. Those are the things you should ask her to help us with. I never mentioned Lafitte, hoping I could persuade you to reconsider the issue. I doubt if she will help us now, even if Lafitte's name is never brought up, but I know for a certainty she will refuse if we expect her to use her friendship as a weapon."

"You have something in mind, Captain?" asked Howe, mulling over what had been said.

"I believe if we offer Captain Danty an opportunity to find Travers she may help us." Cloud was taken back by the quick and angry response of the senator.

"It's out of the question! Farthington will tell you himself that we don't need ships in the Caribbean right now, not when the British are beginning to blockade our eastern ports."

"And what good is her experience if she refuses you and spends the entire war in prison?" Cloud asked angrily.

"She would do that?"

"She'll tell you yourself if you don't change your approach."

Senator Howe eased back in his chair. "Travers is in the Caribbean. Lafitte is in the Caribbean. If she could bring us Lafitte then—"

"No! Lafitte must stay out of this. Find another way to get his help. Captain Danty will not do it."

"You ask too much for her, Captain!" Howe cut in sharply.

"I do not," Cloud answered quietly. Howe said nothing and Cloud went on, resigned to the fact that nothing would change. "When do you want to meet with her?"

"Robert Davidson has asked the President to have dinner with him on Thursday. Granger, Farthington, and I will also be there. Originally we had planned to discuss what we would do if you were unsuccessful, now that has changed. It will be a good time for a meeting with Captain Danty. We can discuss her role after dinner. Why are you frowning, Captain?"

Howe's question caught him off guard. He had been

unaware he had shown his displeasure so openly. "I doubt that Captain Danty will take kindly to the pretense."

"The pretense?"

"What else can you call it, Senator? She knows she is not your guest, yet you would ask that she perceive it that way. You would give her dinner, small talk, let her drink her wine, in return for her cooperation. She would rather you brought her in chains than as a guest."

"That is hardly something I would consider."

"Consider only that she will perceive it that way."

"If it's chains she wants, Captain, you may assure her that is what she'll have if she refuses."

Cloud stood immobile, fighting not to show what he thought about the senator, realizing somehow it was dangerous to show this man too much. "What time Thursday do I bring her to this"—he wanted to say charade—"dinner," he finished, hoping the hesitation was not noticeable.

"I believe seven-thirty is what Davidson had in mind." He checked his calendar, making a great show of it. "Yes. Seven-thirty, it is."

As soon as Cloud left the office Howe scribbled a note and called in his secretary. "Find Bennet Farthington. He should be hanging on Eustis's heels somewhere. Don't look at me blankly! He's the War Secretary, for God's sake! Give Bennet this." Howe threw the paper across his desk and his secretary hurried out. He got out of his chair and began to pace the room in angry strides.

She had to bring them Lafitte. He was the point of all of this—that, and having Danty herself in custody. If everything the captain said was true then they might have to settle for only Danty. The meeting would prove very interesting.

Walking toward his home, Cloud wondered if he should tell Alexis what had happened in the meeting. He already was sure she suspected there was something more involved in obtaining her pardon than simply supplying them with information and helping them fight a few ships. He shook his head. She would have to hear it from them. He could not be the one to tell her what they wanted.

He stopped suddenly, passing a dress shop. Taking a few steps backward, he went inside. He had not given any thought to what she would wear to meet the President until now and he knew she had nothing suitable for a dinner. He thought of her greeting the President and the others in her fawn britches and white shirt, perhaps with her rapier at her side. He chuckled softly at the thought, then felt himself tensing at the picture he created. She would be magnificent in anything she wore. He wondered idly if Howe expected her to appear with her dagger drawn.

He got the attention of the shopkeeper, a small woman with shrewd violet eyes, and explained what he wanted. She showed him pages and pages of drawings of gowns and he imagined each of them on Alexis's slim, elegant form. He stopped in his search, pressing a finger to the gown on the page in front of him. The gown in the picture appeared to be made of a heavy material, possibly velvet, but it was not the richness of the material that caught his eye. The style, the lines of the gown, matched Alexis. It had short, puffed sleeves, a rounded neckline; and below the empire waist the dress hung freely.

"This is the one," he said with certainty.

"It is very beautiful," the woman agreed, eyeing Cloud with satisfaction. "Will your wife be choosing the material?"

"Ahh . . . no," he stammered and could hardly believe he had done it. The reference to Alexis as his wife took him by surprise. "I will choose. I don't want a heavy material like the one in this drawing. Do you have something very delicate? In blue perhaps?"

She nodded and left him, returning quickly with a swatch of sky blue material, so sheer it seemed to him only a film of air in his hands.

"This is exactly what I want," he said, letting it slip through his fingers into her hand. "Can you have the gown ready by Thursday afternoon? Also the suitable undergarments?"

The shopkeeper was aghast, the curved lines of her rounded face were drawn tight with shock. "It is impossible! That is only three days away. It would take at least a week and I need your wife for a fitting."

"Alexis can not come in for a fitting and I must have the gown ready on Thursday," he persisted. "I am willing to pay extra for your inconvenience. Alexis and I have been invited to a dinner at the home of Representative Davidson. The President will be there. Perhaps Dolley." He knew it was a lie but it was interesting to see how Dolley's presence at the occasion suddenly made the impossible very possible. He knew the woman was thinking what a wealth of orders she would have if the President's wife saw one of her gowns.

The woman smiled, her keen sense of business was surfacing quickly. "I think it can be done, but it will mean some trouble for me," she said, alluding to the fact he had agreed to pay for it.

Cloud laughed, marveling at the way the woman's devious mind responded. "Any price, madam. I must have the gown and I assure you Alexis will be the best model you have had in years."

"Then you understand why I am agreeing to this insane pace."

"Of course. Now as to the measurements . . ."

The woman listened closely, jotting down notes, as Cloud described Alexis's proportions with uncanny accuracy. She was immensely pleased to meet a man who knew his wife so well and who appeared to be as astute as herself. She raised her eyebrows slightly when he asked for a modification in the design of the dress he had chosen.

"The back must be higher," he said.

"But Captain, it is not the style or—"

"Madam, I am already paying an exorbitant sum for this gown. We both know it. Humor me on this point." He was not going to explain the scars that made it impossible for Alexis to wear a low-back gown.

The shopkeeper gave in, as he knew she would. The captain was very insistent over what seemed a minor detail to her. If his wife was as he described, then any change seemed worth it in order to have her wear this gown. A pity, she thought, that she would never see her wear it.

They haggled over the cost of the undergarments and slippers, and although she knew she lost money on this part of the transaction, she more than made up for it by the price he was willing to pay for the gown. He had no sooner left the shop than she called for her assistants to begin working on her masterpiece.

Cloud stopped one more time on his way home when the glint of silver caught his eye in a jeweler's window. He stared for a long time at the necklace before he walked in to purchase it. He thought of what he had said to Howe about Alexis preferring to come in chains. He wondered if the senator would see the significance of the slender silver choker. Alexis would understand what he meant by the gift. As he slipped the velvet case inside his pocket he conjured up the image of her standing before him.

Golden hair framed her oval face. Her amber eyes were like soft flames, lighting the room with delicate sparks. The sheer blue gown hung softly from the curve of her shoulders and the low, rounded bodice revealed the tawny hollow of her throat and the gentle swell of her breasts. He could see the faint movement of the pulse in her throat as she lifted her hand to her neck to touch the silver chain caressing her skin. Her lips parted slightly and her eyes lowered, as if in supplication, then her hand dropped once more to her side. He followed the movement of her bare arm, allowing his eyes to gently touch her slim waist, only hinted at by her movement in the gown. His eyes dropped still lower to the long, straight line of her legs, legs he could not see except through the silhouette provided by the dim light behind her. The gown showed nothing, yet revealed all of her. The empire waist

enclosed the curves of her breasts while the long blue folds
of material defined the form they hid. Her fingers slowly drew
again to her throat, and she touched the chain lightly, raising
her eyes to him, telling him she understood its meaning, a
tremulous smile playing on her lips. He caught the glimmer
of a tear in her eye, brighter than the facet of a diamond.
The image shattered.

What right? he thought. By what right did he have to present
her with the necklace and announce her bondage to him?
The answer came to him as almost a physical jolt. Though
he had said it to her often and to himself more times than
he could count, it never seemed more real than at this
moment. He pressed his hand against the case in his pocket.
He loved her. Hadn't she once said his love was more binding
than any chain could be? He had not fully understood then.
He did now. He would offer her the necklace but the decision
to wear it would be hers. She would have to decide if she was
ready to accept all the necklace signified between them, even
if she could not say the words he wanted to hear.

Briskly he continued his walk, his thoughts turning to more
mundane matters, like the emptiness in his stomach and the
fact he had had very little sleep in the past few days.

Alexis tilted her head toward the door at the sound of
a knock, anticipating Cloud's entrance. She started for the
entrance but Harry by-passed her and got there first. She
gasped when she saw Mike on the threshold, his eye almost
swollen shut, his lip and jaw cut. Behind him were Frank
Forrest, and a few others. None of them looked any better.

She stopped Mike's intended explanation by forcefully leading him to the kitchen where she could see to his battered
face. "What have you all been up to?" she asked, pushing
Mike into a chair. "None of you look as you did when I left
you this morning!"

Forrest smiled, seating himself at the table. He moved his

jaw back and forth, making certain it still functioned properly. "There was a disagreement at the wharf. We settled it."

Alexis lifted an eyebrow suspiciously. "Nothing is worth all this damage to your bodies," she said firmly. "John, get me some wet towels so I can see whether these men will ever be fit for duty again."

"I assure you this was worth it," Mike said, looking directly at Alexis. The others agreed emphatically.

Alexis did not understand why they were all staring at her when they answered, but Landis and Harry saw immediately that she had been the cause of the disagreement. They exchanged knowing smiles, and Landis patted Mike on the back.

"I hope you settled the difference of opinion in your favor," Landis said to Mike.

"Oh, yes. We did," he answered, grinning.

"Well, I don't like it," Alexis broke in, shaking her head as she washed away the dried blood on Mike's lip. "And you all have been drinking. I suppose the losers were forced to buy."

Forrest laughed, then winced. "Not at all, Alex. We bought them a few rounds—to soften their defeat."

Alexis looked at all of them, taking special notice of Tom, who was doing his best to avoid her eyes. "I think you'll all survive. Mike, you're finished. Tom, get over here and sit down. I want to see what you call a toothache."

"Sorry, Alex," he said when he took his seat.

"Just open up, Tom. Let's see how many teeth you've knocked loose." Alexis pronounced him fit. "You may as well look as presentable to your captain as possible, although I don't know how you are going to hide those black eyes. Frank, you've got a real shiner. You're next."

Frank saluted her smartly and took Tom's place. Alexis and Landis nursed them all until she was satisfied they retained some resemblance to their former selves.

When she was finished she smiled at them. "And to think you are supposed to be guarding me. I'd have the lot of you keelhauled!'' The laughter in her eyes belied the seriousness of her tone.

"It'd be worth it," Forrest answered, "if you were around to take care of me afterward."

"You're impossible, you old goat!" she laughed, tossing a wet towel in his face. "All of you are just impossible!" They joined her laughter and when it subsided she shooed them out of the kitchen. "I'll wager you haven't had anything in your guts but ale, and I intend to remedy that. Forrest, you go with the others. I'll cook myself. These men have suffered enough for one day."

The others gave Alexis a grateful look and pulled the blustering cook down the hallway before he could protest. She could hear his grumbling and the good-natured taunts of the rest of the men as they seated themselves in the drawing room.

Later they ate in Cloud's spacious dining room and the men insisted Alexis preside at the head of the table. Their talk was light and friendly as they embellished the actions of their fight. Alexis listened intently, trying to discern the reason for their violence. She remained in the dark until Mike, feeling the effects of the wine served with dinner on top of the ale he had drunk earlier, accidentally blurted out, "And when he called her the captain's whore, I couldn't . . ."

His voice drifted off into silence, broken by the sound of Alexis's fork clattering to her plate. Mike sobered instantly and looked around the table for support. The others glared murderously at him, leaving him to smooth the incident over. He watched Alexis pick up her fork and place it beside her plate, never lifting her eyes.

"I'm sorry, Alex. I didn't mean . . ." He faltered, not knowing exactly what he wanted to say. He was relieved when she rescued him.

"Don't apologize, Mike," she said evenly, folding her hands in her lap. "You did nothing but repeat what you heard." She paused, gathering her strength. "So you fought for the captain's whore. I suppose I should be grateful or at least flattered that you saw it as a reason for abusing yourselves, but I can't thank you for fighting something I should have faced alone."

Frank caught her eyes and held them. His boyish smile had faded, and he spoke earnestly. "We fought because we knew it wasn't true, Alex. And you're wrong about it being only your fight. We are powerless to do anything about your being a prisoner, but we could do something about how those men saw you. It was for ourselves that we fought, as well as for your name and the name of our captain. Our respect was on the line back there too. The men who saw you led away had no idea who you were. They thought we had wasted our time, not sighting any British ships, refusing to do battle. They did not realize we had finished one of the most valuable missions of the war, and no matter how we hate our assignment, we all retain some pride that the woman in question is Captain Alex Danty. They still know nothing about you, except that you are certainly no whore."

"Thank you, Frank. I thank all of you for understanding that," she said quietly. She brightened, dismissing the last of the pain she associated with being named a whore. "I still think I'd have the lot of you tied to yardarms!"

The tension broken, they finished their meal and Alexis listened with interest to the news they had obtained concerning the war.

After dinner she retired to the drawing room as the men flipped coins for the chore of doing the dishes. They were still haggling when she heard Cloud enter the house. He did not see her in the room as he passed, heading straight for the sound of confusion in the kitchen.

"What's all this?" he demanded, looking at the men jammed into his kitchen. "And where is Alex?" He took a second glance at their faces and continued, his displeasure obvious. "And what the hell happened to the lot of you?"

Landis explained. "We are in the process of finding someone to do mess duty since Alex prepared our dinner. She is in the drawing room, taking a moment of well-deserved rest, and what happened to the men is a fight after we left them this morning."

"Thank you for that very concise report," Cloud said without humor. "Frank and Tom can do the dishes. Forrest, you can get me something to eat. We'll leave Alex to her rest, and, Mike, perhaps you can explain the reason for the brawl since you seem to have the largest bruises."

Mike was ready to begin when Alexis's voice stopped him. She passed Cloud at the entrance to the kitchen and said, looking at everyone but him, "There was a disagreement between your crew and the seamen on the dock as to the nature of my presence on board the *Concord*. Your men settled it admirably. There is nothing more to it than that."

Cloud looked from one man to the other, waiting to see if they would add anything to Alexis's explanation. They were silent. Finally he said, "Forrest, bring my dinner to the study. And some wine for Alex. She will be with me." He took Alexis's arm, gripping it more tightly than he had intended and led her to the study. He shut the door, roughly, behind him and when he faced her his eyes were hard, relentless in their gaze, and his mouth was pulled in a grim line.

"And the nature of your presence as those seamen saw it?" he asked as though no time had elapsed between her last words and the ones he was saying now.

She pulled free of his grip, stepping backward. "Cloud," she said softly. "Don't be angry with any of them. What else could those men think, other than I was someone's whore?" She saw the anger in his green eyes replaced with terrible hurt, and she knew he suffered as much at those words as she. She held her hand to his cheek, meeting his steady gaze. "I am at least glad they saw fit to name me *your* whore."

He clasped her wrist, placing the palm of her hand against his lips, then drew her close, wrapping his arms around her, as if to protect her. "I never wanted those words applied to you," he whispered into her ear. "Never." His lips brushed her forehead and her cheek before they covered her mouth.

It was a tender, gentle contact, and it made both of them

ache with desires too long denied. Alexis felt her legs weaken as Cloud's teeth tugged lightly on her lower lip, tasting her sweetness, savoring it, drawing her strength. She held on to his upper arms for support, but when the taut muscles offered no purchase she slid her hands over his shoulders, leaning her body into his, and clung to him as if he were her bastion. Cloud groaned softly into Alexis's mouth when he felt her breasts swell and brush his chest. It was sweet torture to have them pressed against him, offering more proof of her need. In return his hands slipped to her buttocks, cupped them, and pulled her tight against his thighs. This time he swallowed her desperate moan.

There was a moment of surrender for each of them in the kiss, a moment when neither was strong enough to pull away, even though both knew where the kiss would lead. At that time Alexis did not care if she ever saw Travers again and Cloud did not care about the method he was using to make Alexis join him. But it was only an instant, and for each of them their goal prevailed. Slowly they parted. Cloud leaned heavily against the door while Alexis placed a physical distance between them, one she emphasized with words she had spoken before.

"I cannot be yours again, Cloud. Not until this thing is done."

"I know that," he answered quietly. He reached for her face and brushed aside an errant lock of hair. His caress was given sound by the gentle sigh that escaped her parted lips. "I want you so much," he added in response to her quickened breathing. "So much."

"Stop, Cloud. Don't say anything else! If you really love me, please stop!" she pleaded, admitting how vulnerable she was to giving up everything but him.

He nodded and walked past her, careful not to brush against her, knowing it would only take one small contact with her flesh to make him cast aside her pleas.

"How did your meeting go"—she hesitated—"Captain?"

She took a seat in a chair opposite the couch he was now reclining on.

"Not as well as I hoped," he admitted, staring at the ceiling. He crossed his hands behind his head and lazily lifted one leg over the back of the sofa.

"Not as well in what way?" Alexis leaned forward in her chair.

"The senator and I did not agree on a few points."

"Concerning me?" Her voice was almost inaudible.

"Of course concerning you," he replied curtly, then regretted it when he looked over and saw Alexis's disturbed frown. "I have no other reason to see Howe except where you are concerned."

"I do not need a champion," she answered emphatically.

"What makes you think I took your side?"

"I only thought . . ." She stopped. She did not know what she thought.

He sat up suddenly, his face hard and unyielding as he spoke swiftly to cut through any illusions she had. "Perhaps I had better clear up any doubts you may be harboring, Alex. I want you. I love you. Don't you dare frown. You know it as well as I, perhaps better. But right now, with my country at war, I also want you just as all the others do. I have told you before your assistance could make a difference for us and I meant it. The knowledge you have gleaned after almost two years of fighting alone is knowledge many of our commanders have learned only after years of service. You would be an asset to our cause, which I must add, is not simply our indignation at the British removing men from our ships and impressing them. It is also our indignation over the Orders in Council which substitute favoritism for skill by letting some shipping firms through blockades and denying that right to others. Neither France nor England recognize our position of neutrality in their war and Yankee traders fall prey to privateers on both sides. England presumes it has the sole rights to free trade on the Atlantic. If the outcome of this war is in our favor, I will be a richer man than before, because it will free

Garnet Shipping to pursue ports all over the world without
the threat of British interference. I am in this war to protect
what I own and see that it prospers. Do you understand what
the United States has to gain or lose depending on the outcome? Do you see what you have to gain?"

Alexis said nothing. She was not thinking only of Quinton
Shipping, which would become more prosperous because of
the increased competition she intended to beat. She was not
thinking only of the people who would have a better life on
Tortola as a result of her success. She was staring at Cloud,
thinking that her cooperation could gain her what she wanted
most: the man who was presently searching her face, waiting
for an answer.

"I see," she said, not taking her eyes from him.

Cloud nodded. There was a long silence, a pause of painful
understanding. Cloud lay back on the couch and asked, almost
rhetorically, "Alex, if the President were to present the facts
to you as I just did, and ask for your assistance, what would
your answer be?"

"Mr. Madison cannot do that."

His eyebrows furrowed. "Why not?"

"I was brought here by force, Captain. You well remember
the threat you used against me. I expect it will be used again
in an attempt to make me comply with your President's wishes.
Of my own free will I would have joined your struggle and
made it my own. The battle would have been worth the risk.
But I would have joined you only after finishing what I set
out to do. I would have completed my goal first, then I would
have fought for your country. Don't you remember? It was
the United States I tried to reach when I was thirteen. I would
not turn my back on the kind of life I expected to find here."

"And you don't think it is here now?"

Alexis looked around the room, seeing four walls closing
in on her. "Where is my liberty, Captain? Where is my right
to make a decision freely, without the threat of imprisonment?
Your President has not offered me that."

"And if he could?"

"He would have to allow me to seek Travers first; then I would assist you of my own volition, just as I would have if you had never brought me here."

Cloud was ready to tell her this was precisely what he had told Howe, but a knock at the door interrupted him. Forrest entered with a tray of food and wine. After the cook left Cloud sensed the opportunity to explain his position had left with him. Between bites he answered Alexis's questions about the house, thanking her for working so hard to make it presentable again.

"Do you own a home in Boston as well?" she asked, placing her glass carefully on the polished table at her side.

"No, I stay with Emma and Blake when I visit. They live where my parents lived, in the house I grew up in."

"But when you eventually settle in Boston, would you give up this house?"

"How did you know I plan to live in Boston?"

Alexis smiled. "Because of the way you spoke of Garnet Shipping a while ago. You have no intentions of giving it up forever, if indeed, you ever gave it up at all. You could not run the line from Washington."

Cloud laughed. "When I talked to Emma last she told me Quinton Shipping was cutting into our business. I did not tell her, but I knew for a fact, the owner was rarely around to see to the business personally."

Alexis's smile grew wider at the compliment. "I have some very good help and some from quarters I did not desire."

Cloud frowned at the offhand reference to Lafitte. "Let's not talk of Lafitte," he said, pushing his tray aside.

"Why do you react that way when I mention him? He gave me assistance when I needed it. Surely you must realize I did not ask him to let my ships pass unharmed. He chose to do that on his own and I am not sure I understand his reasoning."

"Whatever his reasons, he will reap the rewards."

"What does that mean? I don't understand."

"You will soon," he answered quietly. "You will soon enough." He had less doubt than ever that she would not betray the man who allowed her business to prosper and who gave her her liberty when it was denied by himself and the country whose basis for existence was that very word.

"You never answered my question," Alexis said suddenly.

"Which one?"

"The only one I can hope to get an answer to it seems. About living in Boston."

He grinned. "I would live there. I would give up this house without a moment's hesitation."

"Then why do you have it? You don't spend much time here."

"I keep it because I want a place I can come to and know it is my own. It is infinitely more satisfying than staying in hotels or boardinghouses, waiting for a new assignment. Even the most seasoned veteran of the sea longs for a place where the floor doesn't constantly move under his feet. What about you? Don't you feel that way?"

Alexis lowered her eyes, remembering the home she had on the island, the rainbow colors, the freshness. Without Francine and George it meant nothing to her.

Cloud was on his feet immediately. He drew her from the chair and gently forced her chin upward. "Alex, I'm sorry," he started, feeling words were inadequate to erase the torment in her eyes. "I hoped you'd never see your home again. At least never alone."

"I wanted to go see it," she replied, removing his hand from her face.

"You shouldn't have."

"But I had to. I could never live in that house again. But I did have to see it and seal my pact with the man who was responsible for the loss of my family."

He wanted to hold her close and allow her to cry in his arms as he imagined she must have cried when she saw the empty house. She seemed fragile suddenly, not at all like the infamous pirate the rumors made her out to be. Her lips were trembling and her body responded with a small shudder. Her eyes alone told him this was not the time to pull her slender

figure against him. They were shining with the same light h
had witnessed as she stood on the hill and made her oath
These amber eyes spoke of her strength and not of her wea
ness. She needed nothing from him she could not find withi
herself, and that knowledge made him desire her all the mor

"It's late," he said, when there was nothing in the way
a reply he could offer. "Have you chosen a room?"

"Yes. If you'll excuse me, I will go up now." She permitte
Cloud to hold her arm and lead her to the stairs. She calle
good night to the other men and they answered her in tur
She was almost to the top of the stairs when she heard Cloud
rich voice bid her good night. She smiled, not looking bac
and continued to her room.

Chapter Twelve

Breakfast the following morning was a raucous affair. Cloud, Alexis, Landis, and Harry, enjoyed themselves at the expense of the men who had imbibed too heavily the day before. Alexis could not help laughing at their stifled groans as pots and pans clattered about the kitchen.

Because she had given her word she would meet with the President before attempting another escape, most of the men were relieved of their duty at the house. They were told what to do Thursday evening, but Alexis knew none of it. Cloud avoided answering her questions about when she would meet the President, purposely withholding the information in order to make escape more difficult for her.

The evening meal passed quietly, with most of the men gone. Only Landis, Harry, and Mike remained. Alexis took over Forrest's position in his absence, eager for the opportunity to do something. During dinner as well as afterward she paid little attention to the discussions at hand. She continued to search for ways to leave Washington, a task made extremely difficult by Cloud's refusal to let her out, even under escort. She thought often of her crew and of whether they would

really obey her orders to stay away. She relied on their good
sense to prevail and decided her only chance lay in getting
on board some other ship near Washington. It all came down
to finding a way to get to the harbor again.

When she glanced up she caught Cloud looking at her,
smiling as if he knew what she had been thinking. "There
must be a way," she answered his smile.

Cloud laughed, ignoring the puzzled stares of the others
who had not realized Alexis's silence meant she was plotting
some new plan.

His laugh was comment enough for her. It was a sign of
his encouragement to keep trying. When she lay in bed that
night, hugging his shirt close to her body, she was still tossing
alternatives in her head.

On Wednesday evening Cloud and Alexis sat alone in the
study. She was sitting cross-legged on the floor at his feet, a
book resting in the crook of her legs. She held her head in
her hands, elbows propped on her knees, oblivious to his
presence in the room as she read. He thought perhaps she
was oblivious to the room. It was only a temporary escape, he
realized, for when she shut the book she would find herself
in the same predicament as before.

"Amusing?" Cloud asked in response to her laughter.

"Infinitely. *Romeo and Juliet,*" she said brightly, shutting the
book of plays and confronting the reality before her.

"Strange. I read that. I don't remember it being at all
amusing."

"That's because you weren't thinking how nice it would
be to have a potion that would permit you to appear dead.
It occurred to me how it would help me get away and solve
all my problems."

"I will have to keep you away from books if those are the
ideas you're getting." Cloud gently ran his fingers through
the curls that lay across her back. He pulled his hand away
when he felt her shiver. "There's something you have to
know, Alex," he stated emotionlessly, as if he were about to
tell her tomorrow's tide table. When she turned to face him

he went on. "You are going to meet Mr. Madison tomorrow evening."

Alexis nodded, unsure of her own feelings at hearing his words. Part of her was glad the wait would be over and rose to meet the challenge, while another part recognized this challenge could be the one to defeat her.

"You and I have been invited to dinner at Robert Davidson's home." He saw her bristle as he knew she would and he continued quickly. "Senator Howe, Bennet Farthington, and Richard Granger will also be there. They will want to discuss your help after dinner."

"I hope they don't expect me to feel gratitude after offering me a meal," she said angrily. "I suppose I am to think of myself as a guest. I would rather—"

"You don't have to tell me, Alex," he interrupted. "I recall telling you the senator and I disagreed over a few points and tomorrow's dinner was one of them."

"Why do you understand so well, and they not at all?" she asked hopelessly.

"They are merely conducting politics as they think it should be conducted. A meal and a few glasses of wine have obviously induced cooperation before."

"Force, to a hungry man."

"I suppose, though I doubt they see it that way."

Alexis got to her feet, book in hand and crossed the room. She placed the volume back in its position and turned to Cloud slowly, thoughtfully. "You said something to me the other day," she said. "It has not been out of my mind long. It was in reference to Lafitte. You said—"

"I said: 'whatever the reasons, he will reap the rewards.' Is that what you were referring to?"

"Yes, that's right. I want to know now if he has something to do with tomorrow's meeting." She dreaded the answer she was prepared to hear. She braced herself against the bookshelves, feeling the hard slats at intervals across her flesh.

"He has a great deal to do with it," Cloud said, watching his words take their toll. Her mouth sagged slightly, emitting a short gasp, and she closed her eyes briefly as if she were trying not to see fully what she knew she had to.

"Why didn't you tell me this before?"

"I had not planned to tell you at all. I hoped to persuade the senator to see things differently. I haven't given up entirely.'"

Alexis heard the statement but none of the hope he spoke about was evident in his tone. "What is it they expect?"

"For you to convince Lafitte to come to Washington and offer his help in the Caribbean, guarding New Orleans."

"I can't do that! Not to him! Not after everything he's done for me!"

"Now do you understand what I said about him reaping the rewards?"

Alexis nodded. "But that's only a part of it, Cloud. Don't the President and the others realize Lafitte will help them when it benefits him to do so? He has nothing to gain by British involvement in New Orleans. I know he would offer his help. I know it! But not if they use the same tactics they used on me. He would laugh at a show of force. No pardon would mean anything to him at the price of the freedom he now enjoys." She caught her breath and walked over to Cloud. Kneeling on the cushion beside him, she took his hand and held it to her face. "I can't say yes to all that, Cloud. There is nothing that will make me seek Lafitte for them."

"Are you still willing to meet with them tomorrow?" he asked, pulling her across his lap and laying her head on his chest.

"Do I have a choice?" she said spitefully.

"Only the one that has been open to you from the beginning. You could try to get away." His breath forced wisps of golden tendrils to fly across her lowered face. He brushed them aside with the tips of his fingers, pausing when he felt wetness on her cheeks. He said nothing, but he knew she was thinking the man who professed to love her so dearly would do everything in his power to prevent her from realizing that choice.

After a long silence Alexis lifted her head, making no

attempt to hide her tears or her anxieties from him. "I will meet with them tomorrow. Only to be with you a few hours longer. After I give them my refusal I don't suppose they'll allow me to stay here."

"No, I don't suppose they will." Cloud rested his chin on her head, stroking her hair gently. When her even breathing confirmed she was sleeping, he took her to her room and placed her in bed. Assured she was resting comfortably he returned to the study, wondering if he had been right to prepare her for what was most likely to take place.

It was late morning when Alexis woke. When she went downstairs she found Landis sitting alone in the kitchen, his feet propped on a chair he had pulled close to him. He was lost in thought, sipping from a cup of coffee, and did not seem to notice her entrance.

"Where are the others?" she asked, after observing him for some time.

Landis tipped his cup slightly at the sound of her voice, pouring the dark liquid over his fingers. He wiped them off on his trousers; then he put down his mug and looked up at her. "The captain's gone to town, and Harry and Mike were sent back to the *Concord* for word of any . . ." His voice dropped off.

"Word of what?"

Landis shrugged. "You probably suspected. Word of any of your ships. The captain is still expecting your crew to show up."

"Do you think they will come?"

"I can't give up hoping—as well as dreading—they will." He rose, offering her a chair, and set about making a cup of coffee for her. "Are you familiar with the legend of King Arthur?"

Alexis laughed. "Wot English lass ain't, Oi'd loike ta know? Really, John. Is that where your mind was when I came in?

Medieval fairy tales?'' She paused, thinking over the legend. "Oh, I see. It's an interesting comparison."

"Then you know to what I refer."

"I gather you mean the part of the tale when Lady Guinevere was sentenced to death by King Arthur. He hoped her lover, Sir Lancelot, would rescue her even though he knew he would have to do battle with his finest liege afterward."

"Yes, that's it."

"I wish you wouldn't make comparisons with myths that have such horrible endings," she said, frowning. "Arthur and Lancelot were both killed on a battlefield outside of Camelot. That is not what I want for the *Concord* and my ship, which is precisely why I ordered my crew to stay away. And as for me being Lady Guinevere—well, the idea does not set well with me."

"Why not? You could join a convent, as she did, when everything was lost to her."

They both laughed at their foolishness.

"That would indeed be a prison for me, John." She fell silent, reflecting she might have no choice but to accept prison. She would not cooperate with the demands placed on her. "There is a way out of the legend," she said slyly, peering over the rim of her mug. "You could always give me a plan for escape." She leaned back in her chair, closing her eyes when he just stared at her blankly. "It's all right, John. I didn't expect an answer. I keep forgetting you are one of Arthur's men."

"To the last," he said quietly, solemnly.

Alexis stood over him and dropped a light kiss on his forehead. "I'm glad."

Discussion ended, she prepared herself a light breakfast while Landis amused her with stories bearing no relationship to their present problem.

After the meal she retired to the study. It was some hours later that Cloud found her curled on the window seat, face pressed against a pane of glass, looking at some vision only she could see.

He stared at her for several minutes, etching this particular moment deep within him. He memorized the tilt of her head, the lift of her shoulders, her slim fingers as they drummed lightly on the sill, providing the only sound in the room. That sound seemed to pound mercilessly in his head until he realized it was not her fingers he heard, but the beat of his heart, in perfect time to the rhythm she created. He knew a moment of some fear, thinking if she ceased her gentle tapping his heart would also stop. He spoke to break the power she held over him in that moment.

"Good afternoon, Alex."

"Oh!" Her fingers stopped and she drew away from the window. "I didn't know you had returned. Good afternoon."

He walked toward her and kissed the top of her head. He sat down on the seat beside her. "I didn't expect to find you here."

"I said I would stay."

"I meant I did not expect to find you in this room. I thought you would be in your room, preparing for this evening."

"There is time," she said carelessly. "I am not especially anxious for the day to hurry on."

"Have you thought of what you would wear tonight?" He knew her answer but he wanted to hear her say it. He enjoyed hearing words from her lips that would come from no other woman.

"I haven't thought about it at all. But now that you bring it up, I don't give a damn what I wear."

Cloud laughed amiably at her fierceness. "That is why I have taken care of the details for you, unless you prefer to attend in your trousers and boots."

"Would that be so terrible? To give them the hardened Captain Danty they expect?"

"No, but you would be giving them something that doesn't really exist. Captain Danty is not a woman taking refuge in men's clothing. She is a woman using them to merely suit her purpose, isn't she?"

"You know that better than anyone," she said quietly. She

lowered her eyes to hide the longing she felt for him. She spoke then, not to him, but to herself. "And my purpose tonight?" Neither answered, both knowing her purpose: escape. She looked up to see a small smile forming on his lips. His smile offered a partial reality to her hope. It said she could try to do it. "May I see what manner of clothing you think will serve my purpose this evening?"

"Later. Don't worry, it's not sackcloth and ashes. I won't have them feeling sorry for you." His green eyes hardened for an instant. When the hardness vanished Alexis felt the skin of her wrists tightening around her bones. She looked down and saw his hands gripping her firmly. "Alex, whatever purpose you put the gown to tonight, you must remember I will be the one to recognize it. I will be the one to stop you."

"Who are you trying to convince, Cloud?"

He dropped his hold abruptly, realizing he was speaking aloud the doubts he had from the beginning concerning his ability to keep her.

Alexis slid closer to him. "Hold me now. Yes, your arms around me. I want to feel your strength." She pressed her mouth to his neck. *And no matter what happens, I will still love you.* It was sometime later when she realized she had not actually said those last words, that they were only a thought as she held her lips against his warm flesh. But he responded to the thought as if he had heard it. He gathered her close, eyes closed, mouth buried in soft strands of yellow hair, silently acknowledging himself as both her jailer and prisoner.

A soft but insistent tapping at the door acted like a wedge between them, driving them apart. Reluctantly they separated and Cloud walked to the study entrance.

"What is it?" he called through the door.

Landis answered. "Alexis's bath is ready, Tanner. It's late. You both should be preparing to go."

"All right. I'll send her on her way." He turned to Alexis. "You heard him. It's time to get ready."

"My clothes?" she asked, standing.

"John will have already laid everything out for you."

She nodded and walked to the door. Her hand lingered on the handle, as if she were fighting a desire to remain. He saw her draw in her breath. It was this action, rather than her hand on the knob, that seemed to open the door.

Alexis quickly went up the stairs. When she reached her room she discovered it took no effort at all to open the door. Her eyes went first to the steaming tub of water, then to the fresh towels placed on the floor at the tub's side. Her glance continued to her bed. The object she saw lying there made her gasp. She approached the gown slowly, as though her movement might cause it to float away. She reached down to touch the airy folds of blue, then stopped, touching the filmy undergarments instead. They would seem real beneath her fingers. She thought the sky blue gown would not.

She undressed, folding her clothes neatly to prolong the anticipation of putting on the gown. She stepped into the tub, unaware it was still too hot to be comfortable. She washed herself lazily, never taking her eyes from the azure confection on her bed.

What had he thought when he bought it? she wondered. She touched her face with water to erase the smile that came to her lips. He had thought of no one but himself. The notion pleased her. He had known how she would look in that gown and the fact that he knew made her shiver helplessly.

What would the others see? Would they see Captain Danty? Could they be misled by the appearance of her in a film of blue? If there was another purpose to the dress besides Cloud's pleasure, it was deception. How the deception would take form she wasn't sure. She only knew the gown could be used as a weapon, possibly more dangerous than if she had carried her dagger. She would know how to wield that weapon when the time came.

She rose from the tub and dried herself briskly. She slipped on the undergarments, taking care not to disturb the gown. Sitting in front of the mirror, she arranged her hair, requiring a long time to complete a task that was new to her. Finally she was satisfied. She shook her head to make sure every curl stayed where she had positioned it.

In the mirror she caught sight of the gown behind her and she could not put off wearing it a moment longer. Cloud would be coming for her soon. She knew what he wanted to see.

She stepped into the blue slippers before she gently lifted the gown and slid it over her head. It seemed to her the dress required no further assistance from the hands as it floated over her form, hugging her breasts, but only caressing her hips and thighs.

She stood, facing the door, waiting for him to come. She never glanced at the mirror. Her mirror would walk into the room and she would see herself reflected more vibrantly in sea green eyes than in the finest glass.

She forgot, until she saw him standing before her, that her own eyes and face were also a mirror. She took in the hard, minimal leanness of his body accentuated by his dark blue trousers and high, glossy boots. His chest was hidden by white, starched ruffles, fresh and crisp. His jacket, the same dark color as his trousers, emphasized the firmness of his shoulders and arms. But what caught her attention and held it was the gold braid. It was meant to outline his jacket and declare his rank, but she could only think it outlined the man, surrounding him with a golden light.

She started to cross the distance between them but he stopped her with a glance that told her he had not completed his silent critique. She remained motionless, her arms at her side, while she watched his eyes remove every piece of clothing she had just put on.

Cloud, when he entered her room, knew only that his mind had conjured up an image once more. It took him several moments to realize this was not a vision he was seeing, but reality. He saw in her all the things that made her Captain Danty: the firm tilt of her chin, raised slightly under his scrutiny; the tautness of her smooth arms, even while they seemed to hang freely at her sides; eyes, bright with determination.

Her feet were planted some distance apart and he saw the legs that made it possible for her to stand firmly on a pitching deck.

He smiled. When she approached him he stopped her because he wanted to look at her again and know how the others would see her. This time he saw the tilt of her chin not as defiance, but as a beckoning call. Her arms were no longer taut, but soft, pliant flesh with no purpose except to encircle a man. The amber eyes he had first seen as determined now seemed openly hungry to him, and he was no longer aware of her legs, only the interval between them.

He felt as if two unseen hands were twisting his gut. He would be the only man tonight to know her as Captain Danty. In the blue haze that enveloped her slender body they would see only feminine purpose. If she had gone in black, her blood red sash around her waist, they would have seen only the pirate, never suspecting the woman. But he knew both, and his two visions melted into one as he stepped forward and took her hand, placing his lips in her palm.

"You are very beautiful. Both of you," he added in a whisper.

Alexis withdrew her hand. "How will you address me this evening?" she asked, the hand holding his kiss closed tightly at her side.

"As Captain Danty."

"Good." She started to go but something held her back. There seemed to be some hesitation on his part. "Is there something wrong?"

He reached inside his jacket and withdrew the velvet case. "I brought you something else to wear tonight. After I purchased it, I realized that the decision to wear it is yours alone." Offering no more explanation he handed her the case.

Now Alexis hesitated. She looked to him for a sign that she should either open it or set it aside. When he said nothing, she opened it. Her lips parted in surprise and she drew in her breath. She traced the slender line of the silver chain with her finger. She looked up at him.

"And I thought the shirt made me yours." She gave him the necklace and turned her back to him. She felt a tightening in her chest as he brought it around her throat. She could see their figures reflected in the mirror across the room but she was only conscious of a bright silver flash at her neck and the hands that fastened it. His hands dropped to her waist.

She spoke to his image in the mirror. "Why did you think I would not wear it?"

"I didn't know that you wouldn't." He stared at the slender linkage which held her immobile. "I only knew that I could not force you if you chose not to."

She turned to him, her hand went to her throat. "I have been wearing this chain long before you understood it existed."

He nodded, knowing it was true. "I also know it will not stop you from doing what you have to do."

Bright tears formed in her eyes. "You have just set me free."

"Have I really?"

Then Alexis knew his admission of her right to be free had bound her more surely to him than the circle of his arms around her waist or his lips in her hair. But to be with him later meant leaving him now. It was this she found so difficult to accept.

He pulled away from her, sensing her torment. After he brushed aside her tears he led her downstairs.

Harry and Mike watched Alexis descend the steps with a reverent gaze. They looked to Landis, who had once described her as an avenging angel, and thought they would never doubt anything the man had to say. Landis was smiling, recalling the young woman with angry eyes and fierce promises. If he could have dressed her then he would have chosen no differently than his captain did now.

The three men stood silent, taking great pride in knowing the woman was Captain Alex Danty.

"Captain Danty, you're lovely." It was Harry Young who

found his voice first. He spoke as if he had never been more sure of anything in his life.

"Thank you, Harry." Only Cloud knew she was thanking him for calling her Captain.

"Your carriage is outside, sir," Mike said when he could think of nothing to add to Harry's statement. He saw the slim hand that gripped the banister and he remembered the time he had taught that hand to grip a pistol. It did not seem incongruous to him now that the hand should be part of the woman who stood before him. He would not have understood how anyone could look at that hand and not also see a weapon or the wheel of a ship as a natural extension of it.

Landis followed them out to the carriage and helped Alexis in. When Cloud was ready to snap the reins, Landis turned to Alexis suddenly and asked, "Lady Guinevere?"

"Never!" Before she could say any more Cloud had started the horses and Landis was left behind, with the memory of her earnest expression as she had answered him.

"What was he talking about?" asked Cloud.

"He has some notion about me shaving my head to join a convent," she replied. "Never mind." Laughing, she slipped her arm through his.

Alexis held Cloud's elbow firmly as they were led by Davidson's butler to the drawing room. On the threshold she dropped her hand, smiling grimly at him. When the door was opened and they were announced to the four men inside, her mien was gracious, suggesting the honor was hers.

Cloud observed the astonished faces of the men and knew immediately why Alexis had responded as she did. Not one of these men believed the woman he had brought to them was Captain Alex Danty. Very well, he thought, it has begun.

Robert Davidson was the first to recover from the vision Alexis presented in the doorway of his drawing room. He crossed the room and took her hand, kissing it lightly.

"It is a pleasure to have you here, aah, Miss Danty," he said as she withdrew her hand.

"But how could I resist such an invitation as the one you sent?" she asked. Only Cloud heard the steely edge in her voice. "You went to a great deal of trouble to secure your pleasure."

Davidson smiled uncomfortably and introduced the others. Alexis greeted them all warmly, observing Richard Granger's nervous, darting eyes; Senator Howe's cold, appraising stare; Bennet Farthington's flirtatious, almost hungry gaze. It was Bennet, handsome, well built, and obviously envious of Cloud, that she singled out to proceed with the deception.

"Gentlemen," she said, standing beside Bennet, brushing his tailored smoke gray trousers with the azure folds of her gown. "I believe someone is missing. I was told the President wished to meet me."

Howe smiled soothingly. "The President has just informed us he cannot attend. You just missed his messenger."

An alarm, faint in sound and brief in duration, went off in Cloud's head. He was hardly aware of its existence before it was gone and the senator was continuing his explanation.

"He has given us authority to present his views in his absence, Miss Danty. Rest assured, we will be speaking for Mr. Madison."

Alexis nodded, making a small *moue*. She glanced covertly at Cloud and her eyes seemed to say: this changes everything.

"Let us not discuss business before dinner," said Bennet offering Alexis his arm. "I believe dinner will be the perfect occasion to determine the answer to the question which is plaguing all of us." He had to say no more. They all wanted to put aside their purpose until they were satisfied as to the woman's identity.

Alexis was beginning to enjoy this situation immensely. Her rather confused smile convinced the others she understood none of what was said. Davidson led them into the large dining room. Bennet held out a chair for Alexis, then took a place beside her. Across from her Cloud observed her game with wry amusement as she flirted mercilessly with the others. He had only seen this side of her once, briefly, when he had first known her, and he had punished her for it. The coy coquette had returned. She even appeared to have won the senator over with her light, innocuous conversation. After dinner, while the table was being cleared by the servants, Alexis rose from her chair and walked to the large bay window at the end of the dining room. Cloud saw her tense stance as she stared out the window.

Alexis sighed. How could they doubt who she was? How could they doubt Cloud? Nothing she had said or done this evening should have mattered if they trusted the man who was sent to bring her. She knew then that what she was prepared to do was as much for him as it was for her. Both their prides demanded appeasement.

Bennet went to stand beside Alexis. Over the voices surrounding him Cloud strained to hear her conversation with the aide to the Secretary of War.

"It's a lovely garden, isn't it?" he asked, following her gaze.

"Why, yes it is."

Cloud smiled at the brief pause she took before she answered. He knew she had not been looking at the garden, but the distance to it. She was seeing a path of escape, not a path of brightly colored flowers in the last of the evening light. He noticed, as he was sure she did, the window was bolted shut. He breathed easier. The terrace beyond was out of her reach. When she faced the room again he saw her looking for other exits, all the while carrying on a harmless discussion with Bennet.

Ashtrays were being placed on the table when Farthington escorted Alexis back to a chair. Cloud noticed she had asked Bennet for the seat closest to the window and furthest from him. He looked at the bolt again and saw she had not tampered with it.

Those present seated themselves once more, each with a glass of wine except for Cloud and Alexis. Davidson reached for a box of cheroots. He hesitated when he saw Alexis wrinkle her nose slightly.

"Do you mind if we smoke, Miss Danty?"

"Not at all, if someone would be kind enough to open the window." The senator moved to gallantly comply with her request.

Cloud shifted uneasily as Howe slid the catch and swung the windows wide, creating an unobstructed entrance to the terrace and the lawn beyond. Soft August breezes filled the room. The scent of flowers from the garden smelled like freedom to Alexis and she inhaled deeply. The same scent smelled of danger to Cloud and he could scarcely breathe at all. Then the fragrance was all but obliterated by the overpowering cigar smoke.

"Miss Danty," Howe said pleasantly when he was seated again. "Before we can proceed we need to establish you are who Captain Cloud claims you to be. I am sure you must realize how difficult it is for us to imagine you as the captain described you to us. He mentioned your beauty, of course, but he hardly described you as you are now."

Alexis nodded and waited for Cloud to answer this blow to his credibility.

"She is Captain Danty, Senator. Why do you think otherwise?" Cloud's easy answer mocked the tension in his every muscle.

"I know you were against this from the beginning, Captain. You also told me of an attempted escape. Perhaps you let the real Captain Danty go free and substituted her with this woman."

"Ask her yourself."

Howe leaned forward in his chair, folding his arms on the table and addressed Alexis. "Are you Captain Danty?"

"Yes."

"Can you prove that to us?"

"What manner of proof do you require, Senator?" Her voice was laced with derision but Howe was oblivious to it.

"Tell us something of your background," Richard Granger suggested.

Mechanically, as if she were reciting memorized material, Alexis told them of London and Tortola and her search for Travers. She described her escape from the *Hamilton* but made no mention of Lafitte. She told them of her imprisonment on board the *Concord*. At no time did she embellish the facts, instead she gave the information simply and honestly.

Cloud listened to her lifeless recital as he watched the faces of the others. She told them no lies and yet she said it in such a way that not one of them believed her. When she was finished he said, "I trust Captain Danty has satisfied you."

"On the contrary," Davidson answered, stubbing out his cheroot furiously. "She has told us nothing she could not have learned from you."

"I did not learn it from him," Alexis objected adamantly, too adamantly for them to believe her.

"What do you know of Lafitte?" asked the senator sharply.

Alexis's eyes grew wide. "Why, Lafitte is a pirate. He is very well known." Her expression and voice spoke of innocence and the others turned angrily on the captain they had trusted.

"Did you forget to tell this poor girl about Lafitte's part in her story, Captain?" Bennet sneered, placing a comforting hand on Alexis's bare arm. He had been right after all. Cloud could not bring in the real Captain Danty. The girl at his side, trembling beneath his hand, was far too naïve and lovely to take command of a ship, let alone make threats against a British commander. He had known it the moment he had seen her standing in the doorway emanating a warm elegance. What man would follow this woman anywhere but to bed?

Alexis turned her face away from Farthington, his thoughts so openly displayed in his eyes she could not bear to look at them. He interpreted her action as a demure invitation to carry out his thoughts.

Cloud smiled grimly. "I told her nothing. She is Alex Danty, Captain of the *Dark Lady*, the *Diamond Maria*, the *Ariel*, to name but a few of the titles she uses for her ship."

The words were barely out of his mouth before Alexis decided it was time to press her advantage. She covered her face with her hands to hide her disgust. What sounded like choked sobs to the others was in truth her bitter laughter.

"Don't blame Tanner!" she cried. "It is not his fault I could not remember everything!"

Cloud was prepared for her. Now that the lies were going to be told, she would be believed. They had asked for this. Silently he applauded her, wishing he could truly help her with what she was working toward. The most she would be able to have was a brief moment to secure credibility for her performance.

"Captain Danty, it won't work. I know what you are doing." He scowled at her but Alexis saw he was saying, "Naughty child."

"What I'm doing?" she asked shrilly, covering her laughter. Her body trembled with delight at this dangerous game and Cloud's half-hearted attempt to stop her. "What I am trying to do is save both our necks before this deceit goes on any longer!" Not a truer statement had been uttered all evening but its real meaning was lost on everyone but Cloud.

She stood, facing the four men who had arranged for her capture. She avoided Cloud but knew he was watching her more intently than any of the others.

"I must apologize, gentlemen," she said quietly, her voice tight. "It is not in my nature to lie. I have been part of a deception this evening and I had not the strength to escape it until now." She paused to see if any of them realized the deception was their manner of approaching her: the false charges, treating her as a guest. They did not. She began to cry, her sense of shame immense as she continued. "Tanner has known me for many years—please don't object, Tanner— I cannot bear it any longer. When he failed to hold Captain Danty aboard the *Concord* he came to me and asked for help. He thought I would serve because I have the same general coloring as the woman described to you. He requested I take her place at this dinner and do as you ask. After that it would be a simple matter to be lost at sea and you would never know you had the word of an imposter. I agreed because he is my dear friend, but I cannot stay here and listen to these accusations any longer."

She collapsed in her chair, wiping away her tears with the handkerchief Bennet offered. She was forgotten as outraged faces and angry voices turned on Cloud.

"Did you think you could get away with it?"

"How stupid did you expect us to be?"

"This is your commission!"

"No wonder you asked that Captain Danty not be asked to bring Lafitte!"

"Treason! A violation of your orders!"

Cloud scarcely knew who was saying what. He kept his eyes on his folded hands resting on the table. The men wanted no answers. They wanted proof, and out of the corner of his eye he saw Alexis stand and walk to the open window. How like her, he thought. She could walk out of this room, probably leading Bennet by the nose, and they would forgive her everything. But she wanted to give them the proof Howe had asked for when the meeting first began. Her pride demanded it. He heard her voice, clear and distinct above all the others. How could they not hear the commanding authority of her voice?

"Gentlemen! It is senseless to lay blame upon Captain Cloud. You asked the impossible of him. He could not hold Captain Danty any more than any of you could!" She measured her steps to the terrace, leaning against the frame of the window. "Senator Howe." She calculated the darkness beyond the well-lighted room and saw it would offer adequate protection. "I said I had been part of a deception"—she saw the street beyond beckoning her with comfortable shadows— "this evening and that I had not the strength to escape it. . . ." She looked at the curious faces turned in her direction. They were still drawn tight in anger at Cloud; then they sagged suddenly with compassion for her. She wanted to retch. "What

I should have said was that I was not given the opportunity until now!''

As she ended her statement her body shuddered with sudden power and in a single, fluid motion she leaped over the terrace rail. She felt the thrill of freedom and thought the sensation was brought to life by the sound of Cloud's laughter. She ran across the wide lawn, his laughter growing weaker, marking the distance she traveled from the oppressive house.

Cloud saw the coiled tightness of her muscles before she jumped. The sky blue gown seemed to lift her and aid her flight over the rail. He could imagine her running, graceful and purposeful. His first impulse was to go after her. Instead he forced himself to remain seated and let her have her brief victory. His laughter, however, was not forced. He thoroughly enjoyed the sight of the apoplectic faces turned in his direction.

''What the hell, Captain?'' Farthington's eyes flashed dangerously. ''Is she or isn't she Danty?''

''I have already answered that, Bennet. I believe she has proved it.'' He stopped laughing but his eyes continued to mock Farthington.

Bennet's jaw went slack, his face paled. He sank back in his chair, knowing he had been duped, a suspicion dawning on him that he had duped himself.

There was a murmur of disbelief around the table. Cloud heard the words but paid no attention. He stretched out in his chair, arms folded casually across his chest, long legs before him.

''She is quite a woman, Captain,'' said Howe. ''You warned us all but I had a hard time believing it until this moment.''

''How can you say that?'' Granger said, annoyed. ''She lied to us. Came in here like she was a queen instead of a common pirate in league with Lafitte. Her dress was just short of indecent!''

''She did not lie to you until the very end,'' Cloud said quietly. ''You made it impossible for her to continue with the truth. Captain Danty is no fool. She took the only opportunity she's had for days to escape. Right under all your noses."

"Under your nose too, Captain! If you knew what she was doing, you should have stopped her!" Davidson slammed his fist on the table to emphasize his point.

"I knew."

"And you let her go!"

"I did."

"Damn you, Captain! We want her back! Get her!"

"I already have." His words were greeted by stunned silence. He was the only one comfortable in it.

"What do you mean?" asked the senator.

"Just what I said. You will have Captain Danty back within the hour." He did not move. He made no attempt to leave his chair and carry out his statement. He made it seem as if he could bring her back by the sheer force of his will. The truth was harder for him. He wanted to run from the room, from the house, stop Alexis, stop his men, and send her out of Washington himself. He did not want to see her again in this room, with these men. He remained still and did nothing. It had already been done.

Farthington put down his cheroot and gulped his wine. "Captain, about your commission, I didn't realize. I will not say anything to Dr. Eustis."

"No, you won't."

"You say she'll be here within the hour?"

"Yes."

Bennet stared at Cloud, hating him for his self-assurance, his concise, arrogant responses, and for knowing all along what the bitch had been about. Bennet smiled tightly, dropping his eyelids slightly, regarding Cloud through a hooded gaze. The tables would be turned. When she returned the captain would find he had done his work too well.

"How can you be so sure?" asked Howe.

"I know my men." Cloud waited to be asked for more proof than this but the senator appeared satisfied. "While she is gone I would suggest you rethink your position concerning

Captain Danty. Because of your treatment of her this evening she will be harder to convince than before. It would be wise to end any notion you have about Lafitte.''

The four men said nothing. They sat in stony silence, furtively glancing at one another, committing themselves to their original purpose without one word passing between them.

Cloud walked to the window and stared out at the garden. *Don't let them catch you!* He turned suddenly to see if the others heard him; then he realized he had not said the words aloud.

When Alexis was several blocks away from Davidson's she paused for a moment to catch her breath and decide on the direction of the wharf. Then she moved swiftly, barely glancing at the shadowed faces of the people she passed. She listened for evidence of Cloud pursuing her, but he did not come. This she did not understand. She was sure he had known what she was planning to do, possibly before the idea had settled firmly in her own mind.

The evening had been worse than she'd expected. She looked down at her slippered feet and flowing gown as she ran. A soft shroud of blue. Was that all it took to hide the truth? How could they ever doubt Cloud? What was it about those men that made them suspicious of others?

Outrage spurred her on. She saw the harbor in the distance. She knew she would not take a Quinton vessel. She would wheedle, lie, beg, cajole to secure passage on any ship but one of her own. She would allow none of her merchants to take the risk of having her aboard.

She slowed her steps, forcing herself to be calm when she reached the waterfront. Then she stopped, held back by a force she could only identify as a tightening around her neck. Her hand went to the silver thread at her throat. She saw him; then she realized it was not actually Cloud she saw. She saw his men. It was the presence of his command that she sensed.

So this was why he hadn't followed. The thought made

her smile sardonically. Four crewmen from the *Concord* were approaching her slowly. Not as predators. Merely as four men who knew a lady and wanted to act as her escort.

She turned and ran. She heard their hurried footsteps mingled with her own light ones. She heard them plead with her to stop, to not make them run her down, but she was heedless of their entreaties. She ran harder, ignoring the searing pain in her legs and side, compelling herself to continue, to take one more step. The necklace seemed to cut off her breath and she wanted to tear it away. Instead she struggled harder to fill her lungs with air.

A heavy hand grasped her wrist and she started to fall. The hand shifted, catching her waist, preventing her downward motion.

"I'm sorry, Cap'n Danty," Tom drawled breathlessly.

Alexis looked up at his grim face. The pale moonlight gave it a grayish cast and his eyes were narrowed, his sadness evident in his tight, bitter smile. He dropped his arm from her waist.

"How did you know I would come here?" she asked when she caught her own breath. The other men surrounded her, but not closely. They were not happy to have found her.

"I didn't know. None of us did. Some are down by the *Concord,* others are stationed at different piers. You just happened to come down to ours."

It was obvious he wished she hadn't.

"Is Mr. Landis here?" She remembered the legend and suddenly it was important that he did not see her now.

"He is somewhere around. He wanted to stay at the house but the captain said it would be the last place you would go."

"Well, Captain Cloud was wrong. That is precisely where I want to go! Right now! Before you take me to him!"

"We can't, Captain Danty," one of the others objected. "We have orders to take you back to Davidson's immediately."

"Damn your captain and damn his orders! I want you to take me to his house—then I'll go with you!"

Tom shrugged. "What do you say, mates? It couldn't hurt. What do you want at the house, Captain?"

"You'll see," Alexis said bitingly. "You'll all see!"

Alexis broke through the circle of men and walked boldly toward Cloud's home. They followed her. They knew she would go with them when she had taken care of whatever was drawing her toward the house. Her face revealed only one emotion: anger. They could not know it was directed solely at the men arguing at that moment with Cloud.

Breathless, Alexis reached the front door. She twisted the knob and found it locked. "Find an open window!" she told them. "I want to get in there if I have to break the door down!"

Two of the men stayed with her while Tom and another walked around the building. They returned in a few minutes.

"Nothing open on the first floor, Captain Danty There is a window open in Landis's room, upstairs. The lattice might hold me," Tom suggested. "I don't want to break down the captain's door."

"Lead me to it, Tom. I'll climb the thing myself!"

"But your gown," he protested.

"Damn the gown! Damn the man who had me wear it! Show me that lattice!" She did not know her eyes were like bright sparklers or that her lips had formed a sneer. She only knew that whatever they saw in her face prompted them to action.

She followed Tom to the back of the house and tested the strength of the lattice. "It will hold me," she said certainly. She threw off her slippers. She put the hem of her gown in her teeth and began climbing, oblivious to the thorns and briars scratching her arms and legs. She imagined fleetingly she was on the rigging of her ship.

She slid into the opening headfirst. When she was on her feet she called down to the others, telling them to wait at the front door. She ignored their protests and demands for entry, leaving them gaping on the ground below.

She went to her room and began digging furiously through her clothes. She practically ripped the gown and undergarments from her body. She pulled on her black trousers and shirt, tied the crimson sash around her waist. After jerking on her high black boots she yanked the remaining pins from her hair, letting it fall to her waist. Viciously she tied her scarf over the top of her head and knotted it in the back, not bothering to take the time to hide her hair. She was almost out of the room when she stopped and turned back to look at the crumpled gown lying on the floor in a careless heap.

She walked back, slowly bending to pick it up. She smoothed out the folds and carefully placed it on the bed. *Don't damn the gown. Don't damn the man who gave it to her. Damn those who can't see beyond the gown or into the man. Damn them for not seeing the truth.*

She turned, running out of the room and down the stairs. She opened the door, propelling herself across the porch and down the steps. She knew the others were following her, but she did not acknowledge them. Her legs led her swiftly and surely to their destination.

Tom and the others had stared at her for a moment before finding their wits to follow. Seeing her now, in her midnight attire, they understood how she could evoke fear in an otherwise fearless man. They had never seen her dressed this way before. It was an outfit she only used against the enemy. They had imagined from the stories they heard what she would look like. They had not been able to imagine this.

She was incredibly feline, a stalking night creature. She did not appear to be walking; prowling was the word her movement suggested. When she glanced over her shoulder at them they saw brilliant yellow eyes catch the moon's light and shoot it in their direction. They were glad her fierceness was not aimed at them.

Tom escorted Alexis to the house. She permitted him at her side only to gain entry past the surprised butler. Tom stood at the entrance to the dining room, frowning at his captain while Alexis stared intently at the others with gold, angry eyes.

For the first time, Cloud saw Alexis as he imagined she must look boarding a British frigate. There was energy in every part of her body He realized with some shock that she was standing motionless. The energy was in her eyes and the faint tightening of her facial muscles as she worked her jaw. The black outfit she wore stressed her power, and the crimson sash her commitment to revenge. He got to his feet, dismissing Tom, and offered Alexis his arm. She accepted it, calmly taking the seat he offered her.

Howe got up from his chair and shut the window, bolting it securely. Alexis's laughter filled the room. "You seem to be taking me more seriously, Senator."

"They all do, Captain Danty," answered Cloud, taking his seat across from her.

"As you always have. Thank you for the reception at the pier. I should have known."

"I warned you."

"Yes, you did. I was expecting you to do it personally."

"How did you manage to get back to the house? I believe you were dressed in blue, if my memory serves me." His green eyes were bright with laughter. It was as if only the two of them were in the room now.

She smiled. "I simply told Tom and his mates that we were going back to the house. There, I climbed the lattice to the second floor, changed my clothes, and came back here like a child, filled with remorse and guilt for having run away."

"That is hard to believe, Captain Danty," said Granger, deciding he had had enough of their self-congratulatory conversation.

"What do you find difficult to believe?" she asked with wide-eyed innocence. "That I climbed the lattice? That I changed my clothes? Or that I am filled with remorse and guilt?"

"The last, Captain," he said, agitated.

"Good," she said sharply. "I see there has been some progress made in this room since I was last here." She paused, absorbing their altered expressions. "Now. What do you want?"

They told her, ignoring her objections.

They told her they would give her a ship. A frigate. A war sloop. Whatever she wanted.

"I have the ship I want."

They told her they would give her an unprecedented honorary commission.

"I am a captain."

They offered her the finest crew available. She could choose among the ranks.

"I have the men I want."

They said they would pardon her.

"I ask no pardon. I have committed no crime against you."

They told her the price of what they offered—she would have to give them information on British movements.

"I am aware of the movements of only one man."

They told her that Lafitte could be an additional asset to their fight.

"Yes. He could be."

They explained why the pirate would not let an American officer approach him.

"I would not allow a British officer to approach me."

And they told her she would take to Lafitte the terms of his pardon. His help for his life. The agreement to be completed in Washington.

"I will not."

Throughout the discussion Cloud's eyes never left Alexis while she focused on everyone but him. She sat at some distance from the table, one slender arm stretched out from her shoulder in a straight dark line. Only her fingertips touched the edge of the table, as if any more contact than that would contaminate her. The arm was unyielding, never bending. Her other arm was bent at the elbow, her hand in her lap. It was this arm he expected to see unfold suddenly and slash out at their faces.

He studied her face as she refused their offers. Her eyes were devoid of any expression save disgust, including disgust at herself for bothering to answer their questions. Her cheeks were smooth and soft; her chin lifted at an arrogant angle.

Her sun-kissed skin, glowing in the room's lamplight, seemed especially bright against the dark background of her clothing. In contrast to the golden flesh of her throat was the silver necklace. It captured the light, held it, then scattered it in quick, sharp flashes whenever she lifted her head defiantly.

He could only think in terms of love and hate. He hated them for forcing this on her. He loved her for throwing it back in their faces.

"I will not take to Lafitte any terms which you propose," she said.

Exasperated, Bennet shook his head, running his fingers through his wheat-colored hair. "Why not?"

Alexis stood, placing both hands on the table for support. She explained clearly and accurately why Lafitte would not help them at this time. She spoke exactly as she had earlier to Cloud. "Wait," she finished. "He will come to you. He will offer his assistance. Don't be too stubborn to accept it."

Richard Granger leaned forward angrily in his chair, a brandy in hand. "Are you saying this because he helped you return home and even now is helping your shipping firm establish itself while other businesses flounder? Are you saying this because he is your friend?"

"No. I say it because it is true."

"But he is your friend."

"That has nothing to do with what I am telling you."

Howe lighted himself another square-cut cigar. "Do you realize what will happen if you refuse to help us?"

"I have not refused you—yet," she corrected him. "But, under no circumstances will I consider Lafitte a part of any assistance I could give you." She walked around her chair and put her hands on its high leather back.

"It is everything or nothing," Howe objected.

"Dammit, Senator!" Cloud said, clenching his teeth. He saw Alexis jerk at the sound of his voice. "Let her speak. Let her tell you what she is willing to do!"

"I wondered when you would come to her defense, Captain."

"I am not defending her. She doesn't need my defense. What she deserves is an opportunity to state her terms." His eyes glinted angrily, daring anyone to raise further objection.

Alexis latched on to the silence provided as if it were as tangible as the chair beneath her fingers. "Senator Howe, I am willing to offer my services in any manner you wish, with the exception of Lafitte. I could do nothing for you there. I will help you as soon as I have found Captain Travers. This is what I want. It is the only thing I am willing to accept. If your refusal means proceeding with your absurd charges, then do so. But understand that it is you who have refused me. You may put me in jail. But you will fight your war without any assistance from me."

The room erupted into objections. Voice overrode voice until complete sentences could not be distinguished. The two captains viewed each other solemnly. Cloud saw the brightness in her eyes fade. She smiled faintly, a smile of acceptance of something she had never accepted before in her life: total defeat. She turned her head away from him, certain her defeat meant losing him—not just for now, but forever. He willed her to face him again so he could tell her it was not true but she would not turn her head.

Mechanically, Alexis took her seat. She heard little of what was being said, wondering what it would be like in prison, then refusing to think about it. Her eyes focused on a flickering shadow on the opposite wall, and she made herself listen to parts of the conversation.

"Lafitte. She must bring us Lafitte." "She'll change her mind once she realizes we are serious about these charges." "A few months waiting for trial will make her see she must cooperate."

A dull, lifeless voice—she did not know whose—said she would be kept in Davidson's home under guard until the following evening when the charges would be processed and other arrangements could be made. She felt a hand take her by the arm and help her to her feet. The hand was cold, clammy—or perhaps it was her own flesh that felt that way.

She did not turn back. She walked out of the room concentrating solely on the command from her brain to her feet.

Cloud stood, his face calm, a trace of a smile on his lips.

"Gentlemen, you have been very hard on Captain Danty this evening. I believe I can convince her tomorrow to see things my way, if you would permit me to speak with her. I will bring her belongings with me in case she chooses to disregard what I have to say."

"What can you say to her that we haven't said already, Captain?" Farthington asked.

Cloud smiled enigmatically. "If I could have a few hours alone with her I believe I can persuade her to do anything."

Howe raised an eyebrow suggestively. "Oh, I see. Well, there will still have to be a guard at the door, but it can be arranged so no one will disturb you."

"I understand. Any arrangements will be satisfactory. I will leave word of her decision with the guard."

"Make her understand we do not want to press charges. She is forcing us to do it," Granger said anxiously. "Can you make her see that?"

"I can make her understand what she must do." Cloud stepped to the door. "If there is nothing else, gentlemen, I will be leaving now. This evening has been most instructive."

As Cloud was leaving the house Davidson returned to the dining room, slamming the door behind him. He pulled his chair out roughly and sat down. "Well, Senator?" he asked viciously. "She is locked in the guest room with one of your men at the door. I can't keep her there forever. Imagine the scandal if someone finds out she's here. And I can't very well tell anyone precisely who she is. What the hell are we going to do with her?"

"Do with her?" Howe asked, unconcerned. "Why we are going to do what we always planned. She is just as valuable as Lafitte. We'll find another way to approach him if the captain is unsuccessful in convincing her."

"You should have heard our dear captain, Robert," Bennet said spitefully, fixing himself another drink. " 'A few hours alone and I believe I can persuade her to do anything,' he says. That bastard! You'd think the sun rises and sets because he commands it to."

"Shut up, Bennet," Howe said pointedly, riveting his cold gray eyes on the young man. "You're getting ugly."

"I don't think he should be allowed to see her tomorrow."

"I disagree. He did not realize how serious we were until this evening. He will do everything he can to keep her out of prison, and that means convincing her to bring Lafitte. If he fails, then we still have her."

"All right, Senator," Bennet sighed. "We'll do it your way. It will serve that arrogant son of a bitch right if he does persuade her."

Chapter Thirteen

When Cloud arrived at his home Tom Daniels had already spread the word that Alexis had been taken back to Davidson's. As a result Cloud found more men waiting impatiently in his drawing room than he would have liked.

Cloud paused at the entrance, long enough to let them see he was in no mood to make any explanations. Then he strode past them to the other side of the room to pour himself a glass of brandy. No one said a word.

"Captain Danty has refused to meet their demands," Cloud said at last. "The charges will be processed against her and a trial will probably be held in the near future."

"Those bastards!" Harry swore. "Who'd have thought they'd go ahead with prosecuting her?"

"Captain Danty did," answered Cloud.

"Did Mr. Madison—" Forrest was cut off before he could complete his thought aloud.

"The President was not there. The others acted according to his wishes."

"Damnation! Where are they keeping her?" Mike pounded his fist against the arm of his chair.

"It would be better for all of you if you didn't know."

"But Captain!" Tom protested. "We can't leave her! We've got to do something!"

"Aye, sir," agreed Harry. He was joined by a round of approval from the others, giving him courage. He missed the bright flare of anger burning in Cloud's eyes. "She's a heroine, Captain! She's special to all of—"

"She is nothing! All of you! She is nothing!" The harshness of his voice cut through the room. Then he sent his brandy glass smashing against the brick fireplace. "None of you are to attempt to find out where they've taken her! You'd be court-martialed for helping her! No man under my command is going to face that charge! She has accepted what has happened. You do the same!" He never thought he would see the day when their anger would turn on him. Yet he refused to tell them he had one more chance to make Alexis do what she should have done in the beginning. He did not want all his men to cling to that slender thread of hope. "There is no need for any of you to remain here this evening. Go find yourself a bottle and a whore and forget you ever knew her! Good night!"

He left the room without looking back at their incredulous faces.

There was a brief silence. "He couldn't have meant it . . . could he?" Mike's voice was firm at first, then anxiously quiet.

"She is a heroine!" "Aye, that she is!" "I won't accept it!" "We'll do something."

"We'll do nothing."

It was Landis's weary voice that caught their attention. He was shaking his head slowly, his face pale, and the motion seemed to drain him further.

"We'll do nothing," he repeated. "The captain has forbidden it. Whatever else you think you want to do, you cannot go against his orders." He smiled at them. "After all, we're his men. Or had you forgotten?"

He said nothing more. The discussion was over. He got his coat and the others followed his example. They had caught

a small gleam of hope in his gray eyes even while they saw
nothing but hopelessness in the set of his mouth. They did
not know what to make of either impression.

Upstairs, alone in his room, Cloud lay on his bed. He had
discarded his jacket and torn open the collar of his shirt. He
was as relaxed now as he had been when he'd left Davidson's
dining room. His head rested comfortably in the cradle of
his hands, his fingers mingling with the strands of dark copper
hair. His eyes were closed and the smooth line of his mouth
was evidence of his lack of tension.

The only thought in his mind, the thought relaxing him
so completely, was his knowledge that Alexis could be persuaded, by means he did not really want to use, to do what
she must to avoid prison.

Kurt Jordan glanced down at the tousled head at his side.
The wind was taking the boy's hair and blowing strands across
his face, denying Jordan the pleasure of seeing his bright,
eager eyes. Captain Jordan's mouth curled in a satisfied grin
as he looked in the direction of the boy's attention.

"Just a few hours, Peach. We'll have Captain Danty with us
before long."

Peach glanced up. "Do you think she'll be there?" he asked
earnestly. "What if they take her away? You don't think they
arrested her, do you? I mean, what if she's in prison?"

"Slow down," laughed Jordan. "First of all we have to make
some inquiries after we dock. Maybe she already got away. If
she didn't, it won't be hard to find out what happened to
her. There's got to be someone from the *Concord* who can be
forced to tell us something. We'll find her, so stop worrying."

"It's not just that, Captain."

"Well, what else?"

"She's going to be awfully angry with us, isn't she?"

"Furious."

"It doesn't seem to bother you." Peach's voice held a note

of wonder. He could not imagine facing Captain Danty's anger head on.

"It doesn't matter to me at all. Her anger means nothing as long as she's here to give it. I'll welcome her fury just to see those blazing golden eyes again."

Peach turned his face toward the sight of land. The early morning sun was behind him and he reveled in its warmth.

Cloud woke as the first ray of light crossed his face. He was still in his clothes but he felt more rested than he had in days. His eyes were anxiously bright as he thought of all he had to do. He permitted himself to lie in bed a moment longer to put off the pleasure doing it.

His movements as he bathed and dressed were unhurried. He went to Alexis's room and slowly folded her clothes. He discarded the blankets and pillows occupying an old trunk and placed her belongings inside with the care usually reserved for handling fine crystal. The last thing he packed was the delicate blue gown.

After a light breakfast in his kitchen, he threw the trunk into the carriage and headed the horses in the direction of the harbor. Steering away from the *Concord,* he drove toward the piers the cargo ships used. There he inquired blandly about destinations and departures. He was in the middle of one of these conversations when his eyes suddenly focused on a sight he had feared for weeks but now welcomed. He walked away from the puzzled man at his side, offering no explanation, and watched the Quinton merchant—Alexis's ship—glide down the Potomac. He caught a young boy passing by and quickly scribbled off a note. He pointed in the direction of the ship and the boy nodded. After giving him a few coins, Cloud went back to his carriage.

He took a number of side streets to Davidson's home to pass the time. When he arrived he was asked to wait. He waited, feet propped on the trunk in front of him.

"You wanted to see me, Mr. Davidson?" he asked when he

had been escorted to the study and the door had closed behind him.

"Yes. Have you brought Captain Danty's things?"

Cloud thought Davidson looked as if he hadn't slept all night. He smiled, thinking of his own restful sleep. "I have them in a trunk in the hallway. I'll take it up to her, if you haven't changed your mind about permitting me to visit."

Davidson seemed appalled that the captain would think that. "Oh no! You must speak with her. Mr. Madison was extremely disappointed with her refusal to help us."

"You've talked to him?"

"First thing this morning. He was most anxious to hear our report and very distressed that we were forced to hold her. He wants you to make her understand."

"I intend to," Cloud said firmly.

"Good. Then please go to her now. Leave word with the guard as you said you would. I have a meeting this afternoon with Bennet and Dr. Eustis." He frowned, wringing his hands together. "This war has us all overworked."

"Yes, I understand."

Davidson looked at Cloud curiously, not sure what it was the captain professed to understand. "Aah, of course you do, Captain Cloud. I mean after all you will be fighting it."

Cloud smiled, shaking Davidson's hand. "I will persuade Captain Danty, Mr. Davidson. She and I will fight this war together." Still smiling, he left the room.

"What do you make of it, Captain?" asked Ned Allison.

Jordan folded the note and slipped it into his pocket, turning to the boy who delivered it. "Who gave this to you?"

"I don't know his name, sir. He didn't say. Just said I was supposed to give it to someone on this ship." The boy was nervous under the harsh stares of the men. His foot tapped against the deck and his eyes darted toward the wharf.

"Well, what did he look like?"

The boy shrugged his shoulders. "He was tall. Well dressed.

A uniform, I don't know nothin' about rank. He wasn't husky like you, but you could tell he was strong. Oh yeah, he's got hair about the color of this." He held up one of the coins Cloud had given him, the color of copper. "That's all I remember."

Jordan smiled grimly. "You remembered enough, lad. Go on. Get out of here." He waited until the boy made his hasty retreat then he looked at Ned and Peters. "We'll do what the note says. It had to have been written by Cloud. He's got until four o'clock. Otherwise we're going to tear down this town brick by brick until we find her."

Peters nodded. "And we'll use the rubble to bury the bastard."

It took Alexis several minutes after waking to remember where she was and why she was there. Sitting up in bed, she glanced around the room, seeing things she had been unaware of when she first entered.

A beautifully crafted chest of drawers stood against one wall as elegant as the giant four-poster bed on which she sat. On the commode by the bed was a washbasin filled with fresh water. Clean linens were placed neatly beside it. A pale green robe lay over the back of a chair. She sighed at this fresh attempt to win her over.

It occurred to Alexis that in this room she could easily think of herself as a guest, but a knock at the door and the guard's voice announcing breakfast destroyed the notion.

"Good morning, miss," the guard said uncomfortably, as he brought in a tray of steaming eggs and ham. Alexis chose not to respond to his greeting which she regarded as something of a non sequitur.

She thanked him as he left the tray on the table by her bed. When he left she found she had little appetite, and she left most of her meal untouched.

She washed and put on the robe she supposed must belong to Davidson's wife or perhaps a mistress. The room seemed stiflingly hot. As she threw open the window, she saw two guards look up in her direction. It was then that the hopelessness she had experienced the night before washed over her again, but she managed to shake it off as she stepped away from the window. She must never again allow that feeling to overtake her in such immense proportions. How had she let it happen last night? she wondered. Why had she accepted their judgment and treatment of her? She picked up a delicate crystal vase from the mantel of the fireplace and in one violent motion of her arm she hurled it to the floor. Her body trembled as it shook off the last of her feelings of defeat. She was flushed and her eyes were glowing when the guard burst into the room.

"What did you do?" he demanded harshly. His eyes went first to the splinters of glass at her bare feet and slowly traveled upward over her body. He saw the faint quivering of her flesh as a movement in the pale green robe. One arm hung at her side while the other was still caught in the uncompleted motion of her throw. Slowly the arm continued downward until it also rested at her side. Her face held no expression except for the kind of fulfillment he thought it was only decent to show in bed. Her lips were parted slightly and her eyes were lighted in a way that would have said thank you to a lover.

She bent to pick up the glass. "I knocked this off the mantel," she explained. "I am sorry if I disturbed you. Please tell Mr. Davidson I will be happy to replace it for him."

"Yeah, sure. And how are you going to do that when you're in prison?"

She lifted her head a moment to look at him, then dropped it just as quickly to hide her smile. "You're right. I forgot where I was and where I'll be going. No matter. I'll find a way to replace it."

He muttered something under his breath and went back to his post, making more noise than necessary with the key in the door.

After Alexis picked up the broken glass, she sat in a chair

facing the door and waited. She waited to see the one person who could match every emotion coursing through her blood and understand the reason for it. She waited with the same sense of anticipation that had driven Cloud all morning, knowing only that he would come and that the pleasure of seeing him again would be as intense an experience as being joined with him in her bed.

Suddenly she heard Cloud's voice in the hallway. The tension she felt at the sound of his voice, rich and deep, pushed her out of her chair as if she had been a tightly coiled spring and his voice had released her. Then he was there before her, silently closing the door behind him.

There was something in his face she could not identify.

"Cloud—" She stopped. He was shaking his head slowly.

He stepped toward her, not touching her yet, but knowing it was what they both wanted and putting it off a moment longer. "I know," he said. "I knew it the instant I walked into this room. I knew it last night when you were so sure everything was lost, when you couldn't face me, when you could barely walk out of the room. I knew I would come to you this morning and find you ready to fight."

His arms went around her and hers went to his neck. Their lips met violently, brutally, no longer denying the fullness of their passion. His hand found the belt of her robe. He released it and slid his hands inside, his fingers brushing against the softness of her naked flesh, then gripping it harshly, pulling her closer, making her gasp. She felt his tongue in her mouth, exploring, tasting, then retreating only to return more hungrily than before. When his mouth left hers to kiss her eyes, cheeks, hair, she breathed deeply for air, drawing in fully as she would if she had just surfaced from a powerful wave swell. She heard his light laugh, clearly taunting, against her throat as his teeth caught the silver necklace and the skin around it, biting it gently, then bruising her with the force of his kiss. Her fingers went to the buttons of his shirt and fumbled at undoing them. He stopped her with a cruel grasp of his hands on her wrists. She dropped her hands to her sides. His hands went to the collar of her robe, brushing aside the material from her shoulders.

He stepped back to watch the pale green wrapper float without further assistance down the length of her arms, separating at her breasts, sliding past her slender hips, and caressing her thighs and calves. It fell to the floor with a sigh and he thought it was the same sigh he had wanted to hold—had held for a time. Her body was trembling but she made no move to hide it from him, knowing he wanted to see her tremble at the power he held over her. He walked around her slowly, touching every part of her with his eyes, memorizing the texture of her flesh, caressing every curve, every hollow.

"All day," he said, standing behind her. She glanced at him over her shoulder, but he put her head back, making her face the bed. "No, don't move. I don't want you to move except for the movements you can't stop." He saw her shudder as a rippling in her golden hair which hung in a solid glistening sheet against her back. His chuckle was low, throaty. "All day this is what I was seeing, feeling, wanting. You. Everything I did today, will do later, was for this time when I could look at you again and see you tremble. Tremble as you never would in front of them last night. As you never would in front of any man but me. It is the only mastery I ever wanted over you because it means having all of you. All of you, to do anything I want to, knowing that you'll let me because you can't stop me, can't escape me. Do you know that it's true?"

"Yes." Her voice was small, choked. "Yes, I know it's true."

His hand pressed into the small of her back and he twisted her around. "And while you were waiting, it was the same for you. You knew I would come, that I could not stay away. You were waiting to tell me you hadn't been defeated by them, but wanting to be defeated by me. Wanting to be taken by the one person who can stop you from getting away. Wanting him almost as much as you want to get away."

"Yes. I want you. I want you."

His lips found hers again, crushing them in capture. His

hands stroked her breasts, her flesh quivered beneath his touch. He carried her to the bed and took off his clothes slowly, enjoying the way she watched him undress.

He lay beside her, his head propped on one elbow while his other hand casually touched the skin of her throat, her breasts, her flat stomach, and finally her thighs. Her amber eyes, slightly hooded beneath thick lashes, pleaded with him to go on, and he kissed them gently as her legs parted against the pressure of his fingers. His mouth moved to her breasts and he felt her hands go to his head, curl in his hair, holding him there as she pushed herself against him.

"Please, Cloud!" she moaned. This time she heard his laugh, muffled against her thighs, and responded to him, conquered by his will, her thighs opening further to the touch of his lips.

Her hands reached for his head again but stopped in midair and fell against the bed, gripping the sheets, clutching them as if they offered her support as his tongue brought her closer and closer to release. Looking up, he saw her fingers clenching the fabric. He lifted himself above her and her legs wrapped around him as he entered her with hard thrusts. She matched his passion, holding him tightly within her, liking the warmth and strength of his mastery.

Her body convulsed and sobbed as he gave one final thrust and shuddered against her. He held her close as waves of intense pleasure flooded her limbs, making them tremble even in relaxation. She rested her flushed face in the crook of his shoulder until he turned it up to kiss her still parted lips.

"Alex," he said when he placed her head on his chest beneath his chin. "You do want your liberty more than you want me, don't you?"

"Why do you ask it that way, Cloud? You make it sound as if I can't have both." She lifted her head to look in his eyes, and the thing she'd seen before, when he had first entered her room, was still there. She frowned because she still could not identify its meaning.

"What's wrong?" he asked.

"It's you. Something different. Has something happened since last night?"

"Yes."

"Can you tell me?"

"I can, but I won't. Not yet. You'll understand soon enough." He placed her head on his chest again and said, "You did not answer my question."

"About my freedom?"

"Yes."

"I don't understand you. Don't you realize that only by being free to do the things I have to do can I be totally yours? I want to be yours. I want you until you want me no longer and even then I'll go to no one else. How could I, after knowing you? But Cloud, my liberty is dearer than even you. I cannot exchange one for the other. I want both. You wouldn't want me, would you, if I couldn't finish the promise I made to myself? It would always come between us. Being free means I can do it and that means I can come to you with nothing held back. I thought you knew that. I thought you knew it when you let me go the first time, on the *Hamilton*." She heard his sharp intake of breath and she laughed. "You didn't think I knew, did you? I did. It was then I knew you really loved me. Loved me enough to let me go, even though you thought I might never seek you out again." Her hand stroked his side and she pressed her lips to the bronzed skin of his chest. "I would have come back to you freely and begged you to make me your prisoner. I would have begged you to have me for always in the manner you just did. I would have shown you the scars on my back and Travers's blood on my sword as proof of my devotion to things I believe in and things I must have." She moved her leg against his, flesh against flesh, his strength against her own. "Do you understand?"

"Yes. I understand," he said quietly. "I do love you. Remember that. Remember it when you come back with Travers's blood on your sword and I'm not here."

Startled by his last words she pulled away from him and

looked at his face. He was smiling but the sadness she saw in him crushed her chest as if invisible hands were pressing against her, forcing air from her lungs.

"Why wouldn't you be here?" It was an anguished cry. "Where would you be? Don't talk like that, Cloud!"

He pulled her close and kissed her deeply, passionately. She wondered why even the kiss seemed sad. He kissed her face, wiping away tears she had not known she'd shed until he covered her mouth with his once more and she tasted their saltiness on his tongue.

"I'm here now, love," he whispered against her hair.

"Don't say anything more, Cloud. I don't understand and it scares me terribly."

He said nothing more, not because she requested it, but because he thought he had given away too much already and he did not want her to understand. Not now, not when she still could talk him out of it.

"I can't stay any longer," he said, getting out of bed. "I brought you some clothes. You'll be needing them where you're going."

"I suppose I will," she sighed. "I can't very well appear in court in my black attire. They'll put me away before I get within three feet of the judge."

When he'd finished dressing, he dragged the trunk away from the door and moved it to the center of the room. "Aren't you going to get dressed, Alex? Or are you waiting for one of the guards to come in and know what we've been up to?" His eyes teased her gently.

"As if they didn't hear! Not that I care. But if it will make you feel better I'll dress." She walked over to the trunk and started to open it but he stopped her.

"Just put on the robe. I think you'll be more comfortable. It's warm in here."

She complied, not noticing his eyes were on the trunk as he spoke.

"Where are the clothes you wore last night?" he asked. "I'll put them away for you."

"You don't have to." Something in his face made her abort any further attempt to speak. She pointed to the chair that held her clothes. She watched, fascinated at the way he folded everything and placed it carefully in the trunk. She felt as if his hands were on her body, so intimate was his touch on her clothing. His head was turned away from her and she found the courage to speak again.

"Why did you bring such a large trunk? My clothes hardly take up any space at all. My bag was sufficient."

"This suited my purpose," he answered, straightening and turning to her.

It was then Alexis named the thing in his eyes. It was then she understood what his intention was and what it meant. Her lips parted to speak but it was too late. He had already seen the understanding in her face and he was prepared to still any protests before they were spoken. Alexis saw the lift of his arm, his fist tightly clenched, and she saw the sweeping motion of it as it drew closer to the side of her head. Then she saw it only at the corner of her eye as she stared at his face, his lips moving in a soundless *I love you*. Then she saw nothing. Nothing at all.

Cloud caught her before she fell to the floor. He inspected the area where he had hit her before he placed her tenderly in the trunk. He pressed her head forward and folded her arms across her chest. Closing the lid, he whispered, "I told them I could convince you." He took out the key and locked it, then proceeded to drag it toward the door.

"Damn you for a bitch!" he said loudly. "I practically broke my back bringing this to you and now you say you don't want it. Ungrateful slut! Don't you dare throw that! I'll break you in half myself!"

He knocked on the door so the guard would know he wanted out. "Hurry man! She's having a fit in here." The guard obliged and Cloud quickly moved out, taking the trunk with him and successfully blocking the guard's entry into the room. Cloud shut the door violently. "I wouldn't go in there just yet," he told the guard. "She's furious with me for even suggesting she should cooperate. You know how women are."

"I know how most women are. Her"—he jerked his head toward the door—"I'm not sure about. She was breaking things in there earlier."

Cloud inclined his head toward the room. "It sounds as if she's calmed down some. Give her a chance to cry it off. I doubt if she'll be throwing anything else for a while. Make sure you tell Mr. Davidson that she refused to listen to me. She won't help."

The guard nodded. "What are you going to do with her things? Want to leave them here until she changes her mind about wanting them?"

"No. Serves her right if they're not here when she needs them. I'll take them back with me. She can have them when she decides to change her mind about a few things."

"That'll keep her in line. A woman needs to know her place"—he winked at Cloud—"even if the woman is Captain Danty."

Cloud restrained his urge to put the man's eye out. He said evenly, "Especially because she's Captain Danty." He returned the wink and left, pulling the trunk by its handle.

When he reached the stairs he motioned for a servant to help him, and together they carried the trunk out of the house and put it in his carriage. "Thanks for the assistance," he said, climbing onto the seat. He tugged at the reins before the servant could question the contents of the heavy trunk and started off in the direction of the harbor.

When he reached the wharf he did not go to the Quinton vessel. Instead he found helpers, two off-duty seamen, and told them what he wanted.

"Take this trunk to the Quinton merchant over there. They're expecting it. Give Captain Jordan this note." He handed a folded slip of paper to one of the men. "Then get off the ship. They'll be leaving in a hurry."

"This ain't nothin' illegal, is it?" asked the burlier of the two. " 'Cause if it is we'll want no parts of it."

"At least if it won't fatten our pockets," said the other.

Cloud withdrew some gold coins from his own pocket. "Illegal? I'm not sure. But this should take care of your conscience." He dropped the coins into outstretched palms. The men lifted the trunk jerkily. "Easy there! That's very precious cargo!"

They handled it more gingerly. Cloud watched them carry it to Alexis's ship.

"Which one of you is Jordan?" asked one of Cloud's helpers as he and his friend put the trunk on the deck.

"I'm Captain Jordan. What do you want?"

"We were told to bring this"—he kicked the trunk—"up here and give you this note."

Jordan snatched the paper from the man's hand and unfolded it.

Your cargo has been delivered as promised. I would make one suggestion: open the trunk several miles out to sea, so it can explode harmlessly. It was packed carefully and should not have suffered unduly from its confinement. You will find it damaged in only one area. Good Luck.

Jordan placed the note in his back pocket along with the earlier one. He looked at his men then at the men who had brought the trunk. "What are you still here for?" he asked them. "Didn't the man who asked you to deliver this tell you the trunk contained explosives? We're heading out to sea!" He laughed heartily as the two scrambled off the deck. "Heave to, men! We're going to leave Washington intact after all."

His men regarded him curiously for a moment then their eyes focused on the trunk and back to Jordan. "That's right," he told them. "We have everything we came for!"

Cloud saw the men he hired come running down the wharf toward him at the same time he heard a cheer go up from Alexis's crew.

"Why didn't you tell us it was explosives?" they asked in breathless unison.

Cloud laughed. "Would you have carried it if I'd told you?"

"Hell no!"

"There's your answer." He ignored their murderous looks and asked, "They didn't open the trunk, did they?"

"They're not fools. The captain said they were putting out."

Cloud nodded. He glanced down at the activity aboard the ship and then smiled, turning away. He got in his carriage, still smiling, and drove home. They would come when they found her gone and there were some answers he had to have, even if it meant facing charges of treason to have them.

Part Three

Chapter Fourteen

"What the devil?"

It was Alexis's first statement when the lid of the trunk was pried open. She squinted against the bright sunlight and struggled to see the faces of the men who hovered over her. Her hand went to her brow to block out the sun's glare.

"Jordan, is that you?" she asked weakly.

His smile answered that it was. "Let me help you out, Captain." He reached down to do just that but Alexis shook her head.

"I can get out on my own," she said stubbornly. She placed her arms stiffly on the sides of the trunk and tried to stand. Her legs were numb and refused to hold her. She started to collapse but Jordan caught her and lifted her out of the trunk, holding her against his massive chest. She tried to make some sense of her new surroundings as her crew gathered closer. "I don't understand. What are you doing here?"

Peach pushed his way to the front of the circle of men. "We came for you, Captain Danty!" he said proudly. "But you got away! Just like you said you would!"

Alexis looked from Peach's earnest face to Jordan's concerned one. "Put me down, Mr. Jordan. I can stand now." Her command was obeyed at once. She wavered slightly when her feet hit the deck, but she managed to gain control. She pulled at the belt of her robe, fastening it more securely around her waist. With a hand on Peach's shoulder, she addressed her crew.

"I gave you men orders not to come here. Isn't that so?" There were murmurs of acknowledgment. "Do you have any notion of what your presence here could have meant?"

"Aye, Captain," said Ned. "We knew. The risk was worth taking."

"I'm sorry, Ned," she answered. "Of course, you all knew. What I am saying is that it's a good thing Captain Cloud agreed to help you. Otherwise you wouldn't have stood a chance of getting me out of Washington." She did not perceive their questioning glances immediately. "Our course, Mr. Jordan?"

"Back to Tortola first. Then wherever Captain Travers can be found."

"Good. You seem to have it all under control." She looked at her men, searching for one face. She frowned. "Where is Captain Cloud? I have a few things to say to him about the way he packed me."

Jordan's eyebrows furrowed. "But Captain, he isn't here."

Peach winced as Alexis gripped his shoulder more tightly. "What!" she cried. "What do you mean he is not here? Where is he?"

"He never was here," Jordan replied. "He made contact with us when we sailed in this morning. He sent a young boy with a message and later he delivered the trunk through two seamen. We never saw him."

Alexis's mouth went slack for a moment and then drew in sharply for air. Redland stepped forward, thinking she was going to faint. "Then you didn't plan this with him?" she asked softly as everything was becoming clear to her.

"No, Captain. He was the last person we would have approached." Jordan brushed back his hair in a nervous movement. "Didn't he tell you we were here? Didn't you come with him willingly?"

Cloud's words to her made sense now. She stood very still, hands at her sides, her mouth drawn in a tight line of pain. She closed her eyes for a moment. When she opened them, she said quietly to Jordan, "There are some explanations we need to exchange. Come to my cabin in ten minutes." She turned to Peach. "Take my trunk down." To the others she said, "Continue present course until I find out what's been going on. I am too surprised at seeing all of you to be angry." She smiled. She turned sharply and went to her cabin, and the men congratulated themselves on their insubordination with low laughter.

Alone in her cabin Alexis changed clothes quickly. Her thoughts whirled and she struggled to put them in order. She had expected to end up anywhere but aboard her own ship. When she recognized her crew she allowed herself to hope that Cloud had decided not only to free her but to come with her as well. Why had he elected to stay behind? What chance did he have? He was going to be accused of treason for releasing her.

She was saved from dwelling on the final outcome by Jordan's insistent knock.

"Come in. Have a seat, Mr. Jordan."

Jordan settled his muscular bulk into the chair at Alexis's desk. His fingers tapped lightly on the arms of the chair, the only sign of the tension knotting his insides. Alexis sat on the edge of the desk, one leg bent, an ankle resting on the knee of the other.

"What was your plan this morning when you entered the harbor?" asked Alexis.

"We were going to ask some questions and find out where they were keeping you. After that . . ." He paused. "After that we were going to get you out."

"Did you ask questions?" Her voice was low and strained.

"No. Captain Cloud contacted us first. He must have seen us coming in."

"The notes. Do you have them?"

Jordan nodded and reached into his pocket. He handed her the first slip. "You can see he didn't give us any indication you weren't coming willingly," he said while she read.

Do not look for the prize you are seeking. Make no inquiries. It will be delivered this afternoon. Arrangements have already been made. Your visit was a welcome surprise.

"Yes, I see. So you assumed I planned this with him and your being here just made it easier for us."

"Well, yes. I thought at first it might be some kind of trick but I decided to wait and see if he delivered."

"The other note. I want to see it also." She slipped the first note into the pages of her log and read the paper he gave her. Then she placed it with the other and stared at her folded hands for a long time before she spoke. "I am going back, Mr. Jordan." Her voice was quiet, controlled, but Jordan saw the effort it took to say those words so evenly. "I do not know if you are fully aware of what Captain Cloud has done—"

"I'm beginning to see," Jordan said slowly. "You didn't know anything about this, did you? You were not expecting us."

"I was expecting you to follow orders!" she snapped. She slid off the edge of her desk and walked the length of the cabin to the porthole. She sat down on the bench and remained silent until she knew she could speak without becoming angry. "Kurt," she said finally "It is good to—"

He interrupted her. "I know all that, Captain." He let her see, with his wide smile, that he was also glad to see her and that her anger did not bother him. "Now tell me what happened that I don't know."

"The charges against me were more than I was led to believe when Captain Cloud first spoke to me. There are also charges of piracy because of my association with Lafitte. Of course, all the charges were false. It was their attempt to get me to bring them Lafitte. Captain Cloud tried to persuade them to forget Lafitte, to allow me to go after Travers and help them later. He was not successful and neither was I. I was informed the charges would be processed and that I would go to prison. I was placed under guard that evening. Apparently that was too much for the captain." She smiled grimly, remembering it had almost been too much for her.

"I was held at Mr. Davidson's home until I could be taken to jail. That's where you would have found me this morning. There would have been no possible way for you to get me out without killing someone. Captain Cloud, however, was permitted to see me. Apparently they trusted him enough to allow him to bring my clothes, maybe they thought he was their last chance to convince me. I don't know." Her voice was brittle as she finished her recital. She fingered the silver chain at her throat. "There was something different in his manner when I talked to him but I did not have any idea he was going to release me. I never would have permitted it. It is too dangerous for him. He must have known. He did not give me an opportunity to talk him out of it. His fist made reasoning impossible." She glanced out the porthole to avoid meeting the first mate's eyes. She concentrated on the horizon, her face devoid of any emotion.

Jordan said nothing for several minutes. The gentle drumming of his fingers was the only sound in the room. Abruptly, his movements ceased and he spoke with calm assurance.

"Captain Cloud is waiting to be charged with your escape."

"Yes. I believe so."

"Why? He would have been welcome to come with us."

"I think he wants to convince them they were wrong to hold me that way. He wants to give me time to find Travers."

Jordan shook his head slowly. "He doesn't have a chance. You were an important part of their plans. They'll consider his actions treasonous."

"I know it."

"And his actions kept us from doing the same thing. Even the notes he sent us are perfect. We can always say we never knew what was in the trunk. There is no mention of you. Only prizes and explosives and damaged cargo." He laughed suddenly, chillingly. "We thought he meant you were going to explode because we had come after you. He really meant you were going to be furious because he wasn't aboard."

"That's right," she said quietly. She searched his face earnestly. "Do you understand why I have to go back, Mr. Jordan?"

His expression was deadpan. "Do you understand why we are going with you?" Alexis's eyes betrayed her surprise and Jordan's laughter this time was warm and comforting. He smiled openly, his eyes shining with the brilliance of a child setting out on some new adventure. "You don't think we are going to let him hang after he returned you to us? And we are certainly not going to allow you to turn yourself in. They wouldn't trade anyway. They'd have you and Captain Cloud. No, we came to Washington to get a captain out and that's what we are going to do. Objections?"

Alexis grinned. "I don't think it would be prudent to object. I'd only end up with a mutiny on my hands." She stood and began pacing the deck, not in restless agitation, Jordan noted but with a purposeful stride that marked her resumption of full command. Her words were clear and crisp, edged with the undeniable authority of her position. "How far are we from Washington?"

"Not far. If we turned about now we could be back before sunset."

"Too early. We will continue slow and steady and then we will turn and go back when it is dark. I doubt anyone will come after us now. Captain Cloud is the only one who could bring us in and he has probably sent any pursuers on the chase of their life. If there are any ships sighted we are going to outrun them. No fighting unless we are fired upon. Is that clear?" Jordan nodded. "Did you sight many British frigates as you were approaching?"

"Several. They didn't give us any notice. Ran up a Union Jack and gave our destination as London. They let us through. We changed our course again when we were clear."

"Good. We will continue that way. I do not anticipate them as being much of a problem. Our biggest worry from them remains impressment."

"Do you know where the captain will be taken?" asked Jordan.

"No. But his crew is bound to know something by the time we return. We will have to rely on them for information. And Mr. Jordan," her voice was deadly serious, "that's all we can ask of any of them. They don't dare be implicated in any escape."

"I understand, Captain. Do you have a plan?"

"The beginning of one. Only the beginning. I need more time to think." She stopped pacing and faced Jordan, smiling shyly. "I am more accustomed to devising my own escapes, not someone else's."

Jordan chuckled. "Do you want me to talk to the men?"

"Yes. I do not want any man involved unless it is his own choice. Those who do not want to help will have to be left in Washington, otherwise they'll be in danger if we're chased."

"They'll all come," he answered certainly.

She smiled. "I think they will. You can go now. I'll have something worked out in an hour or so. Come back then and we can go over the details. I want you to tell me anything that doesn't sound plausible. We cannot afford one mistake."

Jordan started to take his leave, eager to tell the others about their new plans. He halted when Alexis called to him. He heard the anxiety in her tone and when he turned he saw it clearly displayed on her face. She stood before him with all her defenses down and he felt a certain pride that she trusted him to see her this way.

"You never answered my question," she said quietly. "Do you understand why I must go back?"

He smiled. After a pause he said, "I might even understand it better than you."

She stiffened. "What does that mean?"

"You are going back to the captain because you want to put an end to this farce once and for all. The charges of treason— his death—have to be stopped because they would give the illusion of truth to all the lies that have been stacked against you. And there is another reason you're going back— the one you don't want to name." For the first time since he had known her, Jordan thought he detected a blush surfacing on the planes of her cheeks.

"Am I so obvious?" she asked, meeting his gaze directly.

"This time—yes." Jordan leaned against the door, crossing his legs at the ankles. "Were you worried we might not want to follow you if we thought you were doing this because you love the captain?"

"I didn't know if you would understand."

Jordan's sun-white brows furrowed and lines creased his face. His voice was sharp. "Captain Danty, we have followed you all over the Atlantic because you hate a man. There is a reason for hating him. You have a reason to want your revenge. Now we'll follow you into Washington because you love a man. There are reasons why you love him. You must have a reason for wanting to see him free."

"I should have known," she said regretfully. "I should have known without having to hear it from you."

"Yes, you should have," he said flatly. "All this time aboard this ship together, you shouldn't have had to ask."

Alexis cast him a sharp glance then she laughed. "I deserved that." She sat down. "Now, Mr. Jordan, as to this ship. What exactly are we calling her these days?"

He stood at attention, once again the competent first mate. "Why, it's the *Dark Lady*. We've come full circle."

"Then suppose you go on deck and see that the *Dark Lady's* crew knows what's going to take place this evening. When you've accomplished that we will go over precisely how it is going to take place."

Jordan caught the excitement in her voice. "Aye, Captain," he answered and left the cabin with a new spring in his step.

* * *

While Alexis and Jordan were discussing the plan that would release him, Cloud was counting the stone blocks of his prison walls. It did nothing to keep his mind off the doubts and unanswered questions plaguing him.

Twenty-five. But why had Howe come to the house? He had expected naval authorities to take him into custody. Why had the senator? *Twenty-six.* And the guards with him seemed to be taking orders from him. Howe did not have that kind of authority. Madison must have given him orders to supervise the arrest. *Twenty-seven.* If only the President had been at the meeting. He would have understood why it had been necessary to release Alexis. *Twenty-eight.*

And why wasn't he allowed to see his superiors? Why had the guards told him only Farthington and Howe were permitted to see him? He supposed it didn't matter for the time being. He would be able to explain everything at his trial. *Twenty-eight. No. Twenty-nine. Damn. One.* He would be able to make the officers at his trial understand that freeing Alexis was not a treasonous act. He would make them see that by releasing her to find Travers they would have her help later and it would be given freely. *Two. Three.* What was it about Howe and the others he did not trust? They seemed to want the same things. Seemed to. *Two. No—damn! One.*

A key grated in the gate of his cell door. Cloud looked up and saw the guard named Matt usher Senator Howe into the cell.

Howe glanced around briefly before his gaze rested on the captain. His eyes were cold, mocking. His thick lips formed a derisive smile. "Not very pleasant, is it?"

"Not very. Would you care for a seat?" Cloud patted the end of his cot, the only available space in the room.

"I'll stand. I understand you've asked to talk to your superior."

"That's right. I thought I should arrange for counsel."

"You won't need counsel." He saw Cloud's questioning look. "There isn't going to be any trial."

"No trial?" He was puzzled and a faint alarm sounded in his head. "Then you realize why I had to let Captain Danty go?"

"There isn't going to be any trial because you have already been found guilty, Captain."

"What!"

"Why are you so amazed? You've already admitted you freed Captain Danty. She was a criminal."

Cloud forced himself to speak with deadly calm. "You know that isn't true, Senator. She isn't a criminal, at least as far as the United States is concerned. That is one of the things I wanted to make clear at my trial."

Howe laughed. "Don't you think I know that? Don't you understand that is precisely why there isn't going to be a trial?"

"What are you talking about? Just exactly what is going on?"

"You really don't know, do you?"

"I don't make a habit of asking questions I know the answers to."

Howe frowned. "You won't be quite so cocky after I finish explaining a few things to you, Cloud. First of all there won't be any trial because as you've known all along there were never any real charges against Danty. You were right in expecting to be able to prove that. Therefore, there can't be any charge of treason against you. Although Danty's help would have benefited us we couldn't force her to cooperate."

"Then why—"

"Don't interrupt." Howe warned him sharply. "I don't have to tell you anything before you're hanged." He saw Cloud's attention was riveted on him and he felt a heady sensation knowing he held so much power over this man.

"As I was saying, no one would convict you of treason because no such act really took place. I know what you're thinking—the orders. Well, the orders from Little Jemmy came from Bennet's pen."

"A forgery!"

"You're very bright, Captain," Howe responded sarcastically. "But not bright enough when it counted. Do you know how you were picked for the mission to bring in Danty?"

Cloud shook his head. He could hardly take in what the senator was saying.

"No, of course you wouldn't realize it. You were chosen because, unlike some of your fellow officers we could have picked, you really believed this war could be won. You really thought the United States had a grievance against Great Britain. We knew about your impressment by the Royal Navy but we also knew you didn't see this as a personal battle. You actually thought there might be a favorable outcome.

"You were chosen because we knew we could make you believe Captain Danty's help could bring about that favorable ending sooner. And indeed, Danty would have been of some assistance if that's what we really wanted. You'll have to believe me when I tell you we had no idea you actually knew her. We were genuinely surprised to discover she was a woman.

"It almost made us change our minds until we realized she had to be stopped regardless of her motives or her sex. And there remained the matter of Lafitte who was our second target. You helped us stumble on the means to get both of them at once.

"You see, Captain, winning this war is not our desire. I never wanted to enter it in the first place, and I have a lot of company. My biggest concern, and Robert's, too, when you arrived here with Danty was that somehow you would find out that both of us voted down the proposal for war. There were hardly any votes from New England to support Madison. Because Robert, Bennet, Richard, and I knew there was probably no way to stop a declaration, our primary interest became: how to survive it.

"Contrary to what you believe, we cannot hope to win. The real problem is how to end it quickly. The fewer losses the

British suffer, the sooner this is over and the better chance we have for negotiating a favorable peace settlement. Turning Captain Danty over to the Royal Naval authorities would have been seen as a friendly gesture on our part."

"You bastard!" Cloud spit. "You treacherous bastard!" He glared at Howe, piercing him with icy green eyes. Cloud gripped the edge of his cot, wanting his hands around Howe's throat.

Howe shifted nervously, backing toward the gate, toward the safety of the guards who sat playing cards in the outer room. With one large hand he grasped one of the iron bars.

Cloud threw his head back and laughed. Dark copper hair rippled as his head shook. "I am not going to attack you, Senator. At least not yet. There are still too many things I want to know."

"For instance," asked Howe, feeling much safer on the far side of the cell.

"You said you planned to turn over Captain Danty. What was your purpose for asking her to bring in Lafitte?"

"Danty was right about Lafitte, Captain. That is what made this all so interesting. Neither of you could understand why we insisted that Lafitte be brought in when you knew he would help of his own accord when the time came. But actually that's exactly what we were afraid of."

"And that's why you wanted him locked up," Cloud finished, more to himself than to the senator. "To make sure he didn't help."

"Exactly," Howe added smugly.

"But now you don't have Captain Danty, at least for your purpose of turning her over to the British, and you won't be able to reach Lafitte. Where does that leave you and your friends?" He said the last word with as much contempt as he could muster.

"It leaves us with you," Howe answered amiably, ignoring Cloud's tone. "You will be hanged for treason, Captain, but hardly on the charges you anticipated defending yourself against."

"And the charges are?"

"Giving vital information to the British. The Arnold of Mr. Madison's war."

"You won't get away with that, Howe. I'll get someone to listen to me."

"Do you think I would be telling you any of this if I thought that was even remotely possible?"

Suddenly Cloud felt weary. He wondered if this despair taking possession of his entire being was similar to what Alexis felt when she'd refused to look at him, when she had thought she'd failed. He held on to the thought of her, miles away, heading toward her goal, and it gave him strength. "The guards," he said, clutching at any hope. "I'll inform the guards."

"They won't listen. As far as they know you were already tried and sentenced in Boston. You were delivered here for execution because of the nature of your crime. They won't believe anything you have to say and I have taken the added precaution of warning them to stay away from you. They'll carry out the sentence in the morning."

"Why are you going to all this trouble? Why not just kill me yourself or have one of those fake guards you had pick me up today do it for you?"

"It had occurred to me. You have Davidson to thank for your short reprieve. He realized we could make your death work for us in a way that compensated generously for the loss of Danty and Lafitte." He leaned against the bars, releasing his grip, savoring his return to control over the captain. He allowed himself a brief satisfied smile as he realized how hopeless Cloud's plight was and how secure his own position. "You will be executed as a traitor. The story will be released and there will be a great furor over the fact that one of our most respected commanders decided to become a turncoat. People on the fence over the issue of war will immediately leap to my side. Their anger over what you did may be enough to end this war before it gets too far along. What hope can they have when they find out what kind of men are fighting for them? Your name will be a disgrace. Don't frown, Captain. I plan to exonerate you eventually.

"I'll see that your name is cleared and it will be discovered that Madison himself was responsible for your death. It will be found that you were condemned without a trial. When the public finds out you were innocent their outrage will be greater than when they thought you guilty. What kind of administration is Little Jemmy running? they'll ask. Doesn't the navy know what's going on in its own ranks? How can a man who let a thing like this happen possibly hope to win a war?"

"And you'll be there to encourage that attitude," Cloud replied, disgusted.

"Encourage it?" Howe asked incredulously. "I am going to feed it! I am going to make sure we end this debacle quickly! I am going to pull out every foundation Madison is standing on and I am going to make sure the United States survives this insanity! I am not a traitor, Captain. In spite of what you think. I want to see us with something left. The British will go easier on us if this is over soon."

"Why do you assume we are going to lose?"

"Our eighteen warships against their eight hundred? I don't assume it. I know it."

Cloud chuckled joylessly. "And you are doing everything to make sure you are not wrong."

Howe nodded. "You know, Captain, you exceeded all my expectations. You really were the perfect choice." He pressed his large bulk against the bars and called for a guard to let him out; then he turned to Cloud and observed him coolly. "Even now you sit there as if you were entertaining in your own home. There's an arrogance about you, Cloud, and this time it worked in our favor. You were so sure you could expose the truth of what we had done to Captain Danty. You were so sure you were right in releasing her that you blindly fell into our trap. Well, the truth you've discovered this evening is a little more than you bargained for, isn't that so?"

"You know it is. I didn't think people like you could find their way into our government."

"I assure you, we do. And now that you know it, you'll be more careful in the future, won't you?" He laughed triumphantly.

The guard approached Howe from behind and released the gate. Howe stepped out, shut the gate, and motioned the guard to leave.

"You really haven't accepted this," he said to Cloud. "I'd wager my next term in office that you still think there is some way out."

Cloud shrugged his shoulders and lay back on his cot, stretching his long, lean frame over the rough blankets like a powerful cat feigning disinterest in the prey temporarily out of reach. "Perhaps not for me." His voice was deceptively soft, almost a purr. "But you won't get away either."

Howe stared at the captain a moment but Cloud would not meet his eyes. Then he turned abruptly and hurried down the hallway, away from the cell, not totally unaware he was trying to escape the man he held prisoner.

Cloud's laughter reverberated in the cell. Howe had called him arrogant. Maybe he was. Maybe he was just confident enough to believe there was a way out—at least for the truth. Howe did not know about Landis. He was not aware someone existed who might be able to sort through this before morning. It did not matter to Cloud if Landis was unable to stop the execution. It only mattered that he expose Howe and the others—and that he should not die to serve a purpose he despised.

He closed his eyes and thought of Alexis. Howe can't wear the shirt forever, Alex. I've seen what kind of warped loyalty he hides beneath it. I know it exists. Someone else will discover it too. And when they do you'll know I did not die for nothing. I knew what might happen when I freed you. I warned you this afternoon when I held you in my arms. I held you tightly, knowing I might never hold you again. I didn't know what I was fighting then, only that something was terribly wrong and you could not be a part of it. Somewhere in the back of my mind I clung to the fact that my trial would free me even while I clung to you. I hoped for that but was aware it might not happen. What Howe has told me makes it more difficult to accept, but I can, knowing that you're out of his reach.

Amber eyes suddenly mocked him. Cloud's eyes flew open. Aloud he pleaded, "Don't do it, Alex! Don't come after me! You don't know . . . you can't suspect what you'll be walking into." He wondered why he felt so strongly the conviction that she would come when that possibility had never occurred to him before. He tried to dismiss it, but with his eyes open or closed he saw her face, her chin lifted defiantly, her mouth set determinedly, and her golden eyes blazing with fire fed by anger.

"What!" She flung the word out into the space of her cabin, into the faces of the men sitting at the table around her. She stared at the men one at a time.

Frank Springer sat at the far end of the table, holding his glass of wine stiffly, as if he were torn between bringing the liquid to his mouth or crushing it in his hands. Harry Young leaned casually in his chair; the only sign of tension was in his narrowed eyes. Mike Garrison sat rigidly. His only perceptible movement was a slight twitching of his jaw as he ground his teeth together. John Landis sat at her right, his eyebrows furrowed in concern. He hardly seemed aware of the others as he stroked his beard with one hand while the other gripped the arm of the chair.

Kurt Jordan, on her left, turned to her. His clear blue eyes that had been highlighted with excitement a few hours ago were tinged with a sadness he could not hide from her now. "I thought you would want to hear it from them, Captain Danty," he said softly, letting her know he would have spared her hearing it at all if it were possible.

"You were right, Mr. Jordan," she answered firmly. "Mr. Landis, repeat what you just said. I won't scream at you again."

"Scream all you want," he said. "We've been doing it for hours."

"Yes, well, it hasn't helped you or Captain Cloud. Repeat your statement."

"I said Senator Howe and the others have been using us all. I said the captain is going to hang, not for freeing you, but for something else."

"But you don't know what."

Landis shook his head. "We couldn't get near enough to the stockade to find out what's going on. And now we've got ourselves a new captain, Walter Franklin, and orders to shove off in the morning. It's all very hasty."

"Their orders are to find us," Jordan supplied. He had heard the entire story when he and some of the crew had gone in search of Landis. Landis and the others had insisted on telling Alexis personally. Jordan had agreed to it. They were risking their lives by coming aboard the *Dark Lady,* and Jordan knew it was not a trap they intended.

Frank broke in. "We're to be kept out of Howe's way while he's taking care of the captain."

"What proof do you have that Howe is behind your orders to sail? How do you know he is trying to prevent you from getting to Captain Cloud?" Alexis felt in control again. She was prepared to listen to everything they had to say. She had never thought for a moment it was going to be easy to get Cloud out, but the little information she had already gleaned from Landis told her it was going to be more difficult than she had expected.

"I'm waiting, Mr. Landis," she said, settling back into her chair. "How have you come by this information?"

Everyone's attention focused on Landis. He drew in his breath and began the story he had told once to his mates and repeated for Jordan. For the first time since so much of it became clear he allowed himself to hope.

"I went to the captain's home this afternoon. I wanted to find out how he was bearing up since you were taken prisoner and no longer in our custody. It was then he told me what he had done. He was far from unhappy about it. He said he had put you aboard your own ship and that you were safe miles away. He even jokingly criticized me and the crew for not being aware that your ship had docked. I told him we weren't much concerned about your crew after you were taken away from us.

"I tried to convince him that we should go after you but he told me about the meeting you had with Howe and the others and I saw he was right. When going after you was out of the question I thought I could get him to leave the house instead of waiting for them to pick him up. He refused to leave. He said he would be able to expose the false charges against you at his trial and get the answers he wanted concerning Howe's peculiar use of you. He thought possibly he would be exonerated. He said he did not want to tell you that. He wanted to prepare you for the worst.

"While I was at the house the guards came for him. He made me hide and swear not to admit I knew what he had done. I guess he figured if things didn't work out the entire crew would be in danger. Since he was waiting for them at the door, they didn't bother to search. I stayed hidden in the study with an ear pressed tight to the door. I heard Tanner talking to the senator. I was a little surprised to find Howe present. That is not usual. The captain was taken away, but Howe and one of the guards remained in the entrance.

"The guard asked Howe a strange question. He asked him how they were going to get Tanner *into* the stockade. Howe answered that it had all been taken care of. They were to give the guards at the prison these papers. He must have handed them over to the man, who apparently looked at them because he started laughing. He said, 'You really have thought of everything. This certainly isn't what the captain expected to be tried for!' Then his voice was kind of troubled and he added, 'You know, Senator, Captain Cloud is pretty well known. His superiors aren't going to believe this.' Howe said something like, 'Let me worry about it. You've been paid. So have some of his superiors. The ones who haven't will find out too late.' "

Landis paused to sip his wine. Over the rim of his glass he observed Alexis who had leaned her head back and shut her eyes. Her face was drawn and pale.

"It still doesn't make a whole lot of sense, Captain," he continued. "We don't know why Howe is bringing these false charges against the captain. Maybe he knows Tanner would have gotten free on the matter of releasing you. The only thing we can figure out is Howe doesn't want him free. We can't go to anyone. We don't know who's been paid and who hasn't. There doesn't even seem to be enough time to find that out. It could be the President himself who issued these orders."

"I can't believe that!" Alexis said sharply, opening her eyes. She leaned forward in her chair. "He couldn't be so much of a fool that he would set out to destroy one of his ablest commanders."

"I agree with you," Harry interjected. "In fact I'll go further and say Madison knows nothing of what's going on. But his ignorance isn't exactly in our favor."

"Harry's right," Mike said. "Madison probably doesn't know we were assigned to capture you. That's what Mr. Landis meant when he said we had all been used. Howe and his friends wanted you for some purpose that we can't guess. They used us to bring you to them. If that's the case then they can't let the captain tell what has happened at his trial. He may not even be allowed a trial of any kind."

"Why put him in the stockade?" she asked. "Why not . . ." She could not finish.

"We don't know why he's still alive." Landis helped her. "But we do know that he is. A few of the men have been slipping away from the ship from time to time and they've been able to learn he's still there. Captain Franklin is a little disconcerted by the crew's wanderlust, but he's so excited with his new command I don't think he knows what's really going on."

Landis's attempt at levity was not lost on Alexis but she could not force a smile. "You don't think there is much time, do you?"

The men from the *Concord* shifted uncomfortably in their seats. Alexis had her answer. She addressed her first mate. "In light of what you know, Mr. Jordan, are you having any second thoughts about going after him?"

Jordan shook his head. "If it's possible, I want to get him out of there more than I did before."

"Mr. Jordan is speaking for me as well," she told them. "Captain Cloud is the only one who can tell us what is happening. If Howe, Davidson, Farthington, and Granger have some sort of scheme in mind, then he is the only one who can stop it. I had not intended involving you men in this except for the necessary information concerning the captain's whereabouts—but now I know I'll need more from you."

"Don't ask us, Captain Danty," Frank responded. "You know we are ready to help."

Alexis smiled. "I wasn't going to ask you, Frank. I knew you were prepared to help when you first came in here. I wanted to let you know I have changed my mind about accepting it." She stood and walked over to her desk. She returned to the table with paper, quill, and ink. She laid the blank paper down and smoothed out its edges.

"I want a drawing of the stockade and where the guards are positioned. There are probably more of them than we anticipated. I need to know how many are in the prison as well. Also give us a rough idea of the surrounding buildings and what route we'll have to take from the stockade back to the ship."

Frank seized the paper and began providing the information. As he worked Alexis conferred with Jordan.

"The plan we talked about earlier. Do you agree we can still make it work?" she asked.

"I doubt if Howe anticipates you returning for the captain," he answered thoughtfully. "Surprise will be on our side. I think we'll need more men in hiding in case something goes wrong. The core of the plan is still workable. It would have been easier if Howe hadn't turned him over to the real authorities."

"I agree. What about an additional diversion?" She looked down at Frank's work. "This building," she said, pointing to a square near the prison. "What is it?"

"It's not a building, Captain," Frank explained. "It denotes the lumber pile. They keep extra lumber there for the ships. It's guarded almost as well as the prison. People are always trying to get into the yard and carry some off."

"Mr. Jordan, what do you think? A fire there would certainly cause a disturbance."

"We have the extra powder. We could blow it sky high."

"I don't want it blown sky high," she said firmly. "I want it to look like an accident. If they suspect it was deliberate they'll guard Cloud more carefully. Can we manage an accident?"

Jordan grinned. "No problem. Davie Brandon can do what you want."

"Good. You explain it to him. Ask him to pick three men to help. No more than that. We'll have to leave some on the ship."

"What else do you want us to do?" asked Harry.

"I hadn't forgotten about you." She laughed. "What I don't want is for you or any of your crew to show your faces within two hundred yards of where they have the captain. Do you think your new commander is excited enough with his new command to give all of you a last night in Washington?"

"I'll make him see the merits of it," said Landis. "He knows we were all loyal to Tanner. He'll be eager to start off on the right foot."

"Then I want you to be at your drunken best. I want you to get in the way of every man who comes after us. Send them in any direction except the one we'll be heading."

"That's easy enough," answered Mike. "But what makes you think they'll follow? Aren't you going to make an assault on the place?"

"You mean kill the guards?" Her voice was filled with disbelief. "Hardly, Mike. I am not going to add murder of American seamen to the problems I already have with your government. Our plan doesn't call for killing. We'll knock out as many as we can. That's why I know we'll be followed. We can't hope to get them all."

Jordan added, "There'll be some time before they realize Captain Cloud is gone. We should be able to outdistance them."

"Who is actually going to get the captain out?" asked Mike. He sounded a little skeptical of their plan.

"Prepare yourself," Alexis warned. "My cabin boy is going to do it." She and Jordan laughed as Mike's mouth opened and Frank dropped his quill.

Jordan calmed himself enough to explain the plan. When he was done they looked at him with new respect and grudgingly admitted it was better than anything they had been able to think of.

Frank slid his completed drawing toward Alexis. "How soon do you plan to get started?"

"We'll be ready as soon as you send word back about your leave. We'll go ahead without you if need be but we'll have to know how much help we will be able to count on."

While the others gathered their jackets, he explained his sketch to Alexis and Jordan. When he had answered all their questions satisfactorily he joined the others at the door. "No matter what happens tonight, Captain Danty, it will be a long time before we see you again. We'll be chasing you tomorrow as ordered. What direction will you be going?"

"South. Then to New Orleans."

"Got it. North. Then to London. Wait until I tell Franklin the good news!"

They all laughed easily and "thank you" was inherent in the sound. When Harry closed the door Jordan said to Alexis, "They really like you. It must have been hard on them taking you in the first place."

"It was," she replied quietly, remembering how guilty they

all had felt. "It was very hard. And now it seems they are not even sure why they had to do it."

"Then you believe Captain Cloud's orders did not come from Mr. Madison?"

"I always had a hard time believing they did come from him. Have you ever read any of his articles defending the Constitution?" Jordan replied that he hadn't. "George had some of them. I don't know how he got them but I read them once and I know why he saved them. Any man who wrote about the necessity of adopting your Constitution and its Bill of Rights is not the man responsible for violating my rights or those of Captain Cloud. No, those men I talked to are the ones responsible and I plan to find out why."

Jordan never doubted her for a moment. He gathered strength from her determination. "Before I see to Brandon and the details for the fire there is something else that has been bothering me."

"What is it?"

"When the captain discovers you are with us and not where Peach says you will be, I am wondering if he'll go to the ship."

Alexis touched her temple gently. It was still tender from Cloud's blow. "I've taken care of that. Peters and Wilkes are going to make sure the captain does as I've ordered. They know what to do if he becomes too obstinate."

"Peters and Wilkes," he whistled softly. "And I thought you had forgiven him his rough treatment of you earlier today."

"I'll pay. He'll see that I pay."

Jordan smiled at his captain who was unconsciously staring at her bunk, seeing something he could only guess at. He saw her shiver and when she realized what she had done she looked up at him.

"Go on. Get out of here." She laughed. "That silly smile on your face makes me feel like a little girl instead of your captain."

Jordan got up and went to the door. "Why do I worry?" he muttered as he shut it.

* * *

Alexis kept Peach close by her side while her other men separated and took up their positions in the vicinity of the prison. Everything was going as planned. Harry had reported the *Concord* crew was ready to help, and he had made her a present of the dagger he had taken from her aboard the ship. Now the weapon was securely strapped to her calf, hidden beneath the folds of her dress. She pulled her dark cape more closely about her shoulders and placed a hand on Peach's arm. She was not completely sure whether she was steadying herself or comforting him.

"We'll wait a little bit longer," she whispered. "Are you scared?"

He looked up at her. She could barely make out the lines of his face in the darkness but she knew his eyes held trust in her. She saw a brief flash of white reveal his impish grin.

"Not much, Captain. You're not disappointed in me?"

"Hardly." She refrained from telling him how frightened she was. More frightened of facing these next minutes than she had ever been at the thought of facing Travers. She patted him on the back. "You go on now. Through the yard. Make enough noise so they don't shoot you outright. If Allison catches up to you before the guards do he'll have to be a little rough. Just make sure you scream."

"Hope I know how!" he said bravely.

Alexis laughed. "Off with you!"

Peach ran out of the shadows toward the stone prison. He whimpered and called for help as he moved quickly into the light coming from the building. He hoped the guards would see he was just a boy, even though he felt like a man now. He glanced up to see the three guards lower their muskets as he approached. Relieved by their decision not to fire on him, he increased his crying as well as his speed.

Peach was almost on top of them when he fell to the ground, sobbing brokenly. It was not as hard as he thought. He did not know he would be so scared.

"What's wrong with you, son?" asked one of the guards, stepping forward.

Before Peach had a chance to reply the guard heard other voices shouting and drawing closer. "There he is, Ned! I told you I saw him come this way!" The guard watched as Peach struggled to his feet and tried to get away. He was stopped when the man reached out and grabbed him firmly by the arm.

"Is someone after you?" he asked.

Peach nodded rapidly as if all power of speech had left him, and he attempted to pull away again.

Jordan and Allison came running into the circle of light. They stopped abruptly when they saw the muskets aimed at them. Jordan held up his arms and moved cautiously.

"You can put down the weapons," he called. "Wouldn't have come near this place if that damn fool kid hadn't stolen my watch. Followed him here to get it back."

"I don't have his watch!" Peach defended himself.

"Lower your guns, men," ordered the guard who held the squirming boy. He motioned to Jordan and Allison to step closer. "The boy says he doesn't have your watch."

Allison growled. "You don't expect him to say he does, do you? I saw him lift it right out of my friend's pocket."

The guard laid his musket on the ground and made a quick search of Peach. He found the article in question in his pocket. "This what all the fuss is about?" He threw it at Jordan who caught it and examined it.

"This is it," he said angrily.

His statement brought fresh denials from Peach. "He's lying, sir! That watch belongs to my sister. He took it from her. I was trying to get it back. There's an inscription on it. Says, 'George.' He was my father. He willed the watch to my sister, Francine."

"If you believed that, you'll believe anything!" Jordan said caustically.

"Didn't say I did. The kid could have read it."

"Then give us the boy so we can turn him over to the

police," Allison said. Jordan and Peach tensed, waiting for the guard's reply. They were prepared for either a yes or a no. No would be easier.

"No. You have the watch back," said the guard. "If you two hadn't been drinking so much he wouldn't have been able to take it." It was obvious to him now the men had just come from a tavern. They reeked of ale ten paces off. "Get out of here and don't come back. You're just lucky you weren't shot."

"What are you going to do with the brat?" asked Jordan.

"I'll send him on his way when I know you're not waiting to grab him."

"Have it your way." Allison turned to go. "Hope he doesn't pick your pocket."

When Jordan and Allison were out of sight the guard released Peach. "That was a stupid thing to do."

"I'm telling you the watch belongs to my sister, sir," Peach said, wiping his tear-stained face. "She was furious when they took it. Says the streets aren't safe for anyone these days."

"How long ago did those men supposedly take your sister's watch?"

"A few hours ago. We were on our way home and she was checking the time and all of a sudden she didn't have it any more. They grabbed it right out of her hand! I told her I was going to get it back. She begged me not to."

"You didn't listen very well." He was beginning to believe there was some truth to the boy's story.

"I know. I hope she doesn't come looking for me. If she sees those men she'll scratch their eyes out."

"You make your sister sound like quite a tiger."

Peach laughed, enjoying himself. "She is. Blazing golden eyes and—"

He never finished. The guards all jolted to attention as Alexis's piercing scream reached their ears.

"That's her! That's my sister!" Peach was frantic. "She must have seen me leave the house!" He started to bolt in the direction of the screams but he was stopped.

"Where do you think you're going?"

"I have to go after her. They might hurt her."

"C'mon, Davis. John. It seems tiger lady got herself in a bit of trouble." He turned back to Peach. "What's your name, son?"

"Peach. It's a nickname, sir."

"Well, Peach, we'll help your sister. You wait inside. Matt's in there. Tell him where we're going. We'll have your sister back in no time at all."

"And the watch," Peach called as he ran past them into the building.

The three men started running toward the screams. They were joined by two more guards who heard the same thing. In the darkness they almost stumbled over Alexis who had ceased her cries and was now sobbing uncontrollably on the ground. The five men circled around her and she looked up. She tried to move away, her eyes filled with terror.

The three guards who heard Peach's story were immediately certain he had spoken the truth. Even at night those eyes flashed flecks of gold.

"We are not going to hurt you, miss. My name is Richards. Greg Richards. Those men . . . where? . . ."

"They're gone," Alexis said quietly, her voice trembling. She looked down at her torn bodice and thought what a nice effect it was. She went on. "They tried to . . . tried to . . ."

Richards held out his hand but Alexis pushed it aside. "You're Francine, aren't you?"

"How did you know?"

"Your brother is back at the prison. He told us about you. Why don't you come back with us? He'll want to know that you're safe." His voice was soothing and Alexis almost wished he wouldn't show quite so much kindness.

"Not just yet," she answered. "I don't want to move. Those men, they knocked the wind out of me."

Richards nodded. "Davis, you stay with me. John, you better go back and tell the boy his sister is all right." He motioned to the other two. "Go back to your posts as well."

"Oh, no!" she pleaded. "Don't any of you go. What if they come back?"

"And don't you think the two of us can handle them? That doesn't say very much for us, does it?"

Stall! Her men needed more time to get ready. "It's not that," she answered prettily. "I just feel safer with all of you around."

Richards grinned. "You'll be fine. These men have to get back. We have an important prisoner to watch."

The words were barely out of his mouth when he felt a sharp pain creasing his skull. He did not know the others, so captivated by Alexis's soft voice and appearance were experiencing the same pain.

Alexis pushed Richards's body off her own and stood, brushing herself off. She smiled at her men, Jordan and Allison among them. "It doesn't say much for my ability to hold a man's attention when they all wanted to go back to their posts."

"Don't know about that, Captain," Allison said. "They were so busy looking at you they didn't hear us come up on them."

Alexis glanced down at the bodies. "I'd say you did your work pretty well. I don't think we'll waste time tying them. Let's get rid of the walking patrols next. The fire will take care of anyone else who might see Peach and Cloud leave."

As Alexis was leading her men to the next post, Peach was lifting the butt of a pistol Matt was kind enough to show him high over the guard's turned head. He brought it down sharply and watched in fascination as Matt slumped forward in his chair. Peach did not waste any more time. He thought he had lost too much already, winning the guard's confidence. He quickly grabbed the ring of keys from their place on the wall and he opened the door that led to the cells.

He found Cloud in the next to the last cell, sleeping peacefully. Peach wondered how a man who was supposed to die could possibly sleep. He slipped the key into the gate and opened the door. The captain still did not move. Peach drew closer to the cot. He was in the process of reaching out to touch Cloud when the captain suddenly shot forward, knocking Peach to the ground.

"My God! It's you!" Cloud could hardly believe he saw the small boy sprawled out on the floor in front of him. The boy was glaring at him. He smiled, remembering these were the eyes he had once accused of being lovesick for Alexis. Love was no part of anything they were expressing at the moment.

Peach continued to glare as he got to his feet. "You have a strange way of saying thank you."

Cloud realized the boy was more angry for being taken off guard than anything else. "I'll make it up to you later," he replied, grinning.

Peach ignored him. "Come on. We have to go out front. Be ready to move quickly when the time comes."

"Where is your captain?" asked Cloud as he followed the boy to the front room.

"She'll be waiting for us," he answered tersely.

Cloud pointed to the unconscious guard. "You did that?" His voice held the proper amount of admiration and Peach responded in a friendlier manner, assuring Cloud that he had. "What about the others?"

"They're being taken care of." Peach kept his eyes trained on where he knew the lumber pile should be, although he couldn't make it out in the dark. Occasionally he glanced away from the window and looked at Cloud, who was confiscating Matt's weapon for his own.

"What are you waiting for? Why aren't we leaving now?"

"It's a good thing Captain Danty is planning this. You'd get us both killed. Did you really expect to get out of here after you knocked one guard out?" Peach's tone left Cloud no doubt the boy was unimpressed by his actions back in the cell.

"When you have been assured your death is inevitable you take almost any chance."

Peach shrugged. "I suppose. Still, it's better Captain Danty is in charge."

Cloud laughed. "You're probably right. Now, why don't you tell me what you're looking for so I can watch too."

Peach did not have to answer. Flames shot up in the distance, outlining the piles of lumber. "That's it. No, don't go yet," he said as Cloud started toward the door. "Wait. I'm supposed to make sure most of the guards head in that direction." The flames were bright enough now to let Peach see figures flurrying toward their origin. "Okay. Now we go."

Cloud stepped aside and let the cabin boy, who had the presence of an admiral, lead the way. When Peach started running for a house in the distance Cloud stayed right behind him. Peach reached the far side of the house and caught his breath. They both stiffened when they heard the sound of approaching footsteps. Peach put a hand on Cloud's pistol, signaling him not to be hasty.

"Peach? Captain Cloud?" It was Peters.

"Over here," answered Peach. Peters and Wilkes joined them. Both men towered over Peach and even Cloud found himself having to look up, something he was not used to doing. Peach turned to face Cloud. "These men will take you to the ship. Captain Danty says you are to go with them."

Cloud shook his head. "Where is your captain? You said she'd be waiting for us."

"She's waiting for me. I have to circle around and let her know you're all right."

"Damn! Do you mean she's out there by the fire?"

"Yes, and don't argue. Go with these men."

"I'm going with you," Cloud corrected. The boy was becoming just a little too authoritarian. "I won't leave until I know she's safe. She could be killed!"

Peach looked at Peters, who was becoming restless. He looked back at Cloud. "Captain Danty said you might not obey orders. She's taken care of that too. Peters. You know what you have to do."

Cloud realized too late what was going to happen. Peter's fist connected with the side of his head and he was knocked against the wall of the house. He struggled to his feet in time to see Peach running to his rendezvous with Alexis. As he lunged at Peters his only thought was to get away from her men and make sure she was safe. It was his last thought as Wilkes finished off the job Peters had initiated.

They carried Cloud to the waiting wagon and headed for the ship.

Alexis watched from her hiding place as Davie Brandon and his helpers escaped the flames they had just started. The grounds were in chaos as guards moved in to fight the fire. Alexis and her men had little time to enjoy the sight. They ran toward the place designated to meet Peach.

The flames rose higher and higher, casting their light in sharp, jagged patches across the compound. Away from the light, in their hiding place amidst some straggly shrubbery, Alexis and her crew waited to discover if Peach had been successful. It was not long before they realized their diversion was bringing them an unexpected piece of luck. People from nearby homes, seeing the flames, were hastening to the area.

"They'll be helpful," Jordan observed dryly "They're bound to get in the way."

"As long as they don't get in our way," Brandon answered. "Where the hell is that boy? I hope he took advantage of that magnificent fire."

Alexis shifted her position to get a better look in the direction Peach was supposed to come from. "He'll be here, Davey," she assured him as well as herself. She focused her attention on the people hurrying past them on the way to the fire. "Oh my God!" she gasped, clutching Jordan's arm.

"What is it? What's wrong?"

Alexis pulled the hood of her cape over her head, released Jordan's arm, and slipped further back into the shadows. She pointed to a man on horseback not more than twenty feet from them. He was staring intently at the fire. Occasionally the light flickered across his face and his wheat-colored hair.

"That's Farthington," she whispered to her men. "He'll suspect something!"

"C'mon, Peach!" It was a reverent prayer the way Allison said the words.

A few tense moments passed then Farthington made them realize their worst fears. He jerked the reins of his horse and pressed heels into his mount's flanks. He muttered a few curses and galloped in the direction of the prison.

"Damn him! He knows!" Alexis groaned as she watched him ride off.

"It's Peach!" cried Allison, clapping Brandon on the back.

Alexis turned and saw Peach mingling with the crowd, trying to get to them. She was on her feet immediately. "Ned! Get him! The rest of you, follow me!"

Allison singled out Peach and grabbed him tightly by the wrist. "This way, you little pickpocket!" he chuckled. "You did get what you came for, didn't you?"

"I did," the boy answered proudly.

Peach and Ned met the others on the far side of the compound. After Alexis made sure that Peach had been successful she held back her questions and praise. A shot originating from the area of the prison halted their short celebration. The men needed no encouragement to follow her as she lifted her dress and began running. She smiled when she passed familiar faces as she ran through the streets and alleys—familiar faces that seemed to shout their thanks and encouragement though they remained silent, as if they were oblivious to everything but their drunken camaraderie.

As they raced up the gangway of the *Dark Lady,* Alexis gave the order to sail. The task was undertaken more quickly than she had ever dreamed possible. She strained to hear above the voices of her men, intent on learning how closely they were going to be pursued. But the docks remained quiet. There was no unusual commotion from the harbor as the *Dark Lady* slipped away.

Jordan stepped to the rail beside her. He was also listening for the sounds that would mean a pursuit. "I think Captain Cloud's men kept their word," he said at last. "We're not going to be followed."

Now that they were safely out of the harbor, Alexis felt the tension slowly ebb from her body. She placed her arms stiffly on the rail, leaned her body forward, and raised her head in a way that signaled her victory. The men who saw her pose were reminded of a figurehead at the bow of a ship. They smiled to themselves, thinking this was how they always saw her, though never so clearly as they did at this moment.

"We did it," she said solemnly, speaking to the water, the retreating shoreline, and the brisk night air. She turned to Jordan who was watching her intently, an understanding smile on his rugged face. "We did it, Mr. Jordan!" she shouted as if she had just accepted the fact and all it meant. "Peach! You did it! We all did it!"

A cheer rose up from the crew and Alexis felt herself being lifted into the air on the firm, muscular shoulders of Jordan and Allison.

"Put me down!" she cried, smiling, not caring if they obeyed her or not. She felt light and slightly dizzy when the two men finally decided it wise to set her down. "Where's Peach?" she asked, holding Jordan's arm to steady herself.

"Here, Captain!" Peach called as he worked his way through the men surrounding her.

She pulled him toward her, placing an arm around his shoulders. "Here's the man we have to thank for the success of tonight's venture!" The crew loudly sounded their approval, and Alexis could feel his shoulders straighten as he proudly accepted his praise. "And what have you done with the captain, Peach? I thought he would be on deck to celebrate." This statement brought some laughter from Peters and Wilkes. Alexis could guess what had happened.

"That man is awfully stubborn," the cabin boy answered. "I gave him every chance to go with Peters but—"

"But he had to be persuaded," Alexis finished. "It seems the captain and I expend a lot of energy trying to persuade one another. Where is he now, Wilkes? Were you very rough on him?"

"He's in your cabin sleeping it off."

Alexis laughed. "He should learn to follow orders. Peach, go see to the captain. Let me know when he wakes up."

Peach nodded and hurried away, eager to see Cloud and face his anger when he woke.

Alexis set their course for New Orleans after the men assured her they were more anxious to get Travers than see Roadtown. Satisfied that everything was functioning smoothly in the hands of her crew, she assigned watch duty then spent the next hour with Jordan, acquainting herself with everything that had happened during her absence.

They had just concluded their discussion when she saw Peach motioning to her. She excused herself and went to stand beside him.

"Is it the captain?" she asked.

"Yes, ma'am. He's awake and he's furious."

"What did he say to you?"

"First he grumbled about his head hurting; then he realized where he was and told me to get you. Said if you weren't all right I'd better never show my face around him again. Told me to tell Peters and Wilkes the same thing."

"Then I'd better see him," she sighed. "So you don't have to worry about being in his way."

"He doesn't scare me!" Peach assured her loudly. More softly he added, "But do you think you should see him just yet? He's really angry about what Peters and Wilkes did."

"Then I'll have to inform him they were following my instructions."

"Do you think you should?" he asked warily.

"You did a good job tonight, Peach. We could not have been successful without you. But as I recall you still cannot manage to give me a hot bath when I want one."

In a perfect imitation of Jordan when he was exasperated, Peach pulled his shoulders straight, folded his lanky arms across his chest, and shook his head slowly. "Why do I worry?" he asked as he rolled his eyes heavenward.

Alexis threw her arms up in despair. "He's corrupted you!"

Peach laughed as his captain walked away.

Chapter Fifteen

Alexis paused outside the door to her quarters, bracing herself for Cloud's fury, certain of the form it would take.

Her cabin was dark, throwing all her possessions into a shadowy netherworld. Only one thing seemed real—his presence and she could sense it as clearly as if she were seeing him in the full light of day. She shut the door quietly. Cloud would want the commander to pay.

She tensed, listening to the sound of his even breathing only a few feet in front of her. She noticed her own breathing was ragged and she tried unsuccessfully to still it. She was aware he was coming closer but when his arm brushed her as he reached to lock the door, her gasp mingled with the sound of metal scraping against metal.

"Cloud?" She said his name hesitantly, almost fearfully.

"Shut up." His voice was not abrasive or cruel. The words were not pronounced angrily or menacingly. They reached her senses as a caress—holding her, enveloping her. Cloud placed his palms flat against the door on either side of her head.

His hands moved to her throat and Alexis's breath constricted as if his fingers were pressing tightly against her flesh when actually he was doing no more than unclasping the frog of her cape. She leaned forward a fraction, letting the cloak slip from her shoulders and fall to the floor. He gently pushed her back against the door as if he realized she needed it for support. His fingers found the circle of silver at her neck. Then his hands moved lower, cupping her breasts, and slowly, expertly, he began to unfasten the buttons of her dress. He slid the material down her arms, over the curve of her hips, and allowed it to join the cape at her feet. He knelt in front of her and removed her shoes. His hands recoiled as they reached to touch the warm flesh of her calves and came in contact with the cold metal of her dagger. She heard his low chuckle as he unstrapped the weapon, then she felt the tip of the blade sliding upward along the length of her leg, lifting her slips as Cloud slowly began to rise.

"Raise your arms."

Alexis responded, not to the edge of steel against her waist, but to his steel edged voice. He tossed the dagger aside and lifted the material over her breasts, over her head, and finally past her slender wrists and trembling fingers. Her arms started to fall but he caught them in one hand and held them above her while his other hand removed the pins from her hair, freeing the golden mass to his inquiring fingers.

"I like your hair like this."

It fell across her shoulders and breasts and he caught a section of it between his fingers. He fondled it lightly, rediscovering the texture, the thick richness of the gold he held. His eyes never left her face as he laid the ringlets against her skin and stroked the warm, yielding softness of her breasts.

Alexis heard a soft moan pass her parted lips as the naked flesh beneath his palm quivered and her nipples hardened and thrust forward to meet his caress. His hand dropped lower. The tips of his fingers brushed against the curve of her waist, across the flat plane of her stomach, and rested gently on the warm skin of her inner thigh.

He could see her amber eyes imploring him, begging him,

to take her. Her eyes, with golden flecks of fire, spoke eloquently in place of the voice she did not have the strength to use. He pressed against her more tightly, forcing her back to the door, one hand still holding her wrists, the other at the junction of her legs, and now he added the pressure of his mouth on hers to push her head back. He sensed her momentary struggle, not to be free of him, but to be free to hold him, then her gradual acceptance when she realized he would not allow her this, and finally her willing response to his kiss.

Abruptly he removed his hands and his mouth and stepped back out of her reach. With the loss of support her arms fell limply to her sides and she thought it was only a matter of seconds before she collapsed entirely at his feet.

"Come here. I want you to come to me."

Somehow she found her voice. "I don't think I can," she whispered.

"You can."

And she did. When she reached him she collapsed in his arms, regaining her strength from the contact of his body close to hers. Her arms circled his neck. As her mouth sought his he lowered her to the deck. His kiss was hard and brutal. His hands were no longer tender in their stroking but fierce and violently demanding. Alexis accepted it all, knowing this was his way of regaining ownership over something he had almost lost this evening.

He tore his mouth away and released himself from the circle of her embrace. Standing, he took off his clothes. She watched, her breathing becoming more irregular with each article that drifted to the floor. She stroked his bare, muscular calf, and as he knelt beside her, her hand moved along the tight skin of his thigh. He pushed her hand aside and placed his hands beneath her shoulder blades, lifting her toward him, her head tilted back, and kissed the hollow of her throat.

His lips moved from her throat to her breasts, burning her skin, bruising her flesh. Her fingers held his head, caressed his temples, and lightly drew down the column of his neck.

They raked savagely across his back as his mouth fell on hers once more and his demands increased. He pressed her to the deck and moved between her parted thighs.

"You could have been killed tonight." He thrust into her.

"Yes." They both knew she was responding to his statement as well as his thrust.

"I could have lost you." He moved powerfully again.

"Yes." Her legs wrapped around him, holding him tightly, assuring him in his anguished pleasure he could not lose her now.

"And you'll still go after Travers!" His stroking continued.

"Yes! Oh, Cloud! Yes!" She arched her back and matched his thrusts, answering him with her voice and her body.

Alexis felt herself being lifted higher and higher, supported by nothing but the rising wave of pleasure he was creating. She clung to him, unwilling to reach the crest without him or make the descent alone. She cried out at his final thrust as one explosion after another rocked her body.

A moan, a cry of helplessness, muffled against the warm skin of his shoulder, reached his ears as her mouth pressed its outline on his perspiring flesh. He fell beside her, her fingers gripping his arms tightly in a last effort to hold him to her. When the last of her strength was finally exhausted, her fingers opened, unfolding like the petals of a delicate flower, and slipped from his arms. She remained motionless except for the occasional tremors that spoke of the pleasure which had just passed between them.

His arm circled her waist and drew her close, He felt warm, uneven breathing against his chest, more intimate in its contact than the closeness of their bodies. When she quieted he made a move to pull away from her, wanting to carry her to bed.

"No. Don't move," she whispered. "I want to stay here . . . with you . . . just like this." She heard his low, throaty laughter and sensed his smile as he settled beside her. A little later she said, "I was afraid, Cloud. For both of us."

His arm tightened around her. "You shouldn't have come."

She shook her head violently. "Don't say that! You released me. It was my choice to use my liberty as I did."

"But you didn't even know what you were facing."

"I knew some of it. I knew I would lose you if I didn't return." She placed her hand on his chest, caressing it lightly. He felt the trembling of her voice through the trembling of the five slim fingertips that touched him. "I don't want to be apart from you."

"And you won't be," he assured her. His hand clasped hers and he pressed it close. "Now tell me what you thought you were facing when you came back."

Alexis told him everything that had happened since she'd found herself aboard the *Dark Lady*. She conveyed Landis's suspicions and his crew's help in Cloud's escape. She hesitated a moment near the end of the story, then plunged in, explaining how Farthington had stumbled upon their scheme and almost upset everything. When she finished his mouth covered hers, angrily at first, then more softly, tenderly. She made no protest when he lifted her in his arms and placed her in the bunk.

He did not join her immediately. He searched her room for a lamp. Finding one, he lit it. A soft, golden light filled the cabin and flickered over Alexis's body. Cloud stepped closer to the bunk and admired the tawny flesh that seemed to quiver as if it were being stroked and fondled by the glow. He reached out to touch one of the patches of diffused light falling on her cheek. She held his hand in place, her eyes caressing his face, silently conveying the words she had never said aloud.

"Come," she said quietly. "Lie beside me."

He obeyed and fitted himself comfortably along the contours of her body. Her fingers curled around the thick copper hair at the nape of his neck and brushed against his temple and the lean, tight skin of his face.

"My men? Did they hurt you very badly?" she asked.

"My pride." He gripped her wrists cruelly, reliving that moment when she had exposed herself to so much danger because of him. He released her suddenly and laughed. "I guess I deserved it. Your cabin boy warned me all along that you were in charge."

"Peach told me you were very stubborn."

"A trait you apparently planned for," he commented dryly.

She kissed his lips tenderly. "I tried to prepare for everything."

"Even for what happened in this room?"

"Even for that." She was silent for a while; then she said, "Tell me what they were really after, Cloud. Were your crew's suspicions justified?"

"Completely." He paused then, thinking back to all Howe had told him. Alexis waited patiently, giving him time to sort through the experience. When he finally spoke his voice was edged with the same bitterness she remembered hearing when he spoke of his impressment. The muscles and tendons in his chest and arms tensed beneath her embrace. His arms crushed her as he explained Howe's plan to turn her over to the British in return for considerations when a treaty was signed. When he told her the senator's intention to execute him in the morning her tears fell silently on his skin, scalding him with the white hot intensity of her passion.

"Oh, Cloud! How could they want to do those things to you? What kind of men are they that would not respect the decision of their peers, and would fight against their country when it needs them most?" She wanted to say more but her voice shook while her body shuddered against his. She fell silent, knowing he understood all she could not say.

He kissed her tears, her closed eyes, and trembling lips. He drew out her despair and anger with his mouth as a poultice would draw poison.

"Howe can't touch us now," he whispered. "You've seen to that." She started to argue but it came to nothing as his fingers pushed against her lips. "We'll discuss what to do about stopping him in the morning. I don't want his name between us now."

"You're right," she murmured. She turned sleepily in his arms.

"Tired?" He was grinning.

"Exhausted," she replied, suddenly realizing how true that statement was. She glanced up at his face and saw his green eyes were smiling at her. The smile was a translucent cover for the hunger and longing behind it. She felt powerless and impotent beneath his steady gaze, as if she had no will of her own. Then she realized she did have a will and the want serving as its impetus was her desire for him. She stammered. "Not if . . . that is not if you want . . . I mean if you want . . ."

"If I want to make love to you?"

"Yes," she answered weakly.

"Oh, I do. I do. But I want you to sleep now." He laughed, running his fingers through her hair. "Who knows? Maybe you'll be able to speak in complete sentences later."

She pinched his arm and nestled beside him, her lips curved in a contented smile. Slowly her eyes closed and her lashes fanned slivers of shadow across her face.

"I love you," said Cloud. He noticed the slight curve of her mouth.

When Alexis awoke she threw off the covers Cloud had placed over them. Outside it was still dark but the lamp had never been extinguished and she lifted her head, letting her gaze wander over his lean, well-muscled features. He was a composite, she thought. A composite of valuable metals and precious stones: brilliant emerald eyes; rich copper hair; bronzed flesh hinting of golden undertones where the sun had not touched it; sinewy muscles having the tensile strength of steel. A human alloy cast from the materials men had prized from almost the beginning of time.

He was lying on his back, one arm flung around his head as it rested in the curve of his elbow. The other arm lay at his side, palm up, and Alexis traced the lines of his life with her fingertip. His breathing was even, his chest rising and falling in a slow, easy motion, comforting her with its steady rhythm. His long legs were intertwined with hers and she could feel the pulse beat in his thigh against her own. His face showed no sign of past tension or any indication the future would not be exactly as he wanted it. There were no troubled lines marring the perfection of his classic features.

A small, deep sigh escaped his parted lips. Alexis smiled, understanding what it was Cloud had wanted to capture when he heard her sigh. She felt the same desire to embrace the sound, its origins, and its creator so it would be repeated again and again.

"Cloud?" She whispered his name softly as she nibbled at his ear and rubbed her leg against his. She liked the feel of their flesh touching.

"Mmmm?" he answered, not bothering to open his eyes.

"When we were away from each other for so long . . . when I first escaped you until you returned for me . . . were there other women for you?"

"Two. Three. I can't remember."

"I'm glad there were others."

"Why?"

"Because they would remind you only of how much you wanted me." She was silent a moment, then, "Cloud?"

She murmured his name against his shoulder, tickling his skin lightly with her breath.

"Mmmm?" he answered, eyes still closed.

"If I told you Travers did not matter anymore . . . that I am tired of the pursuit . . . that I don't care if I find him any longer . . . would you believe me?"

"No."

"Good." A brief pause settled between them, then, "Cloud?"

She said his name wonderingly, as if she had just discovered she liked the sound of it. Her fingers traced lazy circles on the surface of his abdomen.

"Mmmm?" he answered, peering into the darkness afforded by his shuttered eyes.

"On the cliff, the day I became Alex Danty again, I swore two things to myself."

"Yes?"

"Do you know I've broken the second promise?"

"I know."

"I love you." The only sound she was conscious of came from the increased beating of his heart, then, "Cloud?"

She breathed his name gently, the slightest catch in the single word. She caught his nipple between her teeth.

"Mmmm?" he answered, still closing her off to his vision.

"They would have picked you for me. George and Francine and Pauley, I mean. They would have wanted me to choose you."

"Why?"

"Francine would have picked you because you're very handsome. You are, you know. She would have told me the qualities that make you beautiful come from your character. George would have chosen you because you're intelligent, honest, and quietly arrogant. He would have said your pride was refreshing because it came from a man who believed in himself. And Pauley . . . Pauley would have singled you out because you would have never backed down from him. He would have said that it meant you knew what you wanted. That was a quality he valued highly. They all would have been right about you."

"And why did you choose me?" His eyebrows lifted almost imperceptibly.

"For all those reasons—and one more."

"And?"

"You wanted me for the same reasons." She was quiet until she could stand it no longer. Finally, "Cloud?"

She said his name anxiously, frustrated. Her palms slid up his chest while her knee moved to his naked thigh and rested there.

"Mmmm?" he answered, his heavily lashed lids still hiding green eyes.

"What do I have to do to get you to make love to me?"

"Is that what you want?"

"Yes."

"Then ask me."

"Will you make love to me?"

"Is there a chance you might sleep until morning afterward?"

"A very good chance."

"Then I will make love to you."

His eyes opened wide in surprise as she sunk her teeth into his shoulder. Laughing, he threw her on her back and began to return the exquisite torture she had been putting him through.

When Alexis opened her eyes the light flooding the room was not artificial. Cloud was sitting on the edge of the bed in the last stages of dressing. He felt her movement on the mattress and turned in time to see Alexis attempt to bury herself in the softness and cover her face with a sheet.

"Isn't it time the captain of this ship was up and about?" he asked, pulling the sheet from her.

Moaning, she clutched the material and tried to draw it over her again. "I think the captain's been drugged." She gave up the tug of war and contented herself by flinging an arm over her eyes.

"Any suspects?"

She lifted her arm, cast him an accusing glance, and covered her eyes again. "All I want to know is: Is it addictive?"

Cloud shook his head slowly. His voice could not have conveyed more seriousness. "I don't know for sure. Let me know how you feel in a few hours."

Alexis lifted herself on her elbows in time to see a wide grin spreading across his face. She pushed him off the bunk. While he was laughing and tugging at his boots she wrapped a sheet around her and scrambled out. She got a few feet from him when she was stopped by a sudden tug on her covering. She spun and tried to release it from his fingers but he held fast and drew her closer. When she was standing over him he released the sheet and pulled her down onto his lap.

"You didn't struggle very hard," he observed.

Alexis wrapped her arms around his neck and rested her cheek comfortably against his chest. "It must be the drug. I feel as if I could use another draught."

"Already?" His tone mocked her but his hands had begun loosening the sheet and caressing her bared flesh.

Alexis nodded. "Already," she answered firmly, lifting her mouth to receive his kiss.

Their lips and tongues had barely tasted of one another when they were halted by a hesitant rapping at the door. Alexis sighed and reluctantly released herself from the circle of Cloud's arms. She looked up into his eyes and laughed at the expression of pure misery she saw there, knowing she was seeing the reflection of her own disappointment. To him she whispered, "It wasn't meant to be, love."

Before he had time to respond she was on her feet, hastily pulling on her trousers and shirt while she carried on a conversation with Peach through the closed door.

"It's your breakfast, Captain," he called in answer to her question.

"And what marvelous things do you have for me this morning?" She shot Cloud a murderous glance as he chuckled at her attempt to stall for time.

Peach looked down at his tray and wondered at her question. She always had the same breakfast: fresh fruit, muffins and tea with sugar. Suddenly he thought he understood and he called back, "Do you want me to return with it later, Captain?"

Alexis's reproachful glare at Cloud absolutely withered at her cabin boy's answer, and Cloud laughed heartily at her sudden discomfort and Peach's attempt at easing it. Alexis hastened to pull on her boots and reach the door before Peach would take Cloud's laughter as a signal to go away. With an impatient sweep of her hand, she motioned for Cloud to sit at the table while she opened the door.

"Bring it in, Peach." She noticed his hesitation and thought she knew the reason. "It's all right. Captain Cloud has quite forgiven us the hard time we gave him yesterday. I hope you have enough for him there. He may not forgive us for not feeding him properly."

Peach stepped into the cabin and eyed Cloud suspiciously rather than apprehensively. Cloud observed the boy's guarded look and grinned at Alexis. "This man is not seeking my forgiveness. Indeed, I don't believe he gives a damn—it was my fault. Is that right, Peach?"

"That's right."

"You're trying to decide if I am good enough for Captain Danty."

"That's right."

Cloud returned his grave expression. "And I suppose there will be all sorts of tests I'll have to pass before I can meet with your approval." Peach's head bobbed slightly. "Then suppose you put that tray here so I can eat my breakfast and start these Herculean tasks you have for me."

Peach was not sure what Herculean tasks were or even if he could repeat the words aloud but he was sure he could match the importance of the tasks Cloud referred to. He placed the tray on the table and stepped back, taking a look at Alexis who was regarding both of them with a curious expression tempered with amusement.

"You can go, Peach," she said finally, touched that he cared who she chose.

He walked past her with the same confident air he had displayed for Cloud the previous evening. He had reached the door when Cloud called to him.

"By the way, Peach," he said casually. "I don't believe I thanked you properly for your assistance yesterday."

"I was doing what was expected of me," the boy replied tonelessly.

Now Cloud's voice was earnest. "I would not thank you for any less than that."

Peach turned, flashing Cloud a huge, wondrous grin; and Cloud knew he had passed the first test.

Alexis shut the door behind her cabin boy and looked at Cloud thoughtfully before she spoke. "I think there is a conspiracy against me. You are going to take Peach away from me."

"Hardly. In fact, I'd say the conspiracy is against me." He smiled. "If Peach is any indication, I am going to have my hands full trying to prove I'm worthy of you."

Alexis took a seat at the table and began peeling an orange. "You'll find Peach an exception. The others trust my judgment. But I suppose he'll keep you busy enough." She dismissed Peach's protective attitude with a wave of her hand. "I think we should discuss what you want to do about Howe and the others. Have you given it any thought?" Her voice was cool and impersonal but Cloud looked up from his plate in time to see the downward curve of her mouth, revealing her concern.

"I've given it some," he answered. "Are you worried about something, Alex?"

"Are you going to ask me to return you to Washington so you can fight them personally?"

"And if I did?"

"You haven't answered my question," she sighed. "But I'll answer yours. I cannot return you directly to Washington. It would be too dangerous for my crew. But I will see you safely to another port, if that is what you really want."

"You would do that?"

"If I didn't I would be guilty of the same thing you were when you took me from my home." She faced his gaze directly and caught the first hint of a smile in his eyes and the relaxed line of his mouth. "You aren't going to ask me, are you?" Her relief was overshadowed by her indignation that he would even pose the question.

"No. I am not going to ask you to do that. But I had to hear your answer anyway."

"Why?"

"I had to know if the alternative was open to me or if I was your prisoner."

Now Alexis smiled at the thought of keeping Cloud behind a locked door with guards posted at the entrance. "You would do better not to bait me or I might be tempted to throw you in the hold." She eyed him wickedly over the rim of her cup and actually seemed to be weighing the thought. His smile disappeared and she laughed, setting down her cup. "What do you have in mind?"

"Can you take me to Charleston?"

She sat upright. "But I thought—"

"To deliver some letters," he finished before she could go on. He waited for her to relax then he continued. "I thought I would write a letter to Madison and to my sister, explaining what the senator is doing. Did you know Howe is from Massachusetts? Ironic, isn't it? Emma and Blake will be able to exert some pressure on him there, and I am sure the President will find a suitable method for dealing with him. The others will fall into line after that."

"Do you think the letters will actually make it to their destination? It's risky putting that all on paper. What if they are never delivered?"

"Howe can't—"

"I did not mean Howe. I mean letters just have a way of getting lost."

Cloud frowned and dropped an orange slice into his mouth. He chewed it thoughtfully. "I suppose it's a chance I'll have to take."

"I might have a way to reduce the risk. My second-in-command, Kurt Jordan, is from Charleston. He may know someone who would see the letters delivered personally. I'll ask him when we go on deck."

Cloud finished his breakfast, thinking that Peach was right for placing his trust in Captain Danty.

"And now, Captain," he said, pushing his plate aside. "What sort of work do you have for me to do?" He laughed at her surprise. "I seem to be a commander without a ship and I can't very well do nothing around here."

"Are you serious?" She could hardly imagine him working for her.

"Very much so."

"Well, I already have a very competent first mate—"

"I was not thinking of anything quite so high ranking," he assured her, brushing back the hair from his temples.

"On the other end of rank then, I have a very competent cabin boy." She laughed. "Except for his inability to draw me a hot bath."

"Perhaps I could be of service there?" he suggested a little too innocently.

"Oh, no!" she answered quickly. "I know what that look in your eye means! I might need Peach's tepid baths if I am going to get any work done." She jumped out of her chair as he reached for her hand. In a few quick strides she was at the door. She opened it, bowing low and motioning him out with a graceful sweep of her arm. "You'll just have to find a niche for yourself somewhere between the two ends. My men will be pleased to help you. Feel free to come to me with any questions you have concerning this ship."

Cloud slipped out the door in front of her, but not before he whispered, "Don't forget to let me know when the effect of the drug wears thin."

Alexis muttered ineffectual curses under her breath and followed him through the companionway, braiding her hair as she went. Once on deck, she motioned to Jordan to come to her and formally introduced Cloud. She was satisfied when the two men seemed to like each other at once and exchanged firm handshakes. How different it had been at their first meeting.

"Captain Cloud is at your disposal, Mr. Jordan," she told him. "He wants to join our crew."

"I don't think the title is necessary or accurate any longer," Cloud reminded her, grinning. "Cloud will do just fine."

"Tanner would be better," she said quickly, thinking she

could not bear to hear anyone give him orders by the name she had always thought of as so intimate. She was not ready for that just yet.

"Tanner, then," Jordan repeated. "Welcome aboard the *Dark Lady.*"

"Thank you, Mr. Jordan. Do you think I might be able to get some clothes like the rest of the crew? This uniform is a bit out of place." He saw Alexis wince at his request. He understood her reluctance to see him physically stripped of his command but he would not withdraw his request.

"I'll see what I can do." He turned to Alexis and noted her discomfort but could not name the reason. "Will there be anything else, Captain?"

Alexis composed herself. "One item before I leave him in your hands. Tanner has explained to me that his crew was correct in their information about Howe. He can tell you the details later. I want to know if there is anyone in Charleston you can trust with the delivery of letters to the President and Tanner's sister in Boston? I am willing to pay very well to see the letters reach their destination."

Jordan only had to think a few seconds before he brightened. "David Hastings is the one you want. He'll do it and you can trust him not to read the contents."

"Will you be able to find Mr. Hastings once we get to Charleston?"

"Finding him won't be half as hard as getting past the British into port."

Alexis laughed. "Then it's settled. We'll manage the blockade. Tanner will have the letters for you by the time we reach Charleston and I'll have the money. You can take our new seaman on a tour. And, Mr. Jordan, you may want to introduce him to Peters and Allan Wilkes. They've exchanged a few things but I don't believe words were among them." Alexis left them alone and went to the quarterdeck to make course adjustments.

Cloud stared after her. "I suppose Peters and Wilkes are the men she foisted on me last night."

"The same," he chuckled. "C'mon. You'll get the grand tour; then I'll put you to work."

Cloud followed Jordan's lead and soon he was acquainted with the vessel as well as how Alexis ran it. He was impressed with the accommodations she had for her crew. Their quarters were larger than most seamen were accustomed to and the bunks actually looked comfortable. The larders were well stocked from the *Dark Lady's* voyage to Tortola and not with the usual fare one expected to find on a ship.

Jordan saw Cloud's eyebrows and he answered the unasked questions. "When Captain Danty had this ship gone over she knew she was asking the men to be away from their families longer than they ever had been when they'd worked for her father. She insisted they be quartered well, fed well, and paid well. For these reasons as well as others she got her crew."

"The British could learn something from her."

"The Americans, too, although our men have it a little better."

Cloud nodded. "You carry cargo?"

"Some. This way. I'll show you." Jordan led him into the hold and showed him the cargo of rich silks, linens, and cottons. "We picked this up in London and got rid of a load of rum. The profits pay for Captain Danty's voyage. None of the other ships on the line provide us with any money. They're used occasionally to pass information. This particular cargo we were going to sell in the islands. Bad weather took us off course and the captain was going to get rid of it in New Orleans. Never did though. Seems even simple merchant vessels aren't safe these days."

Cloud could not miss Jordan's pointed sarcasm. He laughed and motioned toward the wall, to a door partially hidden by some crates. "I'll wager a month's pay that whatever is beyond that door will make a liar out of you naming this ship a simple merchant."

Jordan grinned. "Very good. I won't take the wager." They removed the crates and Jordan opened the door, placing the lantern he carried outside the room. "This is the reason we don't take kindly to boarders," he said as Cloud stepped in.

"My God!" was all he could say while his eyes scanned the contents of the compartment. There were barrels of gunpowder, muskets, pistols of every description, and cannons on dollys so they could replace damaged ones with little time lost. The size of their cache amazed him.

"All of this has come from the British. We actually had to stop confiscation several frigates ago. We don't sell the weapons and we couldn't carry any more safely."

"I wonder that you carry all this safely," replied Cloud.

"Captain Danty had the sides reinforced to protect against fire and misguided cannonballs. It causes us to ride a little lower in the water but it gives the impression we always have a full cargo."

"Why so much? I was under the impression Captain Danty did not use weapons."

"She doesn't—or rather she hasn't—yet. We have been able to stop the frigates with our ruses, and by the time they really understand what we want they are at a disadvantage. Officers are always the hardest to convince, but the crews don't put up much of a fight once they realize Captain Danty is their excuse to return home. Now with war on both sides of the ocean I expect this particular cargo will be used frequently."

"I'm afraid you're right," he agreed grimly. "When did you join her crew?"

Jordan and Cloud moved out of the room. "I was on board the very first ship she took. I've been with her about two years now. First mate—about a year and a half ago."

Cloud noted Jordan said these statements with a sense of pride and respect for Alexis and himself. When he was introduced to the rest of the crew he found these qualities common to all her men. They were sure of themselves, their purpose, and their commander.

Jordan found suitable clothing for Cloud who changed into bell trousers and pullover shirt, then discarded his boots in favor of no shoes at all and went about his work. He accepted his duties with such simple pleasure that Jordan wondered if he really missed his command.

Cloud did miss it. But he considered the situation temporary and he gladly accepted the work as a balm. He used it to heal the wounds Howe had inflicted on him. He could go about his work without concentrating on it and still know it was well done. While he scrubbed decks and mended sails he mentally composed the letters that would return him to the *Concord* and see Howe finished. He ate lunch and dinner with the men, enjoying the time to trade stories and answer, as well as ask, questions. They accepted him as if he had always been among them.

He watched Peach observe all this with his still-suspicious gaze. Attempts at conversation on Cloud's part were met with short answers and apparently no interest. Cloud noticed though, the boy's resistance was slowly fading and his mien was forced to some degree. He was glad Peach was the only one who set himself up as Alexis's guardian.

Throughout the day he was aware of Alexis's presence although he never talked to her after their conversation with Jordan. Occasionally he caught her looking at him while he was doing some menial task. At first she would turn away quickly, but not before he had time to glimpse the openly pained expression on her face. No matter how easily she had accepted his decision to fall under her command it was still cutting her deeply. Later she did not turn away, but continued to stare, gathering reassurance from him until the muscles of her face relaxed and her placid features signaled her acceptance. When he last saw her covertly studying him, he was descending the rigging. Even the distance separating them was not enough to dim the desire that replaced all her previous expressions. When he reached the deck Alexis had disappeared, and Ned Allison was urging him toward some new task before he had a chance to decide if he had imagined the golden fire in his captain's eyes.

Cloud drew an early watch, much to his pleasure and Jordan's amusement.

"If I didn't know better, I'd say you rigged the lottery." Jordan grinned. His arms were folded across his chest and he leaned against the rail while Cloud took his turn at the wheel. A breeze ruffled his sun-bleached hair.

"But you do know better." Cloud eyed the first mate skeptically.

"Of course," Jordan answered lightly. What he left unsaid was: "Because I took care of it for you."

"Thank you."

"For what?" Jordan appeared truly amazed at this gratitude.

Cloud laughed. "For what you'll never admit to doing, except perhaps under extreme torture."

"Probably not even then." He fell silent while he observed Cloud's stance at the wheel. It was a pleasure to see a man who was so much in control of his every movement and yet seemingly unaware of the effort involved. His legs were braced apart: the muscles taut and firm but at the same time yielding to the greater rolling motion of the ship beneath his feet. His hands gripped the wheel in a manner that suddenly brought a woman to Jordan's mind. He chuckled.

"Something wrong?" asked Cloud. He had been oblivious to everything but the feel of the ship until Jordan's laughter reached him.

"Nothing wrong. I was just making an observation."

"Care to share it?"

"You love her very much, don't you?" Jordan surprised himself with his question. He was hardly aware of the separate thoughts that joined to make that statement possible.

Cloud raised his eyebrows. He did not try to hide the fact he was greatly amused. A slanted grin crossed his face. "That is not much of an observation, Mr. Jordan. I'm surprised you phrased it as a question since I have never made it any secret. Sometimes I think the words must be branded on my forehead." He turned to the wheel and kept his eyes ahead, distinguishing between the subtle variations in the dark blue of the sky, the water, and the shoreline. "Does my answer confirm your observation?"

"Absolutely."

Out of sight, but within hearing distance, Peach was thinking Cloud had no more tests to pass.

Cloud entered Alexis's quarters after knocking lightly and receiving a perfunctory "Come in" in reply. She did not look up from her work when he closed the door. He watched her, her head bent over the log, slim fingers holding a quill which crossed the page in a fluid motion. Several minutes passed and she seemed to have forgotten she had allowed someone to enter. Finally she put the quill down and examined what she had written. Eyes still on the page she asked, "What is it?"

"Sorry to disturb you, Captain Danty, but there is a small matter of the British bearing down on us, a storm gathering to the south, mutiny among the men . . ." At the sound of his voice Alexis's head jerked up and she could only half listen to the list of calamities he was presenting. Her eyes followed his as he sat down on the bunk and removed his shirt. ". . . Redland has thrown Wilkes to the sharks, the hull's rotted in two places, we are taking in water and"—he tossed the shirt aside and lay back on the bunk with a small groan— "I am exhausted."

Smiling, Alexis walked over and sat beside him. She placed her hands on his chest, massaging it lightly. "Is that all? There doesn't seem to be anything wrong I can't take care of."

Cloud grinned, closing his eyes. "Good. I knew I was telling the right person."

Her hand moved up his chest, to his shoulders. Her fingers brushed against his neck and through his hair. "Let's take care of the most serious problem first."

"And that would be?" His hands began to unfasten the buttons of her shirt. His fingers slid beneath the material to stroke her breasts.

She pulled away suddenly and addressed him sternly, laughter in her eyes. "I thought it was your exhaustion but there appears much you can still do. Therefore I will see about the others matters.'' She started to move from the bunk but he caught her wrist and pulled her back. His grip was urgent, his fingers pressing tightly against the pulse in her wrist. She did not resist.

They undressed each other hurriedly, frantically, unable to prolong the inevitable joining of their bodies with tender phrases, light caresses, or gentle kisses. Somehow, they realized those things had already been done. Covert glances on deck, when amber locked on green for a fleeting moment, had accomplished the task more thoroughly than words and delicate manipulations of fingers, mouths, and tongues. It was as if their actions the entire day had been in preparation for this moment.

Their embrace was fierce and Alexis found herself straining against Cloud's familiar contours, wanting to know the angle of his elbow with the soft inner curve of her own; wanting to feel the flat of his abdomen flush against the slightly rounded slope of her belly. She tried to get a sense of her own body through the palms of his hands as they skimmed her back, pausing briefly at the base of her spine, then causing her to shiver delightfully as the pads of his thumbs ran the length of her backbone to her neck, then over her shoulders to trace her collarbone. She wondered if he could feel her skin tingle beneath his fingers or detect heat from her flesh that rivaled his own. What did he taste when his mouth touched her lips, her shoulder, or her breast? Did he find her bittersweet or was she tangy, perhaps salty, as she found him. His nose brushed her temple when his tongue outlined her inner ear and she was curious if she had a unique fragrance he might associate with her. She breathed deeply and found Cloud to be a heady combination of briny sea air and his own special musky scent she thought very masculine and attractive. As their bodies meshed and she called his name and her need in the same breath she wondered if she warmed him with her body as he warmed her when he filled her. And he seemed to know what she was thinking because he whispered he wanted this loving to go on forever, that she was necessary for his existence, and the manner in which she opened herself to him, gave to him, humbled him even while he sought to lose himself in her. In the end they were lost in one another.

Afterward they slept deeply, unaware of any reality except the closeness of their bodies and the word that gave definition to their contact.

Alexis shivered and reached out for the warmth of the body she had grown accustomed to. She shivered again. Gradually she realized Cloud was no longer beside her. Slowly her eyes opened only to shut tightly when they met the light of the lamp. She sat up, waited until her head cleared, and opened her eyes again. Cloud was sitting at her desk, his head propped on an elbow, writing furiously. The sweep of his arm told her he was angry and the crumpled sheets of paper scattered around him spoke of his frustration. He paused, as if to gather some thought; then the paper in front of him joined the others on the deck.

"The letters?" she asked when he made no move to get fresh paper.

"Yes. I didn't want to wake you. I'm sorry."

"It's all right. Can I help?"

"Come. Sit here." He reached for a nearby chair and pulled it close to him. "That will be help enough." His voice was strained but his eyes were warm and inviting.

Alexis rose from the bunk, slipping on her shirt, and crossed the cabin to sit beside him. She curled comfortably into the chair, tucking her feet under her. She waited, knowing he would tell her what the problem was when he was ready. Her hand moved to his arm, easing the tense lines in his muscles with light strokes.

"I get so angry," he sighed. "I start writing clearly; then I think of what Howe wanted to do to you . . . to me . . . to his country, and I get so angry I end up sounding like a madman. No one will ever do anything to him on the basis of what I've written so far."

His voice began to rise and he pulled away from Alexis.

"All day, Alex, I have been thinking of what I would write . . . of how to phrase the accusations . . . facts instead of adjectives. Read one! Go ahead! You'll even wonder if I have a lucid thought in my head!" He reached down to pick up one of the discarded letters but she stopped him.

"I am not interested in the attempts that were not good enough for you. Don't insult me. Show me your best." She released his arm and walked to the back of his chair. She put her arms around his neck and bent her head so her mouth was near his ear. "I am only interested in your best. That is all that should concern you."

He waited until he relaxed under the full effect of her words; then he leaned forward, sliding out of her embrace, and picked up the quill. As he wrote he was conscious not of the words, but of the way they seemed to appear effortlessly before him. He made changes, scratched out paragraphs, but he did not have to discard an entire sheet.

Alexis moved away from him, sensing she had ceased to exist for the time being. She poured them each a glass of wine. His went unnoticed, untouched, while she sipped hers slowly, settling back into her chair. Occasionally, during a pause in his thoughts, his hand would reach out to touch her thigh, her shoulder, her hair. She was not certain he was aware of these movements but they'd seemed to give him the same reassurance she had sought earlier from him. She did not know when she fell asleep, only that she must have, for strong arms were enfolding her, lifting her, and when she was in her bunk they did not leave her.

During breakfast Alexis read the final work. When she finished she placed it to one side and looked at Cloud. "Are you satisfied with the letter?"

"I'd still be writing and you'd still be in that chair if I wasn't."

"It's very good."

"I know." His fingers curled around her hand, squeezing it briefly.

Alexis accepted his silent thank you, returning it with a firm smile. "Now to get it to Charleston," she said, sighing.

Cloud frowned. "How difficult do you think it will be?"

"Very. But not impossible. We've run French blockades in British ports, British blockades in French ports, Spanish blockades in any port they feel like congesting. It seems the whole world is concerned with everyone but themselves. I don't suppose it will be too difficult slipping past the British into an American port. We have an advantage because the war is only a few months old—the British will not have their blockade well organized yet."

"What flag will you fly?"

"Stars and Stripes."

Cloud laughed. "You say that like an American."

Alexis regarded him curiously. "If you mean with pride— of course. I have been an American all my life—up here." She tapped her head. "I did not always know it. Even when I left London I didn't know enough about the United States to realize it was the country that would hold the same truths I did. I only knew London had nothing for me."

"But you never made it to the United States. Was Tortola a disappointment?"

Alexis shook her head. "Life in Roadtown was wonderful, but that was more because of George and Francine than anything else. If I ever had the inclination to proudly call myself a citizen of the British crown it was smashed the moment Captain Travers stepped foot on the island. I've thought about it for some time, Cloud. Since I first learned war was imminent between the two countries I knew it was time for me to decide which side I could help. I suppose the English will consider me a traitor but in light of all I value there is only one side I can choose. So from now on we'll fly an American flag—no more deceptions. If we have to fight to get to Travers then that is what we'll do." She grinned. "There is another factor involved, although it didn't take part in my decision. The United States also happens to be the winning side."

"You're confident."

"Aren't you?" she asked incredulously.

"Not as long as Howe is still doing his worst and I don't have my ship to command."

Alexis left her chair and sat on the arm of his. She kissed his forehead. "Then there is nothing to worry about. It won't be long before Howe is finished and you'll have the *Concord*. You probably think you can defeat the entire Royal Navy once you have your ship back."

"At least the part that is causing us trouble." He laughed and shrugged his shoulders carelessly. "You can have what's left."

She pulled his arm and led him to the door. "You are very gallant, Captain, and if I get my man I may take up your offer. Now, shall we see about raising that flag?"

Chapter Sixteen

Two days later, at night, the *Dark Lady* docked in Charleston harbor. There was no celebration at having successfully slipped through the blockade. Everyone on board knew each hour spent in port would allow available Fleet ships to gather, making their departure many times more dangerous than their entry.

While Jordan and Cloud placed the important letters in the hands of David Hastings, Alexis arranged for the sale of her cargo. The silks and linens she had in her hold were eagerly seized by city merchants who were already experiencing the shortage of goods that war brought. But the profit the material brought did not compensate for the price Alexis was forced to pay for additional foodstuffs and medicinal items. Finding someone who could supply the ship took four days and there was another day's delay when it was discovered some of the meat ordered was spoiled.

Reports filtered in from coastal observers that the British were tightening their forces off the Charleston shore as well as around important trade centers farther north.

The day before they were scheduled to leave a Garnet-owned merchant was captured by the HMS *Raleigh* only ten miles from the harbor. The cargo was confiscated, the ship burned, and the members of the crew who survived were allowed to reach land in long boats.

"My God!" Cloud swore bitterly when he heard the news. "They never had a chance, Alex! Garnet merchants aren't equipped with arms to match a frigate. I understand confiscating the cargo, and burning the ship makes sense because they didn't have anywhere to take it. But firing on them before the captain was given an opportunity to surrender—that is unforgivable!"

Alexis massaged the tight corded muscles in his neck. "I'm sorry," she said softly, wishing the words were not so inadequate. "Have they been able to determine how many lives were lost?"

He nodded, closing his eyes as bitter tension left him. "I spoke with Hank Winslow, the cargo master. He said the *Raleigh's* first shot was as unexpected as it was lucky. It struck the mizzenmast which toppled and killed two men. Before they could recover from the *Raleigh's* tactics they were greeted with a three-minute cannonade. Eight men died then, including the captain. Four more died from wounds on their way back to the harbor and Winslow says there's one man yet who may die or spend the rest of his life with one arm. Fourteen men, Alex! Fourteen!"

"Are you feeling responsible?"

"My sister and I own the line. Of course I feel—"

"Cloud, you know that if your captain had been given the option he would have surrendered as ordered. You aren't at fault because someone on the *Raleigh* refused to allow him that chance."

He acknowledged her words by placing his hands over hers at the base of his neck. "I do need you, Alex." She kissed the top of his head then released herself from his hold. Walking to her desk, she smoothed the edges of the map lying on top and studied it for several minutes.

"What are you thinking?" Cloud asked as he joined her.

She sighed ruefully. "It's nothing you're going to like."

"But you do have an idea."

She nodded, turning on him suddenly. "Wilkes and Peach have been asking questions for me. In order to leave here we'll have to contend with more than the *Raleigh*. There are British privateers just waiting to capture a few prize ships. Charleston trade is being cut off by that congestion."

"And you're suggesting . . ."

"I am suggesting we clear the local waters on our way out."

"You're mad. You know that, don't you?"

"Be serious. It can be done."

"Of course it can," he agreed gravely. "But the *Dark Lady* can't do it alone."

"And I never suggested she could," Alexis returned smugly.

Interested now, Cloud raised speculative brows. "How?"

"There are two privately owned schooners in the harbor. Wilkes tells me they're already outfitted to do some privateering. Their guns are good and the crews are experienced. They have only been waiting for the proper time to leave port. There are also several smaller craft that would be battle worthy if they had the arms." Smiling, tongue in cheek, she said, "You may have noticed the *Dark Lady* has some extra munitions. I propose to use some of them now. We can outfit two of the best sloops and still be adequately stocked."

"An armada. That's what you're talking about, you know."

"I'm talking about ridding this area of the British and opening up trade for the city again."

"You've been thinking about this before the *Raleigh* incident, haven't you?"

"Of course I have. I thought at first we could be in and out. But the delays, the reports, and now the *Raleigh*—well, you know the difficulty we're facing. Wilkes has approached the owners of the ships I would like to have with me. They're willing."

"Do they know with whom they're dealing?"

"Alex Danty, you mean?" He nodded. "No, I didn't want them to be swayed by any tales they may have heard. They

made all the arrangements with Wilkes. We'll let them know
it's Danty who's leading them just before we sail, and only then
because I don't want them forgetting who's in command."

Cloud was pensive for several moments. His attention
focused on the map at his fingertips, wandered to the activity
beyond the cabin windows, and finally riveted on the woman
in front of him. A lazy, confident smile formed on his sensuous
mouth as his eyes slowly appraised Alexis.

Her throat became tight, her mouth dry from the possessive
nature of his gaze. "What are you thinking?"

"That I like you in black."

Three days of preparation were required to make the two
sloops ready for battle. From the moment the first cannon
left the *Dark Lady's* hold rumors held the city's imagination.
As word spread of reprisals for the *Raleigh's* actions, townspeople visited the harbor to get a look at the men who were
going to do it.

Alexis had not been able to go on deck for over a week.
There was already too much speculation surrounding her
ship's identity without adding the enigma of a woman.

Those hearty souls who suspected that any move to be made
would occur at night were rewarded for their vigilance when
Captain Danty made an appearance. At first they were not
certain they had seen more than a shadow, an insubstantial
black wraith against an ebony sky, but when questions were
put to the shadow and husky commands were returned, they
knew they were witnessing the authority of Alex Danty.

An hour after midnight Alexis ordered her ship out of the
harbor. The *Dark Lady* was followed minutes later by the
schooners, the *Phoenix* and the *Centurion,* and after that, the
sloops, the *Dianne* and the *Hancock.* Out of sight of the harbor
they separated to the coordinates Alexis had outlined several
hours earlier as Captain Danty.

The *Dark Lady* would be a decoy, an attractive prize ship
for enemy privateers, or a defiant blockade runner that naval

ships would not want to overlook. There was no moonlight to reveal their number, giving Alexis confidence that surprise and skill would see them break the foreign hold over the city before dawn.

Little distance had been covered before Randall's alert from the cap signaled a ship had taken the bait. Alexis allowed the British privateer to narrow the distance between them while she skillfully drew him to where the *Dianne* and the *Hancock* waited to turn the tables.

Once the *Dark Lady* had cleared her nearly invisible partners she swung wide to watch the trap close. Cannon shot ripped the air as the *Hancock* opened up on an enemy schooner. Flashes of light froze the action for the spectators. The *Dark Lady's* crew saw the *Dianne* pull hard to starboard and as the dull sound of metal meeting wood was carried across the water they knew the schooner had been secured with grappling hooks. There were shouts and cries after that, painful to hear, more terrible in some ways because they could not see—only imagine.

It was not until a flare was released from the *Hancock* that any of them were certain of victory. Beneath her mask Alexis's cheeks were wet, stained with bitter tears for those who had died.

The light and the noise of the battle attracted a second ship a naval brig intending to assist the floundering schooner. While prisoners were being taken aboard the *Dianne* the *Dark Lady* diverted her adversary, delivering her into the hands of the *Phoenix*. The *Phoenix*, although swift and ably commanded, could not match the gun power of the brig. The *Dark Lady* was going to return to help when the late arrival of the *Hancock* made it unnecessary.

Victory over the brig was assured after several hours. Aware of the limited time before morning, Alexis ordered the *Dark Lady* to the coordinates where the *Raleigh* had last been sighted. As they left the *Phoenix* was taking prisoners and Alexis had to force her eyes away from the burning brig. She committed the destroyed vessel to memory, its smoking timbers and flaming sails engraved so finely in her mind that when she would recall the event later her stomach would heave.

On the way to their target the *Centurion* was sighted sailing in the direction of the harbor with a privateer in tow. Alexis maintained her course, calculating the increased risk to be acceptable with three of her four companions returning to port with prisoners and prizes.

Randall's next sighting forced Alexis to order her men to their battle stations. She scanned the inky horizon for the ship while the men took positions by the cannons below deck and others manned the on-deck guns. She made a satisfied murmur when she located what Randall had observed and handed her scope to Jordan.

"They're going to give us chase, Mr. Jordan. Have Peach send up a flare to warn the *Hancock* to stay away. She'll be of no help to us, not against that frigate. We're on our own."

Jordan made out the shape of the vessel and thought he actually saw every one of the twenty guns on its port side. It was not a reassuring mirage. Handing the scope back to Alexis he carried out her order. The momentary light from the flare clearly exposed their position to the enemy and he wondered how she would turn that in their favor.

As if in answer to his thoughts Alexis told him, "This ship can outmaneuver any frigate on these waters and they're not expecting us to give more than a token resistance. If I were their captain I would be readying my long-range guns on the forecastle. Give the order to take position to leeward at my signal."

Jordan hoped his shock was hidden in the darkness. He was certain she knew that positioning the *Dark Lady* to leeward was an additional disadvantage. It would allow the frigate to close the distance more quickly.

When the British fired the first shot, missing the *Dark Lady* by only fifty yards, Alexis lifted her arm in signal and they slowed dramatically. Even as the frigate gained on them Alexis remained calm, keeping her pursuers off the port stern with clever maneuvering. She knew now the frigate was not the *Raleigh,* but her sister ship, the *Francis Drake.*

"Are the men ready at the Long Toms?"

"They're ready, Captain." He was wondering what their very accurate guns could do if the *Drake* managed to get broadside at close quarters. They would have no chance then. Still, he observed, Alexis was in control, firing her orders as if this were her hundredth battle with weapons, rather than her first. He wanted to suggest that she move away from the helm. The frigate's shots were coming dangerously close and she was in the line of any damage the shots could do. He opened his mouth to speak but his words were lost in the explosion on deck.

Jordan felt himself being lifted into the air and thrown against the deck. He raised an arm to cover his eyes, rolling with the movement of the ship as splinters of wood flew through the air with the velocity of gunshot. Alexis was unprepared for the force of the hit. Thrown in the opposite direction of her first mate, she made such a violent landing on the deck that air was knocked from her lungs. Gasping for breath she tore off her mask and struggled to her feet. Each successive breath she drew only seemed to increase the pain. She clutched her sides and the pain became even more fierce. Pulling aside her cape she felt blindly with her palms until they scraped a large splinter of wood lodged in her flesh. Quickly, before Jordan got to his feet, she broke off the part that protruded and used her hand to apply pressure to the wound. With her free hand she jerked the cape more closely about her.

"Are you all right, Captain?" Jordan's voice was deep with anxiety by the time he reached her. He had a number of small cuts and bruises but nothing serious.

"I'm fine," she said evenly. "I only lost my wind. You look as if you'll live." She surveyed the damage to her ship. Her men were putting out the fire and none of them appeared to have seen her fall. Redland, a nasty gash on the side of his head, had already resumed his position at the wheel. The *Drake* was closing in, gaining an advantage from their temporary confusion.

Alexis ignored the dull throb of pain in her side, pressing her hand harder against her flesh. "When I give the command we're going to rake them, Mr. Jordan. Order the men to fire in succession as we cross their spar deck. We'll make them regret coming so close."

Jordan conveyed her orders. He had a brief moment to ponder the origin of her expertise, then he saw his answer standing by one of the guns. Alexis was unaware of Cloud watching her intently, conveying his approval. He would have been incapable of displaying more pride if he had been giving the orders himself.

"Now!" Alexis's voice carried over all other sounds at that moment. The *Dark Lady* began her dangerous maneuver, sweeping in front of the frigate at close range. The lighter, faster merchant was able to perform the task easily, in spite of the *Drake's* windward advantage. The cannons were fired in rapid succession as the *Dark Lady* passed. The frigate retaliated with its bow battery but two cannon were no match for Alexis's broadside cannonade.

"We'll sweep her again, Mr. Jordan." She looked through her scope to estimate the damage. "One more pass should leave her crippled. We'll not board. Their crew probably outnumber us three to one. Raise the wedges on half the guns and fill them with hot shot. Aim for their sails, masts, and rigging."

The *Dark Lady* began to turn again. The *Drake* lost its advantage after Alexis's daring retaliation. On the second sweep the damage to the other vessel was devastating. The guns filled with hot shot, cannonballs that had been fired red-hot in the forge, tore into the warship's sails, setting the canvas ablaze. The flames climbed the foremast just as the first rays of the sun appeared on the horizon. The two lights clashed, fighting for domination until smoke enveloped the *Drake*, blocking the sun, naming destruction the victor.

A cheer went up on deck as the *Dark Lady* regained the

windward position and the ship moved quickly out of the frigate's range. Alexis looked around at her men, some of whom were beginning to come up from the lower decks. Even their faces, streaked with gunpowder and sweat, could not hide the glow of victory. A murmur of excitement ran through them as they slapped one another on the back, not so much in the manner of a job well done as in a manner that was meant to assure them they were still alive. She saw Cloud's face among them, but he was not joining the celebration. His gaze was fixed on her as if he knew something was wrong. She was suddenly conscious of her hand beneath the cape pressed so tightly to her side. She countered his concern with a smile and relaxed her stance, but did not remove her hand. Apparently relieved, he saluted her smartly and turned back to the others.

"The *Hancock's* asking if we're all right, Captain," Randall called from above her.

"Tell her yes and signal her to return home. We've done what we set out to do."

The *Hancock* saw the flag they had been waiting for, the colors of the Quinton Line, hoisted until it rested on the gaff directly below the Stars and Stripes. The next five shots from their guns were both a salute to Danty's prowess and a farewell to the *Dark Lady,* now leaving them as planned to go toward the target that had been her reason for being.

After Alexis was sure the *Hancock* was safely on its way she permitted her tightened muscles to relax. As the tension ebbed, her pain increased. She gave her scope to Jordan, aware that it took a conscious effort on her part to lessen the tight, bloodless grip her fingers had held on the instrument.

Jordan took the scope and had a last look at the damaged vessel. The smoke was beginning to clear which meant the fire was being brought under control. Little good it would do them, he thought. The ship did not have more than a few hours above the water, but it was enough to release the boats and save most of them. He brought the scope down, slapping up against his thigh, and turned his attention to Alexis. He noted she was still holding her side but other than that she appeared to be fine. He followed her to a broken section of the rail where they both leaned against it, daring it to give way beneath them.

"That was some fancy maneuvering, Captain," he whistled softly. His voice held a note of awe.

Alexis forced a smile. "Out with it, Mr. Jordan. You didn't think I knew what I was doing."

He was tempted to deny it, thought better of it, and answered, "You're right. I had my doubts."

She laughed but cut it short because of the pain the effort brought her. She just wanted to enjoy her victory a little longer before she gave in. "You should have known better. All this time aboard this ship together, you should have known better." She repeated the words he had once said to her. Her tone reflected none of the seriousness. Her voice was bright, mocking.

"I deserved that," he chuckled.

Alexis enjoyed the sound of his laughter. It was a salve for her pain. "Will you see to the damages? And the wounded?" She pointed to Redland at the wheel. "He's been hurt. Thrown the same time we were. Damn limeys!"

Jordan saw blood from a cut trickling down the side of Redland's thin face. He nodded to Alexis and moved toward the injured man. "Wilkes! Take the helm! Redland's been hurt!" Redland protested but Jordan took him away while Wilkes filled in for him. While he was being led away, Redland cast a suspicious glance at Alexis. He knows, she realized. She put a finger to her lips and her eyes ordered him to say nothing. She moved away from the broken rail and reviewed the damage around her. Just a while longer, she told herself when the pain became harder to bear. Just until everything is safely under control. She found a place where she could sit and oversee her men's work. At the same time she tried to make herself as inconspicuous as possible. It was not long before Jordan returned.

"I thought you were going to let me see to the damages?"

She dismissed his complaint with a wave of her hand. "How many wounded?"

"Redland. Brandon. He was hurt when one of the cannon misfired. A few cuts and bruises on some of the others. Nothing serious. Peters has them in the orlop. We were fortunate. He frowned, glancing down at her side. "Are you sure you're all right? Perhaps you broke a rib during your fall."

"My ribs are fine," she assured him. She straightened her posture, keeping her hand in place. "We did a good job, Mr. Jordan," she said quietly. "Tell them," she pointed to her men. "Tell them they did a good job."

Jordan's brows drew together. "Tell them yourself," he said bluntly, almost insolently. He regarded her pale face for a moment. Something was terribly wrong with her. "Captain, what happened to you? You're not all right."

"I will be." She hunched over as the pain became unbearable. The blood began to push through her fingers as the pressure of her hand became insufficient to staunch the flow. She was too frightened now to examine the extent of her own injury, certain she would faint if she looked at it.

"Captain?" His voice held a note of alarm, but he could not see the blood yet. Jordan grabbed her shoulders and Alex shook him off.

Her voice was almost inaudible. Repairs on the ship had stopped and voices were hushed as the men became aware something had happened to their captain. "Promise me you will see to Travers."

"Captain?"

"Promise me!" Her tone held both the authority of a command and the helplessness of a plea.

Jordan could not have ignored either. "Of course, Captain, I promise." She glanced up at him. Two bright crimson patches appeared on her cheeks, flushing her face unnatually. Her eyes were glazed with a thin wet sheen. Although they were focused on his face he knew she was not seeing him at all.

His answer echoed in her head and she managed a weak

response. "Good," she whispered. "I am going to my cabin. Tell the men to get back to work." She stood, turning her back on Jordan and the curious stares of her men and took three steps before she could not take another. She turned back to Jordan whose face went white as a gust of wind lifted her cape and he saw the blood covering her hand. "I need some help," she grinned childishly. She drew her hand away from the wound, and Jordan could see an ugly splinter still piercing the black silk of her shirt and beneath that, her flesh.

"Oh my God!" He started forward as Alexis began to sway, her smile vanishing. Even before he reached her he was aware of another person at his side. He stopped. Cloud went forward and Alexis collapsed into his arms.

Cloud swore as he looked at her pale face. "Mr. Jordan, is there anyone aboard who can attend her?"

"Peters can. He's in the orlop now."

"Then get him! I'll put her in her cabin." Cloud adjusted Alexis's weight in his arms and hurried toward her cabin. Peters was beside him by the time he placed her on the bunk.

"Find Peach, Tanner," Peters said breathlessly. "Tell him to fetch the rest of my medicine in the orlop. He'll know what to bring." Cloud stood motionless, held immobile by Alexis's unconscious form. "Hurry!" Peters commanded imperiously.

Cloud moved quickly and did as he was told. When Peach and he returned with the supplies, Peters had stopped the steady flow of blood but each time he tried to retrieve a splinter or a thread of material it would start again.

"Peach! Where does the captain keep her liquor?"

The cabin boy brought Peters a bottle of brandy which he used to bathe the edges of the wound. Alexis jerked under this slow onslaught of pain but she did not wake. Peters handed the bottle to Cloud after he took a few gulps. "You need this as much as she does," he said flatly. "Drink up."

Cloud took his advice. After the brandy's warmth fired his veins he passed the bottle to Peach. He was not aware of what he had done until the boy's choking reached his senses. He snatched the bottle away. "Let me have that! She'd have both our heads!"

Peach nodded and kept his eyes trained on what Peters was doing to his captain.

"Hold her hands down, Tanner," he ordered. "I'm going to try to get the rest of those splinters. Damn her!"

Cloud frowned at the man but he placed the brandy on the floor and grasped Alexis's wrists. Peters saw the look and said, "I can tell she broke off a section of the wood. Probably to keep anyone from seeing it. Unfortunately she put pressure on the pieces remaining inside and dug them into herself more deeply."

"Damn her!" Cloud echoed softly, feeling himself pale.

"Exactly," Peters retorted. "Hold her still. She won't wake thank God, but she's going to be able to feel this probing anyway."

Cloud winced as Alexis struggled against Peters's digging. Each moan cut through the three men in the room.

"Peach! Find something for her to bite down on. I can't work hearing her cry out." Peters probed again and extracted a shard almost two inches long from her flesh. This time when Alexis opened her mouth Peach jammed a wadded strip of sheet between her teeth and the only sound that came out was muffled considerably.

Peters worked for the next hour, stopping the blood flow long enough to extract some piece of the ship from her body then working frantically to stop the flow again. Above them the repairs continued on the *Dark Lady*. Her men worked with a vengeance, trying to forget what was happening beneath their feet. And in Charleston the *Hancock* spread the tale of Alex Danty's victory over the *Drake*, unaware of the toll being extracted for breaking the blockade.

Jordan checked on her every fifteen minutes until Peters told him his constant interruptions were doing more harm than good. On his last visit he shivered seeing Alexis's lifeless body and the face of the man holding her wrists. Cloud's features were contorted in a wounded expression more terri-

ble to look upon than his captain's. He shut the cabin door
quietly, fully aware that anything she was suffering was nothing
compared to what Cloud was taking upon himself.

"I've gotten everything out," Peters sighed. "I'll clean it
out again; then I'll stitch it. Peach, get me a needle and
thread. You can let go of her now, Tanner. She's beyond
pain." He said the words gently but they exploded in Cloud's
head.

"Is she going to live?" It was a question he had not wanted
to ask, but seeing that Peters was right, that Alexis was far
beyond them now, he forced the words.

Peters shook his head and took the needle and thread from
Peach's trembling fingers. "I'm not giving up hope, Tanner,
but it doesn't look very good. She's lost so much blood. I
don't know how she lasted through the battle."

Peach, who had been able to say nothing since he'd entered
her cabin, glared venomously at Cloud. Even his words, when
they came out, had a hissing quality. "This is your fault! She
wouldn't be dying if she had left you in Washington!"

"Shut up!" Peters shouted at the boy. "Get out of here if
you're going to talk like that. She'd dismiss you if she could
hear you!"

Peach was not intimidated. "And it's his fault that she's
dying!" He winced at the pain he saw in Cloud's face but he
did not back down. "It is your fault! It is! It is!" Suddenly he
realized he was crying.

"Get him out of here," Peters muttered to Cloud. Peach's
sobs were just as disquieting to him as Alexis's previous moans.
"And don't listen to what he says. It is not your fault."

"I'm not so sure," Cloud answered. "I'm not so sure at
all." He left Alexis's side and crossed the room to Peach. He
placed his hands on the boy's shoulders and drew him close.
He was glad Peach did not pull away. He didn't think he could
stand the rejection. He needed the closeness of someone who
loved Alexis as much as Peach did. "Come on. We'll go on
deck. There is nothing for us to do here. Jordan will come
down with her."

Peach wiped his tears. "I'm all right. I don't want to leave her. I want to be here in case she . . ." He could not finish and his body shuddered with sobs he held back.

"She won't die, you know." Cloud's fingers gripped the boy's shoulders tightly. "She won't." He said the words so firmly he found himself believing them. "Let's go. I have something to tell you. It's the reason I know she won't give up."

Peach nodded and followed Cloud out of the cabin. He stole one last look at Peters working diligently at sewing Alexis's wound; then he shut the door. When they reached the deck, their pale faces unwittingly confirmed the crewmen's worst thoughts.

Cloud spoke to ease their fears. "She's still alive," he told them. "Peters is stitching her now. Mr. Jordan, can I talk to you?" When Jordan joined him Cloud asked Peach to wait for him on the far side of the deck.

"How is she really?" asked Jordan when they were alone.

"It's not very good. Peters says she's lost too much blood. She should have told you she was hurt."

Jordan sighed. "She would never have gone below during the battle. Redland suspected she was injured and was told to keep quiet. I can only guess why she waited so long. The last thing she did was make me promise that we would still go after Travers. She wanted to be certain that would be taken care of before she—before she went below."

"Oh, God!" All color drained from Cloud's face as he listened to Jordan. Would Alexis not fight as hard if she thought her men would carry out her vow?

Jordan was about to comment on the unspoken thought when a voice above them arrested their attention.

"It's the *Raleigh!*" Randall called down. "She's heading for us! Off the starboard bow!"

"Damn! What next?" Jordan muttered as he raced for the starboard rail.

He lifted the scope and examined the ship, still a small blur in the distance. He did not doubt the authority of the voice above him. Randall not only had an uncanny ability for recognizing the enemy, he was also the only man ever to guess Alex Danty was a woman before the unveiling. Jordan passed the instrument to Cloud.

"Randall's right," said Cloud.

"We'll have to fight." Jordan grimaced.

"No!" Cloud's objection burst forth before he realized he had no right to voice one. "I'm sorry, Mr. Jordan. But we can't fight. The ship can stand it and if we repeated our earlier strategy we might even win, but the captain won't be able to survive the shock of a battle. We've got to find another way. Outrun her if we have to."

"That frigate? This ship has suffered some damage. We're not at top speed. We're still fast but—"

"But nothing. Something can be done."

"I can't."

"I can."

Jordan laughed admiringly. "A ship has never been so easily taken over before! Men! Follow Captain Cloud's orders! He says we can avoid a battle and by God, I think he's right!"

There were no objections to the sudden change in command. Cloud threw a grateful look at Jordan. "See to Alex. Stay with her until we're safe."

"You'll need someone to relay orders," he objected.

"I'll use Peach," replied Cloud. "Go to her. And Mr. Jordan, if she comes around, take back your promise." He smiled. "And tell her I love her."

"Tell her yourself! She'll be around to listen!"

Cloud nodded and took his place at the wheel. He called to Peach. "Station yourself partway down the deck. Listen to every order I give and repeat it at the top of your lungs. Can you do that?"

"Aye, Captain," he answered. He started forward but paused in midstride. He turned back to Cloud. "I didn't mean what I said before. About it being your fault."

"Yes, you did. You didn't say anything I wasn't thinking. It's not important now."

Peach had no reply. He went to his station and braced himself against the rail as the ship turned sharply under Cloud's skilled hands.

When the ship lurched Jordan found himself flung against the wall in the companionway. He could hear Peters's curses from inside Alexis's cabin and he hurried along to ease the man's anger.

"What the hell's going on up there?" Peters demanded after Jordan entered.

"It's the *Raleigh*. She's coming after us," he explained. He examined Alexis, who for all appearances, might have only been sleeping. "How is she?"

"Weak. Did Tanner tell you I don't think she'll make it?"

"He told me. Is there anything I can do?"

"Yeah. Tell me what you're doing down here if there's a ship on our heels."

"Starboard bow," Jordan corrected him. "I wanted to fight—"

"Good God! That would kill her now!"

"That's what Tanner said. He's in charge at the moment. He's going to try to outrun them."

"A frigate?" he asked in amazement. "After the damage we've suffered?"

"A bloody frigate. And he's not concerned about the damage."

The ship tilted again and Peters reached out to secure Alexis before she rolled on her side. "Damn! She can't take much more of this either. The slightest movement pulls at the stitches."

Jordan looked down at Alexis's side and saw a tiny circle of red widen on the sheet covering her. Peters threw the sheet aside and staunched the droplets forcing their way through the tiny stitches.

"Find some sheets and rip them in long strips," he told Jordan, who was watching helplessly. "We'll have to strap her to the bed. She can't take this tossing." His eyes lifted toward the noise overhead. "I hope he knows what he's doing."

Jordan began tearing the sheets. "There's no one aboard with more to lose if he doesn't."

Peters nodded. "Peach was pretty rough on him. Blamed him for Captain Danty's injuries."

"Peach could not have been one tenth as rough on him as he is on himself."

"I know. That's why I sent them both out of here."

Jordan handed Peters several strips of sheet and together they wound them around Alexis and the bed until Peters was satisfied she would not be tossed with the ship. Peters covered her again and for the first time since he had entered the cabin he moved away from her side. He glanced around the floor, found the bottle of brandy that had rolled away, and helped himself to its contents.

"Here." He gave the bottle to Jordan. "Drink up. It dulls the pain." He took the unused portion of the sheet and ripped it into smaller sections. These he dipped in water and used to wipe Alexis's face free of perspiration and grime from the battle.

"Does she have a fever?" asked Jordan.

"Not yet. If she makes it through the night she'll have to battle one later. I don't think for one minute she'll get through this without infection. Look on the table. That's what I dug out of her. I can't even be sure I have it all."

Jordan walked to the table and examined the splinters. The largest was three inches long and almost an inch wide. There were two others almost as long and many smaller, equally lethal slivers. He grimaced.

"She would have been better off getting a dagger wound. It wouldn't have done half the damage. At least it wouldn't have left part of itself in her." He replaced the cloth on her forehead with a fresh one. "For God's sake, Jordan, have a seat. There's nothing you can do that can't be done sitting." His gruffness had the effect of pushing Jordan into a chair. "That's better. Now tell me what Tanner's doing up there."

"I told you. He's going to outrun them."

Peters smiled. "Told you he could do it, huh?"

"I don't doubt it."

"Neither do I, Mr. Jordan." The ship heaved again but Peters observed with satisfaction that Alexis remained still. "Just hold on, Captain," he murmured. "He says he can do it."

An hour passed. Then another. Alexis clung tenaciously to life. Jordan and Peters took turns bathing her face and checking her wound. Above her Cloud was using every skill he had to keep the *Raleigh* from gaining ground. After the first hour he had known there was little chance he could outrun the British vessel. His goal now was to maintain the distance separating them until dark, when he would attempt to lose them. He glanced at the sun. Almost noon. There was a curse and a prayer in his softly uttered sigh as he swung the wheel. His grip alternated between a stranglehold that threatened to break the spokes with its unrelenting pressure and a caress that urged the *Dark Lady* into difficult maneuvers with its unrelenting coaxing.

Jordan observed this peculiar command of Cloud's while on one of his visits topside to review their situation.

"Well?" Peters demanded when he had returned.

"Tanner says the best he can do until dark is keep the ship at a safe distance."

"Is he doing it?"

"Yes."

"They why do you look as if the British are going to beat down the door any minute?"

"Because he's the only thing between us and the British. How long can he push himself that way? Christ! You should see him up there! He looks as if he could kill the entire Royal Fleet with his bare hands or break down in tears and never know the difference. How long can he keep that up?"

"Cloud?" It was only a whisper but it riveted both men to the source.

"There's your answer, Mr. Jordan. He'll go as long as she can." To Alexis he replied softly, "He's not here, Captain. Soon."

Alexis shook her head. Her eyes opened slowly and her gaze alternated between the two men, seeing neither.

"She doesn't know who we are," muttered Jordan.

"That would be asking for quite a lot." Peters lifted the bottle of brandy to her lips and managed to pour a few drops in her mouth before she passed out. "She needs rest and for that we'll have to trust Tanner."

The hours until sunset passed with agonizing slowness. On deck there were occasions when the men believed the *Raleigh* had abandoned its pursuit only to discover minutes later this was not the case at all. Each disappointment was met with a succinct epithet and a renewed effort to see that it was their last. In Alexis's cabin the time was spent in much the same manner. Peters and Jordan took turns at her side, seeing to her comfort. There were no lucid moments for their captain and when she became tormented by pain Peters administered drops of laudanum. When she slept peacefully the two men silently berated themselves for not being able to do more.

Several factors were involved in Cloud's decision to change his strategy. The night was plagued by a sliver of new moon and lack of cloud cover, providing the *Raleigh* with sufficient light to track the *Dark Lady*. Hope of breaking free of their ghostly shadow gone, Cloud was forced to consider alternatives. Alexis's worsening condition throughout the night not only made the selection of a new course imperative, it helped determine the destination.

It was not yet midnight when Cloud informed Jordan of his plan. He had not slept for forty hours but tension was keeping him alert.

"I've decided to take the *Dark Lady* to Roadtown," he said. "Alex will make a better recovery there." He would not admit aloud there was any possibility but that she would recover. "Engaging the *Raleigh* is still out of the question. It would be like putting a pistol to the captain's head. I've thought of a way we might be able to stop the *Raleigh* without firing a shot."

Jordan had listened attentively, but now he was skeptical of Cloud's last statement. "Without a shot?"

"That's right. I was thinking of Horse Shoe."

Jordan's eyes widened. "Use the reef, you mean? Damn! That's a good thought."

Cloud smiled wryly. "I'm glad you think so. I've already committed us to the new coordinates. We could arrive there in three days if the weather holds. Roadtown is only a couple of hours beyond. Once we have taken care of the *Raleigh* it will be safe to see Captain Danty to her home."

Later that night Cloud was able to leave his post for a brief visit with Alexis and a few hours of sleep on the floor by her bed.

"Is there nothing else I can do?" he asked Peters before he left.

"Nothing. I can bathe her fever and ease her pain with laudanum. Beyond that there is nothing."

Cloud stared at Alexis while he held her hand and squeezed it gently. He thought his heart would stop beating when he felt the pressure of her touch respond reassuringly. The conviction that he had not imagined her response was what he needed to keep on going when the weather changed shortly before sunrise.

At first the slackening sails were hardly noticeable and only minor adjustments were necessary before they billowed fully in the wind. But as the hours wore on the wind tapered to a soft breeze and it was as if the anchor had been suddenly dropped. In a matter of minutes the breeze had disappeared and the *Dark Lady* drifted listlessly on still water.

There was no way of knowing how long the calm would last. It was not unheard of for a ship to be trapped in one for weeks. That the *Raleigh* was experiencing the same conditions did little for the *Dark Lady's* morale. The *Raleigh* had more men, and in a calm, men with muscle *are* the wind.

Cloud ordered men into a longboat which was then lowered over the side. Grasping the oars, the men rowed to the bow of the ship and attached a tow line. Wilkes, Brandon, Ned

Allison, and the others making up this first shift grabbed the oars again and heaving, grunting, and sweating, began the almost impossible task of pulling the *Dark Lady*.

Through his glass Cloud saw the *Raleigh* was up to the challenge. Two of their boats were being used to tow the frigate and more men were waiting to replace those who dropped.

While the crew in the boat put forth their best effort, one shift of men was allowed to rest while a third shift filled buckets with sea water and painstakingly carried them up the rigging to wet the sails. The heavier material now caught even a suspicion of a breeze.

The calm lasted two days. During this time strong men dropped to the deck from exhaustion while the *Raleigh* came dangerously close, and Alexis's reassuring gesture to Cloud was never repeated.

Several hundred miles to the north, in a newly constructed town with muddy streets and cheap boardinghouses, an event was about to take place that would change the static nature of the present.

In Washington the morning paper had carried a brief account of the battle to free Charleston's harbor, and now, on a tray carrying the President's lunch, there was one letter among many which held special significance.

"Get me Senator Howe!" was the outraged response to the letter's content.

And it was as if that bellow filled the *Dark Lady's* sails.

The calm was over.

Cloud recalled the longboat and where they thought they had no energy, no hope, they found reserves of both.

That night Cloud stayed with Alexis while Jordan maintained the margin of safety Cloud had achieved for the *Dark Lady*.

Alexis had also been released from the effects of the calm. Now she stirred restlessly, shivering, trembling, and then growing still only to grow hot. When her breathing became labored he held her hand and stroked her forehead. When she cried out from pain he sparingly administered laudanum. He talked to her most of the night in low and gentle tones. He talked of his childhood, his first girl. He described his home, his parents, Emma, the streets of Boston. He told her about the wharfs, his first voyage, Landis, Harry Young, and the others. He told her things that would have made her laugh if she had been awake and he told her things that would have made her clutch his head to her breast if he had been in her arms. At times he hardly knew what he was saying, only that some part of her had to hear and realize it was his voice. It was only when he felt the warming rays of the sun at his back that he fully realized she had survived the night.

Cloud slept then. When he woke it was late afternoon and he had to accept Peter's explanation that he needed his sleep more than they had needed him until now. Jordan had held their advantage admirably and they were within hours of Horse Shoe reef.

Horse Shoe reef was a bed of razor-sharp coral stretching in a perilous arc for thirteen miles. Located some twenty miles from Tortola, between the tips of Virgin Gorda and Anegada Island, it was a treacherous welcome for vessels entering the Caribbean from the Atlantic, its unique shape creating currents that were often swift and unpredictable. Like a tropical iceberg, Horse Shoe reef only rose above the water in a few places while the great bulk of its mass lay hidden, a series of hills and valleys ten fathoms deep in areas. Even in clear weather the reef was visible only to those who knew the meaning of the pale water surrounding it. Others, not familiar with the formation, had to depend on excellent navigation charts. Only in recent years had the reef been included on maps, and three hundred ships and many more men were mute testimony to this negligence.

It was Cloud's intention to make this natural obstruction do the work of cannon and hot shot. He planned to skirt the reef, draw near, then retreat, always keeping the *Raleigh* at a distance that would make firing her guns a useless exercise, but allowing her close enough to tantalize and seduce her into making a deadly error of judgment. The strategy was risky, the outcome uncertain.

"She's following us, Captain! Just like you said she would!" Peach stared at the man beside him admiringly.

"Hard to starboard!" Cloud ordered as he felt the ship being pulled by a dangerous current. When the *Dark Lady* had shaken off the water's clutch he glanced over his shoulder at the *Raleigh*. "Now we'll see if they follow. If they don't know the exact location of the reef, then they've learned there is some danger waiting for them."

But the *Raleigh* did not slacken her pace, having pursued too long and hard to retreat now. When she reached the point where the current had tugged at the *Dark Lady*, nothing at all rocked the frigate.

It was like a game of chess, a tournament marked by stamina, patience, daring, and eerie silences. For an hour the *Dark Lady* flirted with the reef, swinging in graceful arcs, the pattern of her taunting movements marked by her frothy wake, sparkling bread crumbs for her opponent to follow. The *Raleigh* matched her steps, not gracefully, but competently and powerfully, as if she scorned the edge of strength which belongs to beauty.

It happened without warning. A powerful upsurge of water captured the *Dark Lady*, and the *Raleigh* was forgotten and Redland and Cloud battled for life at the helm. Her sails strained and her rudder groaned at the position it was expected to take. Her crew was pitched forward and sideways while in her belly the other Dark Lady cried out in terror and pain for three people who could never answer. Then, as if she were shivering in revulsion at the current's domination, the *Dark Lady* shuddered from stem to stern and pulled free moments before the reef would have claimed her. It was only then that anyone dared to look back and see how the *Raleigh* had fared.

Sounds travel in water. The great wrenching and scraping of the *Raleigh's* keel as it drove into the coral reef reverberated in an underwater chasm. The slicing of her underbelly and starboard side delivered a message of splintering wood and shredding metal in fanlike waves to nearby animal life.

On the surface those sounds were muted. What the crews of both ships thought they heard clearly, they heard only in their imagination.

Water rushed into the *Raleigh's* hold and the frigate began to tilt at a dangerous angle before the boats could be lowered. The *Dark Lady* looked on as men began to abandon their ship and strike out toward her. By the time four boats had been released, filled to overflowing with men of the *Raleigh's* crew, the surrounding water was dotted with the bodies of men who had been trapped in the current and was red with the blood of those who had been cut by the reef. One of the boats overturned before Cloud's men could reach it with a hook. Sharks claimed all but fifteen of those lives. The remaining boats were towed until they were in sight of land and then were set free.

One hundred twenty men reached Anegada Island as the *Dark Lady* sailed to Roadtown. Horse Shoe reef held two hundred of their mates.

"Did you really have a girl named Prudence?"

Cloud's chair fell backward as he leaped from his place near the window to the fourposter where Alexis was lying. She spoke as if she had been awake for hours, listening to some conversation and only now deciding she wanted to contribute.

He knelt beside the bed and placed a hand on her forehead. She was watching him curiously, as if she did not know why he looked so concerned.

"Sally! Her fever's gone! Sally!" he called for Mrs. Grenlon.

Alexis brushed his hand aside with an air of impatience that made him laugh.

"Yes, Alex. Prudence."

She placed a finger on his cheek and traced a line Cloud thought was imaginary until he saw her finger come away wet.

"You're crying," she said softly, wonderingly. She found

his hand and held it, feeling no need to say anything more as she drifted back to sleep.

It was this scene that Sally Grendon viewed from the threshold of the bedroom. She dabbed at her round violet eyes with a corner of her apron and closed the door quietly.

When Alexis woke later she demanded to be allowed out of bed. Sally would not hear of it and called Cloud and her husband to restrain her. The threat of both men holding her down was enough to make Alexis promise to stay put, but when Sally told her how long she had been unconscious she was hard pressed to make Alexis keep her word.

Cloud visited her for several hours, entertaining her with carefully selected episodes of the days she had missed. He told her nothing of the *Raleigh,* preferring her to remain ignorant of the dangers they had faced while she was still weak. He described the hospitality they had received from the townspeople and the Grendon's generosity in opening their home to Alexis and him while Sally took over caring for Alexis.

"I think she suspects," he whispered conspiratorially, brushing his thumb lightly along the sensitive underside of her wrist.

"Suspects what?" she whispered back, equally secretive.

"That I want to crawl into bed with you."

She fell asleep with an attractive flush highlighting her features.

From that day on Alexis was permitted a few visitors each afternoon, and to insure that she received enough rest Sally gave her laudanum. Alexis took the drug but complained bitterly until it had its desired effect.

It was not until Alexis had been improving steadily for six days that Cloud enjoyed his first restful sleep. During the night he turned on his side, dreamily thinking his room had never been so warm or his bed so comfortable. He was asleep again before he could question the difference. When he woke to discover Alexis curled in his arms he was furious that she had left her room. Then she turned in his embrace and he wanted only to kiss the parted lips she presented.

"You shouldn't be here with me," he said gently. "Why did you leave your bed?"

"Do you really want me to answer that?"

Cloud sighed. "No, I guess not. It was all I could do to keep from joining you."

"You should have. I'm much better."

"You won't be if Sally finds you here."

"Oh, she's pampering me too much. Don't let her give me any more of that drug. I've missed so much already."

"She pampers you because she cares and she'll be here any minute looking for you. And it's just as likely she'll have my head as yours."

She traced his mouth with her finger. "I couldn't bear that. Help me back to my own room."

Cloud washed and dressed quickly then carefully gathered Alexis into his arms and carried her down the hallway to her bed. "Let me look at your wound. If you opened it because you got out of bed then I won't stop Sally from drugging you. She consented wearily and he lifted her shift to remove the bandages. "No harm done," he said after inspecting the livid gash. "She'll be able to remove the stitches in a few days. You're going to have to be more careful, Alex. You were very, very sick, and you can't pretend you weren't."

"Promise you'll stay here tonight."

"I won't promise, and if you don't obey Sally I won't even sleep in this house."

"All right. You win. Do you suppose Sally will allow me to have a bath?"

"No, she won't. She'll give you a sponge bath later."

"Please ask her to come here, Cloud. I can't stand another day of being fawned over."

"Most people enjoy it," he said as he left the room, ducking to precisely the right moment to avoid the feather missile she threw at his head. In a few minutes he was back with Sally only a step behind him.

"If this is about getting out of bed you can think again, Alexis Quinton," Sally said sternly as she smoothed her patient's sheets.

"I will never understand how someone with such a round chin can be so stubbornly set in her ways."

Sally looked at Alexis askance. "On this island stubborn and Alex Danty are synonymous."

Cloud laughed and Alexis sighed to keep her mouth from curling at the corners. "When will I be able to take out my ship, Sally?"

"Give it some more time, Alexis. You've waited this long for Travers; another week won't matter."

"One week. Then we're sailing. May I visit my ship today, perhaps review the repairs that were made?"

"You'd fall over before you reached the front door. I will not hear of it."

"Then what will you hear of?" she demanded, frustrated at being under someone else's supervision. "May I have a real bath?"

"No. You cannot get your stitches wet."

Alexis dared Cloud to say I told you so. "May I work with Frank on the company books?"

"Yes, but in bed."

"Am I allowed to get up at all?"

"No. I will not be responsible for what would happen if you do."

Alexis ignored the groan that came from Cloud when he heard Sally's last sentence. "Then it's settled," she replied quickly, raising herself on her elbows. "I'll be responsible."

Too late Sally realized her mistake. She turned to Cloud for assistance. "Can you talk any sense into her?"

"I haven't been able to yet."

There was a long pause while Sally examined Alexis's wound closely. Finally she said, "Have it your way. But remember later that you forced me to do this."

"Don't worry. I won't try anything strenuous. I'm glad you realize I can take care of myself."

Cloud was appalled. "You can't be serious, Sally! You can't mean to allow her out of bed."

Sally confirmed this with a nod of her head. "You heard her. She's relieved me of the responsibility. She may do whatever she likes." Her tone registered defeat but when Cloud opened the door for her she gave him a dimpled smile. It was a smile of victory.

Cloud stared at the closed door, as if it would give some clue to the woman's behavior. No answers forthcoming, he focused his attention on Alexis's struggle to get out of bed.

"You won't get any help from me," he told her coldly.

"I was not aware I asked for any," she snapped. But she could not conceal her grimace as she walked to the small cherrywood breakfast table only several feet from her bed. Nor could she hide her problem finding a position in a chair that caused only minimal discomfort.

"Why do you insist on being so stubborn, Alex?" Cloud asked her after he joined her at the table. "You've bullied Sally into going against her judgment. You are in no condition to be issuing orders—in or out of bed!"

"I won't stay in this room a second longer than I have to." She lifted her chin defiantly.

Cloud pushed away from her in disgust.

"Where are you going?"

"I don't know. Anywhere. I do know that I'm not staying around to watch you kill yourself. You promised not to do anything strenuous. Since you have already managed to get out of bed without toppling to the floor I assume you will want to try other, equally insane things."

"But I thought you would share breakfast with me."

"I've lost my appetite," he replied crossly. He opened the door but his path was blocked by Sally's husband. Cloud stepped aside to let Frank enter.

When Frank realized Cloud was intending to leave he shook his head frantically. "My wife said you would be eating breakfast here. She doesn't think Alexis should be alone."

"And why is that?" Cloud remained poised between taking the initiative to leave and shutting the door.

"Sally just said she was not to be left alone."

Alexis broke in. "It's all right, Frank. If he wants to leave he can. You stay with me and we'll go over those books you wanted me to see."

"Oh, no!" Frank answered quickly. "That is, er—there's nothing to do right now, not until we hear from Scott Hansom. He's ten days late returning from Baltimore. When he arrives we'll have a clearer picture of our profits."

Alexis would have liked to inquire as to the possible reasons for Hansom's delay, but she was sidetracked by the tray placed in front of her. The aroma of freshly cooked bacon stopped her from voicing an objection when Cloud shut the door and returned to his place at her side.

"Sally made these biscuits this morning," Frank murmured, placing two on each plate. "And this tea is freshly brewed and piping hot. Sally says you're to drink it that way, Alexis. She told me if you insist on getting out of bed you should have as much strength as you can."

"You see, Cloud," Alexis said, lifting her cup. "She hasn't given up on me completely. She'll worry and fret and complain, but she'll help me do what I want."

Cloud said nothing in return. He was more interested in Frank's barely successful attempt to keep from laughing. He glanced from the man's angular face to Alexis's hands holding her cup and when he made the connection between Sally's earlier confident smile and the steaming cup of tea, he raised his own cup to his lips to hide amusement and satisfaction.

After Frank was gone Cloud enjoyed his meal, ignoring Alexis's attempts to justify her actions. When he was done he pushed his plate away and leaned back in his chair, eyeing her expectantly.

"Why are you watching me that way, Cloud? It's unnerving. It's as though you hope I'll collapse any moment."

"I believe it is inevitable."

She paid no attention to his smug tone. "I'm afraid I will

disappoint you then. A good meal was all I needed. Indeed, I'm hardly in any pain at all."

"Oh, yes. I'm certain the meal is responsible for your lack of pain. Just think: a filling meal, a hot bath, a trip to the *Dark Lady,* and a decent burial beside the people you vowed to avenge."

"Stop it!" she ordered. "That was cruel! Why do you insist on being so mean?" She shoved her plate away in anger, causing silverware to clatter to the floor.

"Mean! You call it mean because I don't want to see you hurt? You call it mean when I point out your perversity will be your undoing? I'm cruel because I remind you of a promise?" He shrugged. "Maybe I don't love you enough. Right now I'm not sure I even like you. I should probably tie you in bed and leave you there. Then I wouldn't have to listen to your curses. I heard enough of them while you were ill."

Alexis's eyebrows arched dramatically. "What did I say?" she asked softly.

"Nothing you haven't said to my face on occasion. I deserved it then. It's just disconcerting to hear it when I haven't done anything. And now you accuse me of being mean. Madam, if you want to know the truth, I would like to beat some sense into you since reason doesn't seem to be working!"

Stunned, hearing words from him she had never expected to hear, Alexis bolted upright in her chair. "You wouldn't dare!"

"I would dare it, Alex," he answered. There was a pause between each word for emphasis. "I would dare it, if I thought it would help." The hard lines of his face softened as he continued to meet her penetrating stare.

Alexis wondered at the change in his expression. She felt as if she were going to melt beneath his emerald gaze. She put the back of her hand on her forehead. It felt unnaturally hot. She smiled weakly, forgetting her anger, part of her even recognizing she was being unreasonably obstinate about her present situation. She got to her feet and moved to his side.

She had a fleeting thought that it was odd she felt no pain at all, but the thought was lost as he pulled at her hips and gently sat her on his lap.

"Please don't be angry with me, Cloud. I know you think I deserve it, but I have to do things my way. I don't want you to worry so much. I'll be all right."

"I know you will," he said with assurance. She missed his smile because he pressed it into her hair.

"Of all the things I said while I had a fever . . . did I tell you I love you?" She whispered the words against his chest while she dismissed the euphoria taking hold of her as merely an indication of the intense pleasure she felt at being in his arms. She listened to the quickening of his heart, her ear pressed to the smooth material of his shirt.

"No. That was something you didn't say."

"Then I'll tell you now." She lifted her head, placing her hands on either side of his face, drawing him close. "I do love you. I love you . . . I adore you . . . everything about you."

Cloud smiled. "I have a confession."

Alexis laughed brightly. "Saying you love me won't be much of a confession."

"Don't anticipate me," he cautioned, kissing her forehead. He paused, another thought taking precedence; then he said, "Tell me again."

"I love you. Again? I love you. I worship you! I need you. I won't tire of saying it, Cloud." She felt pleasantly warm in his embrace. She knew her face was flushed, reflecting her desire and the overwhelming contentment she experienced when she was close to him. "I love you," she offered once more with no prompting. It sounded as young and earnest as the first time she'd ever said those words.

"Sally drugged your tea."

"What!" She intended it to be a cry of indignation but it came out as a groan of despair. She pushed away from Cloud and tried to stand. The euphoria was replaced by a heavy drowsiness and she recognized the drug was as much responsible for her flushed face as Cloud. When she realized her legs would not support her she accepted defeat, collapsing onto his lap, rather than fall to the floor. "I think you're right. How could she do this?"

Cloud suppressed a grin at her plaintive cry. He carried her to bed and after he had covered her with a blanket he asked, "You're not angry?"

"I'm furious." The statement sounded inadequate to her own ears as she had to stifle a yawn. "Tell Sally I'm furious with her. She shouldn't have done this to me. I hate that drug. I hate not being in control . . . not being able to do things."

"I know, but she warned you that you were forcing her. Don't fight it now. Just rest."

"Don't leave me!" She gripped his hand tightly to prevent an escape he never considered making. She struggled to keep her eyes open. "I hate this so much. It's not natural to fall asleep this way."

Cloud heard the genuine alarm in her voice and he placed his free hand over hers. "I'll stay, Alex. I'll be here when you wake. Promise you'll wait until Sally says you are well enough before you try to do things again."

Her eyes closed. "You ask so much."

"Promise me," he insisted gently.

"I promise." Cloud had to bend close to her mouth to hear the words but upon hearing them he relaxed, certain she would keep her commitment.

In the following days there were many times Alexis regretted her promise. She accused Cloud of extracting the words under duress but he refused to listen to her. The knowledge that she had given her word, no matter the circumstances, and her fear of the laudanum kept her confined to her room. When Sally pronounced her fit for cautious exercise she made no pretense of hiding her excitement. Similarly, Sally made no attempt to hide her displeasure when she overextended her time at the ship. Both women were irascible and irresistible by turns and Tanner Frederick Cloud opted to stay well out of the way when they disagreed.

The day before the *Dark Lady* was scheduled to leave Tortola, Cloud and Alexis were picnicking on their favorite section of the beach, the area below the crow's nest, when they were interrupted by a soft tread across the sand behind them.

Turning together, their faces showed opposite poles of emotion to the newcomer. Cloud frowned, irritated by the stranger's intrusion, while Alexis smiled, elated he had returned safely.

Getting to her feet, she ran lightly across the white sand and hung her arms about his neck pleading, "Keep that horrible Captain Danty away from me! I won't stay with him another moment!"

Cloud laughed with both of them. "You're Scott Hansom, I take it."

The laughter died in Hansom's throat. He put Alexis to one side and took a menacing step toward Cloud, refusing to show he was impressed when Cloud didn't move. "And you're the son of a bitch that took Captain Danty and exposed her to those bastards—Howe, Farthington, and what's-his-name? Richard Somebody or Other."

"Granger," Cloud supplied dryly, getting to his feet. "And you forgot Robert Davidson. Another bastard."

"You should know."

Cloud's reply was cut off by Alexis. "But Mr. Hansom," she reasoned, quickly perceiving the important issue, "how is it that *you* know?"

Reaching into his back pocket, he threw several folded newspapers at Cloud's feet. "It's all there, Captain Danty. Everything. It's what made me late. I left Baltimore for Washington when I first heard the rumors and I stayed there until I was certain the business was handled justly."

Alexis tugged at Hansom's sleeve. "Here, sit down! Don't make us read the accounts now. Tell us what happened!"

Hansom eyed Cloud as if he were something to be stepped over before he did as Alexis suggested. Alexis seated herself beside him, while Cloud, in amused deference to the appraisal he was receiving, sat a few feet away.

"I heard your name linked with the senator's several times. That's when I thought you must be in Washington. I knew there was going to be trouble the moment *his* men"—here the scathing tone was accompanied by a distasteful jerk of his head in Cloud's direction—"started asking questions about you. I don't suppose you ever received my message?"

"No, she never got it," Cloud answered for Alexis.

Hansom gave him another narrowed look before he continued. "I found out that you had been in Washington a few weeks earlier, that you had been brought there by *him* and were going to get some idiotic pardon for crimes you never committed by men who had no authority to offer one.

"Bennet Farthington confessed the whole of it to Little Jemmy himself. Jemmy's war secretary, Eustis, resigned over this issue and some earlier conflicts. When Davidson discovered Farthington implicated all of them after Howe and he had tried to cover themselves, he killed himself. Apparently he couldn't face the humiliation of the trial the others had to endure. The trial lasted four days and the jury was less than one hour returning a guilty verdict. All three men were given prison sentences for conspiracy to commit treason. If there had been proof that they had contacted the British, they would have been hanged."

It took Alexis a while to take it all in. "It's really over," she murmured wonderingly. "I can hardly believe it. They can't hurt us any more, Cloud." A frown drew her eyebrows together as a terrible suspicion occurred to her. She grabbed for the newspapers on Cloud's lap. "What do the accounts say about Captain Danty? Do they know?"

Cloud moved to kneel in front of her, stilling her frantic hands as she searched for the articles. "It's all right, Alex. I looked through them already. I think it was a mixture of pride and fear that kept them from admitting all they knew. The world has Bennet Farthington's sworn statement that Captain

Danty is small and wiry and scarred so terribly in the face
that he no longer resembles a man.''

Scott Hansom was relieved to find he could laugh with
Captain Cloud after all.

Chapter Seventeen

Cloud took a few moments to become accustomed to the dim light as he entered Alexis's quarters. Instead of the usual lamps there was only soft candlelight and if Cloud had been asked to name the quality of the light, he would have answered: seductive.

Alexis was standing at the table, her head bent, adjusting a candle in its brass holder. Her slender fingers were wrapped around the candle and the tiny flame flickered across her face as she secured it in its position. Cloud smiled at the purposeful set of her mouth, so familiar to him now. His eyes darted from her mouth to her throat where the moving orange light caught the silver chain, sending a spark in his direction. Emerald eyes continued their slow appraisal as Alexis straightened and stepped back to view her handiwork. She glanced up. Her face held no surprise at finding him in the room although she had not heard him enter. She saw appreciation of her appearance in the warmth of his eyes. His gaze had changed from casual to one she could only describe as reverent. Skirting the table, she took a few steps in his direction, the sky blue gown veiling her body whispered its presence with every movement. Unbound, her hair formed a golden aura about her oval face and shoulders. Her eyes were bright, anxious, when his eyes returned to hers, and his eyebrows arched in a question he could not have asked with his voice.

Alexis held out her hand, which he grasped firmly in his own, and led him back to the table. Cloud noticed the two goblets filled with dark, red wine only when she reached out to place one of them in his free hand.

"We are celebrating," she said quietly, pressing her glass to his. The contact of the goblets seemed as warm and intimate as the touch of their hands.

"The occasion?" He raised the wine to his lips.

"Several things actually." She tasted her drink sparingly, savoring just the hint of it in her mouth, over her tongue. "A few hours ago I completed my first full day back in command."

"As if you had never left it."

"Thank you. We are also drinking to the fact we are only one week from New Orleans and possibly Captain Travers."

"And the end of your search."

"Yes. Then there is the matter of the *Raleigh.*"

"Who told you?"

"Peach. You should have said something, Cloud."

"There was nothing to say. I did no more or less than I was able to do."

Because he said it simply, as a matter of fact, Alexis did not thank him for being capable of so much. "And finally, we are alone."

"Completely?"

"Mmmm. Last night was our last in separate bedrooms."

"That," he said with emphasis, "is worthy of celebration."

"Exactly what I thought." Stepping closer, she curled her fingers around the open collar of his linen shirt, spreading the material so she could see more of the tawny skin of his chest. She bent her head, pressing her lips to the slight hollow of his breast where his heart pulsed beneath warm, salty flesh.

Cloud's laughter was deep in his throat when she looked up, golden eyes misty and glowing, but with a glint that named him the target of her actions. He made no move to embrace her or give any outward indication he was affected by her nearness. She wanted to win him and he was moved by the notion she still thought it necessary. He calmly lifted the goblet to his mouth and drank deeply. He set it down and said, "I like it when you look at me that way."

"What way?"

Again the throaty laughter. "You don't know, do you?" Alexis shook her head. Strands of hair kept time with the ship's slow motion, falling across her cheek and mouth. He smiled faintly, brushing aside the wisps. "You look as if you had no idea I was lost the very moment I entered this room."

"You were?" Her tone was softly incredulous.

"Yes."

"Oh."

"I see part of it in the way you hold your mouth." His hand moved to cup her chin while his thumb traced the line of her mouth. "It's set in the same determined way when you face me as when you face anything you perceive as a challenge. It's not at all the look of a woman, so heady with desire, she can't control the muscles of her face. It's more purposeful. I like it. I like being the challenge, the purpose of your determined smile."

Alexis could only return his stare as she listened to his words. He released her jaw, sliding his hand up her face. Her ear rested in his palm while his fingers intertwined with her hair and now his thumb slowly outlined her brow.

"Your eyes too. Instead of being heavy lidded, drooping, slack with sensuality, your lids are open, almost tense, as if you were afraid the slightest drop would mean you might miss something. Your sensuality is in the clearness of your eyes. Behind that misty sheen your gaze is steady, conscious, and there is a special light in them when you see something you want."

"The light? Is it there now? Do you see it?"

"Yes."

"Good," she whispered, turning her lips into the palm of

his hand. "I want you." She voiced what he had known since he'd walked in, what she had planned for since returning to her cabin. Her fingers began to move over his shirt, unfastening the buttons until she could part the material fully. When she pulled it free from the band of his trousers, he shrugged out of it while her hands caressed the smooth muscles of his chest and slid lower over his abdomen.

"Do you always get what you want?" His lips moved over her cheeks, her jaw, her closed eyes.

"Not always." Her breath was warm against the curve of his neck and her arms drew around his back. She could feel the rough lines of his scars with the tips of her fingers.

"Liar." His thick voice made it sound like an endearment.

Alexis did not realize he had unfastened her gown until it fell softly to her feet. Her body shuddered at the touch of his hands on her shoulders. When she was naked he lifted and carried her to bed, but when he would have released her Alexis held on, refusing to break the circle of her arms about his neck. She pulled him in with her, rolling on top of him, covering his face, neck, and chest with quick burning kisses.

He lifted his hips under her urgings to allow her to remove his trousers. When she had drawn them off her hands pressed against his thighs, his knees, his calves. Her touch was firm, her lips warm and moist, and Cloud, although enjoying her aggressiveness could not remain passive a moment longer. He changed her frantic, devouring pace with lingering kisses. His tongue traced the scar on her shoulder while his finger ran along the tender line of her freshly healed wound.

"You're beautiful," he murmured against her shoulder.

"I'm scarred."

"So am I." He brought her hand around to his back, forcing her to touch the reality of his statement.

"You're beautiful," she said. Her mouth sought his and the contact was tender and light and loving.

His fingers circled the curve of her breasts, lightly teasing in their stroking, tempting her to move forward into the palm of his hands. When he rolled her swollen nipples ever so

slightly between his thumb and forefinger she arched, straining to one side as the pleasure of his touch tugged at her
very being. Cloud smiled at her action, enjoying her pleasure
and determined to feed it. His smile closed over one of her
breasts, worrying her tender flesh with his tongue, flicking it
delicately until she squirmed beneath him and reached for
his head, trying to pull him away.

"I need you now, Cloud," she told him breathlessly.

He might not have heard her or he may have chosen to
simply ignore her entreaty. His mouth merely moved to her
other breast, giving it a similar loving treatment while his
hand caressed her thighs. Under his insistent touch Alexis's
thighs opened to him and his fingers found her warm and
moist and ready. Her heat and energy excited him and he
moved to allow her to feel what she was doing to him.

"I need you, Alex. Touch me."

Alexis did not need Cloud's encouragement. She was eager
to return his caresses. Her hands and fingers moved nimbly
over him, feather light at times, deeply massaging at others.
Under his encouragement, in the manner he had taught her
she shifted to please him intimately with her hands, then her
mouth. She drew out the pleasure, having her revenge for
his earlier erotic teasing. When his control broke under her
languorous ministration, he released a low growl deep in his
throat and pulled her from him, rolling with her until she
was beneath him.

Their bodies met, arching, clinging, resuming the hungry
urgent pace Alexis had set in the beginning, until, after climax, their exhausted limbs could offer no more than the
gentle contact of thigh against hip, curving arm against curving waist, cheek against breast.

"Marry me."

Those two words shattered the silence and penetrated the
mist of contentment surrounding Alexis. She felt no pain at
first. The words had the effect of an accidental cut, slicing
the skin so cleanly and quickly there was no knowledge of
injury until the line of vision included both the knife and the

blood. She forced her eyes to look down at Cloud's head, resting comfortably on her breast, and the throbbing began.

"Alex?" He could barely hear his own voice above the pounding of her heart against his ear.

"No, Cloud." He started to lift his head but she wound her fingers in his hair and gently forced him to remain where he was. She did not want to look at him yet. She doubted she was strong enough to repeat her words if she had to look at his face.

"I don't understand." He tried to maintain an even tone as she continued. He was only partially successful. "I've given it some thought, Alex. You could turn over your command to Jordan and he could marry us on this ship. Or we could be married in New Orleans in a week if that would be better. Why did you say no? You never gave me any reason to expect that answer."

"Please, Cloud. I said no because I anticipated you wanted to be married soon." She hesitated, waiting for the constriction in her throat to pass. When she continued her voice was clear but the sign of her pain was in the tears stubbornly clinging to the corners of her eyes, then falling past her temples, into her hair.

"You want to be married before we find Travers. Isn't that so?"

"Yes."

"Why?"

Cloud refused to answer. Unconsciously his hand moved to her healing scar and his fingers followed the path of the reddened line. When he realized what he was doing he withdrew his hand abruptly. It was too late. He had already given her the answer she had expected.

"Afterward, Cloud. I'll marry you afterward."

"I can't change your mind?"

"No. I love you too much to be your wife for only a short time."

"Then don't go after Travers." His tone was bitter.

"Don't say that to me again."

"I hate him." He lifted his head now, searching her face. He saw her tears, the clear blood of her wounded senses. He sat up, drawing her beside him, and cradled her head against his chest while she clung to his arms and the tears continued to flow, cleansing the hurt and easing the pain. When it was over his kisses were first a soothing balm and later more drugging than the laudanum. The sleep that followed the gentle unhurried uniting of their bodies was completely natural and Alexis found no reason to fear it.

Salt spray hit Alexis in the face like a thousand stinging nettles. Wind tugged at her cape and she struggled to continue standing upright. Six days had passed since she had resumed full command. Now the storm was laughing at her, she thought, making a mockery of her skills, pitting her ability against a force which had no regard for her command. The *Dark Lady* pitched wildly, throwing Alexis to the deck. She grabbed a rope and pulled herself upright, the task doubly difficult because both the rope and the deck were slick with sea water. She hoarsely issued new orders that were relayed by Jordan as he fought the wind to approach her.

"Captain, the ship can't take much more of this pounding. Water's coming in!"

"The pumps are working, aren't they?"

"Of course," Jordan had to shout to be heard above the rising wind. "They're just not working fast enough!"

Rain was hitting both of them in torrents. Alexis squinted to see through the solid sheet of water glistening all about her. Lightning created a jagged patch of light across the sky. The masts of the *Dark Lady* seemed to be thrusting themselves brazenly against the night sky, almost daring the wrath of nature's destructive forces.

"We're changing course, Mr. Jordan!" Alexis shouted. "Our only chance is Barataria!"

"But that's—"

"Yes, it's Lafitte. It's either him or Davy Jones!"

Jordan thought Lafitte was infinitely preferable to the bottom of the Gulf and he told her so. Alexis laughed and made her way to Wilkes at the wheel to change course. She had to repeat herself several times to be heard above the thunder but finally Wilkes understood and fought to control the wheel and head them to their new destination.

She slipped on her return to Jordan but she felt strong arms reach out to stop her from sliding across the deck.

"Captain," Redland said, placing her on firm footing once again. "Are you all right?"

"Fine! What are you doing here? Shouldn't you be helping secure the sails?"

Redland paused, letting the thunder have the first word, then he proceeded. "It's Peach! He's been hurt! He fell from the rigging. Maybe a broken leg. Tanner's taken him to your cabin!"

"I'm going to see him. Mr. Jordan, maintain present course! I won't be long!"

She pulled her cape tightly around her and bent her head, bucking the strength of the wind head on. Redland stayed close beside her, his hands stretched out in her direction, in anticipation of another fall to the deck. His anticipation was correct, but he was worrying about the wrong person. Redland lost his footing, stumbled, and careened toward the rail. Alexis was beside him almost immediately.

"My hand, Redland! Grab it!"

Redland reached out. His body was prone on the deck, his back to the rail. If he had not fallen when he did the momentum of his body would have carried him over the side. Alexis grasped his hand firmly and pulled him to his feet.

"Thank you, Captain!" His words were lost in another violent burst of thunder and he did not bother to repeat them.

Jordan hurried over to where they stood. "My God! I thought we lost you!"

"Damn near did!" Redland shouted back.

The three of them stood there for a moment, catching

their breath and at the same time trying to determine the safest way to get to the hatch without further mishap. Redland stepped forward, pushing off the rail at the same instant lightning struck the ship. The loud report following the flash of light was not thunder this time. Alexis, blinded for a moment by the light, recovered her vision in time to see a section of the mizzenmast hurtling toward them. Instinctively, they leaped out of the way but as they did so the ship pitched again and when their bodies should have connected with the deck they found themselves on the other side of the rail, well on their way to being swallowed by the rough, frothy sea.

Members of the crew who had been close enough to see what happened immediately threw over life lines. Precious minutes were lost before they realized none of the three would be able to grasp the lines. The ropes were practically invisible to those who threw them over. Peters quickly took charge and had the boats released from the davits. Even as he and Randall and Brandon were being lowered against the side of the *Dark Lady* he knew it was probably too late to find his captain or his friends. Brandon kept his eyes riveted to the point in the water where he thought they must have gone under. When lightning flashed he cursed the fact he could see no more than whitecaps. Peter's assumption he was on a fool's mission was quickly realized when the lowered boat came into contact with the water and was buffeted about until it began to crack under the strain. It smashed against the hull of the *Dark Lady* even as they tried to move it away. Brandon and Peters grabbed at the extended ropes when they knew only death awaited them if they did not get back aboard. Randall made his grab for the line at the same moment his attention was caught by a figure riding on the water toward them. While Peters and Brandon were being pulled aboard, Randall reached for an oar and held it out over the water. With one hand he held onto the rope with such tenacity he could feel the fibers digging into his palm.

His grip was severely put to the test as the boat gave way beneath him and a groping hand reached for the extended oar. From above him, Randall could hear his mates encouraging him, and when light split the sky he saw it was Jordan who held the oar. Randall pulled him close to the ship as another line was thrown for Jordan to grasp. When he was sure Jordan had a firm grip on it he released the oar and his mates pulled him up the side of the ship.

Jordan felt strong hands grasping his arms, pulling him over the side. He teetered on his feet for what he thought was an eternity then, in spite of his resolve to do differently, he passed out.

His collapse coincided with the moment Cloud chose to come on deck. The men around Jordan parted and Cloud had a full view of the unconscious first mate as well as the bent figure of Peters kneeling beside him.

"What happened?" he cried, hurrying over to the men. First Peach, now Jordan. The storm was heaping abuse upon them.

His question was greeted with silence. Not only silence, he observed, but avoidance. The crew was more uneasy than the storm alone would have made them. Some were already returning to their posts, careful it seemed to not even glance in his direction. The looks he did manage to catch were vacant stares, as if their eyes were not seeing him, but seeing past him. He sank to his knees beside Peters.

"Is he alive?" he asked.

"Aye. He'll make it." Peters's voice was strained as he pressed Jordan on his back, forcing sea water from his stomach and lungs.

"What happened?" Cloud asked again. This time he made sure his voice was such that it demanded an answer.

Peters pointed to the fallen section of the mizzenmast. "Lightning. Knocked out part of the rail. They went overboard."

"They?" He lifted his head and searched the faces of the men standing around him. The glances caught briefly then the contact was broken. He turned back to Peters. The man's face was drawn and ghastly pale. What Cloud had first thought was rain streaking across his face he suddenly realized were tears. A sickening feeling came over Cloud. He made no attempt to control it, rather he let the strength which accompanied the feeling control him. He was on his feet, dragging Peters with him.

"They!" he shouted, shaking Peters by his shoulders.

Peters made no move to extricate himself from Cloud's powerful grasp. "Redland," he answered tonelessly. "And Captain Danty."

"Oh, my God!" He immediately released Peters only to begin chucking his boots. His action was so quick no one realized his intent until he started toward the rail.

Randall lunged for him. "Tanner! We tried! You can't do anything!" Cloud shook him off. "For Christ's sake! Somebody stop him!"

Brandon barreled into Cloud, knocking him to the deck. They wrestled but the others stepped in when it was obvious Cloud was going to be the victor.

"Let me up! Goddamn you! Let me up!" he shouted. "You can't leave her out there!" He struggled against the viselike grip of the four men holding down his arms and legs until he was exhausted. He slumped against the deck, his energy gone, his strength washed away as the rain stung his face and arms. Brandon helped Cloud rise, his outstretched hand saying more than he could have managed in words.

Cloud returned to Jordan's side. "Take him to his cabin," he told Peters as quietly as he dared and still be heard. "Then look in on Peach. He's in her cabin."

Peters nodded and motioned Davie Brandon to help him. They lifted Jordan and carried him toward the hatch. Before he descended Peters looked back over his shoulder at Cloud. His eyes were focused on the fallen section of mast and his hands were clenched in tight fists at his sides. Every muscle in his body was pulled taut, facing the wind defiantly, aggressively. He raised one arm in a slow, almost painful motion and opened his mouth as if to utter some oath. The stance was that of a man who was ready to kill; Peters was surprised to hear him say, to the accompaniment of a sweeping motion of his extended arm: "Clear this out of here!" Peters smiled faintly, tasting bitter tears on the edge of his lips. Cloud was in command. He had his ship. He had a crew who would follow him. Travers didn't have a prayer.

"What is it, Pierre?" Lafitte asked wearily, rising out of his tub. He took the towel offered to him by his servant, André, and began drying himself. "You really do have a habit of interrupting me at the most inopportune times."

"Ahh, Jean. But when has it been for anything unimportant?"

"I concede, *mon frère.*" He threw the towel to one side where it was hastily retrieved by André before it could water-mark the polished floors and began to dress. "What is it this time? Has Governor Claiborne issued a new warrant for my arrest?"

"You make jokes," sighed Pierre, settling himself into one of the expensive Louis the fourteenth chairs. He stretched his meager, wiry frame in a motion that reminded Jean of a cat staking out his sleeping territory.

"You do not seem overly concerned," he noted. It was merely a rhetorical observation. Jean was unaware of anything that could make his brother excited.

"That is because the problem is being taken care of at this very minute."

"Then why bother me with it?"

"Because one of the problems . . . no, actually all of the problems . . . are asking to see you."

"Enough," Lafitte ordered sharply. "You are talking in riddles. Has someone come to Barataria uninvited?" He was pulling on a fresh shirt, plainly agitated with both the buttons and his brother.

"Help him, André," Pierre said, enjoying Jean's anger. As the servant rushed in to aid Lafitte, Pierre continued. "Do you remember Captain Danty?"

"What kind of question is that? Without me she would not be Captain of anything."

"Her ship is here," continued Pierre, as if Jean had said nothing. "At least her men say it is her ship."

"Why do you doubt?"

"Because one of the men aboard has identified himself as Tanner Cloud. I believe that is the name you mentioned to me when you spoke of Alexis. Was not he the commander she escaped from?"

"You have a good memory. I believe that is the name."

"I have been thinking perhaps this was just a trap he was setting to find her."

Jean turned to the mirror and straightened the collar of his shirt. "I will not need you now, André. Go to Jeannine and tell her there will be guests for dinner." André bowed slightly and left the room. Jean turned back to his brother. "You may be right, Pierre. From what Alexis told me he was a very determined man. You say he wants to see me?"

"The man is not alone in that. His whole crew wants to see you. Their ship was damaged in yesterday's storm. They were limping in here when we intercepted them. They did not put up a fight. They said they were coming to see us anyway."

"Where are they now?"

"Down in the bay. I would not let them off the ship until I found out what they were up to. They will not tell me anything except that they will tell you everything."

"It is good to see their trust is not misplaced." Lafitte grinned. "*Allons*. We will talk to these men. We have not shown them much hospitality so far." He tucked a pistol into the waistband of his tailored trousers and followed Pierre out of the room to greet his unexpected guests.

When they reached the crest of the hill overlooking the bay, Lafitte stopped and surveyed the ship beside the one belonging to Pierre. He saw the broken mast, the damaged sails, and the gaping space that should have been railing. He also noted the lines of the ship, the unmistakable craftsmanship that made it a Quinton vessel.

"Mon Dieu!" he swore under his breath. His lips creased in a thin line and his dark brows drew together. "It is her ship, Pierre. She had made alterations consistent with the goal she had in mind, but it is without a doubt the ship I placed in her hands."

"Then where is she?" asked Pierre. He frowned, looking at Jean's face. His brother's expression was such that Pierre expected only the worst.

"That is what we are going to find out." He started over the hill, breaking into a run as he approached the shore. He remembered the golden hair and sparkling eyes he had often likened to champagne, much to Alexis's discomfort. The defiant tilt of her head, the lift of her chin, the cool gaze she used to keep his men at a distance, were still etched in his memory. But her seriousness, her purpose, her determination to avenge those she'd lost, were more clearly part of his recall than any of her physical attributes. As he and Pierre were rowed out to the vessel he remembered the things he had taught her and the way she had hung on every lesson, knowing her life depended upon it. Pierre had once laughed at him for being so interested in Captain Danty's whereabouts; but then, Pierre had never met her. It was his crew's great respect for Alexis that made them never consider he had returned her ship to her out of weakness. It was his crew that kept their ears open for news of Travers, and it was they who decided that Quinton vessels would not be part of any booty. They shared a sense of pride when they heard of Captain Danty's exploits, realizing they had something to do with her success, but also knowing she would have found a way without them.

Lafitte grabbed the rope ladder thrown over the side of the ship and scrambled to the top. He swore he would kill them should he find this was some kind of ruse to hurt Alexis.

Landing lightly on his feet, he quickly surveyed the men around him. Their faces, pale and gaunt, only served to tighten the knot in his stomach. He knew then something beyond his power to avenge had happened to her.

"I am Jean Lafitte," he said simply. "Pierre says you want to see me." Beside him, Pierre was ready to step forward and introduce Cloud. Lafitte, however, had already eyed the man he thought possessed the name. He stepped forward, holding out his hand. "You are Captain Cloud, I believe."

Cloud reached for the hand and shook it firmly. "I am. But how did you know?" He did not mention that he would have known Lafitte anywhere from Alexis's brief allusion to the pirate's mocking blue-green gaze and lifted eyebrow.

"We have an acquaintance in common, *n'est-ce pas?*" He dropped Cloud's hand. "You are as she described you. It could only be you who would dare to pull her from the rigging when she was about her business." He saw Cloud wince. "I do not know if that look is because the memory of your action is particularly distressing or . . ." His voice trailed off. He did not know how to phrase the thought in his mind. He spoke again, this time dearly to discover what the presence of her ship meant.

"This ship? It is the one I gave to Alexis, *n'est-ce pas?*"

"It is her ship," Cloud answered.

"And what is an officer of the American Navy doing aboard her vessel? And where is Captain Danty?"

"May we talk below? There is a lot to explain."

Lafitte hesitated, casting a sidelong glance at Pierre. "I will go with the captain. It will be all right." He motioned to Cloud to lead the way before Pierre could protest and in a few minutes he was alone with Cloud in a cabin that had the presence of Alexis all about it. He saw her handwriting on the open page of her log, bold yet distinctly feminine. He thought she had chosen her furnishings in much the same manner. There was nothing in the cabin that reminded him of the man who had sailed this ship for Quinton. It was clearly Alexis's domain. He took a seat and told Cloud to do the same, then repeated his question.

"Alex is dead." Cloud heard the sharp intake of breath

and he continued dully. He forced himself not to think about what he was saying and to concentrate only on getting the words past the tightness in his throat. "We were on our way to New Orleans. We had reason to suspect Captain Travers was patrolling these waters." He met Lafitte's eyes directly, letting him know he understood how the information had been received. Lafitte bowed his head slightly in acknowledgment. The storm put us off course and Alexis decided to head for Barataria. We had encountered some minor damage at that time which she thought could be repaired here. Lightning struck our mizzenmast and when it fell it knocked out a section of railing, Captain Danty, the first mate, Jordan, and another crew member were thrown overboard. We managed to get Jordan. There was nothing we could do for Alex and Redland."

Lafitte listened attentively to the lifeless account, noting the pained, weary expression in the green eyes facing him. That Cloud had had no sleep was obvious. That he had lost someone he cared for was even more obvious and enormously difficult to look upon.

"What were you doing aboard her ship? You must understand that I have to be sure . . ." Again he faltered, disliking himself for even doubting Cloud's motives.

"That I am not making this up? That I would tell you this wild story to get at Alex?" Cloud felt anger welling up inside him and he fought to control it. Part of him realized Lafitte was being cautious to protect a woman he did not want to believe was dead. Briefly he told the pirate all that had happened to bring about his presence on the *Dark Lady*. When he was done Lafitte nodded and rose from his chair.

"I am truly sorry," he said quietly. "I wish it could be as Pierre and I first thought—that you were only trying to discover her whereabouts. I wish I did not believe you." Both men were silent, each thinking private thoughts that they knew somehow were the same.

Finally Lafitte broke the silence. "Come. You will be my guest for a few days—you and the crew. It will be some time before the ship can be repaired, and perhaps in that time, we will be able to learn something of Captain Travers. I assume that is what you want to do." Cloud nodded. *"Bien.* It is as she would have wanted—not for herself, but for the ones she loved. There is a representative of the Royal Navy due here tomorrow. Perhaps he will know something that will be of help."

Dinner had been a decidedly gloomy affair. Cloud listened closely to the conversation between Jean and Pierre which centered mainly on the arrival of the Royal Navy captain. Apparently the British had conceived a plan Senator Howe would have admired. They wanted to secure the pirate's help in maintaining a firm base in New Orleans. The British were willing to name the pirates subjects of the crown and give them residency in British colonies. The brothers joked about the audacity of such a proposal. Jean was interested in meeting the representative in order to put the question of aid to an end once and for all.

Cloud was grateful for the discussion because he could not have contributed any thoughts that would not have reminded everyone of Alexis. Jordan and Peters were also invited to dine and more than once Cloud caught them staring off into space while they made a pretense of eating the delicious food Lafitte had provided for them. Jordan excused himself and his lack of appetite with a statement about not being fully recovered from his near drowning, and the others graciously accepted it. Peters managed to get away from the table early saying he had Peach's leg to attend to. Again the excuse was accepted. When he was gone, Cloud and the two Lafittes were left to manage the uncomfortable silence.

"You have no wish to get away?" Jean asked as he refilled wineglasses.

"Every wish," Cloud replied honestly. "I hadn't yet found a way to do it tactfully."

The brothers laughed, and Jean said, "Tact has its place."

His voice became somber and he lay his hand on Cloud's wrist, offering support in his grasp. "But not here—among friends—who share your grief. I suggest you take a tour of Barataria. It is quite beautiful, especially now, at dusk. You will find much to your liking." He knew he was not cleverly handling his suggestion that Cloud be alone but he believed what he said about tact. "I also insist you spend the night here. One of the servants will prepare a room for you. When you return I will have some news for you concerning our visitors tomorrow. I am expecting it shortly."

Cloud nodded. He thanked Jean for his understanding, not with words but with his eyes. Then, he left the spacious dining room, the wide foyer, and stepped out onto the portico. There was a slight breeze, the air was cool and fresh, and Cloud took pleasure in being able to breathe it.

He walked aimlessly, hands in his pockets, thumbs out, and let the wind tug at his open collar and whip at his thick hair. He stopped suddenly, not knowing precisely why, when he reached the top of a grassy knoll overlooking the bay. The sun, barely noticeable on the edge of the horizon, had colored the sky with red, orange, and in some places, pale mauve that would become a rich indigo and later deep purple. In sharp relief against the striking background were two ships rolling listlessly off shore. In direct contrast to their somber silhouettes he could hear voices drifting across the water to his place on the crest of the hill. They were too loud, too raucous, too determined to be carefree, to be coming from Pierre's ship. They were the voices of the crew of the *Dark Lady*. Voices that were consciously hiding their misery beneath boisterous laughter and being totally unsuccessful at it.

He sat cross-legged in the grass and continued to stare out over the bay. He felt oddly protected up here—away from the men, the ship, but overlooking it all. Safe, but in control. The feeling passed and he jerked his head up when he heard the sound of someone approaching from behind. Before he could turn a voice spoke and he was strangely at ease to discover it was Lafitte.

Lafitte sat down beside him, his eyes taking in the same view Cloud had been admiring. "I thought I would find you here. You were thinking of her." It was not a question.

"Yes." Cloud was startled by his answer. Until then he had not been aware that Alexis had been on his mind. "She had a place like this. On Tortola. She called it her crow's nest. She would sit there and watch the ships and wait for her friend and plan her future. She always thought she would be safe in her nest ... nothing could harm her there." He paused, drawing in his breath. "She was wrong."

"And you?" Lafitte asked quietly. "Do you feel that way now? Protected? Safe?"

"I did for a while. Only a moment. There isn't any place where one can be fully protected."

"At one time I thought Barataria would offer me that," Lafitte thought aloud. "A refuge from the rest of the world. It is not like that. The world intrudes."

Cloud listened to the words, regretful but not bitterly spoken. There was some memory that remained unsaid. He had heard stories about Lafitte's family, murdered by the Spanish, and now he thought they were true. Lafitte had ceased to allow the world to intrude upon him. Now he made the first move.

Cloud unfolded his legs and stretched them out before him, leaning back on his elbows. He let the silence that seemed to create a seal of friendship over them continue a few minutes longer before he spoke.

"You said you would have news for me when I returned to the house. I assume you did not want to wait to tell me."

Lafitte nodded. "It is about the British representative. I told you they are anxious for my assistance."

"You also gave me reason to believe you would not consider it."

"That has not changed. Alex was correct about me. So were the men who tried to use you. I will help when the time comes. Perhaps the British do not realize it, and I think the Americans are not proud of it but I am an American. There has been no question of it in my mind since Jefferson purchased the Louisiana territory.''

"I'm glad."

Lafitte laughed but the sound was hollow. "Captain Travers is the representative."

"What!" Cloud sat upright. His fingers dug into the earth. He would have been overjoyed to hear he would meet Travers here but something in Lafitte's tone warned him.

"You must understand, Tanner, there is no way I can let you exact your vengeance here on Barataria," he said. "No matter how much I dislike what the British are suggesting, and no matter how much I would like to run Travers through with my own sword, it cannot happen here. I gave my word when the meeting was arranged. I gave it to his superior that whoever was sent would be treated cordially and no harm would come to him or his men."

"You can't be serious! You would stop me when he is right under my nose? I can't believe you mean what you are saying!"

"I mean it," Lafitte answered firmly. "You and your men will be confined to your ship if you cannot give me your word that no harm will come to him while he is here."

Cloud's lean fingers curled around a stone. He clenched it a moment then he hurled it toward the water. Perversely it made him angrier when it fell with a soft thud into the sand, several yards short of the incoming tide. He said nothing.

"Your word," Lafitte persisted. "Do I have it?"

Cloud groaned. "How can you even think of letting that man step foot on your land? How can you expect so much from me when you know what she was to me . . . to her men . . . to—"

"To me? Yes, she was very special to me. I have followed her since the time she left me. I have wanted nothing for her but what she wanted for herself. I have provided her with information. My men have seen that her shipping line prospered in these waters. And still that seems nothing in return for the ill she suffered because some half-witted men sought to destroy me. It will not be easy, having him here, knowing what he did to her, knowing what she has done for me, but I have given my word. Now I am asking yours."

"How long will he be staying here?" Cloud asked slowly, the beginning of a plan pushing at the edge of his consciousness.

Lafitte did not miss a beat before answering. The same idea had formed long before in his mind. "How long until your ship can be repaired?"

Cloud smiled and turned to face Lafitte. He saw the mocking smile and raised eyebrow greet him. "You have my word. Nothing will happen to Captain Travers so long as he is your guest."

"Captain, we've sighted something off the port bow!" The voice was excited and decidedly English.

The captain pushed away from his desk and examined his first lieutenant with cool disdain. "Something does not tell me much of anything. What is it you think you see?"

"It looks like a body, sir! We cannot be sure. Do you want us to have a look?" The captain sighed. "I am coming up. Man one of the boats and take it out."

The lieutenant took his leave and the captain closed his log furiously. First the storm to delay them and now something else to keep them from their assignment. In a sudden burst of anger he leaped out of his chair. The delay grated on him and by the time he reached the deck he was in the surly mood his officers and crew were well accustomed to.

He stood at the rail, watching the men row closer to the bobbing object in the distance. The sun's glare off the placid water made it difficult to see exactly what they were rowing to. The combination of the bright morning sun and the gentle movement of the water also made it difficult to believe there had been a storm the night before. He lifted his telescope and sought out the object again. Still he could not make it out clearly and his men continued to row. Probably nothing more than a piece from a ship that had not been fortunate in the squall. He cursed softly. If they had wasted time for that he would have the first lieutenant's head.

His men had stopped rowing and one of them was reaching out for the object. The captain adjusted his scope to get a clearer view.

"Bodies," he announced coldly to the officer at his side.

"Bodies?"

"Plural. Two of them. They are taking them in." He paused then he lowered the telescope to his side. "They've dropped one back in but they are keeping the other. There must be some life left in him."

"Shall I summon the surgeon?" the lieutenant asked eagerly. He wished he had not sounded so concerned. He knew his captain would only sight it later as a weakness. He wondered, not for the first time, how, with all the truly capable and honorable men he could have served under, he had been cast under the ruthless command of the man at his side. It was only a brief thought as his attention was drawn to his captain's answer.

"Wait until we see if he makes it here alive. No use rousing the surgeon if it is only to pronounce the man dead. We have a lot of men capable of that."

"Yes, sir," came the quiet reply.

Word of rescue had passed quickly among the crew and now many of them were waiting along the rail in order to get a better look. The boat was raised in short order and the faces of the men viewing the body slumped against one of their mates carried the same expression familiar to the crew of the *Dark Lady* at each unveiling.

"My God! It's a woman!" Several voices cried out the discovery at the same instant.

The two seamen on either side of Alexis began to lift her out of the boat but at their touch she raised her head and shook it slowly. When she spoke her voice was hoarse and raspy, not at all like the clear tones that were part of her command.

"Myself," she said. "I'll get out myself."

The men did not release her but they steadied her and allowed her to take a tentative step toward the edge of the boat. She managed that well enough but she hesitated when she realized she would have to jump from the boat to the deck. She glanced at the men at her side and her desire for help was in her glance. They picked her up by the arms and lowered her into the arms of one of the men on the deck. She murmured a thank you and freed herself from his supportive embrace. She looked around at the concerned faces hovering over her. As if the throng of men was not suffocating enough she found the silence even more so. She tried to ignore the nausea in her stomach and the cramping in her muscles. A hand reached out to help her when she thought she would collapse.

"Take her to my cabin," said the lieutenant when he had pushed through the men. "Henry, get the doctor."

Alexis heard the words, sensed the concern, and was ready to obey. Then she saw him.

He had just entered the inner circle and the men parted so he had a clear place to stand. He was staring at her as if he had seen a ghost and Alexis thought she must look exactly like such an apparition.

She drew away from the hand at her side. Summoning the last of her strength she walked toward him. Her amber eyes narrowed and locked on his cold black ones.

"Captain Travers," she said softly. Then she spit on his glossy boots.

Ian Smith looked down at the pale face and almost lifeless form occupying the bunk in his quarters. "Why do you suppose she did it, Dr. Jackson?" he asked.

Hugh Jackson finished hanging Alexis's wet clothing over the edge of the two available chairs before he answered. "How the hell should I know? You say she called the captain by his name?"

"She did. Then she spit. Then she fainted." The lieutenant

laughed uneasily. "It is not something I am likely to forget. You should have seen our captain's face. I thought we would be calling you for him." He waited until Jackson's laughter had ceased. Their mutual dislike for Travers was something they shared with all but a few of the men aboard, but they only felt comfortable sharing their animosity openly with each other. "How do you suppose they know one another?"

Hugh Jackson sighed. "You are asking questions you should be asking either the captain or this girl. Obviously they're the only ones with your answers."

Smith was going to ask about the scars on the girl's back but he decided against it. It was only another question that was not answerable, at least not yet. He changed the subject.

"Captain Travers wants to know when she will be well enough to be moved. He says she cannot stay here and he wants to put her in the hold."

"He will have to be patient like the rest of us. She is suffering from mild exposure. Depending on how far along that storm was before she fell overboard she could have been in the water up to twelve hours before we happened along. I can hardly believe she has survived at all. Judging from the marks on her back though, I would say she has been through a lot worse." He lowered his voice when, as if she could hear him, she stirred. He hastened to her side and secured the blanket where she had kicked it loose, freeing her calf and foot from its confines. "I cannot figure out why he wants her out of sight. What does he think she'll do?"

"Now you are asking me something I don't know. Send for me when she comes around. We will decide for ourselves if she is well enough to be taken out of here."

"Where is the captain now?" asked Jackson.

"In his cabin, cursing the delay and the cause of it. He is determined to be on time to meet Lafitte. Tomorrow afternoon, as scheduled. No matter what."

Jackson ran his fingers through his dark hair, salted with strands of white. He set his jaw firmly and said through clenched teeth, "Good. The longer he leaves her in our care—the better."

Ian agreed and left the cabin, intent on finding someone among the crew who could help identify the girl's relationship to the captain. Six hours later, when he was summoned by the doctor he was none the wiser. Too many of the crew had been with the *Follansbee* for years and Travers had only assumed command of the frigate eighteen months ago. Furthermore Travers had discovered the questioning and had warned Smith to end it immediately or suffer the consequences. Since there was only one set of consequences for officers and ordinary seamen under Travers's command it had been easy to assure the captain he would not pursue the subject, nor would he question the girl.

Walking into the cabin, he saw Alexis sitting up in bed, sipping broth from a mug.

"I hardly expected to find you up and eating," he said.

Alexis returned the smile he flashed, remembering this was the man who offered his help before she had seen Travers. He was young, perhaps only ten years older than herself. He had a boyish face, rounded, without the harsh lines of age she would have expected to see among the crew who served the man she hated. He was only slightly taller than she was but he made up for what he lacked in height with a dignity she thought would have been crushed ages ago. His hair was flaxen, his eyes bright blue. They still hinted of some of the eagerness she had often seen in the men who served her— and Cloud.

Suddenly she said, "You haven't been with him long, have you?"

Eyebrows flew up, blue eyes regarded her curiously. "You mean with Captain Travers?" Alexis nodded. "No, I haven't. Only in the last six months."

"I thought so . . . since you sailed from Liverpool."

The doctor and the lieutenant exchanged puzzled looks. "That's right. But how do you know?" asked Smith.

Alexis handed her mug to the doctor and lay back in the

bunk, pulling the blankets securely around her. "It is easy to see from your face," she replied. "You could not have been with him long. You have the look of a man who still enjoys the sea. He would have killed that in you. Now the doctor here, I would guess that he has been with Captain Travers for years. In fact, I will say the gray hairs wouldn't be on his head if he had been serving with anyone else. A good man will gray, looking upon too many bloody backs."

Jackson opened his mouth to say something, then he shut it just as quickly. It was true, what she said. But how had she known?

"Our faces don't explain how you knew I came aboard in Liverpool," Smith said quickly. He was still too much of an officer to let her know he had wondered how long he could stay with Travers.

"Where else could you have come from?" she asked blithely. "The HMS *Follansbee* sailed out of Liverpool."

"Who are you?" cried the lieutenant, forgetting the consequences of his question. He need not have worried. Alexis only graced him with an elusive smile and an equally elusive answer.

"You would not believe me if I told you."

Jackson started to pursue her statement, but Smith cut him off with a warning glance and a hasty explanation. "Captain ordered that no one talk to her. That includes you."

"That is understandable, under the circumstances," Alexis interjected. "Hasn't he told you anything about me?"

"Nothing."

"And he is not likely to. It is what I would expect from him. He should not be concerned though. I did not intend to blurt everything out."

Smith briefly wondered what she meant, then he dismissed it. "He does not want you to stay——"

The doctor interrupted, asserting his position. "She can't be moved. She is not well yet, in spite of her banter. She has told me she has given doctors rougher times and I believe her. Morning will be soon enough. Maybe even too soon."

"Moved to where?" asked Alexis. "Is he planning to lock me up somewhere? Can it be he actually fears me?" She almost laughed. The thought was extremely amusing, just as the memory of his indignant, outraged, and finally astonished expression was when she had spit on his boots. She'd had only a fleeting moment to view the raised eyebrows, the cold, piercing eyes; the hawklike nose, nostrils flared in anger; the thin, cruel lips, parted for an instant as he uttered an oath. She had only seen those things briefly before she'd fainted, but now she recalled them and allowed herself to enjoy them to the fullest.

Smith shook his head. He laughed lightly, though somehow uncomfortably, at the ludicrous suggestion that Travers feared anyone. Certainly not this slender woman with unusual amber eyes that were almost gold in certain lights. He tore his own eyes away from hers. How strange they were. He thought about them no more, but when he spoke to her he fastened his attention on some point on the wall behind her.

"You will have to get your answers from the captain. He will want to talk to you in the morning."

"That should be all right," she said more to herself than to her companions. "I should be able to greet him properly by then."

Her speech had the clarity and resonance of a person deep in thought. Both men noticed she seemed to have dismissed them. The doctor rose from the side of her bed and found more blankets to cover her. She thanked him absently. It was some time after they had gone before she noticed their absence.

"What do you make of her?" the doctor asked when they stepped out of the room. "She seems to know what kind of man Travers is, all right."

"She seems to know too much. How did she know this was the *Follansbee*? Did you tell her?"

"No."

"Then how did she know?" Smith was exasperated. "I don't understand it, Hugh. I don't understand any of it."

The doctor gave him a look that said, And you think I do?; then he left the officer alone to think on the matter while he searched out a mirror to discover if the years with Travers really did show on his face.

Smith thought of little besides the young woman occupying his room. Shortly after midnight, no answers to be found in the calm expanse of the sea, he returned to his cabin. It seemed he had only been asleep a matter of minutes when he felt a hand nudge him awake. He almost tipped the chair he sat in as he came fully to attention.

Alexis suppressed a smile. "Do you think I might have some more of that broth?"

Ian reached for the cup at his side, spilling some as he groped in the dark. He murmured an apology about it being cold and offered to warm some for her.

"Don't go to the trouble," she said, accepting the cup. After a few sips she asked, "What time is it, Mr.—"

"Smith. Lieutenant Ian Smith. And it is about two in the morning and I am surprised you did not know either the time or my name; you seem to know everything else."

"I am not a clairvoyant, Lieutenant."

"I find that hard to believe."

"Yes, I suppose it must seem that I am. Just to prove I'm not, I will ask you another question. Where is this frigate bound?"

Ian laughed. "You won't get that from me . . ." He paused for a name and he was surprised when she gave him one. "How do I know you do not make a habit of preying on British vessels under the guise of a half-drowned waif, Alexis?"

"Is that what you think?"

"It had occurred to me. Nothing else makes much sense."

"No, I guess it doesn't."

Ian shut his eyes and when he opened them the cabin was still dark and his confusion just as deep. "I still don't understand any of this, Alexis," he said at last.

"I don't expect you to. And the captain does not want you to," she added hastily. "Just let me thank you for coming to my rescue when you did and end it at that." She finished her broth and placed the mug on the deck. "It will be clear in the morning."

Ian wondered if he had imagined a threatening tone in her voice. He suddenly did not feel tired any longer. He excused himself to continue his brooding on topside.

Alexis lay back against the pillow, frowning into the darkness.

So close, she thought, and yet her dreams and most of her waking moments were filled less with Travers than with Cloud. During the hours she had been left alone, even as she'd tested the strength of her limbs, even as she'd prepared for the final confrontation, she had wondered if Travers had been worth the separation, the danger, the uncertainty that always invaded her time with Cloud. Somehow it had become more important to know that Cloud had managed to get through the storm safely than it was to see Travers dead by her own hand. It had become more urgent to let him know she was alive.

Looking back on it, on their last night together before the storm interrupted their sleep, she realized he had tried to tell her those things. Even the way they'd made love seemed to be in preparation for another span of time they would spend apart. His hands had moved along her flesh in that peculiar way he had, as if he were pressing a memory into his palms. She had been frightened momentarily to discover her hands and fingers were doing the same thing. Pleasure that evening was inadvertent. It was not pleasure they sought with their touch. It was only the touch.

She got out of bed, stumbling in the dark until she found her boots against the leg of a chair. She reached inside one of them and retrieved her dagger. They either had not found it or had thought it was unimportant. She traced the blade lightly with her finger, the cold steel warmed beneath her touch.

"One last chance," she whispered, holding the blade against her lips. "If I fail and still survive, my love, I will not attempt it again. Only I must take this chance. Do you understand? I must!'' She slipped into her shirt and trousers, pulled on her boots, and tucked the dagger back inside. Her movements were deliberate, unhurried, a ritual in preparation for a challenge that still retained some meaning for her.

She returned to bed and covered herself with the blankets to combat the cold taking possession of her from within. Before she fell asleep she added the names of Redland and Jordan to the reasons she had for wanting to see Travers dead.

Chapter Eighteen

Cloud dressed, his trousers and shirt mysteriously clean and pressed, his boots polished. He found a comb on the bureau and hastily ran it through his hair. His fingers touched the stubble of growth on his face, and as if in answer to his wish for a shave, André appeared at the door to his room with a hot towel, strap, and razor.

"Monsieur Lafitte asked me to look after your needs," the servant responded to Cloud's questioning glance.

"It's not necessary. I can do it myself."

"It is not for you to do," he replied, frowning. Had these Americans no sense of what was correct? André tried to imagine Lafitte shaving himself—could not—and motioned Cloud to have a seat.

Further protests were out of the question as the hot towel was wrapped around Cloud's face, softening his beard. He relaxed and enjoyed the warmth and later André's skill as he quickly removed all traces of the stubble. Cloud took the mirror André offered and with a low chuckle pronounced himself human again.

At André's insistence he followed the servant to the dining

room and joined Jean and Pierre in a late-morning breakfast. The conversation inevitably came around to the expected visitor.

"Is there any danger you will be recognized?" Lafitte asked Cloud.

"I can't imagine I would be. It has been over two years and the little he saw of me was when I was unconscious, face down on the ground." He paused thoughtfully, pushing his fork through the eggs on his plate. "I know I gave you my word, Jean, but I had no intention of being here when Travers arrived. The temptation might prove to be too great. I will be down at the ship, hastening the repairs."

"As you wish. Perhaps it is better that way. As you said, the temptation might prove too great." His hand curled tightly around his knife. "And who could blame you? It is distasteful to me to have to ask such a thing of you."

"Forget it. I understand. I think I can have the *Dark Lady* ready for the open water in three days. Can you keep him here that long?"

"Of course."

"And where will his ship be anchored? I don't want him to see the *Dark Lady*. He may recognize it."

"I am going to meet him in my ship," Pierre answered. "I will lead him to one of the inlets we seldom use. Your ship will be safe from his prying eyes."

"Thank you."

Pierre shrugged. "Orders," he said, eying his brother with amusement. "Pleasurable, but orders nonetheless."

Lafitte cuffed his brother on the arm. "He likes to pretend he does nothing but follow my wishes," he told Cloud. "When we are alone it is he who calls the tune."

Pierre laughed at the outright lie. "What he means is I have a habit of interrupting him at the most unseemly moments to discuss business. Do you remember the time at Madame DuBonnet's Jean? Why—"

"That is quite enough, Pierre." He cut his brother off. "The captain does not want to hear about your indiscretions."

Pierre pretended to be appalled. He mirrored Jean's mocking grin which traveled to his gray eyes. "My indiscretions? *Mon Dieu!*"

He was going to say more when Cloud interrupted and excused himself, saying he had to return to the ship.

"Come back this evening" Jean called after him. "I will have news for you about the meeting. I will see to it that you do not meet Travers."

Cloud thanked him and left. When he had gone Jean turned to his brother. "You will stay with me during the conference."

"If that is what you want. Do you expect some trouble from Travers?"

The pirate looked surprised. "From Travers? *Non.* You will be there to make sure I do not kill the man myself." He rose abruptly and turned on his heels sharply, leaving Pierre alone to wonder what sort of woman this Captain Danty was that she could command men even from the grave.

While Cloud was hurrying toward the *Dark Lady* Alexis was calmly observing the features of the man not five feet away from her. At the same time, he was making a critical appraisal of her. Neither had spoken since he'd entered Smith's quarter but only he found the silence oppressive. Alexis let him suffer a while longer, enjoying his discomfort, and kept her narrowed eyes trained on the chiseled, obscenely arrogant face in front of her. Now that he had recovered from the shock of seeing her it did not seem her presence bothered him overly much. She supposed he saw her as a minor problem, a temporary inconvenience, to be disposed of without a second thought or a backward glance. It would not be that easy, she wanted to say to him, if you knew who I really was—if you knew I was Captain Alex Danty. Instead she said: "I am surprised you remembered me, Captain Travers. After all, it has been some time since I last saw you. I would not have suspected you thought much about me in that time."

"You flatter yourself. I have never thought about you. I just have a good memory for faces. Yours is one a man would not likely forget—even when it is dredged up in the middle of the Gulf of Mexico.''

Alexis shuddered involuntarily at the sound of his voice. Memories, unbidden, came flooding back. ''Why did you forbid your men to talk with me?'' Was that her voice? she wondered. So cold, aloof, edged with ice. And yet she knew it was only a covering for the fear that was gripping every muscle, every nerve. Did he suspect? She could not let him know she was afraid. But why was she afraid at all? Cloud. It was not Travers she feared, but never seeing Cloud if she failed. She straightened her shoulders slightly and pressed the side of her calf against the blade in her boot. Her mind was made up. She would not fail.

''You should be able to understand that for yourself.''

''I suppose it would not do for me to explain how you killed my mother, my father, and my friend. You would not want your crew to know how you brought down your whip on a woman, would you? They might think you less of a man ... Or me more of a woman for surviving.''

''Shut up,'' he growled. He leaned against the desk behind him, casually crossing his feet at the ankles and folding his arms across his chest. He had been truthful with her when he'd said he had not thought of her until she had appeared from nowhere. Even now the recollection of that particular day was hazy in his mind, but one memory stood out—the memory of her defiance. The strange amber eyes glistened now with the same look. Travers vowed to crush it once and for all.

''Shut up?'' she asked coolly. ''How long do you expect me to remain silent about what you did?'' What am I waiting for? she asked herself. Just reach in the boot. Reach in the boot and be done with it. Something stopped her. She could not do it.

''Actually, I am surprised you remained silent this long. You had plenty of opportunity to discuss your troubles with the doctor or Smith. It is really a pity you didn't because I assure you, you will not get another chance. I have already decided what I am going to do with you. The Admiralty would not think very well of me if word of what happened on Tortola got back to them.''

"I had no intention of taking my grievances against you to the Admiralty.'' She did not add that she thought he was wrong. He would probably be given only a reprimand, not the loss of commission he deserved.

"I suppose you didn't. Otherwise you would have done it long ago. Tell me, how is it that you came to be in a position to be rescued by my ship?"

"That is no concern of yours,'' she answered tightly.

"I think you are wrong. It very well could be my concern. The vessel you were on? Was it destroyed by the storm?''

"I have no way of knowing.''

"Brothers? Family? A husband on board?''

"I have no brothers. You killed my family. I am not married.''

"Then it is still Miss Quinton. I'll assume the vessel you were on was one of your merchants and even if it did survive the storm, I am sure your friends do not think you did.''

"Even if they did . . . you have nothing to fear from them.''

"Meaning I have something to fear from you? I doubt that, Miss Quinton. You are hardly in a position to carry out your veiled threats aboard this vessel.'' He regarded her thoughtfully. "Your skin, it's rather dark. Do you spend a great deal of time out of doors?''

Alexis was too startled by his line of questioning to answer him. He went on.

"The marks from the whip? Have they healed?''

Her eyebrows drew together. Why was he asking her these things? "They have healed. Your work is still visible, if that's what you meant.''

"That is exactly what I meant. They fit into my plan for you very nicely.''

"What are you talking about?''

"In a few hours we will be reaching our destination. I propose to leave you there."

"Where?"

"It doesn't matter. You have no choice in what will happen." He smiled mysteriously. "Slaves never do."

As he turned to leave, his words penetrated Alexis's shocked senses. Slave! He meant to pass her off as a slave! She needed no other thought to guide her next actions. She reached for her dagger and held it lightly in her hand. Poised, she called to his retreating figure.

Travers turned, instinctively ducking when he saw the blade. Alexis had already accounted for this action and had adjusted her aim slightly lower. What she had not accounted for, could not have adjusted for, was the sudden presence of Ian Smith returning to his quarters. Forgetting the captain might still be there, Smith did not bother to announce his entry into his own cabin. Flinging the door open, he saved his captain's life and nearly lost his own.

Once released from Alexis's grasp the dagger had no choice but to follow the course she had set for it. Alexis watched in horror as Travers was knocked to one side and the dagger, narrowly missing him, found its mark, not in Travers, but in the lieutenant's abdomen.

Smith staggered backward against the doorjamb, not taking his eyes from Alexis. Before he slid to the deck she was at his side, lowering him gently. Travers was on his feet, fists clenched, face livid with rage. He stared at the dagger imbedded in Smith, knowing it was meant for him.

"Bitch!" he cursed. He raised his hand to strike her.

Alexis lifted her head, not cowering from his raised hand. "Don't just stand there," she ordered, forgetting who was in command. "Hit me or don't. Then get Dr. Jackson. Hurry!"

Travers did not move for what seemed an eternity to Alexis. Slowly his hand came to his side, and when he left the cabin she knew she had only escaped his retribution for the time being. She brushed the perspiration from Smith's brow and shook her head sadly.

"It wasn't you. It was never meant for you."

Her tears fell on the lieutenant's chest and he managed to find his voice while he tried to forget the burning pain in his gut.

"Why? Why do you hate him so much?"

"Not now. You mustn't talk. Please, don't die. I couldn't bear it if you did! I have never killed anyone! I only wanted him!"

Smith smiled weakly. His hand clutched the hilt of the dagger. "I won't. In exchange for the truth. I will live if you'll tell me the truth."

"What?" she asked anxiously. She tried to see his pain-contorted face through a veil of tears. The boyish features were no longer in evidence. His skin was drawn tight, his mouth set hard as he pulled at his lower lip with his teeth to keep from crying out. "What is it you want to know?"

"Your name."

Alexis leaned over him, putting her mouth near his ear. In a hushed voice she told him her name. When she drew herself up to look in his eyes to see if they registered astonishment at her disclosure she could tell nothing. His eyes were closed and he was unconscious.

She did not protest when Travers returned with the doctor and several other crewmen and she was led away from the injured man. She said nothing when she was thrown into a vacant storage compartment and the door was locked and the light was taken away. She sat in a corner, listening to the sound of the retreating seamen and wondered how long it would be before Travers decided to be rid of her. While she thought of that Cloud's face eluded her. The only face she saw was the lieutenant's.

"She didn't give you any trouble?" Travers asked his men when they returned from taking Alexis away. They shook their heads. "Good. Stay away from her. Pass the word to everyone aboard the ship. She is mad! She meant to kill me with that damn knife of hers!" He pointed to Smith, now lying on the bed, and asked the doctor, "Is he going to live?"

"I think so, Captain. It's not as bad as it looks."

"Keep me informed."

"About the girl, sir," Jackson ventured. "Is she to be given anything? Food? Water?"

"No! Nothing! It won't matter to her. I tell you the girl's mad!"

When Jackson was alone he returned to the treatment of his friend, wondering who the captain was trying to convince with his loud statements about the girl's sanity.

Cloud met Lafitte in the dressing room adjoining his bedroom. He was exhausted from the work he had shared equally with the men. The hold of the *Dark Lady* and the splintered railing had been repaired. They all had worked as if possessed. Even Peach had refused to remain in bed with his injured leg. Jordan fashioned him a crutch and the boy pounded nails and mended sail right along with everyone else.

"A hard day?" Lafitte asked when Cloud collapsed into a chair.

"A very hard day. We're making progress. We might even be done ahead of schedule."

"*Bien.* Travers is not pleased with my evasions. I think he wants to leave here as soon as possible."

"Don't let that happen," Cloud said earnestly.

Lafitte smiled. "I will do everything in my power to prevent it, *mon ami,* though it is torture to have him under my roof."

"I could take him off your hands."

"No. You will have your chance later—when he is far from Barataria. Rest now and do not join us for breakfast. Travers turned to his ship this evening, mentioning some unfinished business he had to attend to, but he will be here in the morning. I only hope Pierre will join us. I have not seen him take such an instant dislike to someone before. He dreads tomorrow's meeting."

"As I am sure you must."

"I would not endure it a moment longer if your ship was

ready. He is a cruel man. He talks lightly of disciplining his men with harsh floggings as if that will endear him to me." He sighed. "What a lot of fanciful notions others have about pirates." He joined Cloud's laughter, thankful the man retained that capacity; then he went to his own room.

The following evening the news was much the same.

"He is growing very impatient," Lafitte said.

"Our repairs will be completed tomorrow evening. Can you keep him one more day?"

"Can the crew work without you?"

"Of course. Mr. Jordan will supervise."

"Bien. I want you to meet Travers."

"What on earth for, Jean? I don't think I could tolerate being in the same room with him. Why do you ask it?"

"I persuaded him to stay an extra day because I said I received a lucrative offer from the Americans. I told him I expected the arrival of their representative tomorrow. You must not make me out to be a liar."

"All right" Cloud agreed reluctantly. "When do you want me to come?"

"In time for dinner, *naturellement.* Jeannine is preparing the most delicious ham. You will enjoy it."

"I doubt I will eat a bite."

While Travers was in his third afternoon meeting with Lafitte, Hugh Jackson decided it was time to check on the condition of Alexis. He was careful to make sure no one saw him go in the direction of her quarters. Travers had a few men who were loyal to him and the doctor feared his captain's reprisal as much as anyone.

He listened at the door for some sign of life inside before he dared enter. When he caught the sound of tiny whimpering he unbolted the door. Holding the lantern high, he stepped inside. He had barely taken three steps into the cabin when he was attacked from behind and knocked on the floor. The lantern dropped and rolled but it did not go out, so Alexis had enough light to see it was not Travers she had gone after, but one of the two men who had shown her some kindness.

"I'm sorry, Doctor," she apologized wearily. "I thought you were the captain."

Jackson got to his feet and brushed himself off. "You seem to have a habit of making that mistake. I wouldn't mind if your intent wasn't to kill." He bent over for the lantern and lifted it high, inspecting her in the flickering light. "My God! What happened to you?" Her right eye was bruised and discolored and her jaw was swollen. Her once-white shirt and fawn trousers were spotted with blood and he could see slight scars in the material that had been rendered by a whip.

She dismissed her appearance with a wave of her hand but she faltered unsteadily on her feet. "Please, Doctor. Captain Travers would not tell me. How is Mr. Smith?"

"He is much better. Stubborn man. Wanted to come down here himself, but I told him I would look in on you. You are lucky he is alive. You would be hanging from the crosstrees otherwise."

"I am aware of that." She released her breath slowly. Relief that Smith was alive and recovering made her relax. The pain she had been trying to hide from the doctor gripped her in a dozen different places. She moaned and started to fall to the deck.

Jackson caught her and eased her down, placing the lantern on the deck. The fetid air in the room was turning his stomach but he managed to fight the nausea while he held her head in his lap and stroked her hair. He had no medicines with him and he was undecided whether he should risk going back for them.

"I want to help you," he said quietly. "I don't know what I can do."

"It's all right. You should not be here. If the captain finds out he will have you punished."

"Did he do this to you?"

She nodded. "That first night . . . after I hurt Smith . . . he came down here. He said he did not want to punish me in front of everyone."

"Sssh. Don't talk. Have you had anything to eat? No, don't talk. Just shake your head." She shook her head. "Water?" Again she shook her head. "Dear God! What does he want from you?"

"He wants me to b-b-beg him." She was shivering now so Jackson took off his jacket and covered her.

"I'll be back," he said, laying her head on the floor. "I'll get my medicines and—"

"No, you mustn't. The captain—"

"I don't care about that. You can't survive down here without some treatment."

"No!"

"Hush! You don't have any say-so. I am taking the risks."

"P-p-please don't!" She reached for his hand and held it in a vise grip. "I don't want you hurt because of me."

"What makes you so sure the captain will have me flogged? I'm the ship's physician. He needs a doctor."

"A man like him doesn't care. He whipped me, didn't he?"

Jackson examined the dozen or so tears in her shirt and trousers. The skin beneath was broken in only a few places. Travers wielded the whip not to scar her, only to frighten her and cause pain. "These are nothing," he replied. "I know they hurt a great deal but they won't leave marks. Just let me treat them so they don't become infected."

"N-n-no. You don't understand. I didn't mean what he did recently. My b-back. You've seen those scars?" Jackson nodded. "Who do you think put them there?"

Before the doctor could utter a response he heard a sound in the companionway. Quickly he doused the lantern and took his jacket. "I will be back later with something for you," he whispered; then he peered out the door and left, locking it behind him and successfully avoiding a confrontation with the approaching seaman.

When the door opened again, Alexis cringed at the sight

of the towering figure in the doorway. The seaman said nothing as he lifted her less than gently and carried her out of the room.

"Gawd, you smell," he said when he deposited her in the captain's cabin.

She wanted to retort that he would smell the same after being locked in a room for three days, but she was too weak to do anything but nod abjectly.

"Bath's ready for you," he said, pointing to the copper tub on the far side of the room. "Captain sent word you are to join him soon. He said you're to clean up and make yourself presentable. I put what you're to wear on the bunk."

Alexis glanced in the direction of the bunk. On it lay a simple cotton day dress. It had short puffed sleeves edged with lace and a rounded bodice. She stared at the sugary yellow confection and wondered who Travers had purchased if for.

"A sister, or cousin, I think," the seaman answered, reading her thought. "You can be sure it wasn't for his mistress." He thought that seemed to please Alexis. He took another look at her matted hair, dirty face, and the blood splattered at intervals on her trousers. "I'll be back in two hours. You should be able to do something with yourself by then."

Alexis found her voice. "May I have something to eat or drink?"

"Captain didn't say anything about that."

Alexis refused to plead. She eyed the bath water, hoping it was not brackish. "Where are you taking me?"

"To the captain."

"I know. But where is he? Where are we?"

The seaman chuckled. "That is the captain's surprise."

As Lafitte predicted the spiced ham was excellent, but Cloud, also true to his word, found eating it a tedious chore. He concentrated on the mechanical procedures of lifting the fork to his mouth, chewing, and swallowing. It was easier to concern himself with procedure than to be drawn into the conversation with the man seated across from him.

Cloud offered nothing to the topic when it centered on women but he listened with interest to the banter between Pierre and the captain of the *Follansbee*. It kept his mind off the impending negotiations.

"And while you were in New Orleans," Pierre was asking "did you have an opportunity to attend a quadroon ball?"

"No. But I have heard a great deal of the beautiful women who can be purchased there. Is it a common practice?"

"Common in New Orleans."

"And the women? They do not object to being sold?"

"On the contrary," Pierre answered. "These women have it better than most. They will be purchased by men who desire them as a mistress and probably treated better than most wives. Their mothers supervise the bidding, and I assure you it is discreet"

"The women are of mixed blood, then?"

"Quadroons or octoroons. Skin the color of café au lait a dusty gold," Pierre said dreamily "They are indeed beautiful."

"You would be interested in such a woman?" asked Travers. He hid his anxiousness. The young woman was getting ready to join him shortly and he wanted to make sure his instinct about the Lafittes were correct—that they would not turn down such a gift as he could offer them. He almost regretted hitting her, but that could easily be explained.

"Pierre already has a mistress," Jean broke in. "What is the point, Captain? I would hardly expect you to produce such a woman."

Travers laughed. "I hardly expected to be able to myself but as it happens, I have a very attractive stowaway on board my vessel."

"A stowaway?" Lafitte asked, astonished.

"That's right. She hid aboard the *Follansbee* in New Orleans. We discovered her in the hold after the storm. She was badly bruised from being tossed around. I can't take her with me, and I thought I would be able to leave her here. She would have a better life than with her former owner."

"Former owner?" asked Cloud, unable to remain silent any longer. He wondered at the concern Travers seemed to have for the girl. If only he had shown that much compassion for Alexis. "The girl is a Negress?"

"Yes. But a very light-skinned one. An octoroon, I believe."

"Did she tell you that herself?" Pierre asked.

"No. She has talked very little. We were able to discern that much from her ramblings while she was ill. As I mentioned, she was badly bruised and I instructed the ship's surgeon to treat her. She has the mark of a whip and what little she said convinced us she was fleeing an abusive owner."

"And you want me to take her off your hands?" Lafitte said.

"I would appreciate it," Travers answered smoothly. "I do not want to send her back to New Orleans and I cannot keep her on the ship. It is too dangerous and she does present a problem for my men."

"All right," Jean agreed. "I will take her. She can help Jeannine in the kitchen."

"Once you see her, I doubt if you will want to relegate her to cutting vegetables."

"That will be my decision," Lafitte said sharply. "Pierre, go with the captain and bring the girl to the drawing room. Captain Cloud and I will wait for you there."

"She should be waiting outside. I told one of my men to bring her here."

"You were so sure I would take her?"

"I thought you might want some proof of her beauty first."

Lafitte sighed, hating the British commander a little more with each passing moment. "Since she is outside, you will come to the drawing room with us. Pierre, see to the girl. Have André prepare a room for her. If she is ill from her voyage have her rest. I will talk with her in the morning."

The three men retired to the drawing room to begin the business at hand while Pierre went to the entrance hall. He opened the massive front door and stepped out onto the portico. He saw the woman immediately She was huddled in an oversized cloak and leaning against one of the columns in a manner that suggested she needed it for support. The seaman at her side saw Pierre and offered the woman his arm. Pierre noticed she grasped it heavily.

"I will take her," Pierre said, rushing to her side. "You can return to your ship. She will be staying here." The seaman nodded and left hastily. "Mademoiselle, can you walk?" Alexis tossed the hood of her cape back and eyed the man who held her warily. Pierre caught his breath. Whatever else he thought of Travers he could not deny the commander had an eye for beautiful women. The strength of her grip on his arm did not seem consistent with her fragile appearance. He brushed back tendrils of golden hair from her cheeks, careful not to touch her bruised eye or jaw. When she was better he decided he would have to discover more about her. It was doubtful she was an octoroon, not with those yellow eyes and hair.

"Come, chérie. You will not have to return to New Orleans. You are safe now."

Safe? Alexis wanted to scream. Where was she safe? With some man Travers had convinced she was a runaway slave. What was the use of trying to explain the truth now? Travers had probably anticipated everything she would say. There was no one to believe her. Holding Pierre tightly she followed him into the house.

"Wait here, mademoiselle. I will find André and have him prepare a room for you. I will be back in a few moments."

"Merci," Alexis whispered, and then Pierre was gone. She stood alone in the foyer for several minutes and still he did not return. Her legs threatened to buckle beneath her and she leaned against the wall, closing her eyes on the luxury surrounding her. Wherever Travers had brought her it was obviously a place of some wealth. Unable to stand much longer Alexis ventured forward to the closed double doors on her left, seeking a place where she could sit.

She thought she heard voices but it was too late to stop

her entry into the room. She had already turned the handle
and leaned forward.

Deep in heated discussion it was some time before the three
men noted the entry of the caped figure. Alexis, however,
had heard and seen enough to decide she had gone insane.
It was Travers who saw her first."

Uneasily he got to his feet. "Aaah, gentlemen. There she
is. The woman I was telling you about. Come here, child."

Alexis recognized the command in his voice, the warning
nature of his tone but she could only stare helplessly from
Cloud to Lafitte and back to Cloud again. They appeared to
have no better a grip on the situation than she did. She felt
hands on her waist behind her and realized it must be Jean's
brother who had brought her in.

"I am sorry, Jean. She must have wandered in here. She
really is not well. What is wrong? You look as if you have seen
a ghost?"

Pierre's fluid voice was all Cloud and Lafitte needed to
bring them to their senses.

"Alex!" Cloud cried, rushing forward to take her from
Pierre.

"Oh, Cloud!" She fell into his arms. He held her close,
allowing her to know he was real, then he carried her
trembling form to the sofa.

"Alex?" Pierre looked at his brother questioningly. "Captain Cloud knows her?"

"Pierre, Captain Travers, I have the very great pleasure to
introduce Captain Alex Danty to you." Lafitte said the words
calmly enough, but Pierre sensed the rage burning beneath.
He glanced at Travers who was only capable of mouthing the
"Danty." He now realized the kind of trick in which the
commander had been trying to involve them. Pierre was not
surprised when he saw his brother take down two of the rapiers
mounted on the wall above the mantle and toss one of them
to Travers. Pierre knew that anything he might say now to
Jean to stop him from killing the captain would fall on deaf
ears, so he busied himself moving furniture out of the way

to widen the arena. He paused in his work once to look at the woman known as Captain Danty and suddenly he knew how she commanded men, even in her absence.

Cloud turned from Alexis the moment he heard the slash of Lafitte's rapier. "No, Jean," he said, looking at Travers. "It is my right."

Lafitte eyed Cloud, then Travers. The British officer was preparing to duel and seemed unconcerned as to who his opponent was. "As you wish," Lafitte replied, tossing Cloud his rapier. "I will not hold you to your word under these circumstances."

"No, Cloud!" Alexis cried out. She tried to get up as Cloud stepped away from her and moved pantherlike to the center of the room.

Lafitte quickly took Cloud's place at her side, placing his hands on her shoulders, forcing her to lie still. "You must not stop him. He would not have stopped you, Captain Danty."

Travers faced Cloud. "Why do you call her Captain? And why Danty?"

"Because it is her name, Travers. The name she took for herself after you visited her island," Cloud replied in a deceptively soft voice. He motioned Pierre to move to the far side of the room. Now there was nothing blocking his advance toward Travers.

"But her name was Quinton."

"So you do remember! Good! I won't have to do much explaining then. I can concentrate on other matters." Cloud took his stance. "I have been waiting for this."

Travers's rapier cut through space in a fluid, silky motion. The sound it made punctuated Cloud's demand. He stepped forward, thrusting as he did so. It was not a stroke designed to kill. Travers was only testing the balance of his weapon as well as the strength and agility of his opponent. Cloud's subsequent movements warned the captain they were evenly matched. Youth was on the side of the American. Experience on his own.

"You are a liar!" Cloud taunted Travers. He sidestepped

Travers's next move easily and began to advance, forcing the captain toward the fireplace. "She did not hide aboard your ship! She was thrown off her own during the storm! Tell me, Captain, how did she come by those bruises on her face?"

Travers did not answer. Cloud's anger gave him the opportunity he needed to move away from the mantle. He managed to move out into the open and with more freedom available he achieved a glancing strike on Cloud's arm.

Lafitte was forced once again to hold Alexis in her position on the sofa. He watched her. Even in her distress she would not call out to her lover, knowing the distraction could mean his death. Still, there was a strength in her that refused to be harnessed, as if by sheer force of will she could cause Travers to go to his knees and ultimately to his death.

Cloud laughed off the scratch lightly. "You will have to do better, Captain, if you hope to leave Barataria alive. Did you know while the Royal Fleet was losing valuable ships she was only after you?" The point of his rapier struck Travers in the shoulder. Cloud pulled it out immediately and let him have a moment to recover. "No, I suppose you didn't. Otherwise you would not have slept so easily these years since you killed her parents."

Travers ignored the small pain in his shoulder and advanced on Cloud. "What is your interest in this? What lies has she told you to make you defend her?"

"Lies? You fool! I was there, Travers! Do you understand? I was there!"

Travers looked at him blankly. The memory of the help the Quintons' received registered at the same time Cloud pierced his side with the tip of his rapier.

Again Cloud gave Travers a chance to strike back, circling him slowly. "Those marks were for her parents, Travers. They do not begin to equal the marks you left with her. The lashes you delivered to her back!" He thrust, missed, and lost his balance, stumbling to the floor before he could right himself. Travers lunged but Cloud rolled to one side and quickly regained his stance. "That was your chance, and you missed it. I still have one mark to put on you. The fatal one. For her friend.''

Alexis stared, transfixed as the two men continued their struggle. There were no more words between them. Each was in earnest to see the other defeated. Cloud had only toyed with the captain thus far. The wounds he had inflicted were minor, their pain minimal, and they did not appear to slow Travers. The only sounds she was conscious of were of the labored breathing of Travers and Cloud, and the sharp, biting sting of the clashing rapiers.

She had almost forgotten the presence of Lafitte until his fingers closed on her shoulders painfully as Travers's weapon made a deadly sweep down Cloud's thigh. She welcomed the firm grip because it took her mind off the open wound and the spreading crimson line.

Cloud launched a new attack, perceptibly favoring his good leg, but not to the point that it cost him his balance. As Cloud advanced Travers retreated to the entrance of the drawing room and in a moment both men were in the foyer, out of the line of vision of the three spectators. Pierre quickly entered the foyer and almost as quickly Lafitte lifted Alexis and carried her to the doorway.

Travers was trapped against the banister of the wide, winding staircase. He teetered for a second, unsure whether to move up the stairs or down. His indecisiveness gave Cloud the opportunity he had been seeking. With lightning-like motion his blade cut a jagged path through the air and found its mark in Travers's chest. This time he did not pull it out.

The captain sagged against the banister, his sword falling noisily on the polished floor below. He clutched the thin blade in his two large hands and pulled it out. Groaning softly, eyes filled with hatred, he made one last effort and tried to toss the rapier at his opponent. It fell only a few inches away from his own feet.

''That was for Pauley,'' Cloud said as Travers struggled to remain upright and, falling, fell heavily down the stairs.

Lafitte released Alexis. She ran for the protective embrace

awaiting her on the stairway. Enfolded in Cloud's arms, she was oblivious to Jean and Pierre as she was to the figure at the bottom of the stairs. His kiss gave her the nourishment she had been seeking, and she forgot the time she spent in the hold. She forgot everything but her need for him.

"Your leg," she whispered against his chest.

"Your eye," he countered, his lips touching her hair.

"It's nothing. But your arm—"

"It's nothing. But your jaw—"

She pulled away from him, laughing, and he joined her. She took his hand and led him down the stairs into the drawing room, past the bemused faces of Jean and Pierre. Still laughing, they collapsed on the sofa, thoroughly enjoying the sound of their voices as a reassurance their time had finally come.

Cloud brushed aside the tears that had formed at the corners of Alexis's eyes and called to Lafitte. "Jean! Are you and your brother going to stand there and stare as if we've gone mad or are you going to find someone to care for our wounds?"

"Neither of you appear to be experiencing any great discomfort to me," Lafitte answered smugly. He sent Pierre for André anyway.

"What are you going to do about Captain Travers, Jean?" asked Alexis when the pirate had pulled up a chair and seated himself across from them.

"I will take the responsibility for his death. Something like this would be expected from me."

"No!" Alexis and Cloud protested at once.

"There is no other way. I can protect myself here. Tanner, you would be sought by the British and Alex, you are still a criminal."

"I think there is another way," Alexis said. "If you will bring the ship's doctor here and the lieutenant, Mr. Smith, I think I can persuade them to come up with something that will satisfy the crew and the Admiralty."

Lafitte eyed her skeptically. "What can they do?"

"I'm not sure but they were friendly to me. Smith knows who I am, and the doctor was willing to risk a great deal to care for me." André came into the room. At Lafitte's direction he began cleaning and bandaging Cloud's leg and arm. While he was working Alexis related how she had been brought aboard after the storm and how Smith had come to know her identity.

Lafitte listened carefully and decided to follow her suggestion. "Pierre, send someone to bring the two men here. Tell them nothing. We will explain everything when they get here."

Pierre was on the point of leaving when he offered a hasty apology to Alexis for believing Travers's story about her. Alexis accepted his embarrassed regret graciously and warned him to take special care of the lieutenant when he brought him from the ship.

When André had finished with Cloud, Lafitte brought him an ottoman to rest his leg on. Then the servant turned his attention to Alexis.

"Are you cold, mademoiselle?" he asked.

"No."

"Then I think you would be more comfortable if you would remove your cloak."

Alexis hesitated, not wanting them to see the scratches on her arm and the top of her breast. The other marks were hidden by the dress.

"Is something wrong, Alex?" asked Cloud, sensing her reluctance to be rid of the cloak.

"No. I'll take it off." She unfastened the button at her throat and stood, tossing the cloak to an empty chair.

"Dieu! Did Travers do this to you?" Lafitte asked tightly. Alexis nodded and sat beside Cloud again, aware of his anger in the tight grip he placed on her hand. "He is better dead then. He was of no value alive."

André made a compress for her eye which she held in place after being ordered to do so by all three men. He cleaned the scratch on her arm and applied a salve but he balked, blushing, when it came time to care for the thin line that started at her shoulder and snaked to the curve of her breast.

"It's all right," she told him. "I will take care of it later. There are others I have no wish to reveal here."

Lafitte dismissed his servant. "Others? Why did he do this to you?"

"To punish me for trying to kill him," she answered simply. It was of no consequence now. She leaned against Cloud's shoulder, drawing her legs beneath her dress on the sofa. "Jean, I want to thank you for taking care of my crew. I am most grateful."

"It was my pleasure."

"Could I impose on your hospitality and ask for something to eat? It has been days."

Jean was on his feet immediately. "Why did you not say something earlier? I will prepare something for you now." He left them and went to find Jeannine.

Cloud chuckled. "Your friend says tact is not necessary between us, Alex. If you wanted to be alone with me you could have just said so."

"I would have, if that's what I wanted. As it happens I really am very hungry. I was reduced to drinking my bath water." She wished she had not told him that. His eyes were opaque with pain for her.

Cloud closed his eyes for a moment, squeezing her hand gently. When he opened them the hurt had vanished and he said lightly, "And I thought you were only interested in me. You have seriously injured my pride."

"You'll recover." She ran her hand lightly along the length of his thigh, her eyes shone with a promise that gave meaning to her words. "I will make sure of it."

When Lafitte returned with a tray of food Alexis slipped to the floor at Cloud's feet and placed the tray on the cushions of the sofa. The two men watched in amusement as she attacked the cold meat, bread, and cheese ravenously. She had no way of knowing what pleasure they derived from watching her do such an ordinary thing. The fact they thought never to see her again made her every move, every word, important in some way.

When she finished eating she put the tray aside and returned to her place beside Cloud, sharing a glass of wine with him. Their conversation, aimed at filling in gaps in information, was almost concluded when it was interrupted by the arrival of Pierre, the doctor, and the lieutenant from the *Follansbee*.

Alexis dropped the compress from her eye as she rushed to the drawing-room door to greet them, her gaze resting momentarily on the body behind them.

"What happened?" Smith asked as Alexis took him by the arm and led him to a chair.

"I will explain everything to you. First, are you all right? I did not want you to come if it meant endangering you."

"I'm fine. Nothing could have kept me away. I told you I would be all right."

"Yes, you did. And do you remember what I told you?"

Smith hesitated, eyeing Lafitte and Cloud.

"It's all right. They know. Everyone here does except Dr. Jackson."

Jackson laughed and the action seemed to take years of age away from him. "I know too, Captain Danty. Don't blame Ian. I wheedled it out of him after you were taken away this evening. After what you told me in the hold I had to find out more. We've been able to piece some sort of story together on the little information we had."

"I am ready to tell you everything now and I am going to take shameless advantage of our short friendship and mutual dislike for your captain. Would you please get a chair, Doctor?"

Alexis made hasty introductions. When everyone was seated in a small circle she explained the situation to the doctor and Smith, starting with her reason for assuming the role of Captain Alex Danty. With Cloud's reassuring presence beside her she told the story slowly and clearly, knowing this was the

last time she would ever have to go over all that happened
since she'd met Travers. Jackson and Smith listened thoughtfully, not condoning her actions at any time, but giving the
impression they understood the course she'd taken. That was
all she wanted from them.

Cloud finished for her. "Your captain told us Alexis was a
runaway slave who hid aboard your vessel. Having no idea
she was really Danty, his only thought was to get rid of her
and hide what he had done to her and her family. As soon
as we saw her and her condition, we knew he had mistreated
her. I completed what Alexis tried to do aboard your vessel."

"And I sanctioned it," Lafitte added, unwilling to place
the sole responsibility on Cloud's shoulders. "It was a fair
duel. Your captain fought well. As you can see, Captain Cloud
did not escape unscathed."

Smith nodded and looked at Jackson. "Is there a problem,
Hugh?"

"A fair match. There is no problem."

"I agree. Monsieur Lafitte . . . Captain Cloud . . . Alexis,"
he addressed them, looking at each in turn. "There are very
few men aboard the *Follansbee* who will mourn the death of
Captain Travers. In a sense you have freed us all. The doctor
and I will take care of the body. He will be given a proper
burial at sea, and we will falsify the cause of death. No one
need ever know what took place here. In return for our silence
I would like some assurance that Captain Danty has retired
her command. Is that possible?"

"Captain Danty's career is over, Mr. Smith," Alexis said
quietly, her voice trembling with emotion. "I will not seek
out the men who were with him that day. They can live with
the guilt of what happened. For them I think it will mean
something. You have nothing to fear from me."

"Good. Monsieur Lafitte, may I have the answer you were
prepared to give my commander concerning the reason for
his visit?"

"The answer is no. I will not give aid to the British. I suspect

I will be asked again but you can tell your superiors I will remain firm."

Smith nodded, then he turned to Cloud. "And you, Captain? We are at war. Do I have the right to ask that the *Follansbee* be able to leave Bartaria safely?"

"You have that right. And you have my word."

Smith stood and ran his fingers through his flaxen hair. Alexis was quick to notice the eager light in his blue eyes. He was ready to assume command and she silently wished him good fortune. "I have need of nothing else, then. We are done here. If the doctor and I could have some assistance with the body, we will return to the ship and sail immediately."

The goodbyes were brief, but when Alexis stood beside Cloud on the portico, Smith and Jackson each took a turn to whisper in her ear.

"What did they say to you?" Cloud and Lafitte asked her almost as soon as they were out of sight.

"Dr. Jackson told me to put the compress back on my eye."

"And Smith? What did he say?"

Alexis smiled. "He said he would cherish the scar I gave him because he could say he'd met Captain Danty and lived."

Lafitte decided the reunion between Alexis and her crew could wait until morning. With Cloud's assurance that Jordan was well and Peach mending rapidly, Alexis finally admitted her total exhaustion.

Back in the room Lafitte had provided for Cloud, Alexis let him undress her and apply medication to her cuts. Her muscles relaxed under his tender ministrations until she thought she would never be able to move again.

"He was not so hard on you this time, Alex," he said as he smoothed the salve along a thin line on her thigh. "It's a miracle, considering what you tried to do to him."

"He only wanted me to beg."

"Did you?"

"What do you think?"

"I think that's how you got the black eye."

"You're right."

Cloud put the bottle on the bureau and undressed and joined her in bed, pulling a sheet over them. Alexis blew out the candles on the nightstand, then nestled close beside him, fitting the contours of her body to his own.

"I thought you were dead," Cloud said after a long silence.

"I know," she said softly, her voice breaking in her throat. "I thought about it all the time I was aboard that frigate. Revenge was little comfort when I realized I might not see you again. I would not have hesitated to kill Travers if I hadn't thought that. Somehow I couldn't bring myself to do it until he said he was going to get rid of me . . . to pass me off as a slave. Then it all came back. The hate, the disgust—everything."

"It's all over now. You are free of all of it."

"Except you."

"That's right. You're my captive. Do you mind?"

"What do you think?"

"I think we should get married."

"You're right."

Exhaustion and pain were ignored, overridden by a driving hunger that sought pleasure as an expression of all they meant to each other. Cloud's light touch elicited soft moans and gentle urgings. His mouth on hers stilled her whispered pleas until his lips moved to her throat, her breasts, and she could not remain silent. Her hands moved across his back, up his neck, and while he caressed the length of her leg, her fingers wound in his thick copper hair.

"When we're together . . . like this, I feel alive." She expressed herself softly, not wanting to break the special reverence of the moment. "Do you know what I mean?"

Cloud lifted his head and searched Alexis's face. His eyes were darkly passionate and his thickly lashed lids were heavy with his desire as he gazed into her slumbrous amber eyes. "From the very beginning, Alex. I've always known you were necessary to me . . . like the air and the sea. I was only afraid you would never admit it was the same for you."

"I was scared."

"I know." He kissed her briefly, soothingly. "So frightened in some ways—so courageous in others."

She returned his kiss, tasting his mouth with the tip of her tongue, asking his forgiveness for a time when she had not been brave enough to be honest with him or herself. She felt him tremble as his fingers moved caressingly along the edge of her brow, her jaw, then along the slope of her neck. She noticed her own hands were trembling as they traced a similar pattern along the ridges and angles of his face.

Her smooth legs sought the masculinity of his. Her hips and thighs, vulnerable to his pleasure, arched searchingly to find and satisfy him, ensuring that her own desires were met.

When they joined there was no longer the sense of a battle between them. Each only strove to give the other greater pleasure than had been known before. Alexis found it first, her senses assaulted, her mind teetering on the edge of oblivion and moments later, unable to withstand the contraction of her muscles, the demands she placed on him with her mouth, her hands, he joined her.

Breathing slowed, heartbeats found a normal rhythm, as muscles ceased to quiver and tremble. Cloud touched the chain at Alexis's throat and brushed his lips against hers.

"I love you."

Alexis's sigh was as eloquent as the words she might have spoken. She turned in his embrace and rested her head against his chest, her hair fell softly across his shoulder.

"That sigh. It's mine forever."

"You will have to work just as hard as you did tonight to get it. Does that bother you?"

He laughed softly in the darkness and bent his head forward, kissing the top of hers. "What do you think?"

"I think I've found everything I ever wanted."

"You're right."

And the bitter memories were laid to rest, replaced by a

calm acceptance of all that had happened. The kind of peace Alexis had only known in her crow's nest she found once again in Cloud's arms. As if sensing her discovery his arm tightened about her waist, assuring her that she had found her place at last.

ABOUT THE AUTHOR

Jo Goodman lives with her family in Colliers, West Virginia. She is the author of seventeen historical romances (all published by Zebra Books) including her beloved Dennehy sisters series: WILD SWEET ECSTASY (Mary Michael's story), ROGUE'S MISTRESS (Rennie's story), FOREVER IN MY HEART (Maggie's story), ALWAYS IN MY DREAMS (Skye's story) and ONLY IN MY ARMS (Mary's story). She also contributed a short story to Zebra's Christmas collection, A GIFT OF JOY, which included New York Times Bestselling authors Fern Michaels, Virginia Henley and Brenda Joyce. Jo's newest series, focusing on the three Thorne brothers, began with MY STEADFAST HEART (Colin's story) and continued with MY RECKLESS HEART. She is currently working on WITH ALL MY HEART (Grey's story), which will be published in March 1999. Jo loves hearing from readers and you may write to her c/o Zebra Books. Please include a self-addressed stamped envelope if you wish a response.

BOOK YOUR PLACE ON OUR WEBSITE AND MAKE THE READING CONNECTION!

We've created a customized website just for our very special readers, where you can get the inside scoop on everything that's going on with Zebra, Pinnacle and Kensington books.

When you come online, you'll have the exciting opportunity to:

- View covers of upcoming books
- Read sample chapters
- Learn about our future publishing schedule (listed by publication month *and author*)
- Find out when your favorite authors will be visiting a city near you
- Search for and order backlist books from our online catalog
- Check out author bios and background information
- Send e-mail to your favorite authors
- Meet the Kensington staff online
- Join us in weekly chats with authors, readers and other guests
- Get writing guidelines
- AND MUCH MORE!

Visit our website at
http://www.zebrabooks.com

TALES OF LOVE FROM MEAGAN MCKINNEY

GENTLE FROM THE NIGHT*   (0-8217-5803-$5.99/$7.50)
In late nineteenth century England, destitute after her father's death, Alexandra Benjamin takes John Damien Newell up on his offer and becomes governess of his castle. She soon discovers she has entered a haunted house. Alexandra struggles to dispel the dark secrets of the castle and of the heart of her master.

    *Also available in hardcover (1-577566-136-5, $21.95/$27.95)

A MAN TO SLAY DRAGONS   (0-8217-5345-2, $5.99/$6.99)
Manhattan attorney Claire Green goes to New Orleans bent on avenging her twin sister's death and to clear her name. FBI agent Liam Jameson enters Claire's world by duty, but is soon bound by desire. In the midst of the Mardi Gras festivities, they unravel dark and deadly secrets surrounding the horrifying truth.

MY WICKED ENCHANTRESS   (0-8217-5661-3, $5.99/$7.50)
Kayleigh Mhor lived happily with her sister at their Scottish estate, Mhor Castle, until her sister was murdered and Kayleigh had to run for her life. It is 1746, a year later, and she is re-established in New Orleans as Kestrel. When her path crosses the mysterious St. Bride Ferringer, she finds her salvation. Or is he really the enemy haunting her?

AND IN HARDCOVER . . .
THE FORTUNE HUNTER   (1-57566-262-0, $23.00/$29.00)
In 1881 New York spiritual séances were commonplace. The mysterious Countess Lovaenya was the favored spiritualist in Manhattan. When she agrees to enter the world of Edward Stuyvesant-French, she is lead into an obscure realm, where wicked spirits interfere with his life. Reminiscent of the painful past when she was an orphan named Lavinia Murphy, she sees a life filled with animosity that longs for acceptance and love. The bond that they share finally leads them to a life filled with happiness.

TANTALIZING ROMANCE
FROM STELLA CAMERON

PURE DELIGHTS   (0-8217-4798-3, $5.99/$6.99)
Tobias Quinn is Seattle's sexiest divorced man, and he needs artistic rebel Paris Delight to save his fortune and his life. Tension, unraveling secrets and bursting chemistry between the two is sure to end in hot, passionate love.

SHEER PLEASURES   (0-8217-5093-3, $5.99/$6.99)
Set out to find an old and dear friend who disappeared from a private club in Washington State's Cascade Mountains, attorney Wilhelmina Phoenix meets the sexy Roman Wilde, an ex-Navy SEAL working undercover. Treading dangerous waters they find the truth and blazing desire.

TRUE BLISS   (0-8217-5369-X, $5.99/$6.99)
Bliss Winters and rebel Sebastian Plato were teenage sweethearts, until a jealous rival's deceit tore them apart. Fifteen years have passed and Sebastian has returned to his hometown as a bad boy made good. He is set on revenge and has no intention of leaving the woman he has always loved.

GUILTY PLEASURES   (0-8217-5624-9, $5.99/$7.50)
When television personality Polly Crow and ex-Navy SEAL Nasty Ferrito meet, love ensues from the magnetism between them. But Polly has a past she must conceal at all costs and when it creeps closer to home, Polly must trust that Nasty will discover how far a man will go to protect true love.

Available wherever paperbacks are sold, or order direct from the Publisher. Send cover price plus 50¢ per copy for mailing and handling to Kensington Publishing Corp., Consumer Orders, or call (toll free) 888-345-BOOK, to place your order using Mastercard or Visa. Residents of New York and Tennessee must include sales tax. DO NOT SEND CASH.